MW01598304

THE
LAST DAYS
OF
MAGIC

THE
LAST DAYS
OF
MAGIC

MARK TOMPKINS

VIKING

VIKING
An imprint of Penguin Random House LLC
375 Hudson Street
New York, New York 10014
penguin.com

Copyright © 2016 by Mark Tompkins
Penguin supports copyright. Copyright fuels creativity, encourages diverse
voices, promotes free speech, and creates a vibrant culture. Thank you for
buying an authorized edition of this book and for complying with copyright laws by not reproducing, scanning, or distributing any part of it in
any form without permission. You are supporting writers and allowing
Penguin to continue to publish books for every reader.

ISBN 978-0-525-42953-1

Printed in the United States of America
1 3 5 7 9 10 8 6 4 2

Set in Aldus LT Std
Map and title-page illustration by Laura Hartman Maestro
Designed by Francesca Belanger

For Serena,
beyond words

Royalty of 1394
Ireland: High King Art
Meath: King Turlough
Leinster: King Murchada
Munster: Queen Gormflaith
Connacht: Queen Mael
Ulster: King Niall
Vikings: King Myndill

IRELAND
and
The Middle Kingdom

N
S

Sgathaich Scoil,
Liam's warrior
•school

Dunkerry Cave,
Fomorian high king's
residence

Nimhe
Glen

•Derry

•Donegal

Ulster

•Belfast

Armagh,
Patrick's main
monastery

Connacht

Meath

Brú na Bóinne,
faerie capital city

Trim,
birthplace of
Aisling and Anya

•Tara, capital of
Ireland

Gormghiolla,
Skeaghshee
sacred tree

•Ratoath

•Galway

•Dunsany

•Dublin,
Viking
capital
city

The Middle
Kingdom
a hidden
parallel land

•Kildare

Leinster

Munster

•Carlow

Fearna,
slave market

Limerick,
Viking port

The Rock
of Cashel

Waterford,
Viking
fortress

•Wexford,
Viking port

Lough Leane

Cork,
Viking port

Bannow Bay

Great
Skellig,
island
prison

Milford Haven
England

Red stag
of Tara

Illustrated map by Laura Hartman Maestro ©2015

ONLY A FEW CENTURIES AGO, the descriptions of magical beings and their actions within these pages would have been taken as fact.

This story's Celtic faeries and Fomorians (merpeople) are based on old legends. The Goddess Morrígna is drawn from Irish mythology, and the trials of Aisling, one of her physical aspects, is founded on the lore of Red Mary. The angels and demons that appear originate from biblical and ancient sources. Most of the named witches of the High Coven are based on accounts of real women tried or accused of witchcraft.

The biblical library of the Essene at Qumran—its contents popularly known as the Dead Sea Scrolls—contained numerous copies of the books of Enoch and Jubilees, which provide accounts of angels' coupling with humans and producing magical hybrid offspring. The scrolls were repressed for decades and it is possible that some are still kept secret. Lilith, Adam's first wife, has been struck from most modern bibles but she can still be seen in the relief depicting the Garden of Eden on the front of Notre-Dame Cathedral in Paris (carved in 1225).

The account of the Celtic high king Art MacMurrough follows historical record, as does the military strategy relating to England's King Richard II and his designs on Ireland. The use of exorcism to control demons is a practice that originated with King Solomon and his magic ring, circa 950 BCE.

Morrígna
(morr-ē-gna)

A Goddess who manifests in three interconnected aspects to rule over the Celts and the Sidhe:

Aisling and *Anya*—Twin girls periodically reborn in human bodies

Anann—An Otherworld spirit who is the twins' source of power

Nephilim
(nef-ē-lim)

Hybrid offspring produced when fallen angels procreated with humans. All of the magical beings below are different branches of Nephilim.

Sidhe
(shē)

Irish faeries, most of whom live in a parallel land called the Middle Kingdom—accessed through enchanted doorways in faerie mounds—within a structured society. They owe allegiance to the Morrígna. In order of appearance:

SKEAGHSHEE—Tree Sidhe who live outside the Middle Kingdom

Kellach—King of the Skeaghshee

Cinaed—Kellach's brother

Ruarc—Kellach's son

ADHENE—Scholars, the most powerful clan

Fearghal—The Sidhe high king

Rhoswen—Fearghal's daughter and a Sidhe witch

GROGOCH—Stoneworkers and builders

Eldan—A Grogoch noble

Devas—Administrators and bureaucrats of the Middle Kingdom
Gnomes—Skilled ironworkers and weapon makers
Brownies—Ambassadors to the Celtic world
Sluaghs—Guides who usher the dead to the afterlife
Pixies—Tricksters who love leading humans astray
Fire Sprites—Controllers of fire and feared warriors
Leprechauns—Gold and silver artisans and jewelers
Dryads—Tree Sidhe who live in oaks; subservient to Skeaghshee
Wichtlein—Miners and tunnel builders
Asrais—Hedonists dedicated to physical pleasure; concubines

Elioud
(el-ē-ōōd)

Magical creatures who live independently and whose allegiance can be influenced.

Fomorians—Hostile water dwellers
Imps—Servants of demons
Banshee—Messengers of death

Elioud mentioned but not living in Ireland: Giants, Goblins, Trolls, Nereids, Vodyanoy, Sirens, Nuggle, and Nix.

Tylwyth Teg
(tal-with taig)

Welsh faeries that sometimes visit Ireland.

Oren—An English captive

Celts & Other Humans

Celts are the native Irish, and while they are not magical beings, it is worth noting that they and other humans use magic.

Druids—Celtic pagan magic workers
Exorcists—Vatican magicians
Witches & Sorcerers—Other human magic workers

The Nephilim were on the earth in those days, and also afterward, when the sons of God [angels] came in to the daughters of man and they bore children to them. These were the mighty men who were of old, the men of renown.

—Genesis 6:4, English Standard Version

And there we saw the Nephilim (the sons of Anak, who come from the Nephilim), and we seemed to ourselves like grasshoppers, and so we seemed to them.

—Numbers 13:33, English Standard Version

THE
LAST DAYS
OF
MAGIC

Prologue

Manchester, England
2016

When Sara Hill's body washed up on shore, the police concluded—logically, given the lack of injuries—that she must have accidentally fallen overboard and drowned. The previous day she had taken a train from Manchester to Liverpool to catch the ferry to Ireland. The police ascertained that she'd boarded for the overnight passage across the Irish Sea but did not disembark.

On the morning she was to take the ferry, Sara watched the sun emerge above the dreary city, chasing away some of Manchester's November gray. She had not slept since yesterday's unsettling call from her grandmother in Ireland. Sweet milky tea had been abandoned for strong coffee until her whole body vibrated, though she knew it had little to do with the caffeine. She leaned back from the desk that dominated her cramped attic bed-sit and rolled her shoulders to ease the knots of tension along her neck and spine.

Her Grandmother O'Trehy was like a second mother to her. She had left her Irish homeland and moved into the family's London flat for the first fifteen years of Sara's life, when it turned out that Sara's workaholic professor parents were woefully ill equipped to keep up with their energetic infant daughter. Over the years Sara and her grandmother became best friends, tramping through the parks of London while her grandmother recited rich and elaborate tales.

"Sara, do you still have the books I gave you when I left?" her grandmother had demanded over the phone the previous day, without so much as a hello.

"Of course," Sara responded, struck by her grandmother's unusual tone. "I would never lose those."

"Well, get them, right now. There's something you need to see."

"Okay," Sara agreed, recalling where she had stashed them. "Let me call you back in a few minutes."

"No! No, I'm not in Dublin anymore. I'm not anyplace where you can call. I'm sorry, Sara, to be so abrupt. Please, just do this for me. I'll wait on the line."

Sara had never before heard her grandmother sound rattled. She fished the two battered boxes out from under her bed, still sealed as they had remained since her arrival at the University of Manchester as a freshman, six apartment moves ago. She tore them open and, one by one, removed the beautiful books of her childhood, placing them on her desk—books full of Celtic myths, legends, and faerie tales.

"Got them," she said.

"Good. Now get a knife and pry open the paperboard of their covers."

"What? Grandmother, no. You can't be serious. What's this about?"

"Please just do as I ask, Sara," her grandmother implored. "You're not going to believe me until you see for yourself."

Sara didn't respond, dismayed at the notion of destroying her treasured books. She picked one up and examined it carefully, touching its broken spine and tattered pages, recalling that her grandmother must have read it to her a thousand times. The cover featured a faerie prince, tall and handsome, holding the hand of a shy human milkmaid. Their love was ultimately doomed, of course, their children to be transformed into swans—a story Sara had always found strangely appealing.

"Listen carefully, Sara," her grandmother said, breaking the silence. "People came for me, and I barely slipped away. They will come for you, too. They're after those books. There's a whole other set of faerie stories, much older, as old as it gets, hidden in them. You have to look in their covers to understand."

Sara feared that her grandmother must have fallen into some sort of dementia and tried to humor her. "Okay, if that's what you really want." She reluctantly took her knife, cut through the linen covering of the front hard cover of the book, and split apart the interior paperboard. To her surprise, a photograph was hidden inside, showing dense Hebrew script elegantly hanging from an invisible line. It was a portion of an ancient scroll—she knew that much from her studies.

Back when Sara was deciding on where to go to university, she had chosen Manchester because her grandmother had studied there. And just as it had with her grandmother, Sara's major in Middle Eastern Studies led to a graduate program in the region's historic languages, for which she had a flair—a trait that apparently ran in the family.

As dusk gathered outside, Sara, no longer convinced that her grandmother's mind was slipping, hurried to disassemble the covers of all the books while pressing the phone to her ear with her shoulder. "Grandmother, how did you get these?"

"John—Dr. Allegro—and I . . . were . . ." her grandmother stammered, and Sara could practically hear her blushing. "We were more than friends when I was in grad school."

"The Dr. Allegro?" Sara exclaimed. She knew the name well. Decades ago he'd been a professor in her department who had become legendary when he was appointed as the British representative to the international team assembled to study and translate the controversial Qumran scrolls.

"The same," said her grandmother. "So I saw the whole debacle unfold from his perspective."

Sara knew well the events her grandmother referred to. Christened "the Dead Sea Scrolls" by the press in the 1950s, the ancient documents were discovered accidentally, along with the remains of a shelving system and an index, in secluded man-made caves located in a hotly disputed area on the West Bank near Qumran. It did not take long for it to become clear that the caves held a carefully arranged, cataloged, and preserved collection of works making up the earliest biblical library ever found—all the books of the modern Hebrew Bible and the Catholic Old Testament were present.

Sara's grandmother recounted the initial, exciting days when the team worked well together as they began the slow, methodical process of translation, publishing completed sections as their mandate directed. The early results dazzled scholars and the general public alike, and newspapers worldwide reeled off a steady stream of stories devoted to the discoveries being made. Working from text a thousand years older than any previous source material, the team began to fill in gaps in the Old Testament, places where grammatically or structurally there was obviously a missing word or sentence or paragraph.

Soon, though, the publications slowed, then stopped altogether. The press started spinning theories that more than missing paragraphs had been found.

"That's when the Vatican began to take over and John became frustrated," Sara's grandmother said. "By chance, the UN official in charge of the scrolls was Catholic, and he had them shipped off to a Church facility. Unfortunately, John's letters to another team member were leaked to the press and became headlines."

Everyone in Sara's class had seen reprints of those reports. Too interesting for the students to ignore, they seemed to recirculate every year. Allegro wrote, *"I am convinced that if something does turn up which affects the Roman Catholic dogma, the world will never see it."* And then, *"The non-Catholic members of the team are being removed as quickly as possible."*

"The next year, only four years into the project, John was denied further access," Sara's grandmother continued. "And the Vatican took complete and exclusive control of all unpublished scrolls."

"Yes, I know all that, Grandma. But the scrolls have been published now."

"Look at the photographs again, and the work papers. John brought those to me late one night and helped me hide them. This was shortly after his disbarment."

Sara spread out the illicit material. She could tell from the translations, meticulously written out in tiny handwriting on onionskin paper, which had also been pressed into the hiding spaces, that the photographs were of significant Qumran scrolls, the books of Enoch and Jubilees. Ostensibly, the scrolls covering these books had been released years ago and were available to anyone online—Sara herself had read them as part of her coursework—except that large sections of those were missing due to rot or other damage. But not the scrolls shown in the photographs in front of her. These scrolls were virtually intact.

Sara was aware that early in its history the Vatican had excluded these two books from its Bible, even though they had appeared in older and much longer versions of the Old Testament. As late as the eighteenth century, scholars who argued that those older versions were closer to the original writings, and therefore more accurate, had been vigorously discredited as heretics and even burned alive.

"The book of Enoch was allegedly written by the great-grandfather of Noah, but the Vatican repudiated that notion. They ridiculed it as a fifteenth-century forgery at best, or a second-century satirical work of blasphemy at worst," explained her grandmother. "Can you imagine their panic when the copies found among the scrolls dated back to at least 300 BCE? Throughout their history they had killed people to suppress the idea that this book was legitimate!"

Sara's grandmother went on to assert that as the third-most-common scroll discovered, Enoch must have been an important part of a version of the Hebrew Bible that existed before the Christian era and very likely the Christian Bible that existed before the dominance of the Vatican.

"The other photographs are of the book of Jubilees. For centuries it was rumored there was a longer and more complete version of Genesis, but no copies were known to exist, at least not publicly, before the scrolls, where Jubilees was also a common book. You see, Sara"— her grandmother's voice lowered—"the ones you have are the complete works. The Vatican released only heavily damaged copies. But it was never safe for me to tell anyone about these, and then John died of that heart attack."

"But why would the Vatican care?" Sara was making herself a cup of tea.

"That's the point: the fact that they cared so much proves that the content of these photographs must be important. I believe these scrolls may recount the true history of the early days of our world, a time when angels mated with humans against God's orders and produced a hybrid offspring, the Nephilim. Sara, those were the faeries."

"Come on, that's absurd!" exclaimed Sara. "You know as well as I do that ancient origin myths tend to . . ." Sara's voice trailed off. She tried again. "These stories were probably invented to explain the genesis of . . ."

Her grandmother completed the academic principle for her. "The genesis of actual things. And that would mean there were real non-human beings in that time, which were endowed with strange powers. But that's almost as absurd."

"Almost," echoed Sara, plopping into her desk chair, her tea momentarily forgotten.

"Read the translations. There is detail there that will leave you questioning what you know of the Old Testament. And bring the photographs and work papers to me. Leave tomorrow, and don't fly or use a credit card. Take the ferry to Belfast, then a bus to Derry. I'll meet you there."

"Who is after you? What's going on, Grandmother? You're scaring me."

"There's more, Sara. I need to tell you something that even your parents don't know." There was an excruciatingly long pause. "I had a twin sister who disappeared while we were in grad school. It must be connected somehow. I know it must. That's why I held on to the photographs and kept them secret for all these years. In case one day I could use them somehow to get her back."

Sara could her hear grandmother's breathing get ragged. *A twin?*

Sara's grip on the phone tightened, she was shocked and hurt that there was so much her grandmother had kept from her.

"I really didn't know what to do at the time, after a hasty investigation faded out," her grandmother continued. "No one listened to me. I knew she hadn't run away. But now I think those who came for me are the ones who took her. I'll tell you everything when I see you. I just can't right now."

"Grandmother—"

But she had already hung up.

Sara studied the photographs. These scrolls were much more complete than the fragments that she'd seen when she visited the modern home of the Qumran scrolls, the Shrine of the Book in Jerusalem. At the time she'd thought the shrine's architectural symbolism merely interesting—a parabolic wave frozen into a white dome opposing a monolithic black basalt wall—but now it reverberated with meaning. The design represented a prophecy in the scrolls of a war between the sons of light and the sons of darkness, a war in which humans and Nephilim would fight in both factions, along with angels holy and fallen. She wondered if it was a war to come or one that had already been fought.

Sara had read through the night. With dawn sunlight streaming in her attic bed-sit window, she stood, stretched, and packed the translations and the photographs into a weathered leather satchel. What could her beloved grandmother have gotten herself into? she worried. She pulled some clothes out of a dresser and tossed them into her dilapidated suitcase. Before leaving she surveyed the mess on the desk—all her childhood books with their covers split open—and vowed to repair them upon her return.

On the train to Liverpool, as the English countryside rushed by, Sara's concerned mind kept replaying what her grandmother had said. She had trouble enough believing in a God above, let alone in randy angels sneaking out of heaven to have forbidden sex with humans and in their resulting offspring. She withdrew two of her own handwritten pages from her satchel, notes she'd made about the hybrid beings in the scrolls and their striking similarity to the magical beings from her grandmother's old stories: pixies, giants, trolls, goblins, merpeople, and faeries.

The elegant, powerful, and passionate faeries that had populated the tales of her grandmother's Irish homeland were known as the Tuatha Dé Danann, a name shortened by the Celts to the Sidhe. Sara loved the fact that the Sidhe were not the shy, diminutive faeries of today's children's books—they even married and bore children with the Celts, when they weren't fighting them. The Sidhe ruled the Middle Kingdom, a mostly hidden land that occupied a parallel plane with Ireland and was accessed through magical doorways.

Sara's favorite of these tales featured enchanted twins, and now she knew why her grandmother's voice was always tinged with sadness when she told them. These were stories of the Goddess Morrígna, who ruled over both the Celts and the Sidhe. The Morrígna, a triple-faceted goddess, carried three female aspects, much as the Christian God carried three male aspects—the Father, the Son, and the Holy Ghost, what St. Patrick likened to a three-leaf clover. The Morrígna's aspects were Anann, who remained in the spirit realm as the source of power to the other two, and a set of twin girls who were periodically reborn into the human realm during times of great trouble: the sage Anya and the warrior Aisling.

1

Kingdom of Meath, Ireland
September 1387

Aisling fell through the rain in a land bright and dark, where the edges of contrast were sharp, often bloody. She had thought, even at thirteen, that she understood the many dangers of this land where the boundaries of the human and the Sidhe realms merged, as only someone who had been trained since birth to rule both worlds could. Now it was knowing, not understanding, that was carried on the tip of the arrow that had slipped beneath her left shoulder blade on its way to her heart. Launched from her galloping horse, her body attempting to flee the arrow's intrusion, her arc ended abruptly in mud, facedown. Then the pain came, an edge flaying her chest from the inside.

Riding beside her as he always did, Liam, guardian of the Morrígna twins, twisted on his horse to follow Aisling's unexpected flight. A moment earlier his attention had been drawn across the clearing ahead, where he had sensed a rush of fear and desire, a sudden movement of iron, and a flood of intent. He had thrown his dagger even before the assailant he perceived—a crossbreed like himself, neither pure human nor pure Sidhe—had fully emerged from behind the ring of seven standing stones. The knife had caught the attacker just under the chin, lifted him off his feet, and sent his already drawn arrow flying wide. As if a single iron-tipped arrow would ever make it past him and on to her without one of them deflecting it. Now, seeing Aisling land in the mud, he wondered how he could have fallen for such a diversion. The arrow that pierced her back had come from the opposite direction, undetected from the woods behind them.

Two of the four guards who had thundered into the clearing with Liam and Aisling wheeled and charged the tree line. The others, swords drawn, surveyed their surroundings while reining in their horses, whose nervous hooves sprayed more mud across Aisling's body.

Liam sat calmly, turning his mount to scan the woods, then walking it over to where she lay, the shaft protruding from her back. He had inherited his muscular build from his human father, who was of a warrior clan, while his dignified stature came from his mother, a Sidhe—a Celtic term for those the Irish Christian Church called Nephilim or, more casually, faeries. Leaning a forearm on his horse's neck, Liam studied Aisling. The splattering of rain mixed with the sounds of branches snapping as the guards zigzagged their horses through the undergrowth in a futile search for the second archer.

"Are you going to get up?" demanded Liam. "The high king's waiting for us. We can't dally here all afternoon. You're going to make us late for the full-moon ritual, and I don't want to miss the feast. You have to be stronger than this."

Aisling dragged one arm under her chest, then the other, and struggled up to her hands and knees. Water trickled from her deep red hair, leaving pale streaks down the side of her grime-soaked face. Liam could not see her eyes but knew they would have gone from light gray to vivid green. He also knew that she should be on her feet already—something was wrong.

"Poison," Aisling gasped. "In . . . my . . . heart. Spreading. Burning."

"Great Mother Danu!" exclaimed Liam in frustration. "I told the king that we should have you in mail already, even if you haven't been enthroned yet." He reached down and tore the arrow out. She grunted and collapsed back into mud that was beginning to take on a red tint—her red.

"He thinks if one of you is safe, then the other is too. Well, now he'll grasp that he has too narrow a view of 'safe.'"

As a warrior, Liam had to admit that the shot had been remarkable. The archer had to adjust for a target galloping away in the rain.

At that angle the bowman had to miss the shoulder blade and hit the gap between the seventh and eight ribs to catch the only part of her heart not protected by bone. Shot too softly, the arrow would not reach the critical vessel, too hard and the tip would pass through the heart, taking the bulk of the poison with it. He knew of no human archer with such skill.

Aisling was back on her hands and knees, head hanging limp. She reached out and fumbled for the dangling reins of her horse. Raising her head, she climbed the reins with both hands until she was standing, clinging to the bridle, shaking.

Liam studied the unusual arrow, making no move to help her. It had been carefully constructed to be undetectable even by a crossbreed such as himself, whose senses were inhumanly sharp. There was nothing unnatural or even animal to draw his attention, to differentiate it from the wooded background. A hawthorn shaft, he noted; a Celtic assassin would have used elm. No human would dare to cut a hawthorn tree, sacred to the Sidhe, not in this land and suffer the curse that was sure to follow. Instead of feathers, ash leaves, meticulously sliced lengthwise along their stems, were used for flights. The head was made of oak, hardened by centuries buried in a bog and then polished razor sharp. The Sidhe archer had to have been a member of an old-line assassin clan or the arrowhead purchased from one at a high price. Few could afford such a rare thing. Sniffing, Liam was surprised that he could not identify the poison, but there had been a lot of it, judging by the warren of small channels drilled into its head.

But why bother? Liam wondered. Whoever had staged this attack would have known that Aisling could not be killed, not so long as her twin sister, Anya, was safe. And Liam always made sure that Anya was protected in a secure room while Aisling was traveling. *Were they trying to send a message?* He shook his head. No, there had been too much effort and expense; there was serious intent to kill here. Then it hit him: Anya must not be safe. They must have found a way to get to both twins. Liam jumped from his horse, reaching Aisling just as she began screaming.

As he held her, his chest too tight to utter any words of comfort, he feared that he must have failed in his duty, his oath to protect the Morrígna twins. He picked Aisling up and carried her to his horse while her screams faded into sobs.

Earlier that morning the courtyard of Trim Castle was full of wagons being loaded with barrels of ale and wine, casks of fresh-ground flour, bushels of vegetables, and whole sides of beef. Tender piglets crowded into cages squealed high-pitched above the low grunts of their older cousins as all were loaded alongside stacks of the iron roasting spits with which they would soon be intimate.

There were shouts of "Careful! Careful! Quick, grab the other end!" as long banners bearing the emblem of the Morrígna—three strands intertwined in a complex knot—were lowered from the high windows where they had hung for the last year. Folded and wrapped in oilcloth, they were packed into the last of the wagons about to depart for the Irish capital city of Tara, where they would be rehung. Trim was the birthplace of the current incarnation of the Morrígna twins and so was sponsoring much of their coronation ceremony, to be held in the capital four days hence, on their fourteenth birthday.

Punctuating the hubbub came the rhythmic *snap, snap, snap* of pendants on their poles above guard towers, being tested by the wind rolling gray-black clouds overhead. A gust swirled down into the courtyard, whipping the white robe about the old, wiry body of Haidrean, the high druid. He stood with Aisling and Anya, frowning as he took note that tradespeople and nobles alike, hurrying to finalize preparations, either rushed their bow to the twins or forgot altogether. As if the pending coronation festivities were the important thing, instead of the twins themselves. Two handmaids walked up carrying identical coronation gowns.

"Why aren't those packed?" barked Haidrean, causing the hand-maids to cringe.

Anya came to the rescue. "Because I wanted to see them first. Aren't they beautiful!"

"They're fine," replied Aisling, giving the dresses—white silk elab-orately embroidered with gold and silver thread—little more than a glance.

"Get them in their trunk," ordered Haidrean, and the handmaids rushed off.

Though Anya and Aisling were identical twins, few had trouble telling them apart, due to their different countenances. Anya, older by minutes, was as joyful and mischievous as her sister was serious. Aisling bore the tight mouth and often furrowed brow of a young woman who had already watched a man die on her sword. Even though it had been a training accident, she knew that more deaths would fol-low, which would not be accidents but the cost of her destiny. And there was their hair, thick red against pale skin; Anya let hers fall free over her shoulders and down her back, while Aisling kept hers in a long plait, swept up and out of the way. Tall, even for their family, and slender with light gray eyes. They would walk into rooms full of kings never knowing what it felt like to bow, thirteen-year-olds who had not been allowed to have a childhood, trained since birth to unlock their Goddess nature and source enough primordial magic from the spirit realm—drawn by way of Anann in the Otherworld—to rule over both Sidhe and Celts.

With a cry of "Yeeup!" a driver snapped the reins on the back of his pair of horses, and the first wagonload of provisions rolled out the castle gate, followed by others. They would return the next day to load up the tents, great ones for parties and smaller ones for lodg-ing, and soon afterward the castle and village would empty out as people flocked to Tara for the once-in-a-lifetime event.

Liam, imposing in a mail tunic, a battle-ax strapped to his back and a brace of daggers and a claymore hanging on his belt, made a straight path through the bustle leading two horses. People instinctively moved out of his way. Reaching Aisling, whose face had brightened at his approach, he handed her the reins of one of the horses.

"Is everything prepared?" he asked his counterpart, Haidrean.

Over the years they had become surrogate parents to the twins, Haidrean as tutor—primarily to Anya—and Liam as fighting instructor—primarily to Aisling, though foremost among Liam's duties was that of bodyguard. Anytime either or both twins were not with him, he took great measures to ensure their safety within the strong walls of the castle keep, which were fortified with incantations.

"I renewed the enchantments myself. Anya will be fine," said Haidrean. A drop of rain fell heavily at his feet. "You two better be on your way."

"The high king sent word that he will be coming to the full-moon ritual as well. We will stay overnight with him there—"

"So Liam can sleep off the ale," broke in Aisling.

"So he can escort us to Tara," corrected Liam.

Anya threw her arms around her sister. "Can you believe it? Next time I see you will be at our coronation. We will finally be Goddesses!"

"One Goddess," corrected Haidrean.

"In four days, then," said Aisling. She kissed her sister on the cheek and slipped from her embrace.

Haidrean ushered Anya into the keep, knowing that Liam would not ride out until she was secure inside.

"Breakfast before studies," declared Anya, taking the corridor toward their private dining chamber. The guards followed closely behind them.

When they eventually moved to the library, Anya was laughing at a comment Haidrean had made about the bishop of Rome's being unable to read or write.

"It gives him an excuse to keep a stable of young scribes he calls into his bedchamber to read to him at night." Twitching his ample eyebrows, Haidrean added, "Young male scribes."

Anya leaned toward him. "So you're smarter than the pope?"

"They don't seem to elect popes for their intellect," Haidrean responded, and Anya slipped into laughter again.

As he had done in the dining chamber, Haidrean took a large iron key from his pocket, so large that it would not have fit the lock if he had tried. Instead he touched it gently to the door, which shuddered as if it had been struck with great force, indicating that the room was sealed. Anya plopped into a chair at the heavy wooden table, which was ornately carved with intertwined foliage and fanciful animals in the Celtic La Tène style. Screens constructed from stretched sheep intestine, scraped almost clear, were set into the tall, narrow windows, keeping the increasing rain and wind out of the stone chamber on the second level of the castle. What little light entered from the exterior gloom was reflected off the lime-washed white walls and supplemented by four candles in a silver holder on one end of the table and three simply stuck into a mound of wax on the other end. Expensive wax candles, because Haidrean refused to subject his books to the smoky animal fat of cheaper tallow. "The king may grumble, but he can afford it," said Haidrean as he lit another candle and stuck it on the mound.

"Perhaps he can also afford a second candle holder," Anya offered, rolling a ball of fresh wax between her thumb and forefinger.

A large fire radiated heat and a warm glow. On this gray day, it was the only operating hearth in the castle without dogs sleeping in front, as druids do not keep dogs. Books were stacked in large piles on shelves and chests around the room. Hadrian placed two books on the table, the title *Rome* written across their buckskin covers, and opened them to reveal vellum pages dense with script.

Crossing her arms, Anya gave one of her rare frowns. "Aisling gets to ride around with Liam, learning to fight, while I'm confined here with you, learning the ways of these Roman Christians."

"Before you were born, the Morrígna designated you as her sage aspect," said Haidrean, tired of repeating himself on this point, "and Aisling as her warrior. You can't change that."

"That may be, but Aisling's aspect is more fun," replied Anya. "And she'll get to stay up here in the sun."

"Sun?" asked Haidrean, looking at the window.

"My point is that after our coronation I'm meant to reign from a damp underworld. But I have decided that the day I'm crowned, I'll decree that forevermore both Morrígna twins are allowed to live out in the light of the human world."

"The Sidhe need an aspect of the Morrígna in the Middle Kingdom for your rule to be recognized. That is your duty and your destiny and why there are two of you. You and Aisling will be Goddess of both lands. Besides, your new palace won't seem like a damp underworld to you after the coronation."

"You really think I'll feel different then?"

"Of course," Haidrean assured her. "Already you feel Aisling as part of yourself. Concentrate and try to describe it."

She turned her focus inward. "It's like she is sitting right here with me, only more so. She fills half the very essence of who I am. I can't think of myself without thinking of her. She brings strength to me, as I know I bring knowledge to her." Anya shut her eyes. "At the same time, I am also with her. We are galloping through the woods, I feel the wet and cold she feels." Anya shivered and gave a little laugh. "We are urging our horse to run faster, trying to out-pace Liam."

"During the coronation ceremony, you will take the next step," said Haidrean. "You will no longer feel Aisling inside you, because you will not sense yourself as separate from her. You will finish becoming one being. You might not even remember there was a time when you were two.

"Now open your eyes and return to your lesson on the Roman Church." Haidrean leaned across the table and slid a book toward her.

"For centuries they plotted against Ireland, and they plot still. You need to understand them."

Anya pushed the book a few inches back toward him. "The Vatican wouldn't dare attack us, not after we routed Strongbow the last time they tried. And my Irish Christian Church is as much an enemy to the Roman Church as we are. It grows ever stronger and has as many monasteries across Britain and Europe as the Vatican does." Anya grinned as she added, "Is it true what they say about Strongbow, about how he acquired that moniker, that he was gifted below the waist?"

"Remember," said Haidrean, ignoring her question, "the Irish Church will not fall under your rule, so you cannot count on them to fight for you. The Morrígna commands the armies of the Celts and the Sidhe only."

"And the Fomorians. No ships will get past them without my permission," added Anya.

Haidrean loathed Fomorians, the fierce race of amphibious Nephilim who stalked the seas around Ireland, always reeking of rotten fish. They were troublesome creatures, but between Celts and Christians, Haidrean knew they preferred to eat Christians, any Christians. "They were of great assistance stopping Strongbow," he conceded, "so I suspect you can count on them with proper gifts and firm threats. But even with those forces at your command, you'll need to be vigilant and prepared. In the two hundred years since the Vatican sent Strongbow to invade Ireland, the Roman Church has fallen and risen anew, stronger and more deceptive than ever. I believe that you'll have to fight them once more, very soon."

"Surely the Skeaghshee are a more pressing problem," insisted Anya.

"You can worry about negotiations with them after your birthday, young lady. They'll submit to your authority once you're enthroned."

Even as Haidrean said this, he worried that it might not be true. The law called for the twins to ascend to the throne at the age of fourteen, in four days, and Haidrean felt in his bones that they would be tested early and severely. Anya and Aisling were born the Morrígna—the Test had proved that; however, the reincarnated Morrígna arrived trapped in their human shells. From that day they had to be taught to connect to their Goddess selves and to strip away their human frailties fortified by fear and insecurity. They had to learn to act as one, in order to bring the Morrígna to the forefront of their being, and be trained to control the supernatural power that would be fully unleashed upon their coronation.

To prepare for his role, Haidrean had studied the journals of the earlier tutors and discovered that preceding sets of Morrígna twins had found it increasingly difficult to transcend their human limitations. The last set never fully merged. It had looked as if this world was becoming less willing to accept the Goddess. Then, when the current Anya and Aisling were born, suddenly every druid in Ireland began foretelling that they would become the strongest twins in an age. That prediction was the source of his worries as he watched Anya creating another ball of wax. If the Morrígna needed to manifest such strong physical aspects, these twins must be destined to face some monumental challenge.

Haidrean wondered anew if the Skeaghshee—tree-worshipping Sidhe who were in increasing conflict with the Celts—were truly going to submit to the twins' authority or if they were the threat that had called the Morrígna back to this world. The Skeaghshee's insolent King Kellach had not returned the Morrígna heart segment left in trust with his clan as required by law. When that segment went missing seven years back, druids stopped predicting how powerful the current twins would be and instead began trying to foresee how much their strength would be impaired.

No, he thought, the Roman Church would be the main threat. He just hoped he had been a worthy teacher.

"The Vatican doesn't worry me, no matter how strong they have become," said Anya, as if reading his mind.

"They should worry you," replied Haidrean. "The condottieri army of indentured prisoners, mercenaries, spies, and assassins assembled by Cardinal Albornoz reunited the Papal States and returned the pope to Rome from his Babylonian captivity in Avignon."

"The bishop of Rome is back in Rome. How convenient." Anya laughed.

"Few in Europe found it funny. The Vatican's new army killed everyone in their path who'd opposed the restoration of a Roman pope. Since then the Vatican has been consolidating independent Christian factions at the point of a sword. Now the new pope eyes the remaining church holdouts, and the Irish Church is the largest by far. Their home in our land vexes him as much as does our alliance with the Middle Kingdom."

"My forces will keep them out of my lands," Anya said.

"As the power of the Morrígna has kept the Vatican's forces at bay, so have Rome's forces kept us confined to these islands. The Skeagh-shee may be your first challenge once you assume your throne, but I'm sure the Roman Church will be your greatest," replied Haidrean.

Anya leaned her chair back to balance on two legs. "You promised to tell me how you became a druid, but you haven't yet. Tell me now."

Haidrean knew she was trying to distract him to avoid further history lessons; he also knew that underneath her playfulness she was anxious about her pending enthronement. The wind rattled a window screen free, and it fell. He caught it with a spell and sealed it back in place. Corporeal magic had once been an embarrassing weakness of his, but to his wonderment even these enchantments had worked well for him since the twins arrived.

Anya was waiting expectantly. Unable to resist her request, Haidrean began, "I was called, without knowing I was being called, as all true druids are.

"I'd borrowed my father's silver knife and before dawn went out to gather purple betony for a healing potion. As I rested at a well and watched the sunrise, I became aware of a sound. My father was the bard of our village, so even at seven years old I knew enough not to be Pixie-led. Still, there was something"—his eyes stared into a distant past—"something like song, a song that bore the scent of an unknown flower, that drew me. I followed it through a doorway in a Sidhe mound, traveling with new purpose. There was a Middle Kingdom sunset and a moonrise and voices in a dark that seemed to extend forever, until I felt the touch of a woman, the woman who had sung to me. She took my hand, and we danced and laughed and lay together."

"At seven?"

"I was no longer seven. What seemed like only a day and a night had changed me physically. When I awoke to another sunrise, I was alone, back at the well in our land, and my body had passed into manhood. I could still feel her lips against my ear, whispering secrets that I struggle to understand even today. I wrapped my too-small cloak around my now-adult waist, gathered the betony, and returned to my father's house to learn that I'd been gone seven years and a day.

"Soon I began to realize that I saw, felt, heard everything differently. There was new knowledge open to my thoughts, new skills coached by memories of those voices in the dark. A week after my return, the previous high druid arrived bearing a druid's brooch for me. He'd witnessed my change in a dream and offered to teach me to understand what I'd been told in the Middle Kingdom. I left with him for Tara that day."

"And the woman, the Sidhe of your passion?" asked Anya.

"We need to return to your studies."

"Tell me, please. I fear growing old alone in my bed in the Middle Kingdom, while the Sidhe around me remain young. Your story keeps hope alive for my own passions."

"She continued to come to me, some nights, in my dreams. Nights full of the taste of her skin and the smell of her hair . . ." Haidrean's words drifted off.

"Not just in dreams, if your son is any evidence."

"With those from the Middle Kingdom, it's often difficult to tell the difference between dreaming and being awake. I'm not sure it matters to them. My son appeared in a dream one night, a fresh wiggling baby, and was still there when I awoke."

"Does she come to you still?"

"Occasionally, though not to my bed. Now she only stands in the forest, as young as ever, watching our son gather wild rose by moonlight. I often wonder if one day he, too, will go on a long walk and if he'll return at all. You know, I hope to go back to the Middle Kingdom someday—I think possibly when I've learned enough to understand all her whispered words, after you're enthroned and I'm no longer needed."

Anya did not hear him.

Haidrean saw that her eyes had turned vivid green. Behind him he heard the sound of small stones falling to the floor, followed by a sharp crack. He turned to see a fresh, rough opening no more than a foot tall in the stone wall. From it a Skeaghshee emerged and straightened up to his full seven-foot height. Haidrean recognized him as Cinaed, brother to Kellach the Skeaghshee king. Without a word Cinaed strode toward Haidrean, drawing a long, slender sword from the scabbard strapped to his back.

No, this can't be, thought Haidrean. *She hasn't been given the chance to negotiate their grievances.* He turned back to Anya and could see that she was with her twin, her eye color and the pain moving across her face telling him everything he needed to know. Aisling had also been attacked. All was about to be lost. Leaning across the table, he spoke urgently into her ear, "Send Aisling all your strength. Now. It's the only hope."

◈

As LIAM AND Aisling were riding out of Trim Castle, Kellach stood on a low rise not far away in the midst of dozens of fresh tree stumps. The gathering storm whipped his long hair, the brown of oak bark, about his thin face that was contorted with fury, for he was king of the Skeaghshee, Sidhe of the open and wild forests, and before him was a scene of murder. Running his hand over the rough wood he tried to comfort the dying base and roots. He could feel the presence of the tree's ghost, as an amputee feels a missing arm and the sudden, sharp sting of the ax it had suffered.

Skeaghshee were the Sidhe clan most in contact with the Celtic world, as they lived out in the woodland that covered Ireland rather than within the Middle Kingdom. While many Sidhe ate as humans ate, Skeaghshee drew all their sustenance, pleasure, and joy from the trees they loved.

The time has come to stop this slaughter, Kellach thought. *After today the Celts will have no say over my trees, there will be no Morrígna in this world to subjugate our clan, and the truce between the Sidhe and the Celts will be broken.*

Sensing his younger brother Cinaed approach, Kellach said, "I summoned you to make sure you saw this before your sortie. Behold another assault on our clan."

Cinaed bowed and said, "A tragedy, my king. My heart weeps with yours."

"Celts are creatures who think only of their own pathetic needs: wood for their carts and their furniture and their fires and their buildings," Kellach continued. "Some say the truce is adequate, with prayers and offerings each time a tree is taken, but now they have gone too far, allowing the Vikings to cut trees for their ships and even to export wood to the French to make barrels for their wine. More and more often, our clan is left grieving over offenses such as this."

"I understand the stakes, my king. I will not fail you."

"My brother." Kellach grasped Cinaed's shoulders. "Others worship the earth or the sun or even water, but trees, trees are all three brought alive, living, breathing, talking to our people. No offering is adequate for the death of even one of our trees. Celts and their allies will never allow our woods to remain sacred, never truly respect our kind. If the Skeaghshee are ever going to be free, we must act now. You are my champion. Remember what I have taught you and you will prevail."

"My sword is hungry, my king."

Watching him stride away, Kellach felt confident that his moment of victory was at hand.

The rain had started in earnest, pounding the land above as Cinaed stood impatiently in a tight earthen tunnel facing the foundation stones of Trim Castle. He longed to be through with his task. Sidhe do not concern themselves with the height of the passages through which they travel; that is not what troubled him. He was troubled by a faint, nagging voice inside his head. Different from Kellach's ravings and his own obedient responses, this voice told him that he was about to break a sacred oath and that he had been led astray.

On each side of him stood a Grogoch, a shorter—relatively speaking in this confined space—much stockier Sidhe clan, reciting to the stones. For a millennium and longer, the Skeaghshee had intimidated the Grogoch into leaving a warren of secret faerie passages in the stones that they provided to the Celts for their castles, invaluable for spying. Once the existence of these passages becomes known to their druids—humans pretending to be Sidhe witches—they will be found and destroyed, thought Cinaed. It will be a great loss, but worthwhile under the circumstances. Glancing at one of the creatures now singing to the wall, Cinaed willed it to hurry. *Grogoch think as slowly as the rock they love.*

The song of the Grogoch faded, taking with it the enchantment that had been hiding the passage he needed, this was the first time this one had been used. In front of him, a small door appeared, set in the face of a single foundation stone, two feet high by four feet wide. Opening it with a word, he bent and entered.

Cinaed stepped into Haidrean's library at last and straightened up to his full height. He had been delayed, not long, but maybe too long.

He flung a silent curse back down the passage at the waiting Gro-goch, ignored their muffled cry of pain. Some clumsiness or laziness or double-dealing by their kind centuries earlier had left this passage without an exit door in the last stone. He'd been forced to break through into the chamber. In doing so he had triggered an enchant-ment designed to protect the room and, more problematically, alerted the druid Haidrean to his approach.

He pushed briefly against the enchantment with his conscious-ness and realized that he was not going to survive. It had closed too late to keep him out—the druid who cast it must not have considered an attack through the wall—so now it was going to keep him in. Reaching for his sword, Cinaed strode toward the pair at the table, but the old druid was already whispering to Anya, "Send Aisling all your strength. Now. It's the only hope."

Cinaed's sword swept down, severing Haidrean's head. He leaped over the table and thrust at the unmoving Anya. As he carved through breast and bone, he could feel that the Morrígna was already leaving. There was little more than this shell left. *Gods, don't let me be too late*, he thought. Kellach had stressed that the attacks on the twins had to be simultaneous in order to kill them both. Cinaed reached into the cleft he had made in her chest and pulled out a heart that began to shrivel in his hand.

Still, he hesitated. In the fifteen hundred years since the Battle of Tailltiu, which led to the truce between the Sidhe and the Celts, three attempts had been made to assassinate a physical aspect of the Morrígna, yet no assassin had ever held half the Morrígna heart in his hand, as he now did. *What will the two worlds become without the Goddess to connect them?* he worried. She was the ruler of their high kings, the one being to whom all Sidhe and Celts alike owed allegiance, bound by ancient oaths.

Looking down at the heart folding in on itself, he could feel the enchantment fading at the chamber door. Soon the guards who had been shouting for Anya would be able to enter. He thought of the words of Kellach. Raising the heart to his mouth, he bit off a large chunk and began to chew. The dagger of the first guard reached him as he swallowed the last piece.

&

AISLING COULD FEEL Anya's energy flowing into her body, keeping her alive, when suddenly a wound she did not know could be inflicted opened up in her, bringing pain that eclipsed that of the arrow and its poison. In that instant her bond with her sister was ripped away, and with it her connection to the Otherworld. Screaming, she collapsed into Liam's arms, knowing for the first time since conception what it was to be alone, to be less than whole.

Kellach watched Liam carry a limp and sobbing Aisling to his horse. Having made himself indistinguishable from the surrounding trees, the Skeaghshee king stood in the rain at the edge of the clearing. A brief shudder passed through him, like a faint gust through leaves, as he felt the death of his brother, Cinaed. Knowing that Liam could sense the presence of a powerful Sidhe, Kellach was careful to remain concealed. Although he detested all crossbreeds, Liam was one whom he would prefer not to fight by himself. So he waited until the guards regrouped, collected Aisling's horse, and galloped back the way they had come.

Expelling the Morrígna with concurrent attacks had been too much to hope for, he thought. Kellach had preached to his followers that if each of the twins' hearts could be destroyed before its share of the Morrígna could retreat to the Otherworld, the Treaty of Tailltiu would be broken and all the Sidhe clans would at last unite and rise against the Celts and the Christians and reclaim the land they had lost. He, Kellach, would lead them to victory.

As his concealment enchantment faded, Kellach retreated into the woods. He should not have had to sacrifice his brother. He should not have had to deal with the twins at all, he thought, his anger

rising. They were not truly entitled to rule and should not have participated in the Ceremony of Hearts seven years ago, even if they
had survived the Test. He alone of all the kings of the Middle Kingdom had stood up to the Morrígna's tyranny. He alone had refused
to return the pitifully small segment of heart that had been granted
to the Skeaghshee clan for safeguarding, after the passing of the previous Morrígna twins. Without it the Ceremony of Hearts had been
a sham, he told himself.

But now even the high kings would have to acknowledge that the
surviving twin was flawed and, by the laws of both the Sidhe and the
Celts, could not rule either race. Aisling had been wounded as never
before. With her diminished state, he would seize the next chance he
got to kill her and banish the Morrígna for all time.

2

Fourteen years before Liam would become protector to the Morrígna twins, he stood alongside Earnan on the island of Toraigh, off the northwest corner of Ireland. Liam's human ancestors were Gallowglass, warrior elite of mixed descent—traces of Norse, Gael, and Pict—from the isles and highlands of Scotland. When they had established this training school, more than a century ago, they named it Sgathaich Scoil after their old fortress on the Isle of Skye—the Fortress of Shadows.

On this clear afternoon, Earnan, a young instructor, readied himself to face off with Treasa, Liam's fully human niece, who was waiting in the center of the practice field. In her left hand, she gripped an elegantly curved scimitar, an unusual sword for a Gallowglass. A polished chain-mail vest shimmered serpentine over her red padded jacket; loose trousers were drawn tight at her ankles. A heavy silver torc, in the form of a twisted rope, circled her long neck. She clenched and unclenched her right hand into a taut fist, her gaze unwavering.

"What did you do to anger her this time?" asked Liam.

"I don't know. I just asked her if she'd like to share my bed tonight," replied Earnan.

Liam handed Earnan a round wooden shield, two feet in diameter. "Take this and maybe you'll survive with all your limbs attached."

Bare-chested, muscular, and wearing a copper torc, Earnan stood at least a foot taller than Treasa and weighed more than twice as much. He bowed his head for a mumbled prayer to Frey and then reached for his claymore. He raised the weapon, pulled his shoulders back, and rushed at his fellow instructor with a roar.

"Next time offer to go to her bed!" Liam shouted after him. "That works sometimes!"

Sgathaich Scoil boasted over three hundred young Gallowglass students. They were joined by a hundred Celtic boys and girls who showed sufficient skill and whose families had the required funds.

The Gallowglass had emigrated en masse to Ireland rather than convert to Christianity following the Treaty of Perth in 1266, when Norway ceded northwest Scotland to England's Edward I. With unsurpassed fighting skills, they quickly became one of the most powerful guilds in Ireland, as every lord of substance hired a garrison of at least a hundred. Not influenced by local feuds or clan pressure, their loyalty was unquestioned, as long as their contract was in force.

Liam watched the warrior dance between Treasa and Earnan, occasionally calling out instructions to Earnan. To the north of the practice field stood a ring fort, a castle keep, and a section of defensive wall. Beyond that, in a large lake hidden in a dense wood, stood the last type of fortress common in Ireland, a man-made island structure called a crannog. In the water's depths dwelled a group of Fomorians—a race banished from all other Irish lakes—who were known to make the occasional meal out of hapless students attacking the crannog, even though Liam left that challenge for the students' sixth year.

To the east stretched the village that had grown up with the school. To the west before the tree line stood a ring of standing stones in front of what appeared as a small hill, but with a stone-rimmed door set in its side: one of the entrances to the Middle Kingdom, home to most Sidhe clans. No battle, not even a mock battle, could be fought without gifts to bind contracts with the local Sidhe. Otherwise swords might stop a fraction too late or mail might develop weak spots. Liam, of mixed blood, handled these negotiations. His Sidhe mother was a Devas noble, a willowy beauty. His father claimed he had captured and bedded her the day he moved to Toraigh Island to take over the school, though who had captured whom had been a lively debate between Liam's parents throughout his early years, until his mother sang over his father's grave and walked back into the Middle Kingdom. His father had bequeathed the school to Liam, but from his mother's blood-line he was gifted with a variety of foresight. He instinctively knew the next move of any adversary standing close enough to attack him with a sword or ax, making his opponent's life span brief.

Liam was watching a squire run out to Earnan with a replacement claymore—the original one lay some distance away—when something between a sound and a feeling caused him to turn. The full moon had just risen into the late-afternoon sky, giant against the distant Donegal hills across the channel separating the island from the mainland. A flock of rooks wheeled and swooped, boiling black against the silver moonscape. Rolling toward Liam from the rocky coastline, their cries overwhelmed the clang of steel against steel.

As the black mass passed overhead, Liam knew he had been called, an enchanted call that told him he would soon be needed elsewhere. It may have come in the cry of the birds, or in the wind they rode upon, or in the leaves that rustled in their wake. Or perhaps from something else entirely. It was a moment of knowing for those like Liam who could still perceive. Even in Ireland many were forgetting how to—forgetting itself a force as powerful as any spell—but not those who carried the blood of the Sidhe.

Turning to the practice field, Liam saw that Earnan was now on his back with Treasa astride his waist, the point of her sword pressed up under his chin. In her right hand, a dagger—Earnan's own, Liam noted—slowly drew a red line across his chest. Treasa liked to leave a scar if her opponent had fought particularly well. She bent down and began to clean the wound with her tongue, her sword never leaving Earnan's throat.

Earnan may get his wish after all, Liam thought. "Treasa, finish up!" he shouted. "I must leave for Trim Castle before the next new moon, and there's much to be done."

Treasa moved her sword away from Earnan's neck. "When will you be back?"

"I don't know." Liam gestured toward the retreating flock. "I have been called. The Morrígna may be returning."

Treasa smiled down at Earnan. "That means real battles are in my future. I've dreamed of this time."

"For now the school is yours to run," Liam instructed her. "Try not to kill too many students, particularly those with wealthy families."

Liam walked toward the school buildings, troubled. Had it truly been the long-absent Morrígna's call? Or—more likely—the signal of some overeager druid who believed they had identified the Goddess twins? Since the last set, ambition or incompetence on the part of several druids had caused them to misread the signs, dooming the infant girls who were subjected to the Test. Liam dearly hoped this was not such a mistake.

He quickened his pace. If the call in fact signaled the Morrígna's return, then he was destined to play a significant role.

✧

BRIGID, HIGH PRIESTESS of the Order of Macha, lingered in the corridor of Trim Castle, working to still her anxious mind. Extending her senses, she felt the ancient stones of the floor, which remembered each tread they had supported. Reaching out even farther, she connected with the earth below. It welcomed her touch, and its powerful spirit rose to fill and renew her. So much of becoming a druid, she thought, was simply learning to trust: trust the forces of this magical land, trust the messages they brought.

Her childhood name had been Lisir, until she had given it up to become Brigid, the title carried by each successive head of her exclusively female order, the only celibate order in Ireland, Celtic or Christian. *Celibacy is my good curves wasted,* Brigid liked to say. But she took her vows seriously, recognizing that the sacrifice strengthened her commitment to her sisterhood.

Ahead was Una and Quinn's chamber, and she willed herself forward. With two lives at stake in the Test—one of them her own—she could not afford to let fear cloud her judgment. And she owed it to her dear friend Una not to infect her with doubt.

She flung open their chamber door and strode in.

"Brigid!" cried a nude and very pregnant Una from beneath her husband, Quinn.

"Oh," said Brigid, stopping halfway across the room.

Quinn rose from the bed, and Una sat up. Neither of them moved to cover themselves.

"What are you doing here?" asked Una.

"I was called. We must speak."

"Now?"

"Yes. Now." Brigid's eyes turned toward Quinn apologetically.

"Why are you here?" asked Una a few moments later as she gently lowered herself onto the bench beside Brigid, her face still flushed. They sat at a wooden table in the warm kitchen. Behind them two cooks worked at an array of pots hanging inside a fireplace much taller than either and wider than both.

"As I said, I was called. The Morrígna twins are returning."

"Finally," said Una. "It has been much too long." She sat quiet for a moment and then, with a hint of unease in her voice, asked, "Who? Where?"

Brigid was busy pulling cold meat off the leg of lamb sitting on a wooden platter and stuffing it into her mouth. Stalling, she quipped, "You know, eating is a sorry replacement for sex, but at least there's some satisfaction to be had, and seeing others engage always makes me hungry."

"Brigid, tell me."

Brigid wiped her hands and mouth, then reached out and laid her palm on Una's extended belly.

"No. There's only one heartbeat. I feel the spirit of only one life. It can't be," said Una.

"That's how it always is with the twins. You are of the line."

"There are many of the line. You must be mistaken."

"You're to be birth mother to the Morrígna twins, the new incarnation of Aisling and Anya. It will be so. Don't think to escape your duty. I'm here to assist in the birth. And I'm here to make sure the twins are Tested."

All color drained from Una's face.

❧

LIAM RODE TOWARD Trim Castle along the river Boyne. This grand castle, the capital of the kingdom of Meath, embodied the strategic importance of that artery linking four of Ireland's principal cities and the wealth the trade along it brought. Described in the Viking fashion starting from the sea, the river entered Ireland mid–east coast, just north of the Irish Viking capital of Dublin. Inland, it swept in a graceful arc around Brú na Bóinne, the only Sidhe city left in this world, though the forty faerie palaces could easily be mistaken for grassy hills by an uninitiated or uninvited visitor. Then the water flowed past Tara, the capital of Ireland and home of the high king, before meandering to Trim, where the castle controlled a ford, the farthest point that trade ships from the sea could navigate.

Castles could be useful as a last resort, thought Liam as he approached the barbican gate. He preferred to meet his opponents on the battlefield, where they met a quick end. But the Celtic monarchs had to hold court somewhere. Gallowglass had no monarch or formal election proceedings, deferring instead to an organic process based solely on respect, which had thrust Liam into a de facto leadership role for the last decade. During that time he had come to know many of the Irish queens and kings, a changing assemblage as they were elected, not born to their posts.

The sun was setting, but the drawbridge was still down and the portcullis open. The gate guards recognized him and waved him through. "Liam, come join us!" one of them called, rolling a pair of dice. "I need someone new in the game to change my luck."

"Later tonight!" Liam called back, his horse clopping across the bridge. "Unless I get a better offer."

Over the years Liam had supervised at least one royal election in each of the five kingdoms of Ireland. The resulting current cast of rulers were: King Turlough of Meath, who wore his battle scars as badges of honor, and whose castle Liam was entering; Mael of Connacht, the young and feisty queen who had trained at Sgathaich Scoil; King Murchada of Leinster, who kept his hair long so it would stream out behind him like a black flag when he charged; Queen Gormflaith of Munster, who could outwit the rest and had the largest library in Ireland; and the recently elected King Niall of Ulster, who Liam thought was more of a politician than a fighter, part of that rising breed of leaders.

The elected queens and kings, along with high nobles and guild masters, went on to elect the Celtic high king, a position that had always gone to males, though Liam knew of no law that required it. He suspected that it was to preserve the Irish sense of balance, as both the Celtic and Sidhe high kings answered to the Morrígna twins, always female—that is, when the twins were present in this world, which they had not been for many generations.

Since hearing the call, Liam had felt his doubts about its source grow. He looked up at the keep and worried for his friends Una and Quinn and the pending Test of their newborn daughters. Only two outcomes were possible: if passed, great honor for the twins tempered by great loss for the parents; if failed, tragedy for all.

Liam made his way through the grounds crowded with the everyday bustle of a regional capital, passed the substantial stone building that housed the mint, left his horse at the stable, and entered the keep. In the vestibule he unstrapped the battle-ax from his back, unbuckled his sword, and deposited both with the officer of the watch as required. The officer informed him that petitions were being heard in the king's private meeting hall, so Liam bypassed the grand receiving hall on the ground floor and effortlessly ascended the spiral stumble stairs leading to the top floor.

The room was alive with color. The Brehon laws that had governed Ireland since ancient times allowed a person's station to be determined by the number of colors they wore, from slaves, who could wear only one, up to nobility, who could wear seven. While a lord out for a hunt or a lady slipping around to her lover's house might not sport all the colors allowed, a court gathering such as this called for the full display of blues, reds, purples, browns, greens, yellows, and blacks across the tunics, jackets, leggings, and gowns of the nobility, guild heads, and military officers.

Turlough MagRodain, the long-reigning king of Meath, sat flanked by his entourage on a slightly raised platform spanning one end of the hall. The deep scar running down the side of his face, just missing his eye, spoke of his commitment to charging ahead of his troops into battle; the fact that he still lived spoke of his deftness with a blade.

Sitting beside him was his son and a woman whom Liam did not recognize but guessed to be Turlough's new wife, as his previous marriage contract had expired without being renewed. Liam was surprised to see that the Brehon-law judge seated on the king's platform was from Tara, while the chief judge of Meath stood respectfully behind her. *That's fortunate*, thought Liam. Such a member of the high court would be helpful in carrying news of the coming events back to the Celtic high king.

Before King Turlough and the judges gathered a delegation of Irish Vikings including their King Myndill, who had petitioned Turlough to hear their grievances. Liam knew Myndill's history well, as his people had been driven from their Nordic homeland in much the same way as had the Gallowglass, the last Viking faction choosing to remain true to their pagan gods rather than convert to Christianity. King Myndill, stout and bearded, ruled over Dublin, Wexford, Waterford, Cork, and Limerick—his territories connected by the sea.

As Liam eased his way through the crowd to stand in the back of the room, Myndill's son Geir began making their case against the

Skeaghshee, who were interfering with their felling of trees. "It started with our people just getting lost in woods they knew well."

"You have to watch those loose sods," offered a seven-colored noble. Laughter danced around the room.

King Myndill stepped forward and pushed his son aside, as he often did. "My nephew," he declared, his angry, booming voice pressing back the laughter, "was found dead in a wood he had traveled many times. His body withered to a skin-covered skeleton not two days after he led ten of my warriors to protect the woodcutters, woodcutters who were impaled on the branches of the very trees I sent them to harvest from lands lawfully licensed from Lord Maolan." Myndill did not appear to notice that Geir had left the chamber.

"You know that a license is only the beginning," replied the Tara judge. "Without the proper gifts and an agreement with the Skeaghshee, you cut down trees at your own peril."

"There's no negotiating with the Skeaghshee anymore," Myndill retorted. "The tribute demanded by their new king, this Kellach, is unthinkable. In exchange for permission to harvest wood, he required an offering of our children equal in weight. I declined and sent my warriors to protect the woodcutters." The Viking sovereign looked directly at Turlough. "It's only our ships that provide trade with other lands. You need these new ships as much as we do. I ask you, King Turlough, are these Celtic woods or do they belong to the Skeaghshee?"

The room erupted with arguing voices.

A monk in the blue robe of his order and with a fat leather satchel slung from his shoulder wandered over and leaned against the back wall next to Liam. He had been called Patrick as long as Liam had known him, a title bestowed upon the leader of the disciples of the original Patrick, the larger of the two divisions of the Irish Christian Church, the Order of Patrick and the Order of Colmcille.

"Liam, what brings you here?"

"I heard this might be more interesting than the usual gathering."

"A waste of time if you ask me, without any Sidhe monarch or ambassadors."

"Where are they anyway?" Liam asked.

"The Sidhe have refused to meet with the Vikings ever since Myndill took the heads of some innocent Gnome moonlight dancers and spiked them over the Dublin gate in retribution for his nephew's murder."

Liam eyed the tarnished old iron bell conspicuous in a leather holster on the monk's belt. He had heard of the Blood Bell—all had—but he had never seen Patrick wear it before. "Is it true the original Patrick bound a demon into the Bell so he could use it to collect tithes due his church? Its ring is said to be lethal."

"That might have been his purpose, but I am more concerned about protecting my monasteries. A number of dark forces have begun to stir, and we would be one of the first targets if Sidhe or Elioud rebel. Not to mention Vikings and Celt marauders. Best to remind all that the Patricks are far from toothless."

"Some worry more that the Roman Church has designs on Ireland again. Though if they try, I suppose you could just stand on the shore and ring the Bell at any invading ships."

"If the high king wants me to do that," Patrick said with a laugh, "he'd better start paying tithes, large ones. Anyhow, when I carry it, my way along the road from Armagh is never delayed by a loose sod."

"You know, when I ride through the woods, it only takes half as long as when I take the road," said Liam with a smile.

"I often think that you, my friend, are more Sidhe than human. It takes me twice as long, even if some playful Sidhe doesn't cause me to become lost. No matter how much I point out to the Sidhe that the teachings of Christ are similar to their beliefs or how much of our best wine I leave outside our gates for them, they still treat me with little grace."

"Perhaps if you spoke up for the Sidhe now, they would be friendlier to you in the future."

"If it had been any clan other than the Skeaghshee. I can't support them. Not since Kellach became their king. He is fomenting so much unrest, I worry that our land may soon be engulfed in another Sidhe war, without the Morrígna to preside over the races."

"They're great at annoyances and dangerous in small skirmishes, particularly for those who underestimate them," Liam said, nodding toward the Vikings. "But most in the Middle Kingdom have no wish to abandon their pleasures for the rigors and risks of all-out war. They value their long lives, which aren't hard to end with a sharpened edge of iron."

After a fruitless hour, the Viking contingent stormed unsatisfied from the meeting. At a sign from King Turlough, servants entered and began moving long tables from against the walls and into the center of the hall. The royal platform was vacated, and the ceremonial seats were replaced with a table and chairs better suited to dining. In the thick of the bustle stood the steward, seating chart in hand, directing the pages as they guided guests to their appointed places. Liam watched the steward make delicate adjustments in the seating arrangement to accommodate for the departure of the Vikings and for the arrival of unexpected guests, such as himself. Hospitality was a trait essential to those wishing to advance politically, and a skilled steward was highly prized and generously compensated.

Then Liam saw Brigid, as beautiful as ever, standing in the doorway. *So the time has come*, he thought.

3

At first He created her [Lilith] for him [Adam]
and he saw her full of discharge and blood; thereupon
He removed her from him and re-created her a second time [Eve].
Hence it is said: This time she is bone of my bone.

—The Genesis Rabba (circa CE 250)

And Demons shall meet with monsters,
and one hairy one shall cry out to another;
there Lilith has lain down and found rest for herself.

—Isaiah 34:14 (circa CE 382), Latin translation
of the Bible by St. Jerome

Trim Castle, Ireland
The Same Evening

Brigid moved across the crowded meeting chamber, dodging pages as they guided guests to their assigned seats, and joined Liam.

"Was it you or the Morrígna who called me?" Liam asked softly.

"The Morrígna." Brigid's lips brushed against Liam's ear, stirring memories of an earlier time. "I was called as well."

"When will it begin?" Liam asked.

"Soon," said Brigid. "Quinn in particular is struggling. It will take all the courage he and Una possess to subject their twins to the Test."

"Brigid, so good to see you," Patrick broke in, taking both her hands in his. "How is that vow of celibacy going?"

"So far, so good, my dear friend," replied Brigid.

"Well, if you ever change your mind, let me know."

"You'd be the fifth man I tell," she replied, extracting herself from his grip.

"That's better than the last, I suppose," Patrick said, "unless that is the last."

Brigid leaned into Liam and whispered, "You'd be the first."

"Patrick," King Turlough interrupted. "Come sit at my table."

The steward frowned and scribbled a quick note on his chart.

Liam and Brigid were directed to what would have been the Vikings' table. Large platters piled with steaming beef, cabbage, carrots, and roasted hazelnuts were carried into the room, along with jugs of ale and red wine. Cups were quickly drained and filled again as talk returned to the problem on everyone's mind: that Kellach was inciting unrest not just among the Skeaghshee but within other Sidhe clans as well. "How do we maintain the Treaty of Tailltiu without the presence of the Morrígna?" asked the Meath judge from the high table.

Lord Maolan rose to his feet. As the largest landowner in Meath—property inherited from his parents ten years earlier, when he was nineteen—and with growing estates in Leinster and Ulster, Maolan was well known to harbor ambition for nothing less than the Celtic high-kingship. Liam noticed that Maolan had been demoted from King Turlough's table, likely as a result of his licensing trees to the Vikings in direct opposition to Turlough's unofficial but evident wishes.

"The Morrígna has been absent for more than eighty years." Maolan's sharp, thin voice fit his face. "Her time is past. We no longer need a Goddess. You know that in your hearts. We need to take control of our land from all the Sidhe, not only those tree-loving Skeaghshee. Who here is not fed up with having to constantly deal with their meddling ways? Who is happy having to get Sidhe approval on where to build a house? Or having to leave gifts before tilling a field, or being told to whom we can sell our trees?" Scattered supporters raised their cups in agreement. "I say no more negotiating with the Sidhe, no more gifts. We need a high king who can drive them into their underground lair and keep them there, or destroy them altogether."

"And that high king would be you?" Liam spat out, ridicule in his tone.

"You crossbreeds are all spies. As high king I would deal with your kind as well as eliminate the Sidhe from our world."

"How do you propose to do that?" asked the Tara judge. "Have you forgotten the harsh lessons of our history? Forgotten the Battle of Tailltiu, where at least one Celt fell for every Sidhe? Few would have survived if the high kings did not finally see the wisdom of forging a treaty. We must continue to work with our Middle Kingdom brothers."

"We're more powerful now," replied Maolan. "Our druids have learned the ways of the Sidhe. The Vikings will join the fight, as will the Gallowglass. This time we'll achieve complete victory."

"There's no price for which the Gallowglass will fight against my mother's people." Liam was now standing, a dagger in his hand.

"Lords," Turlough broke in. "Ladies. Guild masters. Friends. This matter will be brought before my fellow kings and queens, and the high king, during the coming hurling games at Tara. For now, however, let's not spoil the taste of this fine wine, surely the best in all of Ireland, brought from Siena in Europe as a gift by our gracious Viking petitioners. Given their untimely departure, there will be enough for the rest of you to cover a grand story."

Liam sheathed his knife and sat back down as the room cheered the arrival of fresh jugs of wine.

Turlough made a flourish of filling a large silver mether, a square tankard with a handle on each side. Taking a sip from one corner, he held it forward. "To Ireland: Her Earth, Her Sun, Her Moon, and all Her Peoples who worship them, even the Christians." He passed the tankard to Patrick, who took the next handle and sipped from the next corner. A mether was always passed and the next handle taken in the direction a shadow moves on a sundial.

"Tell us, Patrick, do your holy books speak of the origin of the Sidhe?" asked Turlough.

Patrick stood and passed the mether to a woman on his left, where it began its circuit of the room, now hushed in respect for the promise of a lively tale. It was a combative sort of hush, for if there was one thing that the Celts loved as much as a good story, it was ridiculing a storyteller who stumbled.

"Of course they do," said Patrick. "God created everything, even the Nephilim, which is what we call your Sidhe." He withdrew two substantial books from his satchel, the Irish Christian Bible and the Jewish Zohar, and placed them on the table.

"It's all here in our Irish Bible," he said, placing a hand upon the larger of the books in front of him. "In both the Book of Jubilees and the Book of Enoch, from which Christ himself quoted. The Roman Church, in its desire to hide the existence of the Middle Kingdom, struck both books from its Bible three hundred years after the death of Christ. Our Jewish brothers retain some parts in the Zohar." Patrick indicated the other book.

"Get on with it!" called the head of the blacksmiths' guild, dressed in five colors. "Just tell us the story of the Sidhe! And make it good!"

Patrick raised a hand. "Don't worry, you'll like this one. It's full of sex, incest, violence, and revenge." Having captured their attention, he continued, "It all started when Lilith refused to lie with Adam. They had been created at the same time from the same clay, so they each demanded to be on top." Trickles of laughter played across the gathering.

Patrick went on to explain that when God realized they were never going to produce children for his new human race, he created Eve, a submissive wife for Adam. Lilith, furious that a new man had not also been made for her, fled the Garden and began cavorting with fallen angels, quickly becoming the favorite of the Archdemon Samael. Lilith and Samael devised a plan of revenge. Samael, disguised as a serpent, slipped into the Garden and was easily able to seduce a passive Eve, impregnating her with Cain. God saw that Eve and Adam were not the perfect beings he desired and evicted them from the Garden into the world we know. There Adam fathered his son with Eve, Abel. However, half-demonic Cain killed Abel in a jealous rage over one of their sisters, and he was banished from Adam's new land.

"Lilith, seeing in the young Cain both the humanity she craved to return to and the devilness she desired in her bed, left the demon Samael and took the half-blood Cain. Together they had many children, though all were cursed by both God and Samael."

"So these are the Sidhe?" a woman's voice from the back asked.

"Almost. Lilith's children were malevolent creatures, but the females could take on human forms of great seductive beauty. There is another piece to the Sidhe bloodline."

Patrick described how while Lilith and Cain were procreating, Adam had a replacement son of his own, Seth. Famously venturesome, Seth began to explore beyond their homeland, even though Adam warned him that God would not protect him out there. Seth was dubious about God's protection. He had seen supposedly holy angels, their cocks erect for the first time—all angels had been created male—sneaking out of heaven into his sisters' huts, discovering the excitement a woman could spark in their previously chaste lives. Seth feared that soon there would be more angels seeking sex than sisters to provide it, and he worried about the consequences.

"So he journeyed through the wild lands toward the sea. One hot, clear day, a sound like sharp thunder opened up a tear in the sky. Stars glittered in the slash of black through an expanse of blue. Seth threw himself behind a sand dune. Peeking out, he saw specks darting about the opening, and lightning flashed in shades of gold, green, and orange—a battle of angels. He hid for a time, until the sounds of distant fighting were replaced with nearby laughter. Crawling to the top of the dune, he spied three daughters of Lilith sunning themselves naked next to the sea. One had raven-black hair, one nut-brown, and one flaming red. Their names were Banbha, Fódla, and Ériu.

"Aroused—perhaps bewitched—Seth left his hiding place and was immediately embraced by the women. Hungry for mortal touch, they held Seth in rapture, competing with one another to see who could lie with him the most."

"I bet the redhead won that battle. They always do," declared a man dressed in only three colors, who had evidently enjoyed plenty of wine.

"It's obvious that Seth was the real winner," remarked Patrick. "However, after six days all four were exhausted. Seeing a number of logs washed up on the beach, they decided to make a raft to float in the sun upon the crystal sea. But God had witnessed this unholy union, and, waiting until Banbha, Fódla, and Ériu had climbed onto the raft, he rose up a great wind to blow it away before Seth could join them.

"God would have drowned the three sisters but sensed in each of them that the seed of Seth was already set. Showing mercy, if not actual favor, God drove the raft to the shores of this great island, where they each delivered twins, two boys and four girls. These children, bearing the magical bloodline of Lilith's daughters and the human bloodline of Seth, were the first Sidhe. Flourishing, they grew strong and eventually were able to conquer the native Fomorians."

"Thank the Gods for that," the noblewoman sitting next to Turlough said with a snort. "And where do your books say the Fomorians came from?"

"Those daughters of Eve who lay with a group of fallen angels led by Azâzêl produced hybrid offspring called the Elioud, of which Fomorians are one type. But that's another story for another feast.

"Once the Sidhe controlled the entire island, they named it to honor the last surviving one of their three mothers, Ériu Land."

The room erupted in appreciative cheers, the hammering of knives on tables, and the stomping of feet on the wooden floor. Liam had to admit that he'd always liked that story more than the one his

Sidhe mother had told him, about ships arriving in the mist bearing the survivors of Atlantis. He turned to ask Brigid her opinion and saw that she was swiftly crossing the room.

The door swung open and banged against the wall, catching the attention of the guests. Through it strode Una, carrying twelve-day-old Aisling, followed by Quinn carrying Anya. A wave of silence followed them toward the high table. Liam rose and joined Brigid, who was walking behind Quinn. With her free hand, Una swept away an assortment of dishes from in front of Turlough and laid a peaceful but alert Aisling on the table.

Quinn bent and spoke softly to Una, though he might as well have shouted in the now still chamber. "Are you truly sure?"

Una's legs sagged, and she grabbed the table for support. Liam moved closer in case she collapsed, but Una straightened, met her husband's eyes, and nodded.

Quinn placed Anya on the table and stepped back, where Liam put a hand on his shoulder. "They'll be all right."

Quinn glared at his old friend.

"I promise, they will be all right," Liam repeated. "This is what called me here."

Una announced unsteadily, "Sire, I present the Morrígna twins and request the Test to prove their return and right to rule."

Turlough rose from his seat with outstretched hands to quiet the now buzzing room. The whispers transformed into the scrape of benches being pushed back as everyone stood. Then, again, silence.

No one in the room had been present at the last Test of the Morrígna twins, nor would any of them have been able to recite the rigidly prescribed ritual if asked the day before. Yet today the entire assembly knew what was about to happen, and all understood their role in it.

"Who else speaks for the Test and puts forth their bond?" recited Turlough.

Brigid stepped forward. "I, Brigid, rightful and undisputed high priestess of the Order of Macha, call for the Test. I have heard the Goddess's command in my dreams and will forfeit my life should the Test fail."

"Then let it proceed."

Una carefully unwrapped the white linen encasing each girl, leaving them bare on the table, exploring the air with their freed arms and legs, a dash of red hair crowning their heads. Turning to the assembly, she demanded, "Give me a blade of ordinary iron, nothing with a spell on it."

The seven people closest to her pulled their daggers and offered them to Una. She studied each one, then chose a delicate knife with an ivory handle from a woman she did not know. Una turned back to the baby Aisling, raised the dagger, and paused, the tip of the blade hovering above her daughter's chest. The room held its breath. A tear slid down Una's cheek, followed by another. She gave a small sigh, then pushed the blade through the skin into the tiny heart.

Aisling did not cry, she simply stared back at her mother with large gray eyes that were turning vivid green. Then she yawned and looked over at her sister, whose eyes had undergone a similar transformation.

Una released the handle and stepped back into Quinn's arms, their intense gaze not leaving their children.

"Who will remove the blade?" asked Brigid.

"I shall," Liam declared.

Brigid smiled at the man who had long ago been her first lover and replied, "No."

Liam nodded and moved to stand in front of the table next to the twins, where Aisling was happily cooing while seemingly indifferent to the dagger protruding from her chest. The symbolic first offer, always declined, indicated his unquestioned belief in the Morrígna's return and the dedication of his life to protect the twins. The Test turned to acceptance of their right to rule. In the Celtic way, a challenger was needed.

Brigid looked across the audience and to no one's surprise called, "Lord Maolan, will you remove the blade?"

"Maolan! Maolan!" the audience shouted its consent.

Satisfied that everyone had joined the chant, Brigid waved Maolan forward.

Head held high, Maolan scowled as he approached the twins. He looked down into Aisling's green eyes—which signaled her unity with her sister and with Anann in the spirit realm to form the Morrígna—and yanked out the dagger. A small spurt of blood caught his hand. He stared at the half-inch pink line on Aisling's chest where the knife had stood, then studied the blood on its blade and his hand.

Turning to face the audience, Lord Maolan held out the dagger, a drop of blood falling from its tip. As required, he wrapped his other hand around the sharp blade and broke it away from the handle to confirm to all that it was not enchanted, in the process cutting his own flesh to the bone. The resulting scar was intended to proclaim for the rest of the challenger's life his acknowledgment of the dominion of the reborn Aisling and Anya.

Patrick realized he'd been clutching the silver cross, which he wore on a braided leather cord around his neck, and let it drop. Had this been a Christian rite, he would have declared that he had witnessed a miracle. But the terms used did not matter to him; he was once again in awe of the many ways God manifested his glory in this magical land. They may call their Gods and Goddesses many names—Danu, Frey, Morrígna, among others—thought Patrick, but they were all one God.

The Morrígna, in particular, echoed many of his beliefs. Like the Christian Father, Son, and Holy Ghost, she also carried three aspects, though she sent two physically into this world. Patrick knew all the stories of the Morrígna, though after what he had just seen they no longer seemed like mere myths and fantastical tales. The events that had unfolded fifteen hundred years ago—the dreadful battle between

Celt and Sidhe that had resulted in the Treaty of Tailltiu—now seemed to him to live and breathe.

The Celts had invaded Ireland using the knowledge of iron weapons and enchantments given to them by the fallen angels Azâzêl and Semjâzâ. The final savage battle ended in a draw. Celt and Sidhe faced each other on the frost-ringed, blood-soaked battlefield, strewn with thousands of their dead and dying. It was the poet Amergin who stood on that field between the Celtic and Sidhe high kings and convinced them to make peace, creating the Treaty of Tailltiu. The two races, magical and human, called upon their Gods to help uphold the treaty and to bring a dreadful fate upon whoever broke it. They were soon to discover that the Goddess Morrígna answered.

A huge pit was dug, filled with dry wood, and lit. To the disappointed cries of ravens attempting to feed on the dead, Sidhe and Celt worked together to drag the bodies from the battlefield and cast them into the fire. With each corpse the smoke became thicker.

Toward the end of that gloomy work, the Sidhe high king knelt in the bloodstained mud beside a mortally wounded Celt warrior, a woman he did not recognize. As he stroked her face gently with his soiled hand, her eyes flickered open. Misinterpreting the plea he saw in them, he drew his misericorde dagger—a long, needlelike blade—placed the point under her arm angled toward her heart, and thrust it in to administer a mercy kill. He was surprised when life did not fade from her. Instead she gave a frantic shake of her head. Withdrawing the blade, he suddenly sensed a second heartbeat, a beat carrying a burgeoning female spirit.

It was from that act that the Test originated, Patrick recalled. He picked up the broken blade from the table and examined the tiny smear of Aisling's blood still on its tip.

On the field of Tailltiu, the Celtic high king carried the mysterious woman into a tent close enough to the funeral pyre to keep her warm. When all the dead had been consigned to the flames, the two high kings ordered that the fire be kept burning. If the unknown woman and her unborn daughter died, as expected, they would join their fellow warriors in the flames.

Tended by widows of the battle—a group that became the Order of Macha, now led by Brigid—the fire burned for nine months. Unable to speak, eat, or drink, the woman seemed to sustain herself on the thick smoke that streamed into the tent from the giant pyre. She drew her last breath upon the birth of not one but twin daughters. The Sidhe high king named the first Anya, and the Celtic high king named the other Aisling—the names every set of Morrígna twins has carried.

Patrick knew from his Christian teaching that a God, or in Ireland's case a Goddess, cannot fully inhabit this limited world. That portion of the Morrígna that remained in the Otherworld they called Anann. When Anya and Aisling merged their spirits and acted as one being, it was said that their power was channeled from Anann. And what strength they had, by the time the first twins were fourteen, they wielded magic more powerful than that of a hundred Celtic druids or Sidhe witches.

Over the centuries that followed, the Morrígna returned eleven times, whenever Ireland was threatened—sometimes from afar, but most of the challenges arose from within Ireland's own shores. Given enough time, people chafed at being ruled and came to believe that they would be better off governing themselves, even when their sovereign was a Goddess.

And now it was Kellach trying to break the treaty, Patrick thought. The new twins would have to deal with him. But first seven years of training: Anya to be a druid, Aisling to be a warrior, followed by the Ceremony of Hearts. Then seven more years of training to merge themselves into the Morrígna, when at last they would rule both Ireland and the Middle Kingdom.

Patrick watched as Liam and Brigid, each carrying a twin, left the hall, followed by Quinn supporting a sobbing Una. They would never embrace their daughters again. Tradition dictated that the Morrígna twins' parents be kept away so that human sentiment would not interfere with the twins' learning to become one with the mother Goddess.

As soon as they were gone, Maolan scurried out to have his hand stitched up. The members of the assembly slowly took their seats, some talking in low tones, most lost in silent thought.

King Turlough banged his fist on the high table. "Steward, throw open the gates of the keep. Set the grand hall. Send criers out to every village in the surround. Empty the cellar and the larder. Slaughter a dozen pigs and set them roasting. Tonight we don't sleep, tonight we feast! I will not have quiet in my castle. The Morrígna is reborn!"

Cheers rose throughout the room.

"If you have family within riding distance, send for them now! We'll make a story of this evening. Summon the bard—a song must be written."

Those who had squires dispatched them. Others ran for the stables. All who remained filled their cups.

"Patrick," Turlough said, slapping the monk on the back hard enough to spill his wine, "it is truly the beginning of a new age." He refilled Patrick's cup, then pulled on the gold chain around his own neck, dragging a black leather pouch from under his tunic. "In this is a piece of the heart of the previous Morrígna, passed to me in trust by my successor. Now I'll be the one to carry it to the Ceremony of Hearts."

To be so close to such a relic caused Patrick to catch his breath. The Ceremony of Hearts was an affair of magic and beauty prescribed by the first incarnation of Anya and Aisling.

Each time the Morrígna twins' human shells were exhausted, the twins passed together and their hearts were removed and divided by the Celtic and Sidhe high kings into fourteen segments with a silver knife. The segments were entrusted to seven custodians from each race, but even though the Morrígna had just left, prejudice crept in and the segments were never equal.

Then, on the first winter solstice after the seventh birthday of new twins, the ceremony would take place in an ancient stone pyramid, completely covered with a mound of earth and grass, which stands in the center of the Sidhe city of Brú na Bóinne. Curving along one half of the earthen mound, the lower eight feet is embedded with quartz stones echoing a crescent moon. Through the center of this white arc, a long, straight entrance passage joins with three chambers, a head and two sides, to form the shape of a cross. Patrick had often wondered how the Celts and Sidhe came to use that shape before Christianity came to their islands.

In the dark of the morning, the new Morrígna twins would be led down the entrance corridor to the center of the cruciform. In the arm to the left would sit the Sidhe high king, the Celtic high king in the other, with the head left vacant for the Otherworld aspect of the Morrígna, Anann. Coals that originated in the ancient pyre of Tailltiu, attended to day and night through the centuries by the priestesses of the Order of Macha, would glow in a brazier between the girls. Brigid would set an iron bowl on the brazier. One at a time, the seven Celtic and seven Sidhe custodians would enter, place their Morrígna heart segment in the bowl, bow to each twin, and leave.

When the sun rises, a beam of light penetrates the chamber through a narrow channel above the temple entrance—which occurs only on solstice mornings—and travels diagonally from left to right along a series of carvings representing the Battle of Tailltiu until it illuminates a rendering of the Goddess. At that instant the heart segments transform into two thick ribbons of smoke, which snake toward the twins and are inhaled.

Following the ceremony they start learning to become truly powerful, Patrick knew.

☙

LONG AFTER PATRICK contemplated the events of the Ceremony of Hearts, on the first solstice after the seventh birthday of Una and

Quinn's twins, their ceremony did not go as planned. Moments before sunrise a message from Kellach stated that he would not be returning the heart segment entrusted to the Skeaghshee. Kellach further declared that without this heart segment the twins would not be whole and by law could not rule, a declaration the Celtic and Sidhe high kings decided to ignore. The ceremony proceeded with one less segment and a little less smoke.

From that morning until Aisling and Anya were attacked by the Skeaghshee, days before their fourteenth birthday, many druids tried to divine the impact of the loss, but none had been able to pierce the veil of uncertainty that had fallen over the twins' future. The general conclusion was that the effect would become manifest after their coronation.

But there was to be no coronation without Anya.

4

All the kingdom of Og in Bashan, which reigned in Ashtaroth and in Edrei, who remained of the remnant of the giants: for these did Moses smite, and cast them out.

—Joshua 13:12, King James Version

Oslo, Norway
Three Years After the Attack on Aisling

The Norwegian late-autumn sun had made its brief appearance and was beating a hasty retreat. Jordan, commander of a small mercenary force on contract to the Vatican, hurried alone along the Oslo waterfront. The old inn that was his destination had been built alongside the wall of Oslo's Akershus Castle, where decades of storms howling down the fjord left the inn leaning against the stronger stone structure, causing its stairs, walls, and floors to settle at odd angles. A cold blast through the briefly open door announced Jordan's arrival into the dimly lit ground floor, where a smoky fire provided a hint of warmth to the room.

One of the more persistent women working there hurriedly threw off a heavy woolen blanket, revealing a buxom figure, and sidled through the mismatched collection of grimy tables to intercept him. "Good evening, handsome," and his stalwart Sicilian features saved her from having to lie.

"Not tonight," said Jordan.

"It's been 'Not tonight' ever since you arrived. What's a man like you doing in this hovel anyway?" She moved in close and stroked Jordan's cheek. "I could show you a better inn with cleaner beds."

"I prefer to spend my money on books," replied Jordan, edging around the woman and heading for the stairs.

"Books? And fancy swords by the look of it. Hard to cuddle up with those!" she called after him.

Jordan pulled a candle stub from his pocket, lit it, and started up the dark, creaky staircase, holding out the candle so as to illuminate the odd slope of each successive step with its weak light.

Once in his room, he lit the two candles on his desk from the one he held and then set about building a fire. Commander Jordan d'Anglano was named after his famous ancestor, though he did not like to be reminded of it. His forefather, marshal to Manfred of Sicily, captured Florence in 1260 only to quickly lose it again at the Battle of Tagliacozzo, where, as punishment, he was stripped of one hand, one foot, and both eyes. Jordan, who appeared older than his twenty-six years, still possessed both his hands and feet, as well as his intense brown eyes, in which reflections of the fire glimmered.

Unlocking a trunk, Jordan, an avid student of forbidden books, surveyed the large, neatly arranged collection inside. He removed five and stacked them next to the candles. Opening a Latin translation of Enoch, he resumed reading from the page he had marked earlier with a bit of torn parchment. Unconsciously, he gathered his cloak tightly around himself. While he had demanded the inn's only private room with a fireplace, it did little to thwart the damp chill that flowed through the gaps in the askew wooden walls. The cold faded from his perception as he lost himself in the pages.

He had liberated this stack of grimoires—books of magic—from the witch Marija when he captured her outside Trier, Germany, the previous year. She was the first witch he had gone up against, and the event was a turning point in many ways. While he scissored her neck between his dagger and sword tightly enough for trickles of blood to run down her tunic, she had tried to bribe him by offering to teach him how to work the incantations. He surprised himself by hesitating. He did not pause long, sensing even back then that it would be dangerous to give her time to work a spell, a feeling reinforced by the sight of the carcass of an infant on the table, its tiny body stripped of fat. He slit her throat with enough force to feel his blade scrape her spine. Then, just to make sure she would not come back for him, he hacked off her head.

After reading the powerful spells in her books, Jordan realized that he had been dangerously naïve. If he was going to hunt more of her kind, he needed to learn protective enchantments. He'd been very lucky to catch Marija unawares.

Then again, he had always been lucky—he had never been wounded, not once, in all his battles and tavern brawls. And so often did his thoughts foretell events that he had begun to wonder if he had some special talent in this regard, or even whether he might influence events with his mind. These were things he did not dare talk about—he could not risk being suspected of witchcraft himself.

His luck extended back as long as he could remember, back to when he was a child, if you could count it as lucky living through the almost daily ritual of tossing the bodies of friends onto the piles of rotting corpses lining the streets, piles that already contained the remains of his mother and brother. Too few men were left alive to bury all the dead; too little wood was left around his village to burn them. The Black Death stole his childhood, he once told a woman he thought he loved, though he did not really know what a traditional childhood was; he had never seen one that was not immersed in death.

The plague, which first arrived shortly before Jordan was born, swept a wave of agonizing death across Europe. Afterwards, the risk of new outbreaks loomed over the populace like the hammer of a vengeful God poised to strike down a village or a province at the slightest provocation—a fate that frequently befell those in Jordan's

Sicilian homeland, an island dependent on shipboard trade. He grew up unable to escape the cries of the afflicted: some pleading with God to save them, some pleading for anyone to end to their suffering with a quick death, and neither God nor man caring anymore.

Jordan was fifteen when he became a condottiere and killed his first man for pay. If God did not care, why should he? His family's meager fortune had never recovered from his uncle's failure, and in the devastation of post-plague Sicily his choice was either to live as a mercenary or to watch his ancestral home deteriorate further while he worked on another man's land for a wage that would barely keep him from starving. Jordan had decided long ago that avoiding starvation was not a high enough aim. He discovered he was good at killing, and that he liked it. One successful job led to another. Soon, with his reputation for swift action and discretion, his services were in demand across Europe and even in Britain.

When the townspeople of Trier offered him three times his normal condottiere fee to hunt down the witch who had been stealing their children, he took the job. However, Marija's stash of grimoires turned out to be a treasure far more valuable than the money. They provided him with his first direct experience working enchantments, an ability he had long admired from afar.

The restored Roman Church had begun utilizing the condottieri to expand its territories, so Jordan had made sure the Vatican recruiters heard of his successes, though not of his grimoires—to be caught with even one such book would result in a quick sentence to a slow death. He was impressed that the Church had developed such an effective military-like strategy to convert new lands. First they would send disposable mercenaries to kill as many "unholy creatures" as they could—that is what the Vatican called Goblins, Trolls, and the like. Then a group of zealous exorcists, known as the VRS League, would arrive and drive out the rest. Finally they would subjugate any existing Christian groups and convert the indigenous pagan population, by force if necessary, before bringing in Roman priests. All this was conducted at the direction of the head of the VRS, Cardinal Orsini, making him the second most powerful man in the Roman Church.

Jordan was hired as part of a small force charged with fighting these unholy creatures, which he knew to be Nephilim, though that information was not disclosed by their commander. The rest of the men were content to follow orders and collect their pay without questions. Jordan quickly saw that the beings they were tasked with eradicating were not animals; many looked almost human, and they had intelligence and individuality. While his new grimoires were difficult to understand—and one was in Aramaic, a language he had not learned yet—he gleaned that these beings, most of whom had some form of magical ability, were more prevalent in the world than he had ever suspected.

One of the candles on his desk sputtered out, and he replaced it. He reinserted the bookmark and closed the volume before turning his attention to a tattered grimoire, his favorite, Marija's personal journal of enchantments and counterspells. The witch had recorded them in a clear and formulaic fashion, and he had set himself to memorizing them.

During his most recent mission for the Vatican, Jordan had decided to test one of Marija's enchantments on his commander, one that would prohibit the man from seeing whatever Jordan specified, in this case the clan of Norwegian Trolls they were after. To Jordan's astonishment the spell worked so well that the commander had literally bumped into the Troll who killed him. Then Jordan took over as commander and led the condottieri in slaughtering the entire clan.

That troubled him. Whenever he killed a man he felt a bit more alive, as if once again he had challenged death and come out the victor. But when he killed the Trolls—who had been hiding away from people and were relatively harmless unless attacked—he felt less alive somehow, as if he lost a bit of vitality with each drop of Nephilim blood that was shed.

However, killing was what he did, what he would continue to do, so he had holed up in this cheap inn looking for an answer in his grimoires. The Vatican paid him well, something he was not about to give up, so he needed to find a way to kill these beings without being affected, some way to harden his soul even more.

The clock tower's bell struck 1:00 A.M., yet sleep still held no appeal. He was scheduled to sail on the morning tide. A summons from the Vatican lay on the floor where he had flung it yesterday; he hated being summoned. While he could not ignore the order, he had been taken aback to read that he was to present himself in Venice, not Rome, which could be good or bad, very bad.

A deep tremor of sound rolled through the room from somewhere outside. Jordan opened the shutter and peered out. The wind had died down. Under the stars, green ribbons of northern lights danced, showering their faint light on the city, though not enough for him to see clearly. The sound, low-pitched and guttural, repeated. This time he detected a tone of distress. Too tired to read more, too awake to sleep, he strapped on his sword belt and went into the night.

Jordan strode along the wharf, bypassing the occasional patch of ice, until it opened onto a small torchlit square where two richly cloaked and hooded women stood. He could not see their faces. A priest, the long cowl of his black robe marking him as one of Orsini's exorcists, approached the women. *This could be interesting*, thought Jordan as he moved into the shadows beside a tall stack of crates, close enough to hear.

"Thank you for accepting Orsini's invitation to meet and discuss a truce, Grande Sorcière," the exorcist said without a bow.

Jordan recognized the title. In addition to ruling over the most powerful coven of witches in Europe, the High Coven, the Grande Sorcière was queen of France. This meant that she also covertly controlled the French Church, which competed fiercely and sometimes violently with the Vatican for territory and souls, or at least for tithing payers. She must be trying to expand her church and possibly her coven into Norway, Jordan concluded.

"You will address Us as 'Your Highness.' Where is your master?"

the Grande Sorcière demanded in French. "We agreed to meet him only because We were already scheduled to be here."

Switching from Latin to French but ignoring the requested royal address, the exorcist replied, "My cardinal sends his most sincere regrets. Demands of the Church kept him in Rome. He has sent a comfortable ship to carry you there for the meeting."

"Orsini did not come because he is a liar. We do not need to look into his eyes to know that. He must also be a fool to think he can trick Us into meeting in Rome rather than here on neutral ground. We have no doubts that there he would question Us, then kill Us."

"My cardinal instructed me to inform you that you've no choice in this."

A rumble of anguish rolled into the square, a sound emitted by a creature in chains led by two robed exorcists. It was larger than a man but smaller than the giants that Jordan had read about. *It must be some other form of Nephilim*, he thought.

The junior exorcists held the creature still by threatening it with spears tipped with obsidian points while their leader locked its chains to a post.

"We've an army of such creatures, impervious to any spell you may cast," said the leader. He swept his arm toward the Nephilim. "I invite you to try."

"Joanna, We do not have time to waste here. Use your flame to take control of the creature," ordered the Grande Sorcière. Her companion held out a box, the light flickering inside revealed it to be made of blue glass. She placed it on the ground and swung open the lid. A flame, about the size of a candle's, crawled out, multiplied, and quickly became a horde of flames slithering toward the bound creature.

Death flames, Jordan realized, remembering the reference in Marija's journal to an enchantment used to temporarily govern any living thing, until the spell killed them. The flames swarmed up the creature's legs and over its chest as it roared in pain, then faded without any further effect.

Jordan was impressed. Death flames were listed as one of the most potent enchantments, and this creature had resisted it. He considered all the mystical dangers awaiting him in the dark places of the world as a Vatican condottiere—not to mention the risks posed by the capricious Vatican itself—and knew the immeasurable value such an unusual creature would be to him.

"If you don't do as Orsini commands, he'll unleash an army of these on your coven in Paris," said the leader.

"We do not believe so. If there were many creatures like this, We would know. Now, We have an appointment with the king to prepare for." The women walked toward the main street leading from the square.

"We'll set the creature on you right now if you don't come with us!" one of the junior exorcists called out.

"Do so and it may survive," said the Grande Sorcière without looking back, "but none of you would." They disappeared from sight, out of the torchlight.

Jordan studied the many shadows of the square, picked his path, and crept out toward the creature.

"Why'd you let her go?" demanded the junior exorcist to his superior, fingering the silver medallion hanging from a chain around his neck, his badge of office with the initials VRS visible in high relief. "With this creature we could've captured her."

"Idiot," snapped the leader. "You don't take the queen of France on Norwegian soil without starting a war that Orsini doesn't want yet." The creature began to bellow and pull at its chains. "Shut it up."

The junior exorcist stuck the creature in the shoulder with his spear. Something black and viscous oozed out, blistering the skin around the wound. The creature whimpered through clenched teeth.

"Stick it again," ordered the leader.

The junior exorcist dropped his spear and fell to the ground dead. Before the others could react, Jordan had his bloody knife to the leader's throat. "Had to do that. I couldn't watch all three of you, and he was sounding dangerously rash," said Jordan.

"Who are you? Are you with the High Coven? You tell that witch she is going to regret killing one of Orsini's men."

"There's nothing I'd regret about killing you, so hand me the keys and perhaps it won't be necessary."

The leader removed the heavy ring of keys from the pocket of his robe, then spun around, slashed them across Jordan's face, and moved to run. Jordan sprang forward and caught his opponent's cowl, pulling him back to slit his throat. "That hurt!" Jordan shouted at him as the man's life gurgled away. The last exorcist darted into a dark alley. Jordan threw his knife, but the clatter of steel on stone told him he had missed. He considered going after the man. The escaping exorcist did not know who he was, only believed he was with the High Coven. Best to let him go, then, Jordan thought.

He picked up the spear and tossed it aside. The creature squatted on its haunches, watching him with solid black eyes.

"I killed them for you," Jordan said.

"That made Ty glad," said Ty, his voice gravelly. "Are you going to hurt Ty now?"

"No, Ty. Would you like me to kill more exorcists for you?"

Ty slowly nodded.

"Was the exorcist telling the truth? Are there more like you?"

Ty shook his head. "Ty has no brothers or sisters. Ty born different than Ty's clan, they scared of Ty. They force Ty to leave, let exorcists capture Ty."

"So there's just one like you, and you've no clan anymore."

A giant gray tear slid down Ty's face. "Something inside Ty always hurts Ty, always pain. Ty not want to live."

"Either you'll live with the exorcists, who'll abuse you, or you can live with me." Jordan had made his voice stern, but he softened it as he went on. "You and I will be a clan, and I won't harm you. I can kill any exorcists that bother you, but you must bind yourself to me. You must protect me from everyone else, human or inhuman. Will you do that?"

Ty nodded.

"You must give your bond. My name is Jordan."

"Ty bonds Ty to Jordan."

"Good," said Jordan, retrieving the key ring from the dead exorcist. "Do as I tell you and everything will be all right. You'll not be chained again."

The prospects of future witch-hunts and his summons to the Vatican's Venice office did not feel quite as worrisome as they had a few hours ago.

The tide went out early that morning. Ty had carried Jordan's trunks into the captain's cabin, then carried the captain's things out, to his muted complaints. In the intensity of the night before, Jordan had not thought about how he was going explain his new bodyguard, but it turned out not to be necessary—no one challenged him with Ty following one step behind.

5

The two strains [angels and humans] united with each other to execute all kinds of iniquitous deeds. The result of the marriages between them were the Nephilim, whose sins brought the deluge upon the world. . . . The flood was produced by a union of the male waters, which are above the firmament, and the female waters issuing from the earth. . . . Upon the entreaties of Noah, God sent down the angel Raphael, who banished nine-tenths of the unclean spirits [Nephilim] from the earth, leaving but one-tenth for Mastema [chief of the Nephilim], to punish sinners through them.

—Book of Jubilees (circa 100 BCE), Dead Sea Scrolls

Republic of Venice
Six Weeks Later

Sunlight rarely found its way down to the dark ribbon of water where the narrow boat slipped silently along. Venice, standing in a lagoon of the Adriatic Sea off the northeast corner of the re-created Papal States, was a city of shadowy passages and the capital of its own republic where trade ruled. Trade that consisted of clandestine activities and information as often as it did in more tangible, but less valuable, commodities.

Jordan, wrapped in his heavy cloak to ward off the December cold, sat impassively in the center of the *sandolo*, unconcerned that the boat's freeboard was pressed down to within an inch of the water, threatening to swamp them. The cause of the boat's distress was the heavy Ty, who stood behind him working the boat's single long oar with one hand. Jordan had only to point a gloved finger to indicate a turn from the Rio Nuovo canal into Rio di San Pantalon and a slight movement of the giant hand on the oar glided the *sandolo* around the corner without a drop of water splashing onto Jordan's boots. The boat turned onto Rio delle Muneghete, traveled a short distance along the long, curved canal, then gently bumped against a small dock. Jordan stepped out, tied up the *sandolo*, and glanced about before opening the door to the building. Ty followed him inside.

When Jordan received the Vatican's summons to this address, he applied his considerable talents to discovering what went on here. He learned that it was in this nondescript stone building, in the midst of a jumble of similarly nondescript buildings, where four decades earlier Egidio Albornoz, before becoming a cardinal and the most feared man in Europe, first came to plot the return of the pope to Rome. The French had successfully conspired to move the papacy to Avignon, leaving Rome and the Papal States to fracture into warring cities. Albornoz's audacious plan was to raise an army of condottieri, reconquer the old Papal States, and then forcibly extract the pope from Avignon, restoring the Roman Church. The English, chafing at the French controlling the papacy, helped by sending Sir John Hawkwood. Hawkwood took the assumed name of Giovanni Acuto and turned out to be as bloodthirsty as Albornoz. When the chancellor of Cesena refused to pledge to the new Roman pope, Hawkwood had the city sacked and every man, woman, and child disemboweled—or, if they begged in a pleasing fashion, beheaded.

Albornoz, named "Angel of Peace" by the Church, restructured the Vatican as he wished, writing new doctrine and canonical laws, the *Constitutiones Sanctæ Matris Ecclesiæ*. Jordan had tracked down an unrecorded draft when he arrived in Venice five days ago. Now he recalled one clause in particular: *"Whoever controls literacy, and the written word, controls history and can reshape the world to the way it was intended to be, to the greater glory of God and his True Church. The common man, all except God granted nobility and those ordained by the True Church, must be kept safe from Satan by keeping them from knowing his demons and their Nephilim offspring. Only officers of the True Church can confront such malevolent creatures without becoming corrupt.*" Albornoz had redacted this article when he decided it was better to create a secret bureau here, in his old building, so that the new Vatican could mount campaigns that were kept hidden from most of the administration in Rome. Campaigns against witches and sorcerers as well as against magical creatures.

Jordan hoped his summons was related to his sighting of the Grande Sorcière in Oslo and that it would result in a mission against the High Coven. Those dark witches would have to be eradicated at some point if the Vatican was ever going to completely abolish the French Church. Plus, it was the kind of fight he would enjoy, both allowing him to use his growing knowledge of enchantments and pitting him against a human enemy who clearly merited death.

But no, Jordan reconsidered, it had to be something else, because his orders had arrived before he'd witnessed the Grande Sorcière sidestep the trap set by Orsini. More likely it would be another campaign against the Nephilim, all of whom Albornoz despised—Jordan had heard rumors that Goblins were causing trouble in the Alps. He would just have to suppress his distaste for killing them.

Unless the Vatican had learned about his experimenting with enchantments. If that was the case, he was going to need Ty's help to leave this building alive.

Cosimo de' Migliorati had been happy as archbishop of Ravenna, a city northeast of Rome, where the pastries were as sweet and hard to resist as the women who brought them. But his happiness was shattered when Pope Boniface IX made him legate, head of a bureau in Venice he had never heard of. It turned out to be an austere department devoid of the niceties of his former life. In his new position, he was in constant fear for the well-being of his immortal soul and nightly prayed that he would live long enough to balance the scales in St. Peter's eyes.

Today the legate was concerned about meeting Commander Jordan and had slipped off to his dressing room for a few moments of quiet contemplation. Gathering his robes up about his waist, he sat over the hole in the board, which in turn covered a larger hole in the stone windowsill. The normally foul odor emerging from this opening was made even worse by his new contribution to the basin built within the stone wall a short distance below. Here human waste collected, any surplus overflowing out a small opening into the canal, its natural decay producing ammonia vapors that rose up to help rid the clothing hanging around Legate de' Migliorati of lice.

The legate wondered, as he often did when the warm fumes enveloped him, if he would not prefer the lice over the stench, which clung to his robes for hours after he left the dressing room each morning. His thoughts returned to Jordan, whom he had not met. The reports painted Jordan as a cunning, volatile, and dangerous man who had most likely betrayed and killed the leader of his previous mission. Just the kind of man whom the legate required. However, the legate worried that when Jordan received his new orders, he might also be the kind of man who would become angry enough to kill him on the spot.

The legate stood, straightened his robes, opened the door to his adjoining office, and strode in. Waiting for him were his personal secretary, Jordan, and the largest man the legate had ever seen, if indeed he was a man, which the legate realized he was not. He wondered how the massive creature had managed to get through the small door to his office.

"Commander, you have done well," said the legate, walking to his desk. "By all accounts the undertaking in Norway was a success, despite the fact that the first commander was . . . well, 'killed' would be a polite word for it, and you were forced to take over."

"Thank you, Your Grace." Jordan gave a slight bow.

"Though you were instructed to seek out and destroy ungodly creatures, not bring one back as a pet. As our Lord drove the followers of Lucifer out of heaven, he has charged his True Church with driving their Nephilim offspring from the earthly abodes they have crept into. What is it anyway?"

"You'd be well served to call him Ty, not 'it,' Your Grace. Ty is bound to serve me. I rescued him from a witch of the High Coven." Jordan delivered his prepared lie.

"A companion, how nice for you. Now, please ask . . . Ty . . . to wait outside so we can proceed with our business."

"You'll have to ask him yourself, Your Grace."

The legate looked into Ty's solid black, barren eyes and decided it was best to ignore the thing.

"As I said, you did well, showing exceptional leadership during great adversity. This office has need of a marshal of your skills and promotes you to the position. Let us hope you fare better than your namesake."

Jordan showed no surprise at the offer. "What office is this, and under whose authority shall I act? What rights and income go with the position?"

"This office has no title or charter, and you shall act solely as I direct. Here you receive no rights and privileges and only that income I deem necessary to carry out your missions. However, once you have served faithfully for a period of time I see fit, you will be awarded the title of Grand Marshal of the Sovereign Military Hospitaller Order of St. John of Jerusalem of Rhodes, along with the lands, livestock, and slaves appropriate to that position. On Rhodes, of course."

"Your Grace honors me." Jordan gave another curt bow. "Shall I have this offer in a written bond?"

"No. The only bond you shall receive is a share in the great burdens of this office." He handed Jordan a vellum page with the pope's red wax seal at the bottom.

Jordan read it quickly. "What's this? An order of excommunication and death . . . by fire?" Tossing the sheet at the legate, Jordan gripped the hilt of his sword and stepped back. A low growl emerged from Ty and reverberated in the room.

The legate spoke rapidly, jamming his words together. "A similar order hangs over my head, as it does over all who serve this office. To know what we must know, to be exposed to Satan's own family, puts us at risk of suffering and death at the hands of the Church should we become corrupted, which would be but a pale foreshadowing of what awaits us in the fires of hell."

The growl grew louder.

The legate raised a hand, a concerned look on his face. "A copy of this order is being held in trust at the Vatican and will not be released so long as nothing you learn during your duties to this office slips from your lips and that you execute those duties faithfully. Also in trust is a papal indulgence, already signed and sealed, granting your immortal soul forgiveness for all your actions from this day forth. Which of the two orders is released and which is destroyed is up to you."

"And if I decline this honor?" Jordan dropped the "Your Grace."

"That is not for you to choose." The legate leveled his gaze at Jordan.

Jordan let his laughter bubble privately in his chest for a moment. He had known he would accept the position the moment he heard the offer; he just wanted to make the legate work for it. Threats were unnecessary. This is what he had been striving for his whole life, a position of power that could even eventually lead to nobility.

Deciding he had kept the legate dangling long enough, he nodded in acceptance of his new position as marshal of the Vatican. Ty's growling died away.

"Good. Marshal Jordan, you stand with me on the threshold of a new world. Now that the Church has been restored in Rome, it's time to prove to all other churches, to every king and peasant across all civilized lands"—the legate's voice grew louder, and he pointed at the ceiling—"to prove to God himself that the Roman Church is the one True Church by eliminating the last of the Nephilim. God has been waiting for a church strong enough and holy enough to realize such a feat.

"What do you know of the history of these unholy creatures?" the legate asked.

Jordan shrugged, his face unreadable. Those words—"the last of the Nephilim"—dampened the thrill of his new position, reminded him it came with a personal cost.

The legate's secretary, a dour old priest, fished around in a cabinet containing large parchment rolls and returned with one. "Ever since Adam and Eve were ejected from the Garden for Eve's transgression, their descendants have been at war with legions of fallen angels to see if our world will become the second Garden or the next hell. These fallen angels cast their seed widely in the weak-willed and malicious daughters of Eve until their unholy Nephilim offspring so thickly populated the earth that God was forced to send the Great Flood to wipe them out, sparing Noah's family. At the last second, God decided to also spare one in ten Nephilim in order to continue to test the faith of his human creations. Achieving a final solution to that test is the charge of our office, to sweep all trace of the Nephilim, in all their forms, into hell. To fail would be to fail God's very purpose for all of us here, I assure you."

The legate unrolled the parchment to reveal a chart of Europe, the Mediterranean, Britain, and Ireland. "As a Vatican condottiere, you've already fought some of these Nephilim bloodlines, Trolls and Goblins, simply because you were ordered to. Now, as marshal, as the military leader of this office and the one giving the orders, you must come to understand them."

He placed a finger on the chart at the location of Rome. "Five centuries before our Lord Christ's birth, Rome set about conquering the known world to create a pagan empire. Their false gods had migrated from Egypt, fabricated religions of mystery and magic. Even though they didn't align with Satan directly, they were able to divine enough sorcery to be triumphant, for a while.

"The Roman Empire's expansion forced a particularly crude branch of Nephilim, the Elioud, to seek sanctuary in caverns, caves, hollows, and dark woods." The legate glanced at Ty, who remained silent, his solid black eyes unblinking.

"Fearing Rome's increasing power," the legate continued, "a clan of cave-dwelling Elioud went to their ancestor Azâzêl, once a strong Archangel until the second fall, to plead for protection. Azâzêl made a pact with an emerging human warrior race in Central Europe, the Celts, granting them the knowledge of working with iron in exchange for protection of his Elioud. Iron—the very word means 'God's metal.'"

The legate unlocked a drawer in his expansive wooden desk and removed a book with a blank leather cover. "This is the Book of Enoch. Written by Noah's great-grandfather only seven generations after Adam's creation, it describes the world before the Great Flood and the origins of your foes, their powers and their weaknesses."

Undoing the two silver clasps that held the book closed, the legate opened it to a page marked with a black ribbon and began to recite: "'And Azâzêl taught men to make swords, and knives, and shields, and coats of mail, and made known to them the metals of the earth and the art of infusing a desire for death into metals, and working beauty into them also. And there arose much godlessness, and they committed fornication, and they were led astray, and became corrupt in all their ways.'"

Flipping through the pages, the legate explained to Jordan, "Sem-jâzâ, one of the most powerful of the fallen Archangels, taught the Celts enchantments and potions. You can imagine how much better off the world would be today had he stayed obediently in heaven.

"And there's more here you'll find useful: Armârôs taught the countering of enchantments and of potions; Barâqîjâl, prophetic astrology; Kôkabêl, the signs of the stars; Ezêqêêl, the knowledge of the clouds and seasons; Araqiêl, reading the signs of the earth; Shamsiêl, the movement of the sun; and Sariêl, the path of the moon. Of course, all of these Archdemons, as well as the others, produced their own Nephilim bloodlines, bloodlines you'll have to eliminate."

The legate closed the book and handed it to Jordan. "No one must see this book. Lose it, or let anyone else read it, and your life is forfeit."

The Vatican is not as good at keeping its secrets as it thinks, thought Jordan, who knew well the results of Semjâzâ's indiscretion. He accepted the legate's offering with feigned gratitude, having read the book no fewer than three times since taking it from the witch Marija. He wondered if it was a better strategy to reveal or to hide this information from the legate.

"With their knowledge of iron and witchcraft," said the legate, interrupting Jordan's thoughts, "the Celts were able to rise up from their foul hovels to conquer a large swath of Europe." He swept his hand across the chart.

"And were the first to sack Rome. I know this history," interrupted Jordan.

"They were the only ones to sack Rome while it was the capital of the empire, the next time not occurring for eight centuries, when legions were no longer garrisoned there. That shows the strength they gained from the knowledge shared by Azâzêl and Semjâzâ," stressed the legate.

"Finally the Roman emperor Constantine received the grace of the Holy Spirit in the year of Our Lord 313 and merged the old Roman religions of mystery and magic with the new, true religion of man: Christianity. Christianity, fortified with small doses of necessary and purified sorcery, was able to overpower the witchcraft of the Celts. The Christians' new capability was wielded by a select group of holy sorcerers."

"Exorcists." The word rolled through the room like distant thunder. "Ty hate exorcists. Jordan, no exorcists." Ty shuddered and took a step toward the legate.

Jordan reached up and placed a hand on Ty's chest. "Don't worry, you won't have to deal with them again, as long as you keep me alive." Seemingly comforted, Ty returned to his motionless state.

"Please continue," said Jordan, gratified by the look of fear that had appeared on the legate's face.

"Yes . . . uh, thank you," the legate said, regaining his composure. "The newly Christian Roman Empire drove the bulk of the pagan Celts, those who wouldn't convert, and the Nephilim out of Europe and Britain until they found sanctuary here," he said, tapping on the chart. "This is where the battle drew to a stalemate in the mid-fourth century."

Now things are getting interesting, thought Jordan, as the legate's finger rested on Ireland. No Roman legionnaire had ever set foot on Ireland—or Hibernia, as they called it—and lived. Nor had any exorcist.

The legate ordered his secretary to bring them wine, then continued, "Ireland was, and still is, controlled by a particularly strong race of Nephilim, known as the Sidhe, faeries that are of Samael's bloodline through Cain and Lilith. The Sidhe are not like the crude Elioud you've encountered. They live in a highly structured society and are intelligent and skilled at making weapons as well as strong enchantments. They've manifested a kind of land for themselves that spans Ireland and the Otherworld. Celts call it the Middle Kingdom."

"Is this an accurate chart of Ireland?" asked Jordan.

"No. This is just a fabricated shape. No one knows what Ireland really looks like. That is, no true Christian."

Jordan looked at the corner of the chart for the maker's name: Ptolemy of Alexandria. He suppressed an urge to laugh out loud. "Wasn't he the one who provided the Church with a mathematical proof that the sun and stars revolved around the earth?"

"Ptolemy was always helpful with that sort of nonsense, as long as he was paid enough gold. We needed to discourage captains from trying to sail to Ireland, so we had him add a ring of dangerous rocks to the chart and remove anything interesting from the interior, like the capital city, Tara. Uncorrupted Christians cannot enter Ireland without the consent of the Sidhe, and once they do, they become corrupted. Not that an accurate chart would do anyone any good. The forces that protect the coast are not natural. And a sea-dwelling race of Elioud called the Fomorians—nasty creatures—attack any ships that don't have permission to approach."

"I suppose that's why only Viking ships carry trade with Ireland," said Jordan, accepting an ornate silver goblet of red wine from the secretary.

"Not just any Viking ships—only the Irish Vikings are allowed to land. They've retained their pagan ways. Ireland has become a refuge for every unholy group that continues to resist the spread of Christianity: Scottish Gallowglass, Welsh Woodwose, Norsemen. All of them are now fortified on this one island." The legate stabbed his finger into Ireland on the chart.

"Not to mention the Irish Christian Church," suggested Jordan, half smiling at the legate. "I'm sure they come into this somewhere."

The legate cleared his throat. "Of course. It and the French Church are the only two left with enough size and power to challenge our True Church. But the Irish Church is in league with the devil and his spawn. They have formed an alliance with these pagans and Sidhe. We're going to take over the Irish Church and allow the followers of Patrick and Colmcille the opportunity to become true Christians.

"His Holiness the pope has sanctioned a plan developed by Cardinal Orsini: invade and drive the Sidhe from this world, killing any that remain. This will cause the magic of Ireland to die away, taking with it the abilities of the Celtic druids. Then there will be nothing to stop our True Church from finally controlling that elusive island."

"You think eliminating the Sidhe will get rid of the Celtic sorcery?" Jordan asked. "I understood magic to be a natural phenomenon arising in Ireland, not the result of the Nephilim."

The legate looked at Jordan with a puzzled expression.

Jordan handed him back the Book of Enoch. "Thank you, but I have my own copy. And a few other grimoires I gathered to learn about my adversaries."

"That would have been a dangerous admission an hour ago," said the legate. "I clearly have chosen the right man." He returned the book to his desk drawer. "'Natural magic,' as you call it, is as natural and as unholy as original sin, and it arrived in much the same way. It was brought to earth by fallen angels and is still present because their bloodlines are still present. It began to fade in Europe as the Nephilim here were eliminated, an effect first noted by the Romans, then by the VRS League. But it has not gone entirely.

"Ireland is the Nephilim's last major sanctuary. I believe it acts like a beacon, a lingering source of magic for the rest of the world. When we destroy the Sidhe and strip Ireland of its natural magic, the last of it will necessarily disappear from Europe as well, leaving only the exorcists of our True Church to wield enchantments. And all they need to do so are the words of God."

"Other than the High Coven," added Jordan.

"Their magic is unnatural and perverted. We will eliminate them soon enough."

Jordan doubted that the High Coven was going to be that easy to deal with, but he returned his attention to the chart. "Given the forces protecting Ireland, how do you plan to invade?"

"We'll have the English do it," said the legate, a smug look in his eyes. "Their little island always leaves them hungry for more land, and the Scottish and French haven't been very accommodating."

Jordan laughed. "The English will never go. Not after what happened last time—Strongbow's entire armada was wiped out. Not a single ship returned."

"Last time the Vatican made the mistake of placing its trust in the deposed Irish king of Leinster, a human who claimed to know the secret to landing an armada. He was too weak a sorcerer. This time we'll have a Sidhe king lead the invasion. This, my new marshal, is your first mission."

"And how do you expect me to do that?" asked Jordan as the legate rolled up the chart and handed it to his secretary.

"Fortunately, there are some Irish Vikings, high within their nobility, who have secretly come to fear Christ's judgment and, frankly, love gold more than they love Ireland. My Viking spies have discovered that one group of Sidhe, a clan of wood faeries known as Skeaghshee, have rejected the ancient treaty with the Celts and attempted a rebellion. I have passed word to the Skeaghshee that the restored Roman Church does not share its predecessor's desire to conquer Ireland. Instead we share a common enemy: the Irish Christian Church.

"I've made a proposal, using the Irish Church as a ruse: if the Skeaghshee help us conquer the Irish Church, the Roman Church will help them conquer the Celts. We'll receive all the Irish Church's monasteries across Europe and Britain, and they'll regain all of Ireland."

"Unlikely that they'd believe Rome would agree to that."

"It's your job to convince the Skeaghshee of our sincerity. Or lead them to think they can easily betray us after the Celts are defeated. We will, of course, make our move against the Skeaghshee when they least expect it."

The legate turned to his secretary. "Please bring in Prince Ruarc and his . . ." He waved his hand in the air. "His attendants."

After the secretary left, the legate added, "Just remember, my new marshal, that breaking a promise to a Sidhe wouldn't be a sin. Keeping one would be."

Jordan carefully maintained an impassive air as he finished his wine and considered the consequences if the Vatican and the English were to conquer Ireland, that last fully magical land. When the secretary returned, he was followed closely by a lean and weathered man dressed in journeyman's clothing and a frail woman wearing a flowing red robe. A tall faerie entered behind them, moving slowly and deliberately into the room.

"Marshal Jordan d'Anglano," the legate said, "this is Prince Ruarc, eldest surviving son of Kellach, king of the Skeaghshee, future high king of the Sidhe."

Instinctively, Jordan started to bow, only to hesitate and finish with less flourish than he would for a human prince.

"With him," the legate continued, "are Dary Fitz-Stephen, direct descendant of Robert Fitz-Stephen, marshal to Strongbow, and his wife, Eithne."

Jordan's eyes stayed on Ruarc. "How is it even possible for you to enter Venice?"

Ruarc reached out to Eithne, who immediately stepped to his side. Her skin was chalk white, stretched over a gaunt frame. She took Ruarc's hand, and he slid back her sleeve to reveal an emaciated arm and a bandaged wrist, the patch of blood that soaked through not yet having dried brown.

"Eithne graciously sustains me with her own lifeblood, for the sake of all Sidhe."

Jordan glanced at Dary, whose furrowed face had sagged. To Ruarc, Jordan said, "You know what that will do to you?"

"Marshal d'Anglano, we have only just met, yet you express concern over my well-being. Put your mind to rest, I will ensure that I do not become dependent upon it."

Jordan wondered if Ruarc was strong enough to give up feeding on fresh human blood once he no longer needed it to counter the enchantments permeating Venice. He had read in Marija's grimoires that once started, it was a practice impossible to stop.

The reason Albornoz had located the Church's clandestine office in Venice, Jordan suspected, was the protection the city offered against infiltration by all Nephilim, even the Sidhe. More so than the Adriatic Sea that it was connected to, Venice's shallow marshy lagoon had once been a playground of the Elioud: sea nymphs called Nereids and their male counterparts the Vodyanoy, bird-headed Sirens, animalistic Nuggle, and shape-shifting Nix. At the founding of Venice in the second century, these beings provided protection to a group of humans who had made peace with them, allowing the humans to build a city on wooden piles out in the marsh. Then the humans betrayed them.

Vade retro Satana—"Go back Satan"—was the beginning chant in the Christian sorcery known as exorcism. The power of exorcism to drive Nephilim from land and sea was first recognized by Pope

Fabian in 238 when he created the order of exorcists. Exorcism then became part of the official canon of the Roman Church at the Fourth Council of Carthage in 398. With this the Church had new roles for the educated but psychopathic sons of wealthy families, who would ship off their darlings into the priesthood, along with large endowments. The most capable and fanatical of these exorcists formed an alliance and wore a medal of protection around their necks inscribed with the abbreviation of their opening chant, VRS, and thus they became know as the VRS League.

Venice, a city rapidly growing in wealth and power, hired the VRS League in the fifth century to drive out the very beings that had originally protected it from waves of Germanic and Hun invasions. After years of cleansing, the Nephilim were kept out with a constantly maintained weave of blessings, graces, and, clandestinely, enchantments.

By the ninth century, though, some Nephilim had learned that they could survive in protected cities such as Venice by drinking blood from a living human, but doing so carried extreme risk. Human blood was so addictive that after a short while the creature became obsessed only with getting more of it, forgetting their original purpose.

"I could ask the same question of your companion, Marshal," said Ruarc, walking over to Ty and staring up at his face. "Do you let him feed on you somehow?"

"Absolutely not. Ty is an aberration. Enchantments don't affect him in the same way as other Nephilim." Deciding that Ruarc's blood consumption did not concern him—not yet—Jordan continued, "You can land an armada safely in Ireland?"

Stepping back but continuing to study Ty with a look of concern, Ruarc replied, "I can get a small group into Ireland. Only my father has the power to land an armada."

"Ruarc's father, King Kellach, has been imprisoned on the Irish island of Great Skellig," said the legate.

"Trees are sacred to my clan," said Ruarc. "My king was simply trying to protect them from the Celts, as you would protect your own holy places. But how could he, while the Morrígna was siding with the Celts and preventing other Sidhe clans from helping us?"

The legate added, "Kellach is being unjustly punished for his efforts to free the Sidhe from the oppression of the Goddess Morrígna, by attempting to expel her from this world."

"The treaty between the Celts and the Middle Kingdom threatens the very existence of my kind, who live in the woods," said Ruarc.

"I have stressed to the prince our outrage over the desecration of his people's trees," said the legate. "Marshal d'Anglano, you'll go to Great Skellig with Prince Ruarc, free King Kellach, and convey him to England. Your ship will be ready as soon as the spring storms abate. You and Prince Ruarc are to craft and deliver a plan, along with a requisition for supplies and men, to my secretary within a month, and then—"

"No, we must leave this city right away," Dary broke in. At a hiss from Ruarc, Dary looked down and added softly, "For the sake of my wife."

Ignoring Dary's outburst, the legate said, "I look forward to seeing your plan." His secretary opened the office door and led Ruarc's party out.

Jordan waited until they were gone. "What of Patrick's Bell?" he asked the legate. "The Blood Bell?"

"Your knowledge is impressive. Orsini assured me that the Bell will not be in Ireland when the English armada arrives. It's not your concern."

Jordan bowed and left. He was confident he could handle his role, and it would give him the chance to sail to Ireland, which was something he never thought he would get to do. He wondered if a country still steeped in magic would look or feel any different.

Making no more sound than a breeze, Ty bent, twisted, and followed Jordan out the small door. The legate, watching this impossible move, blinked twice.

Outside, on the small dock, Ty rumbled, "Ty not like legate."

"He has granted me a valuable position," said Jordan. As he climbed into the boat, it rocked, and he had to grab the side to steady himself.

"Legate wishes to murder Ty's world," said Ty. He unfastened the rope and stepped in behind Jordan. Other than being pressed down into the rancid water, the boat did not stir until Ty began working the oar.

"That's one way to look at it," replied Jordan. "I didn't know you were paying attention."

"Ty has ears. How does Jordan look at it?"

That question had already been troubling Jordan. This was not only a great opportunity for him, it was a chance to redeem his family's name, perhaps his only chance. But the Church did not just want to conquer Ireland, they wanted to end everyone's access to magic, except for that of their own exorcists. And magic was becoming as interesting to Jordan as status. Back when he was struggling to survive plague and famine, he never thought he would face a conflict between wealth and desire.

"What would you have me do?" he asked.

Ty took so long to answer that Jordan thought he had not heard the question. Then, in a faint, gravelly voice, Ty replied, "Ty not care what Jordan does. Ty not belong in either world."

"You belong with me," replied Jordan.

In the legate's office, Geoffrey Chaucer emerged from a side door.

"Were you able hear everything?" asked the legate. "Thoughts?"

"He's exactly the kind of man you need, if you're going to go through with this gambit," said Chaucer, helping himself to the leftover wine. "Just don't underestimate how hard it will be to convince Richard to join." In the court of England's King Richard II, Chaucer held the posts of Poet to the King, Clerk of the King's Works, and envoy to the Vatican. Richard was the second king Chaucer had worked for as a bureaucrat and diplomat, but his first love remained the emerging English language, and his throaty-voiced recitations of elaborate tales were popular at courtiers' dinner parties.

"How is Richard's mind these days?" the legate asked cautiously. He had yet to meet the inbred and notoriously eccentric king.

"Increasingly difficult to reason with," Chaucer replied laughingly. "Is there no way to take Ireland without him?"

"I have my instructions from Orsini." The legate gave a deep sigh. "Our condottieri are stretched thin with our European expansion. The plague has left few men to recruit. We have no navy yet." He ticked off the reasons on his fingers. "Without the English we can't muster an invasion force or get it to Ireland."

He refilled his own wine goblet. "But we have to attack now," the legate continued, "while the Skeaghshee revolt gives us an opening. The first we have had in two centuries."

"And we know how well it worked out last time," said Chaucer, shaking his head. "Nevertheless, nothing ventured, nothing gained. If your dashing new marshal actually gets Kellach off that Irish rock alive, I promise to secure you an audience with Richard." Chaucer lounged in a chair, took a sip of wine, and observed his friend thoughtfully. "The king might be crazy, but even he will be skeptical about putting all his faith in a tree-loving faerie who failed so mightily in his own plans that he's exiled on a barren island. It will be an interesting discussion. I sail back to London on the morning tide."

The legate pulled a heavy coin purse from his desk. "Someone dropped this on the plaza. Is it by chance yours?"

Chaucer eyed the pouch—the king paid functionaries little and poets less, which was why he was forced to fill three posts. He held up a hand. "No, but thank you. Richard would have me flayed if he found out. Besides, the story material you provide is as gold to me." He raised his goblet in a toast to the legate. "To quote myself: 'The life so short, the craft so long to learn.'" He drained the wine.

"How go the stories?" asked the legate as he retrieved the carafe and poured the last of its contents for Chaucer.

"Very well! Hawkwood provided all the inspiration I needed for the Knight," replied Chaucer, referring to one of the characters in his ongoing series *The Canterbury Tales*. The legate and Chaucer had become close friends long ago when Richard had sent Chaucer to Rome as emissary to Hawkwood when he was helping Cardinal Albornoz wrest the papacy away from French control. Chaucer, sensing a rich vein of subject matter, had made sure he remained his king's connection to the Vatican's clandestine office ever since.

"And with all this talk of enchantments," Chaucer said, looking disappointed at the empty carafe, "I hear the muse's call. I believe I shall write a story containing that magic ring you told me about, King Solomon's, wasn't it?"

"Be careful with your tales, my friend. There's getting to be too much sorcery in them. You don't want to give the Church a reason to flay you either."

"Forbid us something, and that thing we desire."

6

In a spot not far from where Aisling took the poisoned arrow in her back three years earlier, a red stag grazed near the center of a large clearing. Its velvet-covered antlers had sprouted early, encouraged by the unusually warm spring, and by the time the autumn rutting season arrived he would carry a rack large enough to have his pick of the five does that grazed closer to the clearing's edge.

The stag jerked his head up, one foreleg stomping the ground. With a bound, the five does disappeared into the surrounding woods.

"You moved too fast. He sensed you," hissed Tadg into Conor's ear.

"It wasn't me he sensed," Conor hissed back.

The two men squatted behind a cluster of elderberry bushes inside the tree line. They were human but lived outside normal Irish society, in the forests. Conor, tall and lean and the younger of the two at twenty-three, wore a buckskin tunic over black woolen trousers and calf-high leather boots. Short, dark brown hair, still showing some of the curl that had been prominent in his youth, contrasted with the blue of his eyes. Tadg, at fifty-one, was dressed in a more traditional, if tattered, woolen tunic, trousers, and cloak, in faded green, brown, and black. His long, hooked nose dominated a face weathered from living outdoors.

Conor rose and drew his bow, but it was too late. The stag was already leaping into the trees and in a blur was gone.

"Save your arrow," said Tadg. "So much for venison tonight. You're losing your touch. When you were young, you could creep up close enough to kill a stag like that with your dagger."

"It wasn't my fault. Listen. Someone's coming."

A horse entered the clearing, walking slowly. Its rider wore a chain-mail tunic and a full helmet with a keyhole-shaped opening for his eyes, nose, and mouth.

"Is he alone?" asked Tadg.

"I hear no one else," responded Conor.

"A horse is worth three deer."

"In meat, not flavor."

"We could dry most of it, so we'd have it if we need it."

"If you insist. I'm more interested in that knight. I haven't had a good fight all winter." Conor drew his bow again. The arrow caught the horse behind the shoulder, an inch from the knight's leg. It stumbled, then fell, spilling its rider onto the grass.

"Well, that should do it," said Tadg. "Have fun."

Handing his bow to Tadg, Conor drew his sword and started toward the knight, who was getting up, also drawing a sword. "Sir Knight, if that's what you are, do you wish to fight me for the right to this piece of meat you so kindly rode into my clearing? Or would you prefer to just walk away?"

The rider stared at Conor, then dropped her sword and pulled off her helmet, spilling out long red hair and revealing a seventeen-year-old Aisling. She knelt beside the horse. "He's not a piece of meat. I don't know his name, but I know he's a faithful horse with a strong heart." She began to chant an incantation of comfort while stroking the horse's neck. Red foam bubbled from its nostrils.

Leaving his sword thrust into the earth, Conor went down on one knee and covered the horse's eyes with his left hand. From his belt he drew a misericorde dagger. Shifting his hand, Conor thrust the long blade through the top of the eye socket and into the brain. The horse's gasping ceased. Listening to Aisling's chant, now a prayer of thanks for the horse's life, he cleaned the misericorde on the thick grass, replaced it, and stepped back to retrieve his sword.

"Don't be sad, Lady— What's your name?" asked Conor.

Aisling did not reply.

"As you wish," said Conor. "But know that this noble horse, as you've said, will make a fine feast for my friend's family and me, bringing its strength to us. Certainly a worthy end for any animal."

Aisling finished her prayer and turned to retrieve her own sword, one she had secretly slipped out from the armory. Her back to Conor, she took several practice strokes to measure its balance. "You haven't won your feast yet, you arrogant, hedge-born knave," she said calmly.

"If you insist on—" Conor did not finish. Without a sound, Aisling had turned and charged. She started her sword high, sweeping it down in a decreasing radius arc ending in an S-hook thrust. Conor recognized the move too late for a clean parry and had to spin out of the way to avoid taking the point in his shoulder.

Aisling's momentum carried her past Conor, who added to the distance by taking three steps back. He needed to reassess his opponent.

"A little less speed on the charge and you could've caught his torso with a backstroke before he finished his spin," Liam called to Aisling as he walked his horse into the clearing. "Good morning, Tadg, Conor."

"A fine morning it is, Liam," replied Conor. "If you're here, then this must be the new High Priestess of Tara, our half Goddess."

Aisling took a step toward Conor. "A bow is required."

"I bow only to what's left of the Morrígna," said Conor, bending slightly while keeping his eyes on Aisling. "She was much needed. My heart cried at the news of your sister's murder."

Aisling returned a nod.

"I still claim this horse," said Conor.

"Well, are you going to fight him for it?" asked Liam.

"No," replied Aisling. "Let him have it. Otherwise he may have to eat that goat he's been keeping to satisfy his manly desires."

Liam and Tadg broke into laughter. Conor just smiled.

"You took your time finding me," said Aisling to Liam as she sat behind him on his horse, riding out of the clearing.

"I was here, watching. It'll take a lot more than a set of men's clothing and a simple concealment enchantment for you to slip out without my noticing."

"Basic enchantments are all I can muster anymore. But next time I'll fool you," said Aisling without conviction.

She lay against Liam's broad back and turned her face toward the sun, soaking in the warmth of the spring day. "You know those two?" she asked.

"Tadg is the finest fletcher in Meath, perhaps all of Ireland. When you were younger, he made all of the arrows I brought you."

When I was still training to be a warrior Goddess, thought Aisling. *When I was whole, before Anya was torn from me and I was imprisoned in this half-life.*

They rode on in silence. "They were exceptional arrows," she finally offered. "They always seemed to know where I wanted them to go."

"He harvests the shafts from live elm trees and dries them for two years. Sidhe smiths make arrowheads for him, of his own design. For his flights it's said that he has a covenant with the peregrine falcons. They flock to him each morning, and he selects and gently removes only one feather from each, and in return no Tadg arrow will bring down a peregrine."

"Where's his home kingdom?"

"He has none. He and his wife live in the woods, constantly moving to find the next perfect tree to make his arrows."

"And this horse-eating, goat-loving Conor?"

Liam laughed. "The story Tadg tells is that Conor's mother was thought to be a fugitive slave who died in childbirth. No father or owner could be identified. When he was six, he ran away from the farm that fostered him. Soon after that, as Tadg was standing at the base of a tree studying the branches, Conor appeared and offered to climb up and harvest the ones he wanted. Conor has been with Tadg and his wife ever since. But he has no honor price."

"Tadg didn't at least petition the court on his behalf?" asked Aisling, surprised.

"Conor wouldn't let him. Told Tadg that he'd disappear if Tadg tried. And once of age, Conor simply avoided anything to do with it."

"That's odd," said Aisling.

In Irish Celtic society, almost all free persons had an honor price. It represented the size of a business agreement that they could bond by themselves, and it signified the relative value of their testimony in court. In a marriage contract, the person, man or woman, who carried the highest honor price was in charge of all financial matters. Those with a high honor price created income by lending a share of it to others for their business dealings. A child would be assigned a portion of the family's collective honor price at fourteen, or earlier if the family chose.

The Celts loved trade even more than fighting, and all trade functioned using honor price. However, it was not a static amount. It rose and fell, depending on a person's success. Slaves often earned their freedom and their own honor price through hard work or education, which was encouraged for all. A lord could lose his entire honor price and become a slave through a few bad transactions and have to earn it all back again.

If a person was killed without legal justification, then the perpetrator had to pay the victim's honor price to the victim's family. If the perpetrator could not pay, the family was honor-bound to kill him or, as usually happened, take him as a slave until he worked off the debt.

Customarily, only two types of free people were without an honor price. There were the wild, savage tribes, called Woodwose, living in remote forests and worshipping dark spirits. The others were bandits, often fugitive slaves—though with the possibility of earning true freedom there was little incentive for slaves to run away and few measures taken to prevent them from doing so.

Aisling did not think Conor was a bandit even though he had killed her horse, and he did not have the crazed look of a Woodwose. She had been dressed as a knight. Challenging a knight to a fight, with his horse as a prize, was legal if the challenger was of a lower honor price, though it also put the challenger at high risk of a legal slaying.

Liam and Aisling approached Tara from the southwest. The Celtic capital city sprawled across a hill slowly rising five hundred feet from the plains of Meath. The lower structures were simple one-room cottages of post-and-wattle construction, with thatched roofs and walls smoothed with plaster mortar made from mud, lime, and a bit of blood. The buildings became larger and more elaborate the higher up the hill they were positioned. At the summit sat the royal enclosure, wrapped in a meandering stone wall. Within the enclosure were stone buildings with timber roofs containing embassies from the five kingdoms and a great meeting hall built in the traditional Nordic fashion housing a Viking delegation. Surrounding these, filling the royal enclosure except for the courtyard, were inns, shops, and residential buildings for the royal retinue, official visitors, influential lords, ladies, and traders. Gallowglass maintained no delegation, preferring to avoid politics and keep their agreements strictly contractual.

Rising from among the royal buildings and dominating the entire hill were three interconnected towers. The meeting chambers for the elected high king, the treasury, the military, and other high officials were located in the northeast tower. As high priestess of Tara, Aisling occupied the top floor of the southeast tower. The four lower floors housed representatives of the higher-order guilds: harpists, bards, physicians, smiths, brewers, masons, scriveners, and genealogists. Five hundred years earlier, two guild chambers on the lowest floor had been granted to the Irish Christian Church in gratitude for the Latin writing they taught to all—separate chambers because the followers of Patrick and the followers of Colmcille did not get along.

Only Aisling and the high king were allowed residence chambers within the towers.

The chambers and even the number of floors inside the west tower varied depending on the needs and moods of its occupants, Sidhe ambassadors. They were mostly Brownies, whose love of debate and basic understanding of polities distinguished them from other Sidhe. Aisling remembered that the previous winter, when the Sidhe high king arranged for the Celtic high king to meet with the leader of a group of visiting Goblins to negotiate their return to Scotland, the west tower had seemed to contain only one large chamber.

Looking up at the towers, Aisling thought again of Haidrean, her druid tutor killed during the attack on Anya. When she was younger, Aisling looked forward to the time she was no longer required to listen to the old curmudgeon. Now she missed him.

⚭

HAIDREAN HAD BROUGHT Aisling and Anya to visit Tara when they were seven, following their Ceremony of Hearts.

"The Grogoch constructed it out of a single row of stones," he told them as they walked around the base of Tara Tower. The stones, seven feet on edge, emerged from the ground and looped around in a cloverleaf shape, crisscrossing in the center, until they spiraled up over a hundred feet to form the three towers, each thirty feet in diameter. "When it was up, the Grogoch molded openings for doors and windows. So it looks like three towers, but it is really one solid structure."

"Like the Morrígna. Like us," said Anya.

"Exactly," said Haidrean.

"So I'm this tower, and Anann's the far one, and you're that one," said Anya to her sister.

"It was just an analogy," replied Aisling.

"Why does the Morrígna always return in completely human bodies?" asked Anya, her enthusiasm unswayed.

"No one knows," said Haidrean. "However, I believe it is because of our short life span. She prefers to leave us to our own will as much as possible."

"And only our bloodline. Looks like you're going to have to take a human husband," said Anya to her sister.

"It doesn't have to be me."

"It does. I'll be in the Middle Kingdom, so—"

"Both of you can take human husbands," Haidrean broke in. "Anya, you'll be visiting this land often enough."

"See," said Aisling. "You can have one-day marriage contracts."

Anya took Aisling's hand. "Come on, let's go to the bakery." They headed toward a nearby building emitting the inviting odors of fresh bread and honey cakes. "Haidrean, why can't I feel Anann inside me? I'm feeling Aisling more and more."

"You'll never feel Anann as you do Aisling. Anann is evident when the power of the Morrígna moves through you as you exercise your magic. You'll have increasing access to that power now that you've had your Ceremony of Hearts. Do you want to try it?" asked Haidrean.

"Yes, please," replied Anya.

"Aisling, close your eyes. Anya, count silently to yourself the number of loaves on the cooling rack." Anya rose up on her tiptoes and scanned the bread. "Now, Aisling, without opening your eyes, tell us how many loaves there are."

Aisling scrunched up her face. "I'm trying, but I can't see out of her eyes."

"Don't see, remember," Haidrean ordered. "Know what she knows, as if you had seen it a moment ago."

"That makes no sense."

"Do it anyway."

Aisling screwed up her face even more. Anya grabbed one of the small loaves, tore off a chunk, and began to eat it.

"Twenty . . . one," Aisling said. "No. Twenty and a half."

"Yes!" Anya and Haidrean exclaimed together as Aisling opened her eyes to check, their green traces fading to gray.

"You want to see another piece of magic now open to you?" whispered Haidrean.

They both nodded.

Haidrean pinched the back of Anya's arm.

"Ouch!" Aisling and Anya cried simultaneously, and then they dissolved into uncontrolled laughter.

LIAM AND AISLING rode his horse through the stable gate at the south side of the Tara royal enclosure. Here the wall bulged out to accommodate an equestrian complex that surrounded one of the six royal wells. Predating all other structures, their origin lost to history, the wells never ceased to gently overflow their stone rings, even though they opened at an elevation higher than any land for miles around.

Back in my cage, Aisling thought. *Trapped as surely as I am trapped in my marriage.* As if on cue, Aisling saw that Lord Maolan, her husband for the last two years, was waiting, alerted to their return. Liam led his horse into a stall as Maolan approached Aisling.

"Where's my horse?" Maolan asked.

"What's another horse to you?" replied Aisling.

"He's not just another horse, he's Sciobtha, my fastest, and he was promised for a race today. Do you know how humiliating it was for me when he didn't run? I told you to leave my horses alone."

"Well, he wasn't fast enough. He'd have lost you money. You should thank me." Aisling turned to leave.

Maolan grabbed her by the shoulder and swung her around. "Tell me where my horse is. Now."

"Your horse is nothing except meat now. A man named Conor is probably roasting it as we speak."

"Conor? Tadg's slave? Conor killed my horse?" asked Maolan. Spitting onto the floor, he added, "That *cac ar oineach*!"—using the phrase meaning "shit on honor"—an insult that could legally be replied to with a lethal blow, if it were said about someone who had an honor price.

"Conor's not a slave, and I lost your horse to him in a fair fight."

"You're getting expensive." Maolan was leaning into Aisling, shouting and sending small drops of spittle into her face. He looked up at Liam, who had stepped out of the stall to stand behind Aisling. Jabbing his finger into her chest, Maolan hissed, "Make sure you don't become too expensive." He stormed out of the stable.

"Perhaps a five-year marriage contract will turn out to be a bit long," offered Liam.

AT ANYA'S FUNERAL Aisling had stood numb, unseeing, on the royal stand in the Tara courtyard. The touch of the torches to the pyre seemed to jar her awake. She could not recall how she got there. She remembered that it was her fourteenth birthday when she saw Anya—it was the first time since she had ridden away from her twin at Trim Castle, four days prior. Anya was dressed in one of the embroidered white robes that had been made for their inauguration, the day they were to have come of age to rule. *A futile, empty gesture*, Aisling thought. When the flames had climbed high enough up the carefully constructed wooden structure to begin caressing Anya's body, Aisling turned away and left.

Entering the tower and climbing the spiral stairs, she reached out to the curved stone wall, seeking the feel of something solid, but nothing had felt truly solid since Anya's death and she stumbled. She sat on the stair with her eyes closed as a fresh wave of nausea washed over her. *Anya and I were going to rule this land today*, she thought. *Instead I am just trying to get through the day without retching.*

Her equilibrium finally stabilized, and she resumed her climb. When she reached the roof, Aisling turned away from the light radiating up from the pyre and walked to the opposite side. A double line of faerie lights led off to the northeast, floating above the ten-mile path from Brú na Bóinne to Tara. Along it moved a river of Sidhe. As with all Sidhe funeral processions, it was led by Sluaghs, who are skilled in helping the dead find their way to the After Lands. They were followed by Devas and Adhenes, the two ruling clans, then a mix of Gnomes, Fire Sprites, Brownies, Leprechauns, Pixies, Grogoch, and Wichtlein. No Skeaghshee were allowed to attend. For the eight hours it would take for the flames to consume her sister's body, the Sidhe would stream along this path, loop around the pyre, and then return to their domain.

She leaned out through the battlements and looked down at the pools of torchlight that speckled the ground. *Would the ground feel solid if I fell from this height?* she wondered. She sensed someone walk up behind her, felt Brigid take her hand. *I want no more useless words of comfort,* she thought. She said, "I don't know who I am anymore."

Brigid squeezed Aisling's hand. "You're still the Morrígna."

"No I'm not. Not even half. Not anymore. The Skeaghshee not only took my sister, they took the most important part of me."

"I can teach you to connect with your Goddess self again, to be whole, to bring Morrígna's power out."

Aisling shook her head. "If I had any power left, I would crawl up on my sister's pyre and let the flames carry me home. But I don't. Every day I awake standing on a ledge on a cliff face, only the ledge is made of wax and no matter how hard I cling, I keep sliding off and plummeting into a rolling black fog."

"Please trust me, you will recover from this," Brigid pleaded.

Aisling continued as if she had not heard, "There seem to be shapes in the dark, and I try to grab them to save myself." She reached over the edge of the tower into the night. "I grasp nothing, and I keep tumbling, and I am lost. Until I again awake, desperately clinging to the cliff face, only to slide off."

Brigid gathered Aisling into her arms. "Ireland needs you. The high kings have already agreed to a conclave. They'll decide on an important role for you," said Brigid.

"They'll decide. What about what I want?"

"What do you want?"

Aisling closed her eyes and searched for the Goddess she was meant to become on this day, or even for the girl she was a few days before. She could find neither. The first stench of burning flesh reached her from the pyre. She longed to scream: *Tell them to kill me, too! Let me rejoin the Morrígna with Anya in the Otherworld! But that's another thing I am not strong enough to do,* she thought, berating herself for not throwing herself on the fire, or off this tower. To Brigid she whispered only, "I don't know."

Aisling opened her eyes, stared out at the Sidhe funeral procession, and hated them. Hated all of them.

The next week Fearghal, the Sidhe high king, sat at the center of a long table, flanked by the rulers of each of the Middle Kingdom clans. Behind them stood an array of scriveners and attendants. A thin strip of water meandered through the grass in front of the table, barely large enough to be called a stream. Across it stood a mirror-image table occupied by the Celtic high king, flanked by the rulers of the Irish kingdoms—three kings and two queens—and the members of the Druidic Council, of which Brigid was the newly elected head due to the murder of Haidrean. Flat light sank through the turbulent mist that draped over the conclave, giving the impression of a large gray tent in a silent windstorm. They were in the Sidhe's third of the royal towers of Tara.

Fearghal rose from his seat and walked to the middle of the two congregations. "We are agreed, the Treaty of Tailltiu stands." He looked old, for a Sidhe, with a hint of silver in his black hair and thin lines radiating from his eyes, the gold brooch of his office prominent on a brilliant green cloak over his gray tunic.

He was joined by the Celtic high king, who confirmed, "We are agreed."

Together they crouched down, and, cupping their right hands, each drew one drink of water from the stream. When they returned to their seats, the tiny stream no longer flowed, no longer divided the tables.

"And what of the Morrígna?" asked Brigid as she stood.

A wave of soft voices rolled along the Sidhe table. An Adhene stood, whom Brigid knew to be Fearghal's daughter, Rhoswen. Her sharply angled, hairless, nude body was covered with a thick paint in shades of green and brown, signifying her status as a Bhean Draoi, a Sidhe witch. Black tears were painted down her hollow cheeks. "The Morrígna lived between the twins," Rhoswen said. "She was to rule the Celts through Aisling, the Sidhe through Anya. Anya is dead. To us the Morrígna once again sleeps in the Otherworld. We have resumed our vigil, calling to her and awaiting her return."

"Aisling is alive. She carries part of the Morrígna still," urged Brigid. "She can speak for both the Celts and the Sidhe."

Rhoswen shook her head, studying the ground. "Aisling is half dead herself. She no longer brings the Morrígna into this world." Raising her head and locking eyes with Brigid, she continued, "As long as Aisling lives at all, the Morrígna cannot return. You know—"

"Nothing is to happen to Aisling," interrupted the Celtic high king.

"We are not suggesting that," replied Fearghal. "Aisling's life will not be taken by any of my subjects. The Morrígna will return in her own time."

At a whispered plea from Mamos, an elderly druid, Brigid turned to confer with him. Soon she was surrounded by the entire council. Rhoswen waited silently, still except for the painted black tears flowing down her face.

The council members returned to their seats. "My true name is Lasirfhionamhnán," Brigid said to Rhoswen, binding herself to tell the complete truth. A white swan spread its great wings and rose from the space occupied by Brigid's collapsing robe. With one large flap and a short glide, it became a woman, naked, pale, and freckled; Brigid stood in the grass between the tables. Murmurs came from the Druid Council. While all had heard that Brigid had learned this intricate enchantment from the Sidhe—the first druid to master it in five centuries—few had actually seen it.

"Lasirfhionamhnán," repeated Rhoswen. She looked over to Fearghal, who nodded. "My true name is——" Rhoswen made a sound like a boulder rolling in a swollen stream and burst into a brown hawk. She flew to stand in front of Brigid and resumed her painted witch form.

Brigid echoed the sound of the witch's true name, then said, "My entire order, all of our orders"—she indicated the council with a sweep of her arm—"have been performing Taghairm and Coelbreni, but still we cannot see." Taghairm was a powerful divination ritual during which a druid slays and skins a wild bull, wraps the bloody hide around himself, and meditates by a waterfall. Coelbreni is a simpler, and much less messy, ritual of casting hazel rods inscribed with runes. Brigid continued, "We do not know if the Morrígna can return now that one of the hearts has been destroyed." She again called Rhoswen by her true name. "——, what do your people see?"

"Lasirfhionamhnán, we also cannot tell if the Morrígna can ever return," said Rhoswen softly. "Anya's heart was missing a piece, the small segment that King Kellach inherited and hid. That segment survives, which gives us hope in our sadness. A future Ceremony of Hearts may be possible." Rhoswen dropped her head to the side and closed her eyes. Reaching out, Brigid caressed her green-and-brown cheek. Black-painted tears flowed across Brigid's ivory hand and dripped onto the grass.

Fearghal spoke up. "Our nobles are unanimous in their belief that Kellach was behind the attack." There were nods of approval along the Sidhe table, the Pixie queen offering that this sort of atrocity could be perpetrated only by a Skeaghshee.

"The Sidhe are prepared to assist the Celtic forces in his capture," continued Fearghal, "so long as he is not executed. I propose lifetime imprisonment on Great Skellig. Its being a treeless island, that will be appropriate punishment."

Kellach tried to resist the mounting pain as flames roared through the grove of sacred woods. He dropped his sword, clasped his head with both hands, and fell to his knees. Through the flames he could see warriors circling the grove—Celts, Gallowglass, and Sidhe—preventing any escape by his own forces.

"How could you do this?" he shouted, without knowing if his voice would carry to those Middle Kingdom dwellers who had betrayed him. "We could have taken all of Ireland back! The Morrígna is half dead! I made victory possible for you!"

Even without the rest of the Sidhe clans, Kellach had tried to defeat the Celts after Anya's death. For five months his forces, brave hearts all of them, had battled. Now, making this last stand, his warriors gathered around their king. A tongue of fire lashed out toward Kellach but was diverted by a loyal Skeaghshee who called it to himself, breathed it in, wailed in anguish, and died. Others moved to protect their king, to their death.

The agony of his trees overwhelmed Kellach, and he fell squirming to the ground. He caught a glimpse of Liam walking through the flames, protected by a sphere of cool air generated by the four Fire Sprites with him. Liam bound him with a thin iron chain and hefted his convulsing body over a shoulder. As Liam carried him out, the final sounds Kellach heard before he lost consciousness were the screams of both the trees and his warriors.

Once Kellach was imprisoned and most of his followers reduced to cinders, Aisling no longer took long walks in the forests around Tara. It had been the only purpose in her days, a secret hope that somehow Kellach would find a way to kill her, even with Liam and a troop of guards trudging along beside her.

Thereafter she usually stayed in her chambers. Some days she rose, dressed, and sat by the fire; some days she did not. The Celtic and Sidhe conclave had refused to recognize Aisling as the Morrígna, so the Druidic Council had appointed her high priestess of Tara; however, in her depressed state, when her duties required an audience, her acolytes would bring the petitioner to speak with her through a screen.

On the day Lord Maolan entered with her father and mother, eleven months after the death of Anya, Aisling was dressed and waiting, the screen folded against the wall. She knew why he was there. Realizing he would never be elected high king, or even king of Meath, he was seeking another way to obtain power and have influence in the highest echelon of Tara.

"Lord Maolan has asked us to present a five-year-and-a-day marriage contract to you," said Quinn, referring to the longest initial marriage contract permitted under the Brehon laws.

"I've made it clear to him and your father that I'm opposed to this idea," said Una.

"Perhaps a year-and-a-day contract, to see how it goes?" Quinn suggested, more to Una than to Aisling. Aisling's human parents had been trying to reconnect with her since Anya's death, the results awkward at times, disastrous at others.

Maolan moved next to Aisling. "My only wish is to care for you," he lied. "You know of my loyalty." He extended his left hand, palm up, showing the scar along the base of his fingers that he had received during her Test.

Aisling looked into his eyes and saw the cruelty there, saw the pain and unhappiness that awaited her if she became his wife. With a thin smile, she said, "Yes. Five years and a day."

The next month, with a sliver of crescent moon hanging in the midday sky of her fifteenth birthday, Aisling left her chamber for the first time in months and made her way into the high king's private meeting chamber for her wedding. Only a handful of people awaited her.

. . . . .

Liam watched Aisling unceremoniously approach the druid and Maolan. "I'm not going to sanction this," he said to no one in particular, and stormed from the chamber. Striding across the great hall, he stopped in front of a fireplace where Rhoswen stood staring into the flames.

Before he could begin, she said, "You spent fourteen years forcing her to abandon her humanity, and now you expect her to act rational, when she has become ensnared in a void between human and Goddess."

"You think you understand her?" he snapped. "She may not be fully human, but she's not Sidhe at all."

"Is she not?" Rhoswen asked.

Liam wished he had someone to kill.

Rhoswen said, "In your heart she is still the young girl you have been training and protecting. She is no longer that, nor is she the Morrígna. Both of those lives have been stripped from her. Look into your own half-Sidhe nature and you may begin to understand."

"But why Maolan?" Liam's raised voice echoed in the hall.

"I suspect she is so full of darkness that it seems like the only source of wholeness to her, that pain and humiliation are the only ways for her to feel anything," replied Rhoswen. "Possibly she sees Maolan as the next best thing to death."

"So she's lost, to herself and her people," said Liam. "Kellach might as well have killed her."

"Impossible to say. There has never been a being such as she is now. Some new light may emerge into her life. But she has a wound that cannot be completely healed. Nothing exists in this world that can fill the space Anya left. I believe that even if she pulls herself out of the darkness she is drowning in, she will live on a knife edge the rest of her life."

They stood together, staring into the fire.

"I have been trying to see the impact of the missing heart segment,"

Rhoswen said. "Perhaps it would have afforded Aisling enough strength to overcome Anya's death. Given the potential I sensed in the twins on their birth, it is more likely that it would have brought them too close to being a Goddess, leaving Aisling with too little humanity to fall back on, and she would have died with Anya or become completely insane."

Liam was in no mood for useless conjecture; however, Rhoswen's earlier comments were beginning to sink in. He turned and reluctantly walked back toward the marriage ceremony.

After the ceremony Aisling avoided the small feast and hurried to her own chamber. The moon had set by the time Maolan entered. Aisling rose from her chair in front of the fire, slipped from her robe, and lay passively, silently on the bed as Maolan took her. When he was finished, she turned on her side, looking away from him.

Maolan reached down and touched the blood, her blood, on him. He examined his wet fingers, the sight arousing him again. Pushing Aisling onto her stomach, he grasped her hair and pulled her head back. "You will do everything I tell you to do, as high priestess and as my wife," Maolan hissed in her ear as he began to roughly sodomize her.

Afterward, having dressed, Maolan walked toward the door. Before he reached it, it swung inward, revealing Brigid holding a basin of warm, scented water and a stack of towels. She ignored him as he slipped past her. Closing the door with her foot, Brigid placed the basin on the bedside table, then began to clean the prone Aisling.

"My sweet girl. None of this will distract you from your emptiness."

Aisling did not respond.

Continuing to gently clean her, Brigid said, "You still have great power sleeping inside you. Are you going to just give that to him?"

"What choice do I have? What choice have I ever had in what happens to me?" mumbled Aisling.

"Start by choosing to get up and get dressed. To leave this chamber and come with me to my temple, where you'll choose a novice priestess to show you the pleasure a new husband should have shown you tonight," Brigid replied.

Aisling propped herself up on one elbow and turned to face Brigid.

Brigid took Aisling's face in both her hands. "You must learn to bring forth the Morrígna's power again. It will be harder than before, but I'll help you. You must do this, because one day you will face stronger, darker forces than Lord Maolan."

Brigid pulled back, smiling down at her. "First, though, Maolan must learn that he may have secured a right to your bed, but you don't need him there. Let me finish washing you, and we'll go."

Aisling nodded. Once dressed, she left her chamber for the second time in months.

❧

THREE DAYS AFTER her encounter with Conor in the forest, as the sunrise cleared the top of the wall of the Tara royal enclosure, Aisling and Liam entered the stables to see her new horse. Quinn, upon learning that his daughter had lost one of Maolan's horses, had sent his best to her.

Aisling was thrilled to find a two-year-old, jet-black hobby waiting for her in a stall—her father had excelled this time. The favorite horse of the Celtic cavalry, hobbies were compact and very fast. With well-defined muscles under a velvet coat, this was one of the finest she had ever seen. So engrossed was she in examining the horse that it was not until Liam tapped her shoulder that she noticed the men in the back of the stall.

Three sat in the shadows, bound and gagged. A leather strap was fastened around each man's neck and tied to a ring set low on the back wall. Stacked to one side of them was a collection of swords, daggers, and bows. In the far corner, lounging on a pile of straw, was Conor.

Rising to his feet, he said, "My lady, High Priestess, I bring you this gift"—he indicated the three men—"and humbly ask for forgiveness for killing your fine, if somewhat tough and chewy, horse."

Aisling dismissed the request with a wave of her hand. "He wasn't my horse." Studying the men, she asked, "What do you expect me to do with them? Eat them?"

"Keep them as slaves. Or stable hands. I wouldn't recommend continuing to use them in their current profession as assassins," replied Conor. "Or, if you've no use for them, return them to Lord Maolan. It was he who sent them to kill me."

Aisling looked at Liam, who nodded. "You knew this?" she exclaimed.

Liam smiled and shrugged. "I sent word to let Conor know they were coming. He can take care of himself in the woods."

Conor had been moving closer to Aisling. She looked him up and down. Once again she could not help but notice the abundance of life that shone in his eyes. "You weren't hurt in this attack?"

"Not at all. I had them before they could draw a sword."

"Are you sure? No injury at all? Something that's been keeping you from bowing to your high priestess?"

"Ha! Another misdeed that I must atone for," said Conor, not bowing. "I offer a kiss as restitution for my lack of chivalry."

"Liam," Aisling ordered, "if he tries to kiss me, kill him."

"Best I take my leave, then." Conor untied the hobby's reins and swung up onto the horse's bare back.

"What are you doing?" demanded Aisling.

"Well, as the previous horse wasn't yours, you appear to owe me one." With that, Conor rode out of the stable.

"He's stealing my horse," said Aisling to Liam. "Do something!"

Liam bellowed for the stableboy, who popped his head out from the adjoining stall, where he had apparently been listening to the exchange. "Your mistress requires the use of Lord Maolan's fastest remaining horse."

The boy gave a huge grin. "Yes, sir," he said, and ran to the fifth stall down. He emerged leading a tall chestnut stallion and quickly belted a small padded blanket on its back, what Celts used for saddles. With a move every bit as smooth as Conor's, even though this horse was a foot taller at the shoulder, Aisling mounted. "Coming?" she asked Liam.

"You're on your own this time," he replied. Liam slapped the stableboy on the back as they watched Aisling gallop off after Conor.

That evening, as the sun made to hide behind the far west wall of the royal enclosure, Aisling walked her new hobby back into the stables. She did not notice the stableboy running toward her; she was too busy searching inside herself for that strange glimmer and hint of warmth she thought she had detected.

"My lady?" he called, intruding on her thoughts.

"Sorry. Here." She handed him the reins.

He peered around behind her. "And Lord Maolan's stallion, my lady?"

"Oh. I forgot. I'll go retrieve him tomorrow."

7

Jordan sent the requisition to the legate's secretary, who showed it to the legate, who found it surprising. The legate had been expecting a request for soldiers and weapons for the mission to the island of Great Skellig. Instead all Jordan requested were twenty slaves delivered to his ship. The legate sent back a note: *"Is this all you will need?"* Jordan replied, *"Prince Ruarc assures me all he needs are slaves for tribute. All I need is Ty."*

Jordan's requisition had been quite specific: Ruarc required ten women of childbearing age, four young girls, four young boys, and two men not older than twenty-five, all Muslims with swarthy skin.

Najia's skin, usually dark olive, had taken on an ashen cast from dehydration. She felt the slave wagon slow and heard the clang of ship's bells, the call of men working. She cocked her head, wishing that the others would stop sniveling so she could hear better. Her hands were manacled in front of her, as were the hands of all the slaves. A thin rope, in her case about six feet long, attached each set of manacles to a heavy rope that ran down the middle of the group so they could move, caterpillar-like, when the slavers needed them to walk. Unlike the other slaves, her face was covered. Even so, she thought she could untie the rope and try to run away. But that would probably lead to another beating. She needed a more certain opportunity.

Najia's wagon bumped to a stop. A rough hand grabbed her neck and dragged her out. The sack was pulled off her head, and she glimpsed a quay, men unloading slaves next to her, and her captor's coarse face. She instinctively pushed her gaze inside him and saw malevolence stirring excitedly; she perceived that he cultivated that maliciousness to fend off his harsh world, and she knew he would hurt her if he could. With most of her powers repressed and her hands bound, there was nothing she could do to stop him.

He must have sensed her fear, as a dog would, and he laughed, drew his knife, and held it in front of her face. "You scared I'm gonna cut your pretty face? Your throat? Well, I'm gonna." He pressed the blade against her neck. "Unless you do as I tell you. Then I mightn't cut you so bad."

She saw him glance around to make sure the other men were watching. "When you find out what's gonna happen to you on that ship, you're gonna wish I'd cut your throat through and through." He laughed again as he kicked her feet out and she fell hard on the paving stones. "You'd do as well to enjoy this while you can."

"No, not that one!" shouted another man, pushing through the crowd. He grabbed her assailant's shoulder and pulled him back. "Can't you see she's a witch?"

Her assailant seemed to notice for the first time the runes that the slavers had drawn in white paint around her neck to prevent her from working enchantments, more disappearing down the collar of her rough shift. His eyes widened when he realized that several were partially worn off, and he looked down at the flakes of paint on his hand.

Najia saw his terror and rose to her feet, snarling, but was able to take only a few short steps before reaching the end of the rope binding her to the other slaves. The man leaped backward, then fell to his knees, praying loudly and furiously. She squared her shoulders defiantly. She needed to make these men fear her, she thought.

His friend kicked him. "You're stupid, that's what you are. If the runes stopped working, she would've killed us all by now. Best fuck a different one."

"They're not for you." The order came from a well-dressed man walking down the quay. He was followed by what she recognized as a

very large Nephilim. "Load them onto the ship. Now. Or I will introduce you to someone to be terrified of." The men scrambled back
to work.

"Does Jordan want Ty to help load the ship?" Ty rumbled.

"No. Let them do their own tasks," replied Jordan.

The group of slaves shuffled awkwardly along the quay. Najia, at
the tail end, leaned forward to her sister, who was two positions ahead,
weeping. "Stop that," she hissed. "You can't cry and think, and if you
don't keep your wits, you're going to die on that ship." She searched
for her young brother, saw him trudging head down near the front
where she could not get to him.

She looked back at the newcomer walking behind them with his
strange Nephilim companion. He was obviously in command, and there
was something strange about him as well. She shuffled a bit slower,
drifting to the end of her rope. She could not read him. He must be
maintaining a protective enchantment, and without any visible effort.

The cluster of slaves paused at the base of the gangplank. She
noticed Jordan catch her watching him. The slaves started up to the
ship, and she allowed herself to be pulled along while she walked backward. He followed, looking directly into her eyes. Najia tried to read
him again but could not reach any depth. There was just, faintly, behind his eyes, a certain light. This might be her only chance. "Admi-
ral, may I speak with you," she called in excellent Italian.

"Marshal," Jordan corrected her.

"Marshal, would you like me for your cabin?" she asked. "It'll be
a long voyage."

"How do you know?"

"By the amount of food and water they're loading." Jordan's eyes
played over the runes painted on her skin, and she saw him recognize them. A small smile crept up one side of his mouth. She was
about to ask him again when she and the other the slaves were shoved
roughly to the center of the deck. A group of sailors began unlocking

their manacles and directing them down a ladder to the hold. Her hands were freed.

"I'll take this one," said Jordan.

He offered her a scoop of water, which she drank so fast that she had to fight back a wave of nausea. He offered her a second that she forced herself to drink slower.

"Ty, lead her to my cabin and hold her there. Do not hurt her."

She shied away from the giant hand, but Ty's grip on her arm was firm, not painful.

Ty stood statuesque in the center of Jordan's stuffy cabin, holding Najia's arm. Even with his back hunched, his shoulders still pressed against the ceiling. Najia was exhausted, and before her was the first real bed she had seen since her capture, but Ty took Jordan's instructions literally and kept her in his grasp.

She was a piece of chattel in a complex trade network. Slavery had become so common in medieval Europe that the Roman Church had to prohibit Christians from owning Christian slaves or selling them directly to non-Christians. "Directly" provided the loophole. As a result, for the past two centuries this profitable trade had been monopolized by Radhanites, Iberian Jews who ran vast caravans transporting Muslim slaves northwest to Christian Europe, where they picked up Christian slaves and transported them back to Muslim territories, in particular to the Ottoman Empire. Tens of thousands of people, primarily women and young boys and girls, were shipped back and forth along a route centered at the port of Caffa on the Black Sea, the largest slave market in the world, owned and operated by the Italian city-state of Genoa. When the Renaissance began in the fourteenth century, Italian city-states were the largest consumers of humans in Western Europe—all fashionable families had to have at least one slave to be considered successful.

The shouts of men loading Jordan's ship eventually died down, and a swaying underfoot told Najia it was leaving dock. She tried talking to Ty, tried reading him, but he was a complete blank. It was like being tied to a post, as she had been several times since being enslaved.

Jordan entered. "You can let her go." Ty's hand fell away. Jordan pulled Najia's collar down far enough to see the runes on her shoulder, then circled her to see the rest.

"What kind of witch are you?" he asked from behind, his fingers tracing a symbol.

"I'm just a healer."

Jordan's examination brought him around to her side. "I expected you to lie to me. But the next time you do so, Ty will drag you to the hold and chain you up with the others."

She wondered what answer held the best chance of saving her life. He was studying her so intently she decided that she would try the truth. "I see the play of darkness and light in people, and I can manipulate those forces."

"What else?"

"I can work some enchantments, particularly for people I have read, and at times I can foresee their fates," she added.

"Whoever placed these runes on you did not know much about you. They must have drawn every one they knew. Which one actually represses your powers?"

She guided his hand. "This one over my heart."

"What did they miss? How do you still have the power to read people? I felt you trying to get around my protection."

"They should have drawn the symbol for 'night' here." She touched her forehead.

Jordan retrieved a small bottle of grappa from a trunk, moistened a rag, and began to clean the runes off her skin. She had not expected that.

"You believe yourself safe with me?" she asked, regretting the question immediately.

"I wouldn't be much of a marshal to the legate if I couldn't handle one witch. Besides, if you cast any enchantments on me or my men, Ty will crush you. Did you hear that, Ty?"

Ty swiveled his head against the ceiling so he could look at her. "Ty will know. Ty will do as Jordan says. Ty will kill witch."

"Thank you, Ty. Go on out and find a comfortable spot on deck for yourself."

"He seems quite attached," she said as Jordan finished scrubbing off the runes.

"In many ways he reminds me of the puppy I had when I was a boy."

"Did your puppy grow up to be an attack dog? That's what Ty reminds me of."

"No, it didn't grow up. We were starving during the second winter of plague, trade had stopped, shops were shuttered, there'd been no harvest that year. I was out scrounging . . . well, stealing food, but my father didn't trust me to find any, and he ate my dog while I was gone. Made him scrounge for his own food after that."

Najia was silent as Jordan poured himself a pewter goblet of wine. "Where are you from?" he asked.

"Damascus. I come from a family of merchants there. Raiders attacked the procession carrying my grandmother's body to the family tomb in the hills northwest of the city. They captured two of my sisters and youngest brother as well, and killed the rest. One of my sisters and my brother are in the hold."

"I'm surprised they didn't burn you."

"They must have been more interested in money than entertainment. They sold me to the Vatican's slavers, where burning was sure to be part of what awaited me. I was being taken to Rome when the shipment of slaves was diverted here. Was that fortunate for me, arriving here instead of Rome?"

"To be discovered. As you said, it'll be a long voyage. Do you speak anything other than Italian and Arabic? Any that you can read?"

"Greek and French. Some bits of others."

"Can you read Aramaic?"

"It's close enough to Arabic that I can usually work my way through it."

Jordan retrieved the thickest of his grimoires, the one he could not read. "Tell me what book this is."

Gold Aramaic script flowed right to left across the black leather cover, faded but legible. "'Sworn Book of Honorius,'" she read out loud. "There was a Greek sorcerer named Honorius, the son of Euclid the mathematician. This must be a translation of his grimoire."

"How do you know all that?"

"As I was not born male, or the eldest daughter, or the most beautiful, I spent all my time studying. My father was a healer, and more, with a large library."

"Married? Children?"

"No to both. I had five older sisters who needed to be married off first."

Jordan filled another goblet with wine and handed it to her. "When you were being loaded on board, you offered to please me."

"Yes. Do you want me to please you now?"

"It will please me if you translate this book. Do that and you can stay in my cabin."

"You are a strange man, Marshal."

Jordan sat at the small table, motioned for her to do the same. "It will be simpler if you call me Jordan."

Najia's olive skin, restored to health from four weeks in Jordan's cabin, glowed faintly in the moonlight that entered through the porthole out of which her head hung. After emptying the contents of her stomach into the sea, she pulled her head back inside. The ocean had become rougher as their ship drew close to Ireland, unsettling her stomach and interrupting their evening passion. Opening the lid of the water cask, she scooped a tin cup full, rinsed her mouth, spat out the porthole, poured a small amount into her hand, and washed her face.

From the narrow bunk, Jordan watched the moonlight slide across the curves of her body. He couldn't recall when he had spent so much time with a woman. It felt good to be here with her. All the other women he had known would be terrified by his new studies and certainly would not have been able to help with them. During their voyage toward Ireland, they had done little except study the grimoires and play—ever since that first night when she literally dragged him from the table to his bunk. He understood that she was desperately trying to attach herself to him, but it also seemed that she wanted to lose herself in passion when she could, a distraction from the questions that still hung over her.

"Tomorrow night will be the full moon," she said, climbing back into his bunk. "Is that when we arrive?"

"Yes," was all Jordan could say as she stroked him, restoring his erection. She straddled him, and no more was said until after she had satisfied them both.

Najia lay exhausted beside Jordan, his arm across her waist, hers on top of his. "Are you going to keep me or sell me tomorrow?" she asked.

Jordan smiled. "I believe you know the answer to that question."

She ran her hand down the side of his face. "Perhaps my sister could join us?"

"We can't fit anyone else in this bunk."

"She's a wonderful cook. You'll need that when you return home. My young brother is good with horses. He speaks their language and would make a fine stable hand. One day he could be your horse master."

"No," Jordan replied. "I have plans for them."

"I'll let you keep me," Najia said, her voice soft and inviting, "but only if you keep my brother and sister as well."

"Let me?" He laughed. "I own you."

Najia flashed Jordan a look as all softness disappeared from her body.

"You have no idea what will happen to you tomorrow if I don't protect you," he said.

"It doesn't matter what happens to me," she said as she squirmed around to lie on her stomach, pushing Jordan to the edge of the bunk.

With a sigh he stood up. Opening his trunk, he rummaged through the clothes jumbled inside until he found his dagger and the bag of peaches he had stashed. Jordan sat on the bunk's edge and examined a peach carefully. He cut away a rotten bit and dug out a small worm, flicking it at the porthole, missing. Cutting a slice of the remaining good meat, he held it out toward Najia. He knew that even with her face buried in the blanket, she could smell the rare fruit.

She turned toward him, and he slipped the piece into her mouth. "Tomorrow," he said, "you stay in my cabin all day. I make no promises about your siblings." After feeding her the rest of the peach, Jordan climbed under the blanket next to Najia and slept. She did not.

8

At sunrise Jordan emerged onto the deck of the cog. Common seagoing traders, cogs emphasized functionality over comfort and were inexpensive and quick to build. The design was simple: the hull was constructed with lapstrake oak planking, caulked with tarred moss that was forced into curved grooves, then covered with wooden laths and secured by forged-iron clinch nails. The single mast carried one large square sail, which made the ship easy to handle, even in rough seas, by a crew of as few as four. On the stern sat a minimal U-shaped superstructure containing three cabins: the captain's, Jordan's, and Prince Ruarc's. The rest of the crew slept in a common cabin belowdecks next to a small galley and the cargo hold containing the slaves. Ty stayed on the deck.

The ship was no longer pitching and seemed to be sailing down a channel of calm that ran through the rough waves. Ruarc stood on the bowsprit chanting. Jordan could not understand the words but knew they were a poem to the wind and water. The captain stood at the wheel.

"Good morning, Captain. How long until we arrive?" asked Jordan.

"Morning, Marshal. The prince told me that if I follow this course, we'll be through the waves by noon and at Great Skellig before twilight."

Dary exited Ruarc's cabin supporting his skeletal wife. Leading Eithne slowly to the rail, he dropped a blanket on the deck and helped her sit. She leaned back in the sun and closed her eyes.

Ruarc finished his poetic incantation with a flourish of his arms.

Climbing down onto the deck, he walked over, picked up Eithne as if she weighed no more than a lamb, and carried her back into his cabin. Dary said nothing.

Jordan looked out at the calm, enchanted channel before him, framed by walls of thirty-foot waves on either side. Inevitably, his thoughts were drawn to the previous, doomed attempt by Rome to invade Ireland with the English—their armada had sailed across this same sea 221 years earlier. At that time the Earl of Pembroke, known as "Strongbow," thought he could seize Ireland for the Norman king of England, Henry II, who had been gifted the entire island by an excessively optimistic pope through the Laudabiliter grant.

How exactly were the English so soundly defeated, Jordan wondered, *and why had no survivors returned?* This turbulent ring of water couldn't have been the only thing that repelled them, or certainly some damaged ships and men would have made it back to England. *What magic did the Irish use, or was it just the work of the Fomorians?* Jordan needed to ensure that the same fate did not befall the next English armada, because he planned to be on it, so long as the legate was able to convince their unstable king to sail forth.

Dary was still brooding at the rail when Jordan approached him and asked, "Your family are descendants of Strongbow's marshal, isn't that so? Were there many survivors?"

"A few." Dary did not raise his head to look at Jordan. "The Irish sold them among themselves, as slaves."

"And none tried to escape, to return to England?"

"That's not the way of things there. The men eventually earned their freedom, but they had already become *níos Gaelaí ná na Gaeil iad féin*—'more Irish than the Irish themselves.'"

"I need to hear the whole story, what happened to the fleet, before we lead a new armada back."

"I don't care about your invasion," Dary snapped. "I care about what Ruarc is doing to my wife." He walked away.

. . . . .

Jordan's ship had passed through the wall of waves, and the sun had
begun its descent when he spied the seething white flock of kittiwakes
circulating on the horizon. Within minutes Great Skellig seemed to
rise out of the sea like a giant jagged tooth.

　　Located eight miles off the southwest corner of Ireland, the treeless
island had been uninhabited for more than two hundred years when it
was decided that King Kellach of the Skeaghshee would be imprisoned
there. A short stone pier and a few squat stone huts, beehive shaped,
were the only structures on the island, remnants of a Christian monastery that had struggled to survive there, much to the amusement of
the Celts. An effort that was finally abandoned in the twelfth century,
leaving the rock to the kittiwakes, who survived by fastening their
meager nests to its steep faces, using their droppings as cement.

　　Jordan felt vitalized, his senses unusually acute, more so than
could be explained simply by four weeks of rest with Najia. His height-
ened awareness had started as soon as they entered Irish waters and
had been building ever since, but there was no time to think about it
now. He walked to the bow, where Ruarc stood. The captain joined
them, leaving his first mate at the wheel.

　　"What's the plan?" the captain asked.

　　"First we must get by the Fomorians," said Ruarc.

　　"A type of sea faerie," added Jordan.

　　"Not quite," said Ruarc. "They are a type of Elioud, more demonic
blood. They once occupied the surface of Ireland, until the Sidhe
arrived and drove them into the sea at the Second Battle of Magh Tuir-
eadh. Now they live in great caverns, whose entrances are accessible
only from the water."

　　"Yet they align with the Sidhe?" asked the captain.

　　"Treaties between the two races have been common," said Ruarc.
"But the ruling Sidhe clans—the Devas and Adhene—have become
greedy, too much like the Celts, and the tributes they pay to bind

treaties have become too small, such as the treaty to guard that rock. I have sent word to the king of the Fomorian clan who occupy these waters that in exchange for safe passage I will gift him human slaves the likes of which neither he nor any other Fomorian has seen before."

"Did he guarantee safe passage?"

"I have not received word back," said Ruarc calmly, "but I am hopeful."

"If we get past the Fomorians," Jordan said, "there's a relatively small guard on the island itself, a few Celts and about ten Sidhe. Mostly Fire Sprites—they and the Skeaghshee hate each other. We'll land just after nightfall."

The captain looked up at the sky. "It's clouding over. Without moonlight it'll be too dark to dock at the pier."

"Just follow my directions and you will land safely," said Ruarc.

"Once we are docked, Ty will go ashore and retrieve the king," added Jordan.

The captain looked over at the large figure, statuesque on the deck. "He can survive Fire Sprites?"

"Ty is a unique half-breed," said Jordan. "Part giant, clearly, but I've no idea what the rest is. Whatever his parents were, the union didn't take completely, and he was born deformed. With no magic of his own, he embodies its very opposite. He's full of some kind of darkness that absorbs enchantments cast against him."

A quarter mile from Great Skellig, the ship turned into the wind and dropped its sail. The setting sun disappeared behind cloud cover, creating an early dusk.

Jordan returned to his cabin to prepare to meet the Fomorian king. Certain protocols must be followed, even for the king of another race. He pulled off his plain wool tunic and put on one of red silk. His sword and dagger he moved to a silver belt. A black wool cloak trimmed with mink completed the outfit, nothing of which displayed the symbol of the Vatican.

Throughout the process Najia sat in the center of the floor, eyes closed, chanting quietly.

"Praying to your God?" Jordan finally asked, adjusting his cloak.

Najia opened her eyes. "I'm casting an enchantment of protection over my sister and little brother."

"No enchantment will protect them if I fail to keep them from the Fomorians."

"Then I'll cast you an enchantment of good fortune."

"Don't do that. Don't do anything. If Ruarc senses any enchantments, he'll know I'm up to something." Jordan stroked her hair. "Just stay here and trust that I'll do all I can." He picked up his hat and went out on deck.

Jordan walked up to Dary and asked, "How's your wife?"

"How do you think she is?" Anger flared in his voice.

"Why don't you bring her out? The sea air will do her good."

Dary glanced at Ruarc, who was standing at the starboard railing looking out at Great Skellig, then moved toward Ruarc's cabin.

The crew led the nineteen remaining slaves up on deck. They had been stripped and their hands bound. Jordan walked among them; they shivered with cold and fear. He pointed out the two women he thought Ruarc would find most pleasing, and four others, including Najia's sister and brother. He was careful to choose casually and not to look back at his cabin door, which he knew was open just enough for Najia to peer out.

"Take these six back down," Jordan ordered two deckhands. "Allow them to dress, then secure them."

"Marshal Jordan," demanded Ruarc, rushing toward him. "What are you doing?"

"It's not wise to show all we have to offer at the outset. We may need additional trade goods later. Thirteen is a good offer to start."

"That is not the Sidhe way."

"You said Fomorians aren't Sidhe."

"They are closer to Sidhe than human."

"Besides, soon you'll need a new companion." Jordan's eyes moved to the emaciated figure of Eithne cradled in Dary's lap. Ruarc's eyes followed.

Ruarc gave Jordan a nod. "It is good for me to learn the ways of your kind. We will try your plan, but keep the other slaves ready." He glanced over the terrified huddle of naked Ottomans: women, men, and children. "Perhaps you should have left one of the more attractive women."

"Who knows what a Fomorian finds attractive?" replied Jordan.

"We are about to find out," said Ruarc.

A pair of wet, scaly, green hands with clawlike fingernails wrapped themselves around the starboard railing, a slight web apparent between the bases of the fingers. The creature flung itself on deck, followed by another, then more until they crowded the starboard side. Their bare skin dried unnaturally quickly to a nearly human taupe hue, the scales tightening down and almost vanishing. Dark hair hung lank about their shoulders, the occasional crab or bit of seaweed plucked out and tossed overboard.

A large male stepped forward and barked orders to the horde, exhibiting small, sharklike teeth. The Fomorians parted and bowed, revealing an even larger male climbing over the rail. He had one eye, swollen to twice normal size; the second socket was shriveled and empty.

"The king of the clan that rules these waters," Ruarc whispered to Jordan. "As a sign of his strength and commitment to lead, a new king is required to pluck out his own left eye in front of the assembled clan. Over time the other eye swells and gains in power. The longer a king defends his throne, the larger his eye gets."

The engorged eye swiveled toward Ruarc, who bowed and spoke a greeting in the guttural tongue of the Fomorians. At a signal the captain brought forward a sable cloak and presented it to the king. Two obviously female attendants accepted the gift and wrapped it around the king's bare shoulders. The king grunted to one of his men, who then presented Ruarc with a large mother-of-pearl brooch.

Ruarc made a show of removing his own silver brooch, tossing it overboard, and refastening his cloak with the gift.

Ruarc and the Fomorian king began to inspect and converse about the slaves. Jordan could not understand their words, but Ruarc was clearly expounding on the virtues of the offering. The king approached the woman with the darkest brown skin. As she cowered, crying, he slowly ran his hand down her arm, then turned to Ruarc and the two of them shared a laugh.

The king cast his large eye across the huddled knot of humans, seized the dark woman by her throat, and passed her to one of his attendants. At his grunted order, the rest of the screaming, crying, and pleading slaves were dragged over the side. The two female attendants removed the sable cloak, folded it, and placed it in an oilskin pouch. The king and Ruarc exchanged a few words, then shallow bows. The king leaped over the side, followed by the last of his attendants carrying the dark woman.

"What will they do with them?" whispered the captain.

"Stash some of them in their cavern as mates and slaves, eat the rest," replied Jordan, looking down at the horde moving through the water.

The last dim light was fading rapidly from the overcast sky. "Captain, mark the position of the pier and make sail," commanded Ruarc.

"All is agreed with the Fomorians, then?" asked Jordan.

"Yes, we have safe passage until sunset tomorrow. And they have guaranteed our landing. Apparently the king liked the cloak most of all, saying it will be helpful in his quest for the Fomorian high-kingship."

"In that position he could be a valuable ally."

"He has a great desire to lead his people back onto the land. I mentioned that if the Celts are driven from Ireland, there would be room for the Fomorians to return. He suggested discussing it further, over another batch of slaves."

Jordan smiled at Ruarc. "I couldn't have directed the conversation better myself."

"Yes, but I was honest with him," replied Ruarc, not returning the smile.

Torches flared and moved rapidly on Great Skellig.

"They know we're coming," said the captain.

"They were not expecting us to get by the Fomorians," said Ruarc. "They have little time to prepare. How long until we land, Captain?"

"Ten minutes. But it's too dark to dock."

"Just follow my directions and stop fretting."

A shadowy shape moved in the gloom of the stern superstructure. Jordan joined Najia. "We have a long way to travel yet, and I may still find a reason to trade away your sister and brother, or Ruarc may decide to feed from them," he said softly, keeping his face turned toward the activity amidships. He felt her hand slide onto the back of his neck, her lips brush against his ear.

"Ruarc will not survive this night. I have foreseen this."

"Go check on your siblings," said Jordan, and walked off toward Ty.

As the ship sailed through the gray water toward the black that was Great Skellig, Ruarc joined Jordan and Ty. Clearly excited, he had not wiped all the fresh blood from his chin. "I must be the one to free my father," he proclaimed.

"Do as you wish," said Jordan, thinking of Najia's words. Given the size of the splash that Jordan had heard a moment earlier, he guessed that Ruarc had been too enthusiastic in his feeding and that Eithne's drained body had been dumped over the side.

Jordan said to Ty, "Lead Ruarc to King Kellach, then make sure they get safely back to the ship. Kill any who oppose you or try to follow you."

"Ty will do as Jordan says."

Jordan patted Ty's back. "And be on guard. Don't let them hurt you too much."

On a quick order from Ruarc, the sail dropped, leaving the ship to glide. Jordan could feel the island close at hand.

Ruarc called out to the night, *"Solas san aer breithe,"* and a dozen faerie lights appeared above the stone pier not more than twenty feet ahead, revealing a small company of armed Celts. A flash of green moved behind them, and a wave of Fomorians swept the Celts into the water.

The ship groaned up against the pier, entering the halo of light. Arrows swept in from the blackness. Ty batted away one headed toward Jordan's chest, but the first mate and two sailors fell.

"Less light please, Ruarc!" called Jordan. All but one light, floating above the base of the pier at the point where a path led up the rock face, went out, returning the ship to semidarkness.

Ty plucked an arrow from his shoulder, stepped onto the pier, and disappeared up the path, followed closely by Ruarc. Jets of orange flame shot out from the darkness, revealing the pair. Ty stepped between the flames and Ruarc. The fire danced along Ty's skin and faded without burning him, but pain could be heard in Ty's roar. Darkness swallowed them again.

"Fire Sprites," Jordan explained to the captain. "Wood Sidhe have no defense against their one enchantment, but it won't kill Ty."

Blue lightning flashed and green orbs flew, lighting up much of the rock face. Ty continued to roar as the enchantments splashed against him. "Devas and Leprechauns," said Jordan, watching with a mix of fascination and concern. Ruarc's left hand moved in a dance of complex shapes, repelling enchantments. Silhouetted Celtic warriors could be seen rushing forward, brandishing swords, only to fall victim to Ty's giant hands. Ruarc's sword, held in a high guard with his right hand, remained unneeded.

Darkness returned, punctuated by a few cries and the occasional rock rolling down the steep face and splashing into the sea. Jordan sensed Najia approach before he felt her body press against his back as if to shield herself. They stood together studying the night. "I've given my sister to the captain for his cabin for the journey back," said Najia. "I told him it was your gift."

"He believed that? From you?"

"Of course. I washed her, combed out her hair, and led her to him wearing nothing but a skirt. He seemed in a rush to stash her in his cabin and she in a hurry to hide in it."

"Good. And your little brother?"

"Washed, dressed, and peeling apples in the galley as if his life depended on it."

"It may."

Najia leaned forward and whispered in his ear, "Do you feel it?"

"What?" Jordan whispered back.

"Ireland. I've read so much about it. There's no other land left like it."

"I feel something here that's different." They were interrupted by the sudden flare of more floating faerie lights, revealing Ruarc walking down the path. "Ruarc's still alive," said Jordan. Najia did not respond.

Ruarc stopped at the base of the pier. Ty and Kellach emerged into the light and joined him. No Sidhe or Celts followed. Other than cuts on Ty's hands and arms—each cut ringed by small black blisters— and the broken shaft of an arrow protruding from his back, they appeared unscathed.

"My son, give me your sword," said Kellach.

Ruarc bowed. "My father. My king," he said, handing Kellach his sword. "I brought it for you."

Kellach balanced the sword in his hand, then studied its length. "It is a fine blade. Gnome-forged?"

"Yes, Father. Forged by Paracelsus himself."

"Excellent," replied Kellach, and nodded to Ty, who seized Ruarc's head with one giant hand. A look of terror sprang onto Ruarc's face. "You have corrupted yourself with human blood," said Kellach. "Already you obsess on it, and soon you will think of nothing else.

You are no longer of use to your people, or to me." Ty's hand closed in an explosion of pink. Ruarc's body crumpled. With a nudge from Ty's foot, it slid into the water.

Ty glanced at Jordan, then knelt before Kellach. "Fulfill promise to Ty," his rough voice full of melancholy.

Jordan gripped his sword, placed the other hand on the railing. Najia gasped and wrapped her arms around his waist. Kellach raised the sword and swept it down, severing Ty's head, which rolled down the pier. The giant headless body knelt there. A splash sounded as the head tumbled into the sea. Blackness bubbled out of the neck, overflowing the body, consuming it. Kellach threw down the sword, seeing that it was also being devoured by blackness.

"No!" shouted Jordan, as he broke free of Najia's arms and leaped onto the pier, his sword unsheathed. Seizing the collar of Kellach's cloak, Jordan pushed his sword up against the king's throat.

"He was in constant pain, Marshal Jordan," said Kellach calmly, a trickle of blood running down his neck. "Even more so now that you ordered him to kill his own kind. He was half Sidhe. Did you not know? He begged me to ease his suffering. It was a kindness."

"A kindness!" Jordan shouted into his face. "A kindness? Or was it that you could not have a creature on board that could kill you at my whim?"

"You heard him. He did not wish to return to you. Now, Marshal, it is time for us to go. Others on the mainland will be launching ships to catch us." A full moon broke from the clouds, illuminating the island and the sea in silver light. Jordan lowered his sword. Kellach climbed aboard their ship.

Jordan watched the last of Ty's flesh dissolve, the pool of blackness vaporizing, shrinking, leaving behind etched stones. Memories unbidden and unwanted flooded in, memories of the plague taking everyone he loved. The familiar sense of loss returned, like a dull knife carving away another piece of his soul, bearable only by setting his anger free.

Najia waited in the shadows until Kellach passed, then joined Jordan, who had not moved. She bent and scooped up a last handful of the blackness, letting it run through her fingers, her hand uninjured.

"I could've helped him," she said. "If only I had known he was so full of pain."

"Then you should have," Jordan snapped.

"It wasn't possible to read Ty, to foresee this. He was a blank."

"Not much of a witch, are you?" Jordan strode back and forth along the pier, wishing there were someone to fight. He took a couple of swipes at the air with his sword, fantasizing he was beheading Kellach. It did nothing to alleviate the fire in his head. *How dare Kellach take Ty from me!*

Najia touched his arm and said, "Let's go back to your cabin."

He balled up his fist, forced himself not to strike her. "Just because your siblings survived today, that doesn't mean I won't still kill them, or you," he hissed. "I am finished with you." He sheathed his sword and shoved her roughly toward the ship. She stumbled but regained her footing and climbed aboard. Jordan followed her into his cabin.

"Let me—" Najia started.

"Mix a pot of paint," Jordan interrupted. "I'm going to suppress your powers before you go into the hold."

"Our lives are intertwined now," said Najia.

"Don't pretend you can read me or foresee anything about me. You're just trying to save yourself."

"It started that way, yes, but during these weeks together I have seen that we are meant to face the future with each other, whatever perils are coming." Najia drew Jordan's sword, and he did not try to stop her. She pressed the hilt into his hand. "It would be merciful to kill me, rather than put me into the hold. But you know that either way you would lose part of yourself."

Somewhere deep inside, a thin voice penetrated his rage; he knew that she spoke the truth. He flung his sword onto the bunk. "Look inside me, then, and see the type of man you are asking to stay with." He dropped his defense to enchantments.

Najia gazed into his eyes, and he felt her enter. His innermost self was unfolded, opened to a rush of light, simultaneously warm and terrifyingly exposed, unprotected. He struggled not to drive her out for what seemed like an age, yet he knew it was just a moment. She said, "Your whole life you have journeyed to the border that separates light and dark forces, and you are destined to continue doing so for the rest of your days. It is impossible for me to foresee which side you will end up on. Possibilities compound into a fog." She withdrew from inside him, leaving Jordan with a sudden sense of loneliness.

Najia continued, "I can't predict when you might descend into darkness. I can only see that I will be of help to you." She put her arms around him. "You are like no man I have ever known. I am drawn to you and desire nothing more than to journey with you and let the fates take us from this world together, whenever that may be."

A tremor ran through his body as his remaining anger faded. She was right: he did want her in his life beyond this voyage—her thoughts, her touch, all of her. He could feel his body soften little by little as they held each other, gently swaying with the motion of the ship as its sails caught the wind.

9

London, England
June 1391

While the legate endured a plodding, jolting carriage ride through the crowded, muddy streets of London, he worried about the critical meeting ahead. Jordan had succeeded, but now the legate had to convince a demented king to attempt an invasion of an island that had repulsed every caesar, pope, and monarch who had tried over the last millennium and a half. Gazing out the window, he wondered what would happen to him if he returned to Rome without Richard's support. He might not only lose his position as legate, he might find himself on the wrong end of the Inquisition's many instruments of penance.

The legate turned his attention to Chaucer, who sat across the carriage, uncharacteristically quiet. "Have you mentioned anything to Richard about the Vatican's plans?"

"Of course not. If the news agitated him, he'd have my head," replied Chaucer. "You're going to have to carry the day yourself. But take heart, it's unlikely that he'll execute an envoy of Rome."

"Let's hope not," replied the legate, unable to remove the anxiety from his voice. "Best tell me how to play the king's new game."

"Richard and his amusements," Chaucer intoned, his mind clearly elsewhere. "The king sits brooding while before him await courtiers, petitioners, guests, and the like, until suddenly he looks up with a shout, and if he looks at you, you have to immediately drop to your knees. Too slow and you suffer a penalty, one he makes up on the spot, and it's always painful, either financially or physically. This can go on for hours."

"Worth remembering," said the legate.

"Unlikely that game will be on today, though. We're not going to the palace. The king's at the Tower," said Chaucer. "And don't forget, Richard has changed his title from 'Your Highness' to 'Your Royal Majesty.' Get that wrong and even you will suffer a penalty."

The legate hated going to the Tower of London. You never really knew if you were going to be let out. "Why the Tower?" he asked.

"Sir John Clanvowe is to be executed today for being a follower of the Lollard heresy. Also, I believe, for opposing the king's high taxation to support his opulent court."

"But Clanvowe is one of your closest friends."

"Was one of my friends." Chaucer set his mouth in a tight line and looked out the carriage window at the rain starting to fall. The legate barely heard him mumble, as if to himself, "Death is the end of every worldly pain."

They remained silent until their carriage rattled onto the cobblestone road through the outer gatehouse of the Tower, across a stone bridge spanning the moat, through a second gatehouse set in the outer curtain wall, across the outer yard, through a third gatehouse set in the inner curtain wall, and into the inner yard, where three canopies had been erected next to the post-and-arm.

"Damned rain," said Chaucer, climbing out of the carriage. "Now we'll have to wait." Chaucer led the legate through the drizzle to the largest tent, decorated with the king's banners, where members of the inner court were gathered. He and the legate accepted goblets of wine and moved to the edge of the canopy, where they examined the instrument of Clanvowe's imminent execution.

"After being sentenced to death, Clanvowe petitioned the king, requesting that he be allowed a beheading," said Chaucer. "A petition the king denied. You see, this is a game as well. If the condemned shows courage in the face of his suffering, Richard will grant him an early end to the pain."

The legate considered how he might twist today's event to his advantage. The Lollard heresy, if used strategically, could strengthen his arguments to the king. The Lollards had defied the Roman Church and committed their ultimate sacrilege, translating the Bible into English. Freed from the need of priests to explain the words of God, some Lollards—whose secret membership included both peasants and knights—had started thinking they did not need a king either.

"How come the king's attempts to counter the growth of the Lollards?" the legate asked.

"He hunts them down and destroys the translated Bibles when he can find them," replied Chaucer. "But they're proving to be surprisingly resilient."

Richard would get better results, thought the legate, *if he simply outlawed learning to read.* An enhanced strategy for persuading Richard was forming in his mind.

"Where is your new marshal keeping Kellach?" asked Chaucer.

"I made arrangements for them to wait in Conwy Castle."

"And any news on Orsini's plan for Patrick's Bell?"

"No, so don't bring it up."

"Why don't you just send King Solomon's Ring with the fleet, if the invasion ever goes forward? It has enough power to protect the whole armada."

"Orsini would never leave Rome unprotected without the ring, nor would I want him to. Lord knows what demons would seize the opportunity to attack."

The rain had faded, and they were interrupted by the sound of horns. The assembly bowed as the royal procession entered the courtyard led by the twenty-four-year-old king, the incestuous issue of Edward, "the Black Prince," and his cousin Joan, "the Fair Maid of Kent"—the pope had granted them dispensation to marry. Lanky and pale, with delicate features, Richard settled himself in a large, elaborately carved chair at the front of the canopy. To his right sat Anne of Bohemia, his queen. They had been married nine years earlier, when she was sixteen, yet she remained without child. It was whispered, not too softly because Richard did not seem to care, that this was because he preferred the bed of Sir Robert de Vere, Earl of

Oxford, who sat in the chair to Richard's left. Still, Anne was known to be devoted to Richard and he to her, perhaps because she did not mind Richard's eccentricities and even, it was also whispered, joined in them.

Drums announced the entrance of Clanvowe, who walked unchained toward his slow death. Three men carried chopped wood from a storage shed and waited for him to inspect it. "Good and dry. A hot and high fire, if you please," Clanvowe announced in a loud, clear voice, handing the executioner a gold noble, worth six shillings and eight pence. Clanvowe removed his hat and gave it to one of the woodsmen, his jacket to another. He walked on, paused, pulled off his boots, hopping a bit as he moved from one leg to the other, and gave them to the third. Barefoot, he defiantly mounted the five steps up to the small platform of the post-and-arm.

"Chaucer, tell Us of Sir Clanvowe," called Richard in French, without looking away from the continuing preparations.

"He was a valiant knight of the court before being corrupted by Satan," replied Chaucer as required, but his voice carried a caustic edge.

"A valiant knight of the court," Richard repeated with a smile to de Vere. "Then We think he will surely die well. What say you, Chaucer? Do you wish to place a wager?"

"I am sure Your Royal Majesty is correct. I would not dream of wagering against you."

"Hm. Become king and no one will wager with you anymore. Oh, well, let Us begin." He gave a small wave, and a torch was pushed into the stack of wood over which Clanvowe was now suspended.

Richard leaned forward, relishing his victim's attempt to resist the flames. When Clanvowe broke down and began to thrash about, Richard applauded, and his applause was quickly taken up by the entire assembly. "Not bad. Not bad. We have seen better, but not bad. We will let him go for just a bit longer. . . ." he said. "There. Captain, you may help the poor man out. His sins are atoned."

The captain of the guard ended Clanvowe's anguish with a quick thrust of a pike. A smoking fragment of his tunic drifted up in the hot fumes.

Richard rose from his seat. "Let Us escape this stench," he said. "Anne, you will return to the palace. Chaucer, We will meet with the Vatican's legate now in Our receiving room. De Vere, join Us."

The assembled nobles rose and bowed just a bit deeper and longer than they had earlier.

De Vere followed Richard, the legate, and Chaucer inside the neighboring building to a long, dark-wood-paneled room, where fireplaces at each end gave off a heavy warmth for which de Vere was grateful. Executions left him chilled.

"Leave Us," commanded Richard, gesturing to the servants. He strode to a table stacked with food and began pulling breast meat from a roast hen and stuffing it into his mouth.

De Vere poured wine into a goblet, placed it on the table next to the eating Richard, then turned to the legate. "Legate Migliorati, His Royal Majesty welcomes you. Your business must be very important to bring you personally all the way to London."

"The Lollards are not the only ones to threaten England and the True Church," said the legate. "The Irish Christian Church also grows in power across all of Britain and Europe. It owes its allegiance to Armagh, not Rome."

"You have your own mercenaries. Take the monasteries in Europe, and then His Royal Majesty will consider taking the monasteries in England and Wales for you."

"Monasteries are but a small part of the problem. Just as with the Lollard conspiracy, it is their ideas that are the real risk. The Irish Church and its Celtic allies are spreading their heretical philosophy as we speak. Attacking the monasteries in Europe and Britain will only embolden them."

De Vere glanced at Richard, who continued to tear at the food trays. *Having someone killed always arouses my king's appetites,* thought de Vere, feeling his own cravings awaken. He would have to conclude these futile discussions quickly. "What is the Church suggesting, then?" he asked.

"It is critical that His Royal Majesty invade Ireland and destroy the Irish Church at its root."

A piece of half-chewed hen hit the legate on the cheek as Richard broke into laughter, coughed, and spat the rest of the food from his mouth onto the floor. He coughed twice more while bending over with his arms on his knees and then resumed laughing.

The legate furtively wiped his cheek.

Richard brought himself under control with obvious effort, took a long drink of wine, and collapsed into a chair.

"The Church has lost its mind," said Richard. "They tried that with Our Norman predecessors and failed completely. Not even the Roman legions, at the height of their power, were able to take Ireland." Richard waved the back of his hand at the legate. "This audience is over," he said, turning his eyes to de Vere.

"As you know, Legate Migliorati," said de Vere, "His Royal Majesty has always been a devoted supporter of the Church, but what you suggest is, of course, impossible." De Vere extended his arm as if to show the legate out.

"And what if it is not impossible?" the legate asked, standing his ground. "What if the Vatican could guarantee you a safe landing on the Irish shore? What would that do for Your Royal Majesty's empire?"

De Vere cringed at the emphasis on the word "empire." It hinted at Richard's failed attempt to invade Scotland and his retreat from France. Dangerous ground for anyone but a high representative of the Vatican. De Vere dropped his arm and narrowed his eyes. "The Church issued such a guarantee to Strongbow."

"It did not. It simply gave him permission to go," the legate insisted.

"What makes the Church think the result would be any different this time?"

"Strongbow was guided only by the deposed king of Leinster, a mortal king who did not even have enough power to hold a regional kingdom. A human."

The legate addressed Richard directly, "Your armies, Your Royal Majesty, will be guided by a powerful Sidhe king, ruler of all the Skeaghshee, the Wood Sidhe. He has the power to safely land an armada, and his people will fight alongside your army." He went on to explain the attack on Aisling and the destruction of Anya's heart.

The legate was describing the rescue of King Kellach with pride when Richard rose from his chair and slammed his wine goblet down on the table. "And what if we land safely? What then?" Richard shouted, glaring at the legate, then at Chaucer. "Do you want another slaughter? Is that your plan? Our forces would still be facing the combined armies of the rest of the Sidhe, the Celts, and the Irish Church. Not to mention those horrid Fomorians. Why should We do this . . . this favor, for the Church? Chaucer, did he pay you to bring this idiocy before Us?"

"I am sure Your Royal Majesty's spies will report no sudden increase in my purse," replied Chaucer, a hurt look having appeared on his face.

"We will see. So what do you say to Rome's madness?"

"I would not presume to render an opinion. My humble role is simply to deliver Rome's esteemed envoy into your royal presence."

"And We thought poets were supposed to be braver than bureaucrats."

"Your Royal Majesty," interjected the legate, "just eighty miles off your coast, the ideas coming out of Ireland threaten your kingdom even more than they threaten my Church. You have experienced the damage that the Lollards have done to your authority by transcribing just a few copies of their English Bible for their members. Imagine what would happen if all your subjects could read it themselves. The Irish Church educates everyone, even women and slaves.

"What would happen to the very concept of a monarchy appointed by God if the writings of heretics like the Lollards were cheaply and easily available to peasants who could read? Even now, in the Orient, they are perfecting a machine that can produce whole books, hundreds a day, without the need of scribes. The Arabs have mastered making paper much cheaper than vellum and in mass quantities by using water-powered mills. Soon anyone will be able to afford and obtain books."

"We will outlaw such books," said de Vere. "The Church can declare it a mortal sin to possess even one."

"Books are easy to hide," replied the legate. "The spread of literacy itself must be stopped. It is the sacred right of only priests, nobles, and, of course, kings. Whoever controls literacy controls history, and the future."

"Then we will just have to stop this at our shores," said de Vere.

"Impossible," declared the legate. "Just as with the Lollard problem, you cannot stop ideas as long as the Irish Church keeps spreading them. The Irish Church also supports the Celtic heretical practice of allowing anyone to increase his station through effort, while it is truly only God who determines a man's station, and that is through his birth. The Irish Brehon laws are based on the principle of *Is ferr fera chiniud*—'A person is not his birth.'"

"That will never happen in Our England as long as We are king," declared Richard.

"May your rule be a long one, Your Royal Majesty. But what if these ideas continue to spread? Do you want to spend the rest of your life fighting one uprising after another? I am sure you are already aware that the Irish Church is a strong supporter—a promoter, even— of the Celtic practice of electing their kings. If your nobles should get the idea that they could be elected to the throne, not to imply they would be successful, but still, it would cause a constant irritation to Your Royal Majesty."

"Hm," mumbled Richard, turning back to the food table. "We will give your words proper consideration."

The legate bowed to Richard's back.

"Are you in London long?" asked de Vere, ushering the legate and Chaucer to the door.

"I will be staying at the Westminster Priory for the next two days. I understand that the abbey is almost finished, and His Holiness the pope is anxious for me to inspect it."

Having escorted them out of the room, de Vere returned to Richard. The king, no longer eating, was leaning against the table looking thoughtful. "Your thoughts, dear friend?" Richard asked.

"If Ireland could truly be taken," said de Vere, "think of the land and income that would be gained. It would be a mighty addition to your kingdom. Memories would fade of the unfortunate events in Scotland and France."

"True," said Richard. "And a new war would stop the nobles from grumbling about taxes, if there were land for them to gain."

"And if the Roman Church secretly paid for the war, all those taxes would fatten your treasury," said de Vere.

"If Ireland could really be taken." Richard picked up a dish of miniature fruits sculpted out of colored sugar and almond paste and handed it to de Vere. "Go find out if it is possible."

10

Carrying the dish of sugar fruits across the inner yard of the Tower of London, de Vere noticed that Clanvowe's corpse, now headless, lay smoldering on the remains of the fire. He knew that the blackened head would already be on a spike above the outer gatehouse.

De Vere entered a low, windowless stone building. To the guard sitting inside, he said only, "Third cell." De Vere pulled a ring of keys out of his pocket, selected one, and handed it to the man. Following the guard down the short corridor, de Vere drew a violet-scented handkerchief from his sleeve and covered his nose against the rancid smell.

The guard unlocked the cell, placed his torch into a wall bracket inside, returned the keys to de Vere, and left without comment. The flickering torchlight penetrated the darkness just enough to reveal an ancient figure sitting with his back against the far wall, his only clothing a dirty, tattered loincloth. Both legs had been chopped off above the knee, the scarred flesh having withered to expose nubs of bones into which were set iron rings. A chain led from the bone rings to a bracket in the center of the cell floor.

De Vere placed the dish on the stone floor. The prisoner turned his face toward the sound, sniffed the air, and began to crawl toward de Vere, dragging the chain behind him. Reaching the dish, he drew it to his nose and examined its scent cautiously, then propped himself up against the wall next to the door.

"Sugar, my last pleasure," said Oren, turning to face de Vere as if he could still see out of the scarred hollows that once held eyes. "What do you want?"

&

MORE THAN THIRTEEN HUNDRED years earlier on Anglesey Island, Wales, in the year CE 60, Oren leaned heavily on the oak branch he was using as a crutch. Closing his eyes, he concentrated on pushing away the wave of pain threatening to overwhelm him. Regaining control, he looked back across his homeland. Smoke billowed from scores of fires where Roman legionaries were burning the sacred groves. Behind him the sun was setting.

Dawn seemed like an age ago, when he had stood with his now-dead father on the bank of the narrow strait, no wider than a river, that separated Anglesey Island from the western coast of the Welsh mainland. Young, in his first century, facing his first battle, Oren had been full of excitement and confidence. Proudly clutching the new blade his father had made for him, he had been impatient for the Romans to show themselves on the opposite bank.

His family clan were Bwbachod, master smiths of the Welsh faeries known as the Tylwyth Teg. They, along with most of the Tylwyth Teg clans, had formed an alliance with the last of the Britannia druids, whom the Roman invaders had driven from the mainland. For the next two decades, Rome seemed content to leave the alliance bottled up on their island. That was, until Queen Boudica had stirred up a revolt among the Britannia tribes, burning the twenty-year-old commercial settlement of London to the ground and waking the wolf. Rome sent reinforcements, who crushed Boudica's army in retaliation. The Roman commander, Suetonius, had decided to invade Anglesey while he had the men readily available and eliminate the pesky druids and their philosophy of independence from any central authority.

Standing by his father in the mist of the Tylwyth Teg army that morning, Oren felt his excitement catch in his throat at the sight of two full Roman legions, the XIV and the XX, marching toward the opposite bank in tight formations. Under cover of arrow volleys, wizards from Europe, sorcerers from Egypt, and a handful of druid traitors countered the enchantments being hurled by the Tylwyth Teg. The legionaries bridged the narrow strip of water by roping together shallow barges they had carried overland. They surged across, crashing into the combined Tylwyth Teg and druid forces.

A pilum, a Roman heavy javelin, had caught Oren in the leg just above the knee, shattering the bone. Oren's father turned from the mayhem to help him, only to be struck down by two arrows in his back.

Grabbing a stout oak branch from the ground, Oren hauled himself up and limped toward the Celli Ddu faerie mound lying a mile to the northwest, intent on escaping into the Middle Kingdom. The legionaries beat him to it. They had built a fire in the entrance and were swarming over the mound with shovels and picks, digging up the enchanted stones it covered. As he watched, the first standing stone was unearthed and pulled over. With it, all hope that the Tylwyth Teg would hold Anglesey died in his heart.

He hobbled across the island, and every faerie mound he came to was suffering the same fate. His new plan to hide in the woods vanished as the legionaries began to burn the sacred groves. With his opportunities for cover going up in flames, he had to continue lugging his shattered leg west. There was nowhere else to go.

Standing at the base of a low ridge, he gazed back across his beloved island. Physically he had passed exhaustion long ago. He gathered what was left of his mental strength. Over the ridge was his Bwbachod-clan faerie mound, situated on the end of a point extending out the westerly edge of Anglesey Island. He had seen no surviving mounds, nor had he seen Roman soldiers headed this way. The sun was setting on the longest day of his life as he started up the rise, dragging his injured leg along behind him as he could no longer raise it at all. The next hour would decide his fate.

He managed to clear the ridge and advance out the point, its edges sheer cliffs to the sea below. Fear rose in his chest when he saw Roman ships in the bay. *That's how they reached the mounds so quickly,* he thought. With no legionaries in sight, he hobbled on.

I'm going to make it, Oren thought as he approached his still-intact mound. He could see the edge of its doorway. He gathered the last of his strength and pushed his body to move faster. A legionary crept around the mound and rushed at him. Oren locked eyes with him for a moment. Suddenly the man noticed the emerald green grass, stopped, squatted down, and began to examine it closer. Being a Bwbachod, Oren carried his power in his eyes.

A second legionary emerged and charged at Oren, but then that man noticed the beauty of the blue sky spotted with small clouds and stopped to admire it. Oren lurched around the distracted soldier.

"Don't look him in the eye," ordered the decanus as he led his remaining five legionaries around the other side of the mound. They knocked Oren to the ground and slipped a linen bag over his head. The decanus felt for Oren's eyes through the linen and, ignoring his screams, thrust his dagger through the bag into one eye, gave it a quick twist, then the other eye, taking away his ability to work enchantments.

Bound, Oren was carried to the ship and dropped into the hold on top of two dozen other captive Tylwyth Teg, each maimed or painted with runes as needed to prevent any use of magic. At the Roman fort of Isca Dumnoniorum in southwest Britannia, the surgeon who hacked off Oren's shattered leg decided that he would be easier to handle if the other leg were removed as well.

From there the captives were shipped to pagan Rome, valuable chattel for the information they could provide, as Rome continued to struggle with tribes of Nephilim across its empire. The centuries passed, and they were needed less and less. Some died under torture, some found ways to take their own lives, and some were traded away.

OREN DID NOT know how many of his fellow captives were still alive. He had not heard the voice of another Tylwyth Teg since Count Philip of Savoy had shipped him to England in 1283 as a gift to King

Edward Longshanks, who was having trouble with the remains of the Tylwyth Teg during his Welsh campaigns. Oren's resistance to questioning had been broken long ago, so he knew that to be bribed meant that something important was at stake.

Gripping the plate of sugar fruits, he repeated his question: "What do you want?"

Squatting down beside Oren, de Vere took one of the sweets, put it in his mouth, and crunched on it. Oren placed the dish on his lap and covered it with both hands.

"How can Richard invade Ireland?" de Vere asked.

"He cannot," said Oren. "The Romans failed. The Normans failed. Richard would fail as well." Oren slipped a sugar fruit into his mouth. A moan emerged from his throat as the confection melted.

"Why would Richard not succeed, specifically?" de Vere asked.

"Because the Sidhe have what the Tylwyth Teg did not, a Goddess to watch over them. Evidently we were not important enough to any of the divine beings in the Otherworld."

"The Morrígna."

"Yes, the mighty protector of Ireland, but not Wales," said Oren, the old bitterness returning. "She merges and commands the power of the Sidhe and the Celts when her twin physical aspects are present in this world, and if Richard is planning an invasion, they will be present. Even the Fomorians dare not oppose the will of the Morrígna twins."

"What if one of the twins was killed? Her heart destroyed, while the other twin remained alive? And what if the Skeaghshee aligned with us? Then could we succeed in an invasion?"

"This is what you have arranged?" asked Oren.

De Vere remained silent.

Oren placed another sugar fruit in his mouth and let it dissolve, momentarily lost in the warmth of the liquefying sweetness. "Perhaps it could work. So long as the Sidhe do not kill the remaining twin so that the Morrígna can be reborn whole." A plan was forming in Oren's mind. "And you are not being led to slaughter just for their amusement."

Oren paused, hoping to appear to be thinking. "You will need more than the Skeaghshee," he continued. "You will need an alliance with the Fomorians to land your ships safely."

De Vere nodded. "How will we know if all this can be arranged, know if we're not being led astray?"

Oren felt something he had not felt since his capture—he felt hope. Hope and rising strength. "I would know if I were to meet with the Skeaghshee and the Fomorians." He handed the dish, still almost full, back to de Vere. "But it will take more than a dish of sugar for me to do it."

De Vere knocked the dish from Oren's hand, scattering the confections across the cell floor. "I'll force you to do it." He stood up as if to leave.

"You can. But you risk that I have learned to lie like a human during my centuries with your kind and that I will take this opportunity for my vengeance, no matter how painful you make it for me. Instead I offer you a pact that guarantees you can trust me: if I deceive you in any way, or am simply wrong in my advice, you can take my arms."

"I can take your arms anytime I wish," sneered de Vere.

"However, if my guidance proves to be correct," continued Oren, "you will take my life."

De Vere was silent.

"Quickly," added Oren. "You will agree to take my life quickly by beheading me, so I can leave this wretched world for the After Lands."

De Vere considered the proposition. Taking the torch from the bracket, he bent down to Oren, "Agreed, with one addition: if you don't serve us faithfully, I'll spare your life but take your arms and rip out your tongue so that you will never taste sugar again."

. . . . .

The day after his meeting with Richard, the legate sat at the abbot's table in the hall of the recently finished priory of Westminster Abbey, picking at his salmon. With the stench of the Thames rivaling that of the canals of Venice, why risk eating a fish from there? thought the legate.

The provost was droning through the day's Scriptures, his words jammed together and barely audible over the clatter of eighty monks eating in silence. A lay concierge entered the hall, the bang of the heavy door closing behind him echoing through the noise as he scurried around the tables, coming to a stop behind the legate's chair and whispering urgently in his ear. The legate allowed a smile to flicker across his face. *Now the negotiations begin in earnest,* he thought. *I must not seem to be anxious.* Leaning to his left, he whispered to the abbot, "The king's representatives demand an immediate audience. Please send my salmon along with the other leftovers to the charity hall."

Trailed by the concierge, the legate left. Once in the passage, he spoke over his shoulder, "Where are they?"

"In the abbot's new office, Your Eminence," replied the man, trotting a bit to keep up. "I thought the receiving room too . . . too . . . too plain for the likes of them."

"Come on, then, hurry and show me the way."

Picking up his pace, the concierge edged past the legate and directed him down a side passage. On entering the abbott's plush office, the legate was not surprised to see seventeen-year-old Roger Mortimer, fourth Earl of March, standing with de Vere, who unceremoniously tossed a small wooden chest onto the desk. It landed with a hollow thud and slid a few inches, leaving several scratches. *So the decision has been made,* thought the legate, *and we need only talk of money.*

At ten years of age, Roger Mortimer had been named presumptive heir by Richard, should he sire no boys of his own, as most expected

would be the case. At fifteen, Mortimer had been married to the daughter of the Earl of Kent, immediately after the earl purchased the right to
choose Mortimer's bride.

That he faced the two most powerful men in England, other than
Richard himself, was not lost on the legate. He made a point of walking slowly around the abbott's writing desk and sitting down before
motioning for Mortimer and de Vere to do the same, reinforcing the
fact that on Church property he outranked them both.

Silence lingered. Inherent conflict between status and authority
prevented any pleasantries between them.

"I believe I can persuade the Vatican to fund a force of ten thousand men, which will be more than adequate," the legate finally
offered.

"You believe?" shot back Mortimer. "You will have the Vatican
fund a force of fifteen thousand men."

"Of the ten thousand we will fund," the legate replied coolly, "I
know you'll take only eight and pocket the difference. If you need
more men, take all ten."

Mortimer smiled. "The Vatican will fund fifteen thousand, and
we'll take ten. The Vatican cannot afford repeating the mistake of
Strongbow. He took too small a force, as well as too weak a druid."

"And Richard cannot afford to repeat the mistakes he made in
Scotland," replied the legate.

"Exactly," said de Vere.

Perhaps that was not my best argument, thought the legate. But
they were correct; none of them could afford to fail this time. And
there was probably no way to avoid the tax of paying for more men
than actually went, a practice that dated back to the days of the Roman
legions. The overage would be split, some of it flowing all the way
down to lieutenants who would receive pay for one phantom soldier
for every forty they commanded. It was impossible to recruit experienced commanders without such incentives.

"And we will need funds for new ships, of course," noted Mortimer. "All new ships. The crossing may be short, but it's treacherous, even with the help of your Sidhe allies."

"Or is it that Richard wants to regain the support of the trade guilds?" replied the legate. *An astute move*, he thought. While the earls would back the invasion to feed their lust for land, the new ships would gain Richard, and Mortimer, the favor of the merchant class. Shipbuilding employed more skilled tradesmen than any other industry in England.

The legate casually pushed the empty chest to the edge of the writing table, ignoring the new scratches he was causing. "Payment must not be seen to come from the Vatican," he said in tacit agreement. "The Jews within the Papal States will provide Richard with loans. These loans will then be traded to the Church in exchange for the return of some of their confiscated land and property. Once the invasion has succeeded, the Church will return the loans to Richard in exchange for the Irish Church's monasteries. All of them, in England and Wales, as well as Ireland."

"Set up any pretext you like," said Mortimer, "but understand this: Richard will not put his seal to these loans until the invasion has succeeded, until your Sidhe allies have made it succeed. If they fail, the Church will be left with worthless parchment."

The legate shrugged. "If that happens, the Church will not return any land to the Jews."

De Vere pointed at the chest. "Fill it with one hundred fifty pounds' worth of gold and return it to me by midday tomorrow to bond our arrangement. If not, there'll be no agreement, and I advise you not to appear in Richard's court again."

The legate rose and twisted a knob in the wall by the door. A few moments later, there was a knock and he opened the door to admit a steward. "Is the provost finished in the hall?" he asked.

"Yes, Your Eminence," replied the steward.

"Good. Take that to him and tell him I'll join him shortly to explain."

The steward bowed, took the chest from the table, and left. The legate stood by the open door until it became obvious that Mortimer and de Vere had no intention of leaving. "There's more?" he asked with a sigh.

De Vere nodded. "Richard has acquired a faerie ally of his own. You will arrange a conclave with your Sidhe and our delegation. When and if we're all convinced that the plan will succeed, then we'll proceed."

"And what happens to the Vatican's gold if you don't proceed?"

"You mean if you've been wasting our time?" replied Mortimer. "Then it will be retained to cover our expenses."

"Is that all?"

"One more thing," said de Vere. "Your Sidhe must bring the Fomorians to the conclave, where they'll also need to provide assurances of their allegiance."

II

Aisling collapsed onto Conor's chest. She tried to kiss his neck but had no breath left, so she rested her cheek on his shoulder and panted, her breathing in time with his. When her chest stopped heaving, she eased off her knees, shuddering as he slipped out of her. She stretched her legs so she could lie atop the length of his naked body, the warmth of his skin contrasting with the crisp forest air. Her cloak lay in the heather beside them. She felt him fumbling to pull it over their bodies without dislodging her. "Leave it," Aisling whispered. "I want to be just like this."

Safe. The word floated up in her consciousness. Conor allowed her to feel . . . safe. She slid her hands under his shoulders and pressed herself tight against his body. He provided a firm connection to her human self. A secure place from which to explore what remained of her Goddess nature and work to reconnect with the lingering power there. The fissure where Anya used to be was a constant presence, and it would always be so, she thought, letting out a long sigh. *But no longer will I tumble into that chasm whenever I try any but the most basic of enchantments,* she vowed to herself. *No longer will I let myself be smothered in the darkness waiting there.*

Lord Maolan's rough visits to her bedchamber had become infrequent as his efforts to torment her increasingly failed. Her sessions with Brigid's priestesses were also dwindling. While the orgasms they coaxed from her were intense, it was her passion with Conor that fulfilled her. Soon, she thought, she would show him how to please her as the novice priestesses did. Perhaps she would bring one along to demonstrate. Mary, probably.

Dappled sunlight drifted through the trees to create spots of warmth and coolness along her body. She lay with her eyes closed, not quite sleeping, savoring the rise and fall of his chest. She could feel the land breathe with them. The energy of the land and the forest merged with Conor's and flowed into her. She felt connected again, a potent feeling that was returning more often, reminding her of who she used to be. Her mind drifted to memories of training with Anya.

❦

SHE AND ANYA were ten, back before Kellach had been imprisoned and was still building his group of radical followers. The girls rode together toward the coast, galloping a horse length behind Liam and Haidrean.

"They're not old enough," insisted Haidrean.

"Age has nothing to do with it. They can handle this," replied Liam.

"Kellach, no doubt, stirred up this trouble. The Fomorians wouldn't have dared had he not convinced them it could work. He keeps spouting on about how, without the missing heart segment, the twins are not really the Morrígna."

"Whether or not Kellach put them up to it, the Fomorians have decided to test the twins, and they must respond."

"You should've brought a company of Gallowglass."

"That would defeat the point."

The village of Malahide came into view on the shore of Broadmeadow Estuary. Villagers were busy constructing a rough stockade. The village elder came forward to meet them. "Thank the Morrígna you have arrived. The Fomorians have taken another, my nephew."

"How many do they have now?" asked Liam.

"Three. You must get them back." A thick cloud passed before the sun, and the elder shouted a warning to one of the villagers. One voice to the next carried the alarm around the village, Fomorians preferred to attack when it was overcast.

"Tell them to stop building the stockade. It won't help," said Liam. "It won't be needed either."

The four of them rode on through the village and dismounted at the water's edge.

"Make them come out," Liam said to the twins.

Anya and Aisling exchanged whispers, then began to spin.

"No!" Haidrean stopped them. "Don't use physical magic. Merge together to access the power of the Morrígna."

"Fine, if that's what you want," said Anya. She and Aisling stilled themselves and gazed out over the water, green emerging in their gray eyes. Whirlpools bloomed across the estuary, dragging up mud and debris from the bottom.

Half a dozen dizzy Fomorians stumbled out, though not the king of their clan. The largest straightened up and snarled in his guttural language, "How dare you assault us!"

Anya replied, "We dare as we please. We are the Morrígna. Return your captives immediately."

"You two are nothing more than ordinary druids," he growled. He raised a clawed hand and leaped for Anya.

Aisling's sword flashed, and his arm tumbled to the grass. He wheeled on her with a roar. She ducked under his remaining claws and thrust her blade into his heart. He fell to the ground, taking the sword and Aisling with him.

"Jerk it out," ordered Liam. "And next time let the body's weight pull itself off your blade as it falls. Now, keep an eye on the others."

"How was that kill?" asked Haidrean.

"It felt strangely unpleasant, as if we failed somehow," answered Aisling.

"You did," said Haidrean. "Had you used his true name, you would've bound him to obey you, and you wouldn't have had to kill him."

"But we didn't know his true name," said Anya.

"An Elioud's true name, like a Sidhe's, is given to them by their

God in the Otherworld before they're born into this world. The Morrígna knows all the names. When you two merge and bring forth your combined Goddess nature, you only have to remember them."

"Only . . ." said Aisling, wiping the dark blood off her sword.

"Let's try it," said Anya.

"This isn't practice," declared Liam. "The king of their clan is still in the water. Call to him and compel him to immediately return the villagers he took."

And so they did.

❧

MEMORIES OF WHAT she and Anya were once capable of made Aisling restless. The sun had turned and was sinking toward twilight. She ran a finger down Conor's chest, leaving a trail of heat and gold light. Conor opened his eyes. She said, "You called me back, you know."

"Back?" he asked.

"Back to who I'm meant to be. Brigid tells me that my powers may soon be as strong as they were before Anya died."

"Strong enough to leave Maolan for good?"

"Yes. Now that you've asked." Aisling propped herself up, her elbows pressing into Conor's chest, and smiled down at him. "No, wait. You can't afford to pay my honor price if you petition for my marriage contract to be broken."

"You can't afford mine either." Conor rose up to kiss her.

She dodged the kiss. "That's not how the law works. Besides, you don't have one."

"I have more honor than Maolan has, so I must have a high price. You just don't know what it is." He wrapped his arms around her and rolled onto his side, easing her onto the ground.

Aisling wiggled free from his embrace. "I challenge you to a contest. Whoever wins pays the other's honor price to Maolan for breaking my contract." Crawling over to their pile of clothing, she fumbled around until she withdrew her dagger. She stood and pointed it at

Conor. "Tadg told me that you used to be able to creep up on a stag and slay it with just a knife. Is that true?"

"You doubt it?"

"Well, I've never seen you do it."

"The bow is much quicker," he said. "I have to save all my time to lie with you."

"I wager that I can bring down a stag before you," she declared.

Jumping to his feet, dagger already in his hand, having been left within reach, Conor said, "Agreed. Though I doubt there's any game left within two miles with all the noise you were making."

Without a word Aisling slipped away between the trees. Her bare feet made no sound on the moss-covered ground. Locating a deer trail among the deepening shadows, she stopped, reached out with her consciousness, and felt the woods around her as Brigid had taught her. A stag had recently passed, heading north. She turned and raced up the trail. She could not see or hear Conor but sensed his presence moving to her right.

Coming to a clearing, she spotted the stag grazing unconcerned. She could tell that Conor was on the trail just behind her, and she smiled. She had a step on him and was going to win. She tensed for her final rush. She felt Conor reaching toward her. He caught the end of her hair and whispered, "Stop. Something's wrong."

She froze.

Conor did not move or speak.

One of the shadows across the clearing was too dark. She closed her eyes for a moment, reaching out again with her consciousness, connecting with the natural world around her. It was as if there were an empty space in the shadow. She opened her eyes and concentrated on seeing what could not be seen. Using her mind to push away all that was meant to be there, she saw a softly outlined face emerge, then a disjointed body. She reached up to where a ray from the setting sun was striking a tree trunk, scooped up a handful of light, and tossed it into the shadow.

"Woodwose," Conor hissed.

The wild man was all sinew, bone, and tight skin painted with triangles of green between troughs of black tattoos, his head an explosion of hair and beard. A heavy club hung in his hand. A roar came from his mouth. The stag leaped out of the clearing. The Woodwose charged forward, raising his weapon.

Aisling instinctively threw her dagger, piercing his eye. Suddenly silenced, he fell face-first onto the grass. Around the clearing, shadows detached from the trees and rushed toward them. Aisling immediately regretted leaving herself unarmed.

Conor spun her by the shoulder. "Run!" he shouted. She fled behind him down the deer track. The forest around them became alive with pounding feet and crashing brush. A figure in a loincloth stepped in front of Conor. Conor ducked under the swinging club, came up, and plunged his dagger into the assailant's stomach, dragging the blade up several inches before jerking it out and thrusting the screaming Woodwose aside. Only then did Aisling realize it was a woman.

Conor grabbed Aisling's hand and led her off the trail. They ran for a minute, then stopped to listen to the movement in the forest around them. "Stay close," he breathed as they moved on. Stopped. Listened. Moved again.

"Can you tell how many and where they are?" whispered Conor.

Aisling closed her eyes and tried again, shook her head. "Something's hiding them from me. I only sense flutters of . . . of absence, moving in the forest."

"Can you conceal us from them?"

"I've been trying, but that same something keeps clawing away at my enchantment. We have to keep moving."

"Our best chance is to get back to the horses."

"The horses are dead," Aisling replied, knowing it as soon as he had said the words.

"Can we get to our swords?"

She concentrated. "We may be able to. There's movement every-where. It's very hard to pin down."

"Let's try."

They slid forward. Fifteen minutes later Conor paused, crouched, pointed. As she hunched beside him, she could barely make out the pile of their clothing up ahead in the deepening gloom.

"What do you sense?" Conor whispered.

"Traces of movement headed this way. A lot of them. They know we're here."

"I need to know if you're ready for this fight, if you're willing to work enchantments strong enough to kill anyone who attacks you."

"I killed one already."

"Yes, but that was with a knife. I've no doubt about your will-ingness with iron."

"Just get our swords."

Conor sprang forward. There was a bellow as figures moved to their left. Aisling stood, reached both arms into the air, and pulled a fog down on the charging Woodwose. She closed her eyes, and every tree in the surrounding forest seemed to shift a few feet. There were cries and the dull thuds of bodies hitting trunks and branches.

Conor reached their clothing and jumped over the pile, grabbing the hilt of his sword and letting his momentum unsheathe it. Plant-ing both feet, he turned to retrieve Aisling's sword but had to stop and slash the throat of a Woodwose charging out of the fog. A second man rushed him, and he spun, sweeping his sword down to cut open the attacker's chest.

A woman emerged from the fog, saw Aisling, and charged. Aisling stopped thinking and just acted. The woman dropped the sharpened antler she had been wielding as if it had become red-hot. Aisling piv-oted to avoid the charge, brushing her hand across the woman's exposed breast. The woman crumpled to the ground, her heart no longer beat-ing. Aisling sprinted toward Conor.

Being careful to slash, not stab and risk having his sword become stuck, Conor had felled a third and a fourth Woodwose before a fifth surprised him by charging directly onto his sword all the way up to the hilt. Before Conor could free it, three jumped him, knocking him to the ground.

Aisling reached the heap of men and shattered the spine of one with a touch. A sudden impact from behind forced her down hard. She felt bodies piling on her, pinning her arms and legs, pressing her face into the dirt. She could not breathe. A shadow crept across her consciousness. She formed it into the shape of a rook, felt the gust of its wings. With no more air, a wave of shadows swept in and engulfed her.

"ART THINKS that the Roman Church will attempt an invasion, and I agree with him," said Liam as he and Tadg rode their horses along the north road from Tara.

Art MacMurrough, the new Celtic high king–elect, was a bear of a man known for his love of wine and rich food as much as for his skill with a broadsword. The regional kings, queens, high nobles, and heads of the first-order guilds had gathered at Tara two days earlier to express their concerns to the previous high king about unrest among the Sidhe and what the freed Kellach might be plotting. Art had taken the opportunity to orchestrate a vote for the high-kingship and handily beat the throne holder and the only other person on the ballot, Lord Maolan. Art had worried about the possibility of losing to Turlough, the respected king of Meath, but the latter had not run.

Before he could be enthroned, though, Art had to pass the three ancient tests required of all high kings. Preparations were under way for the ceremony, which was to take place during tomorrow's Festival of Bealtaine, marking the midpoint in the sun's progress between the spring equinox and the summer solstice. Liam and Tadg were on their way to meet Brigid's delegation and escort to Tara the King's

Cup, which was kept in trust by the Order of Macha and was required for the coronation ritual.

"I've sensed a stirring, a discontent in the trees and in the land. We may be fighting some of the Sidhe clans as well," Tadg said. "Do you think Art can be the wartime king we'll need?"

"He's a good choice, if his drinking doesn't get the better of him," Liam replied. "He's shrewd and has inspired much loyalty among Celtic warriors, and he can be ruthless."

"Still, this will be a fight unlike any we've seen before. I believe that within the Middle Kingdom sides are being chosen. There are strange, unfamiliar forces at work," said Tadg.

"And some Sidhe are leaving."

"Leaving?" asked Tadg.

"There are pathways in the Middle Kingdom that lead to worlds other than this one. They are little known, and I don't recall a time when I've heard talk of so many taking them." Liam sighed. "Even some of my mother's family are leaving, rather than risk war, risk their long lives."

"And what of the English? Do you believe that they were also involved in Kellach's escape?"

"I don't know. But I fear no outside force. I fear only what Ireland may do to itself," said Liam.

"I fear that Ireland may tear herself apart without the Morrígna to bind her," said Tadg.

"Aisling will do all she can," snapped Liam automatically, weary of this argument. He disdained the implication that Ireland was now vulnerable with only one aspect of the Morrígna on earth, which prevented the full manifestation of the Goddess's power. A growing number of nobles openly suggested that Aisling should return—voluntarily or not—to the spirit realm and allow the Morrígna to be reborn whole.

"Don't get me wrong, you know I love Aisling like a daughter and will protect her with my life. I was just pointing out that we must prepare for war without the Goddess's power," said Tadg.

"Aisling has power she hasn't yet discovered," said Liam. "She'll be enough to ensure that Ireland is protected."

At that moment they rounded a curve in the road and the hostel came into view. Outside stood Brigid in a circle of her priestesses, offering prayers to the setting sun. Liam and Tadg sat up straighter on their horses and urged them into a trot.

"There's one thing I'm looking forward to, and that's fighting alongside you, my friend," said Tadg.

"If you're going to try to keep up with me, you'd better bring extra arrows," Liam said with a laugh. "Lots of them."

Brigid joined them when they reached the hostel. "I wasn't expecting you until the dark of tomorrow morning," she said.

Liam dismounted and gave her a firm embrace. "Tonight's not a good time to have my best horse in the royal stables. Besides, I'd be a fool to pass up an evening of your hospitality."

Brigid smiled and placed a hand on Liam's chest. "I've several novice priestesses who will extend their hospitality to you and Tadg."

"That's not what I meant," said Liam, "but it's most welcome."

A novice priestess in the Order of Mancha cannot become a full priestess, and thus chaste with men and women, until Brigid determines that she has sufficient knowledge of both. As he looked over at the circle of priestesses, Liam was reminded that no lover had ever rivaled his experiences with Brigid when she was a novice and gaining much of her knowledge of men from him.

A rook fluttered toward them. At first Liam thought it must be injured, but as it flew closer, he saw the last traces of twilight through it. The rook gave a faint cry, then vaporized.

"Aisling!" shouted Liam. He swung onto his horse and galloped off, with Tadg following close behind.

Brigid rushed through the enchantment to transform into her

swan form. It did not work; something powerful was countering it. She ran for the stables.

AT TARA the main gate of the royal enclosure was being pushed closed for the night when it paused to let Lord Maolan ride out. He could not recall when he had felt quite this happy. *A God must be smiling on me from the Otherworld,* he reasoned as he rode through the town toward the woods. He was not sure which God, only that it must be one who was jealous of the Morrígna. *I will make an offering when I return,* he silently vowed, *in gratitude for everything coming together better than I could have imagined, with the old high king voted out and Art not yet crowned.*

Maolan thought of the smug way Art had looked at him when he won the election and smiled to himself. *Well, Art, enjoy your night, because there will be no coronation tomorrow, only my knife at your throat. And once I make myself high king, I will do away with the election altogether.*

12

Christians and their Jewish forefathers are much addicted to the sorcery taught them by Moses.

—*The True Word*, by Celsus (circa CE 177)

Conwy Castle, Wales
The Same Day

On the north coast of Wales, the ship that Jordan used to rescue Kellach lay at anchor in the mouth of the river Conwy. Stone walls of a fortified port town, punctuated with guard towers, stretched toward the foothills of the nearby Snowdonia Mountains. Perched on a rocky outcrop, compact and formidable, Conwy Castle brooded over the river and the town it protected. Stone stairs wound up from a small dock at the end of the outcrop and through a sea gate into the castle garden, brimming with hundred-year-old oaks, where Kellach waited to meet with English and Fomorian delegations.

Upper chambers of the castle towers that faced the garden had full-size windows rather than the arrow slits used elsewhere. In one of those chambers, on the third level, Jordan sat cross-legged on the wooden floor, across from him sat Najia, and between them the stubs of seven wax candles burned. He had slipped on a pair of trousers for the ceremony but remained barefoot and bare-chested. Najia wore a modest frock of white linen, which highlighted her dark skin.

Najia's siblings had been shipped off to Jordan's ancestral home in Sicily. He had drawn up papers changing their status from slaves to bound servants, a designation that meant they could not be beaten with impunity by anyone along the way.

Jordan and Najia focused on the light radiating from the candles between them. As they concentrated, the light gathered into a floating sphere that hung suspended, an orb of glowing gold. Areas of blue began to materialize on the surface; then an island of green and brown started to push through the azure. Cracks stretched across the sphere and a tremor set in. Flakes of blue fell off, evaporating before reaching the floor. Jordan frowned, furrows appearing on his forehead and around his eyes. Najia's expression remained calm, impassive. The orb stabilized, and the island started to take definitive shape. Suddenly the sphere disappeared in a puff of candle smoke.

Najia leaned back, supported her body with her hands on the floor, and stretched. Jordan gave a heavy sigh. "What else we can try?" he asked.

Najia shook her head, her dark hair caressing her face. "Apparently it's impossible to manifest an accurate map of Ireland."

"Who blinds our sight?" he asked. "The Sidhe? The Celtic druids?"

"Both have set up barriers," said Najia. "But there's a greater problem with attempting an enchantment this strong from here: too much Ardor has already been stripped from Britain."

"Ardor?"

"The energy that originally animated all life and what makes natural magic possible. There's less and less for those with the knowledge, people like you and me, to draw upon. All magic requires some form of energy. With less Ardor our ability to cast enchantments weakens. You should know that—you're involved with driving it from the world."

"If we can't even create a map of the Irish coastline"—Jordan paused in frustration—"we'll be entirely at Kellach's mercy when we send an armada."

He rose and moved to the window, where he observed the strange gathering forming in the walled garden below. He had sailed here directly from Great Skellig, a journey of a few days, while it had taken the legate nine months to return to Rome from London and squeeze enough money from the Jews of the Papal States to fund the English invasion, then another month to convene this conclave. Yet in that brief time, tended by Kellach, the trees had grown twice as tall and had become fuller and more animated; each morning they twisted themselves into slightly different shapes.

The English lords Mortimer and de Vere had arrived and sat next to Kellach at the round table, quizzing him on the invasion plans. Propped up in a chair beside them was their Tylwyth Teg, Oren, who the English believed could tell if another faerie tried to deceive them. To Kellach's right, the legate was approaching, which meant that Jordan was late. Across from Kellach, between the Vatican and the English seats, a gap remained for the Fomorian delegation. With the sun dipping into the sea, they were expected to pad up the stone steps from the water at any moment.

"The legate believes that when the Nephilim are gone, natural magic will disappear," said Jordan.

"God may have infused the world with Ardor when he created it, or it may have come in the blood of the angels, blood the Nephilim still carry—no one knows," said Najia. "But what I know for sure is that when Nephilim leave a land, Ardor leaves with them. That's what caused the Ardor in Europe to fade almost as much as it has here."

"What of Europe's human witches, like the High Coven? They seem to be getting more powerful," countered Jordan.

"They've less magic than they claim, and they've had to turn to taking lives to power its more potent forms."

"Your father taught you all this? Or did you learn firsthand?"

"Don't worry, I haven't been hiding a dark side from you," replied Najia. "As sorcerer to the emir, my father had to battle dark witches moving into our lands. These witches stripped the fat from stolen infants, who have the most malleable life force. Older people need to be boiled or burned alive to extract any usable energy. Do you want to try one of those methods to create your Irish map?"

Knowing that it was not a serious suggestion, Jordan ignored it, but he could not stop the images reappearing in his mind of the butchered children he had seen in the witch Marija's lair. Trying to think of something else, he asked, "What of the exorcists?"

"They enable their magic through relics, angelic grimoires, and ancient words of power from their God. Forces that were not meant to be used by humans, at least not in the way the exorcists use them, so they do not serve them well, they corrupt."

There were many things that corrupt men, Jordan thought, and surely Nephilim as well. From above he watched Oren nod at something Kellach said, then spoon sugar into his mouth. Jordan did not know what the Welsh faerie's agenda was, but he was sure it was not what de Vere expected.

Jordan knew that Oren had betrayed his own kind at least once already, a century earlier, when he had revealed the hiding place of the Croes Naid. The English king Edward I, known as Longshanks for his imposing height, had celebrated his conquest of Wales by having Dafydd, the last Welsh prince, drawn, hanged, disemboweled, quartered, and his head shipped to the Tower of London to be displayed on a spike. However, relentless attacks by surviving Tylwyth Teg and groups of allied Trolls threatened to destabilize Longshanks's newly won holdings before he could build castles to protect them. Then Longshanks's cousin, Count Philip of Savoy, sent him Oren as a present. With little persuasion Oren disclosed that the Croes Naid, containing a shard of the True Cross of Jesus, had been used by generations of Welsh princes as an effective talisman against Nephilim attacks. Once the VRS League began using the powerful relic, Longshanks had the calm he needed to build this fortress at Conwy. Construction went so smoothly that he finished it in only four years. As soon as Jordan had arrived, he had demanded that the Croes Naid and its exorcist keepers move from the castle chapel to the church in the town. While his excuse was the comfort of Kellach, in truth it was so that he could practice his new art undetected.

Jordan heard the rustle of cloth as Najia pulled her frock off over her head and threw it on top of a chest next to the bed, but he did not turn around. He had too many other things on his mind. She slid up behind him, pressing her breasts against his bare back. Rising up on her tiptoes, she looked over his shoulder at the scene below.

"Once Kellach gets you to Ireland, the plan is to turn on him?"

Jordan had learned during their short time together not to bother lying to her. "Yes. The Vatican and the English will double-cross him and turn on all his kind."

"The Skeaghshee and the Fomorians are betraying Ireland in their lust for power," said Najia. "In turn they'll be betrayed by mortals who lust for land. And the last beacon of Ardor in our world will be snuffed out. Then the breath of the world will fade, and she will begin to die."

Silence hung between them.

Below, shapes rose silhouetted against the last sparkle of a sunset sea and moved cautiously up the stone stairs to the garden, where torchlight glinted from their leader's single oversize eye. Jordan wondered if it was the same Fomorian king who had assisted them at Great Skellig. The answer came as a pair of female Fomorians unwrapped an oilskin package and draped the sable cloak over the king's shoulders.

"Richard's greatest victory begins at this castle," said Najia. "As will his ultimate downfall."

"Prophesying without entrails now, witch," Jordan snapped.

Najia laughed. "I learned to draw upon Ardor through study and practice. You were born with the gift, though you didn't know it. You thought you were just lucky. Then you discovered enchantments, enchantments that always worked the first time you tried them, and your success increased." She ran her hand down his bare chest. "Not a single scar from all your fights. Not one. Yes, I'm a witch, but what are you?"

Jordan pulled away from her touch. That was becoming too nagging a question. He grabbed his tunic off the bedpost and put it on, hurriedly adding the rest of his ensemble.

"What are you going to do when all the bad luck you pushed aside comes back to you? What will you do when there's not enough Ardor left to draw upon?" Najia asked, plopping down on the bed and watching him dress. "What will you be then?"

"My position will be secure. I've an agreement to become grand marshal, bound with the legate," said Jordan, pulling on his boots. "It'll restore my family name."

"Fine compensation for ensuring that the only magic left in this world will be that of dark witches and corrupt exorcists!" Najia exclaimed. "A splendid strategy."

Jordan regarded her sternly, then left the chamber heading for the war council.

By the time he reached the table, negotiations with the Fomorians were already well advanced. Jordan knew what Kellach had offered: if they joined the invasion, they would receive the seaward half of the Irish kingdom of Connacht.

13

Aisling awoke to hell. She was bound to a dead tree in the center of a clearing, her hands tied with a crude rope looped over a branch above her head, her feet tied at the base. Her bruised, naked body throbbed with pain. The waning moon cast its harsh monochromatic light, revealing Conor staked out on the ground, struggling against his ropes. Several dozen Woodwose danced around a fire, chanting and shaking. A high rock face established one side of the clearing, the large black mouth of a cave at its base.

A Woodwose wearing the hollowed-out head of a boar as a mask stepped away from the dancers, pointed to Aisling, and gave a cry. The dancing intensified.

The shaman, Aisling thought. She forced a swallow down her burning throat, then croaked out an enchantment. The only result was a waver in the mouth of the cave, as if black velvet curtains had caught a breeze, but there was no breeze. The ropes holding her remained intact.

A squat figure emerged from the cave mouth. Three feet tall with a chubby, hairless body and pointed ears, he gave a high-pitched, squeaky giggle, revealing sharp teeth. The fear that Aisling had been fighting off overwhelmed her—it was an Imp, a demon familiar.

The Imp climbed onto a long stone slab set before the cave. One end of the slab rested on a rock, causing it to slope. Shallow troughs had been carved at an angle down the face of the slab, joining into one deep trough down the center, which led off the low edge.

The shaman turned back to the dancing Woodwose and placed his hand on the shoulder of one, a young woman. All dancing and chanting stopped. Four men walked her, unresisting, to the slab. The shaman pulled off her loincloth to the laughter of the Imp, who thrust his hips forward to show off his tiny erection, barely visible under his sagging belly. He scurried to the high end of the slab as the men placed the young woman on it, head down.

The Imp squeaked some words Aisling did not understand, and vines crept up across the young woman's body, binding her to the slab. The watching Woodwose restarted their chant, their bodies waving with the rhythm. Laughter trickled from the Imp as he broke into a mocking dance on his perch.

The shaman selected a skull from a pile beside the slab and picked up the stone-headed ax lying next to it. He inverted the skull and placed it under the trough at the low edge of the slab. Aisling's eyes locked onto the eyes of the young woman, where she saw only acceptance, until the shaman's ax severed the woman's head.

There was a thud as the Imp laughed so hard he fell off the slab. He ran around, grabbed the head, and scurried back up to his high perch, where he stood studying the dead face. He giggled, kissed the dead lips, giggled again, and began to suckle blood from the neck, red running down his chin and pudgy chest. The Woodwose resumed their dance.

"Conor!" screamed Aisling. "My enchantments aren't working! There must be a demon in the cave countering them!"

"Keep trying!" Conor called back, pulling futilely at the ropes holding him.

Aisling closed her eyes and tried to focus her energy, but it immediately drained away from her. The chanting of the Woodwose filled her head. When she opened her eyes, the shaman was retrieving the inverted skull, now full of the young woman's blood. He held it up to the cave in a salute. With one hand he removed his boar-head mask, dropped it on the ground, and took a long drink, and then he hurled the rest of the blood into the cave. The blackness covering the opening erupted into a boil.

With a loud screech, the Imp tossed the severed head of the young woman at Conor, hitting him in the stomach. Men pulled the young woman's body off the slab as the vines released her. Others cut Conor loose and dragged him, struggling and cursing, to the slab. Pinned by the returning vines, his head at the high end of the slab, Conor shouted to Aisling, "Whatever they do to me, stay strong, try to protect yourself!"

The shaman again placed the inverted skull under the trough at the low end of the slab. Aisling desperately projected an enchantment of comfort and pain relief but could tell immediately that it did not work.

The Imp's erection returned. He crawled down and sat on Conor's chest, watching as the shaman grabbed Conor's testicles with one hand and raised a flint knife with the other. The Woodwose roared their approval. The Imp giggled and began to masturbate. The shaman slowly brought the knife down.

An arrow exploded from the shaman's throat, and he collapsed before the knife could castrate Conor. Tadg stepped from the edge of the clearing, loosing arrows as fast as he could draw them. Woodwose near the slab fell. Tadg advanced as Liam sprinted from the trees toward Aisling.

Woodwose rushed Liam with abandon. Liam cut through them, sword in one hand, dagger in the other. Bodies piled at his feet, and he stumbled, forcing him to step back to keep his footing.

Tadg was almost to the slab when he drew and loosed an arrow at the Imp. There was a flash, and the arrow became ash in midflight, the iron arrowhead falling to earth. Tadg tried to draw another. His bowstring vaporized. Dropping the bow, he reached for his dagger but was knocked to the ground by charging Woodwose. The Imp jumped down, pulled the dagger from Tadg's belt, and sliced across the back of one of Tadg's legs, then the other, severing his hamstrings. Tadg cried out in pain.

Liam retreated a few feet from the line of Woodwose between him and Aisling, his sword held in a high guard, his dagger low. He looked toward Tadg and Conor and spotted the Imp approaching cautiously from his right. Liam started to loop left, giving him an angle past the mound of dead and dying Woodwose for his charge to Aisling.

"Liam! The cave! There's a demon!" screamed Aisling.

Liam risked a glance over his shoulder to the cave, now behind him. A wave of blackness was flowing out along the ground toward him. He quickly surveyed the clearing, noting the Woodwose between him and Aisling and the Imp creeping closer. Even with his half-Sidhe ability to anticipate the moves of an attacker within blade reach, there were too many adversaries about to rush him at the same time. He looked straight at Aisling, raised and threw his dagger, severing the rope binding her hands. The blackness crawled up Liam's legs and enveloped his struggling body.

Aisling wrenched the dagger loose from the tree, cut her feet free, and stepped forward. Tendrils of black flew through the air from the cave and slammed her back against the trunk, binding her there once again.

Lord Maolan rode his horse into the clearing. A hush descended on the Woodwose. He looked around. The bodies of Woodwose lay strewn about. A shape smothered in black stood fixed where Liam once was. Tadg had dragged himself onto the slab, where he was pulling ineffectively at the vines binding Conor.

Dismounting, Maolan addressed the Imp. "Why are they not dead yet? There will be no coronation tomorrow without Aisling. With no king and no Goddess, your master and I will rise to rule the dual worlds. Stop playing around and finish them."

The Imp gave an exaggerated bow, sweeping one hand to his feet. Rising, he giggled and pointed to Tadg. Two Woodwose grabbed Tadg's useless legs and dragged him off the slab. Flipping him faceup, they tore off his clothing and pinned his arms and legs down.

Using Tadg's dagger, the Imp carved a red arc across his stomach. Tadg gritted his teeth against the pain as small, glistening cavities puckered open along the path of the dagger's point. Blackness crept along the earth toward him. Tadg stared at it wide-eyed. Black tendrils reached out and tore the wound fully open, dragging out intestines, to Tadg's screams. The Woodwose released his limbs and backed off as the blackness enveloped Tadg's body. Tadg's screams became muffled, then stopped suddenly.

The Imp rolled on the ground in uncontrolled laughter.

Maolan raised his arms and cried, "Consume them all!"

"Aisling." A soft voice penetrated the fray. "Aisling, you must stop them." Brigid was standing in the clearing.

"Brigid!" cried Aisling. "Send help, hurry!"

"There's no one who can help here but you," replied Brigid.

The Imp, his head cocked, studied Brigid. "That is not an apparition," he squeaked. "She is really here." He rushed at Brigid. She grabbed him by the ear and held him off to her side. He slashed at her arm, and a red line appeared. She twisted the ear, and the Imp cried in pain, dropping the dagger and falling to one knee.

"Aisling," Brigid continued in her soft, level voice, "you must put a stop to this or we'll all die."

"I can't," sobbed Aisling. "Not by myself."

"You will all die!" shouted Maolan. He took a step toward Brigid and gestured at the cave mouth. "Kill them!"

"Aisling, you have journeyed between this world and the Otherworld for fifteen hundred years. You have the knowledge. You must now find it within yourself if you are going to save us."

A fresh wave of black flowed from the cave and washed around the base of the sacrificial slab. Tentacles reached for Conor. Aisling closed her eyes, tried to still her mind.

"Aghh!" cried Conor through clenched teeth as the first tentacle reached his skin. Aisling forced herself to ignore him and focus on Brigid's teachings, remembering that even if she was not one with the Morrígna, she could still draw upon the Goddess for power and knowledge. She stretched out her consciousness to the Otherworld and compelled herself to experience that connection to the exclusion of the chaos and pain surrounding her. She slipped deeper inward, past any thought, to her deepest memories, memories from before she was born, before her most recent birth. A second tentacle of black slid along Conor's rib cage, smoke rising from the contact. Conor thrashed against his bonds, clamping his mouth shut. Aisling felt Anann, from the Otherworld, breathe into her.

"I know you, Semjâzâ," said Aisling, opening her eyes, which had gone from gray to pale green. "I know your hidden, ineffable name." A shudder rippled through Semjâzâ's blackness, his tendrils drawing back from Conor. "I saw you slip out of heaven with your Grigori followers in your lust for mortal women. I watched as you were eventually rejected by mortals and your Nephilim offspring alike, as you descended into trespassing against birds and beasts and reptiles, into devouring men's flesh and drinking their blood. I know your ineffable name—" Aisling made the sound of lightning striking seawater, a sound no human throat could make. The black tendrils that bound her to the dead tree fell away as small sparks danced within them. She stepped forward.

"No!" shouted Maolan. "Kill her!" With two long strides, he reached the closest Woodwose and pushed him toward Aisling.

Aisling looked over to the man who was her husband and realized she no longer needed him in her world at all. She silently called to his horse, who wheeled around and kicked out with its rear legs. Maolan's head exploded in red and pink as the hooves connected, and his body crumpled. The remaining Woodwose broke and ran for the forest. The Imp twisted out of Brigid's grip and fled into the cave.

Semjâzâ lashed out a tendril toward Conor, wrapping it around his leg to the hissing of scorching flesh. Conor remained silent with clear effort, his wide eyes fixed on Aisling.

"You think you can take him from me?" Aisling laughed, walking into the blackness as it lapped harmlessly at her ankles. Aisling repeated Semjâzâ's ineffable name with more force. The demon withdrew his tendril from Conor.

"It was I who betrayed your rapes to Gabriel, I who taught women how to resist your Grigori horde, I who whispered your secrets to Enoch to warn future generations." The blackness around her feet flowed back toward the cave, sparking and fizzing where it touched her skin.

"I heard Gabriel order Uriel, He Who Carries the Light of God, to bind you in the gloom of Tartarus for seventy generations, heard his words and remembered them."

The blackness drew back across the mouth of the cave, boiled there. Semjâzâ spat out curses understood only by those present in the first days of the world, words that formed into black serpents, only to dissolve into fireflies as they crawled toward Aisling. In the same language, Aisling began to repeat Gabriel's order to Uriel. Her index finger left a luminescent trail as she drew a complex symbol in the air. Twelve tendrils of yellow light slid out from the edges of the cave and began to gather in the darkness. "For seventy generations more, Semjâzâ," said Aisling. "Then we shall duel again." The tendrils of light peeled the blackness off Liam's still-standing form and dragged the last of it into the cave.

Brigid rushed over to where Liam's body had now collapsed onto the ground. She kissed his lifeless lips, then breathed long into his mouth. He gasped, coughed, and gasped some more. "It's not time for you to leave me yet," she said, and kissed each of his eyes. He opened them, struggled onto his hands and knees, and began to vomit a black stream that vaporized into a mist and was sucked into the cave mouth.

Aisling ran over, climbed up on the sacrificial slab, and embraced Conor, who had torn away the newly inanimate vines. "Oh, my love!" she cried, and kissed him, almost laughing with joy, her eyes gray again. Leaving Liam to struggle to his feet on his own, Brigid removed her cloak and draped it over Aisling's shoulders. When she turned to thank Brigid, Aisling's eyes fell on Tadg's torn body, and her joy died in her heart. Conor gently pulled her arms from around him, climbed off the slab, and knelt at the side of the only father he had ever known.

There was movement in the trees. Fearghal, the Sidhe high king, and his witch daughter Rhoswen rode into the clearing followed by ten Sidhe with swords drawn.

A pair of faerie lights added their glow to the clearing. Conor, wrapped in a borrowed cloak, and Aisling, assisted by several Sidhe, gently secured Tadg's body to a horse.

"How did you know?" Brigid asked Rhoswen.

"Aisling must have distracted Semjâzâ from his concealment enchantment. An awareness of the fight bloomed in my mind," replied Rhoswen.

"It was magnificent to watch. She brought forth the Morrígna," said Brigid.

"Not fully," said Rhoswen. "All of the Middle Kingdom would have sensed the return. If she could become whole, the demon would not have even tried to fight her." Rhoswen watched as Conor embraced Aisling, her eyes glassy with tears. "Did she have the eye change?"

"Slightly," said Brigid.

"Incredible. She is . . . gestating into a being of her own design."

14

Tara, Ireland
The Next Day

Outside a village close to Tara, farmers, shepherds, tradespeople, and their families gathered for the Bealtaine fire ritual. As they milled around, they made pronouncements about the relative importance of fertility versus safety, how the fires were larger than last year's, and how surely the gap between the two bonfires was smaller. The piles of wood had stood twice as tall as a man and were separated by a distance of four feet, but that was before they were burning. Now even that gap was obscured by dense gray smoke lit with seemingly impenetrable arms of orange flame that licked across the divide.

A druid standing behind the group reached into his pouch, withdrew a handful of gray powder, and tossed it among their feet, where it flashed into brief flame. "Let's just go!" shouted a six-year-old boy who was attending his first Bealtaine festival. The smoke swallowed him as he disappeared between the towering fires.

With a surge the rest followed, dashing through the flames and emerging on the far side laughing uncontrollably. Gripped by momentum, the group circled to the right and ran through the gap again. Two widowers who no longer felt the need for a fertility rite carefully watched the circulating stream of laughing, coughing, squealing, running, tripping, and skipping villagers for any emerging with their clothing alight, unnoticed until they were tackled and rolled along the grass.

From Tara, high on its hill, columns of smoke could be seen dotting the countryside as the fire ritual was held in every village. Inside Tara's walls a different ritual was unfolding: Art MacMurrough might have won the election; however, he still had to pass three ancient tests before becoming the new high king of Ireland.

The night before in the royal stables—which were not nearly as full as normal—the finest horse was selected, its throat cut, and its blood drained into a jug. The carcass was spitted over a giant roasting pit to make ready for today's feast. While platters of horsemeat would be on the tables as required by ancient custom—horse was once thought to make the eater strong—most would end the day going to the dogs.

In addition to Fearghal and Rhoswen and the Celtic regional kings and queens, many Sidhe nobles were in attendance, though fewer than expected. Tales had been shared, songs sung, and the assembled guests had eaten more than their fill when Brigid brought in the King's Cup for a round of toasting and presented it to Art. Tradition called for the cup to be filled with the blood of the sacrificed horse, a tradition that had faded, as so many had, and for the last two hundred years the cup had been filled with red wine, fortified with only three drops of blood.

With the toasting complete and with much cheering and banging of fists on tables, the first test began. The Brehon laws required that a high king be whole of body, interpreted to mean he must possess his four limbs, both eyes, and all other major body parts. A large bronze tub was brought in, placed in front of the high table, and filled with hot water. Art stood beside the tub, stripped off his clothing, raised his arms to encourage the assembled dignitaries into even louder cheers, and then jumped into the water, splashing the closest of the nobles. Several women, having clearly enjoyed much wine, tried to climb into the tub with him but were pulled away by the stewards.

While the bath itself was not strictly required to prove the first test, it had for many centuries been required by the purveyors of the second test. To become high king, a man must not only be able to achieve his own climax but must also be able to fully satisfy the high priestess of Tara. Currently Aisling.

Two young priestesses dressed in white draped a robe of seven colors—blue, red, purple, brown, green, yellow, and black—embroidered with solid-gold thread, over Art's shoulders as he stepped from the tub. Brigid bowed as they led him from the great hall.

. . . . .

Aisling stood in her receiving chamber with twelve of her priestesses, issuing final instructions. Three turned to one another, whispering conspiratorially. A bed had been placed in the center of the room. The fireplace was at full roar. There was a knock on the door, causing the priestesses, their white robes swirling, to quickly position themselves around the room as required witnesses. Aisling stood by the bed. One priestess glided to the door and slowly opened it.

Art entered alone. He strode straight to Aisling, proud, confident. Confidence that was reinforced as two priestesses removed his robe, revealing the ready state of his erection. One priestess gave a sly but obvious gesture at his phallus, eliciting giggles from several of the others as Aisling had instructed them to do.

"Be quiet," Aisling said lightly, spinning around. "Quiet. He is . . . adequate." In light of his rapidly diminishing state, she added to Art, "Please ignore them. Let me help you, see if I can coax out a bit more size." Aisling reached down and stroked him, but rather than restoring him, she felt the last of his erection fade in her hand.

"Ahhh," flowed around the circle of priestesses. Art glared at them.

"Don't worry," said Aisling. "We have a little time for that to reawaken before the assembly starts to wonder. Here, sit with me and let's talk awhile." She sat on the edge of the bed.

Art scowled at Aisling, whose crooked smile was sending a clear message. Sitting beside her, he asked, "What do you want?"

"Conor needs an honor price," Aisling said.

"Done," said Art. "He can start with twenty cows—make it twenty-five—and I'll include one of my bulls. Then we'll see how good he is at trade."

"No," said Aisling, sliding a few inches away from Art. "He must have an honor price that gives him a seat at your high table. An honor price suitable for the high priestess of Tara's husband, my future husband. Give him the deceased traitor Maolan's land, houses, livestock, and title."

Art laughed. "Maolan's clan would never permit that."

"Maolan tried to betray the Celts to the demon Semjâzâ. Conor stopped him. Maolan's clan should consider themselves lucky you don't take the rest of their lands."

"It was you who stopped Maolan."

"I couldn't have done it without Conor. He's awakening my power. You've become too much of a politician."

"And you ask for too much," replied Art, anger creeping into his voice.

Aisling stood. "I will not lie with a politician. I will only lie with a high king."

"If I don't grant Conor an honor price, even one cow, you won't be able to marry him," Art shot back.

"As you wish," said Aisling. "I'll make my request to tomorrow's candidate for high king."

"What makes you think anyone will agree to this extortion?"

"I defeated a demon!" Aisling shouted, trying to overcome the image of Tadg's torn body that flooded into her mind. "The Morrígna's power is returning in me. Me. Alone. Without my dead sister." A hit of green flashed in her eyes.

"Are you saying that you have the Goddess's full powers?"

"Enough. With time more will emerge," she said, forcing her tone back to calm. "The new high king will need me, given the war you say is coming. The only question is which candidate will be wise enough to see that?"

"And you truly believe the Sidhe will follow you without Anya?"

"There's more chance they will fight for me than you."

Art studied Aisling. A minute crept slowly past.

"Maolan's lands and property shall be forfeit to the high king's estate. I'll grant Conor one half of all this, less one acre and one bull. If he demonstrates good stewardship of these lands and is married to you, he'll be made earl in one year. In exchange he'll swear allegiance to me personally and pay tribute to me of twenty percent of all the estate's income, whether I remain high king or not. Finally, you'll foster your firstborn at my house from his seventh year through his fourteenth."

Aisling moved to stand directly in front of the seated Art. "Our firstborn son, not any daughters," she replied.

"Yes, the firstborn son."

Aisling slipped off her robe. "We have an agreement, then, Your Highness."

Outside the entrance to Tara Tower, a long, grassy courtyard gently sloped down to the royal stables, its edges lined by two-story stone buildings with shops below, residences above. Today the courtyard was flooded with people. Only a small area, halfway down to the stables, remained unoccupied, a circle ringing the Lia Fáil, where the third and final test of the high king took place.

Lia Fáil was a five-foot-tall standing stone, round and phallic, its origin as lost to history as the wells of Tara. From time before memory, the English, Scottish, and Irish kings required a sacred stone for their coronation ceremonies. It provided the king a connection to the earth and its old Gods. Even though the new God, Christ, had usurped much of the old Gods' power in England and Scotland, those two countries still required a stone, though a monarch now sat on it to be crowned. Ireland's stone remained standing, dominant. Tara's French visitors called it *le petit obélisque*.

A few yards from the Lia Fáil, Liam was leaning on Conor's shoulder. "Damn, you're heavy," said Conor, holding the bandage around his injured ribs.

"Sorry," said Liam, shifting his weight. "I still don't have my legs back."

"Go lean on the stone."

Liam shook his head. "You're in a strange mood."

Conor's heart was in a knot, his throat tight. He had never been jealous before, if that was what this was, not when Aisling had lain with Maolan nor with any number of priestesses. But he felt so much closer to her now—bonded to her—and could not stand the thought, the fact, of her lying with someone else, even a high king. And there had been no opportunity to grieve for Tadg, a man who loved him like a natural son and who had died horribly trying to save him. Conor had been too concerned with assuring Aisling that Tadg's death was not her fault, that she could not possibly have defeated Semjâzâ in time to save him. Now, here without her, Conor felt angry and confused.

Shadows grew long. Art and Aisling finally appeared at the tower door. Conor's chest tightened more. Air became scarce. Aisling smiled to the crowd, nodded, and kissed Art. The crowd cheered.

The cheers subsided and the crowd parted, opening a path to the Lia Fáil and the final test. The previous election had been twelve years earlier, and Conor had avoided it, but he had heard. Ireland itself must acknowledge Art for him to become high king. When he places his hand on the Lia Fáil, the land must roar. Well, he, Conor, was not going to add his voice.

Art reached for the head of the standing stone, placed his hand on it. Conor's throat spasmed. He tried to stop it, but could not. He lifted his head to release the cry, which rose uncontrollably within him, as it did within every other person in the yard. The sound radiated out through the city, down the hill, and across the land, as every man, woman, and child, every bird, stag, cow, and sheep, every animal that had a voice, took up the cry and passed it along.

Conor felt a sense of relief and, surprisingly, joy as the spasm left him. He felt Aisling's arms around him. She nuzzled her face against his neck. "My love," she said. "I have a surprise for you." She slid her hand to cover his heart. "My lord."

Busy days followed for Aisling and Conor. Maolan's body was recovered, and with little of his head remaining, his hands and feet were ceremoniously hacked off and burned. The corpse was pressed into a bog.

The pride of Maolan's estates had been a pair of castles, Killeen and Dunsany, which controlled the principal road between Tara and the two southernmost kingdoms, Leinster and Munster, much to the irritation of their nobility. Therefore, upon the announcement that the Maolan clan would forfeit both—Killeen Castle going to the estate set aside for support of the high-kingship, and Dunsany Castle, which was really more of a fortified manor house, going to Conor—the southern nobles lavished even stronger allegiance on their new high king. Art, in turn, let it be known that this move had been in his plans all along.

Queen Gormflaith, ruler of Munster, commissioned both a last name for Conor and a coat of arms for his new, if provisional, lordship, to be recorded in the Tara annals. Conor chose mac Tadg, in honor of the man whom he considered his father and to ensure that Tadg's widow would be recognized as part of his new clan. The chief bard was summoned and produced a coat of arms featuring a green tree and a red arrow on a sky blue shield.

At their wedding in the great hall, Aisling wore a long green dress, elegant in its simplicity, matching the color of the tree on Ireland's newest coat of arms. Conor's white surcoat partially covered his new chain mail, which sparkled in the candlelight as Art performed the ceremony. Aisling and Conor laughed at the absurdity of signing a contract for five years and a day. As soon as the seal was applied to the document, Art embraced the pair of them, and his deep voice resonated through the hall, "Now we celebrate! Bring in the food and wine, lots of wine!"

"One thing we can count on with Art, there'll be a feast at every opportunity," said Liam. He and Patrick waited by the door, away from the thick crowd, which jostled with squires and pages carrying tables, benches, and food.

"I wager ten silver pennies that he leads a drinking song by the third course," said Patrick, snagging a cup from a passing basket and scanning the crowd for a page to fill it.

Rhoswen wedged herself between Patrick and Liam. She addressed Liam without a greeting. "Do you understand that Aisling will still need your protection?"

"She beat a demon!" exclaimed Patrick.

"She is in flux. She must feel secure to continue to develop her powers," said Rhoswen.

"I am grateful for your insight, but don't worry, I don't plan to abandon her," said Liam.

"Conor also. You will stress this to him?" Rhoswen insisted.

"Not tonight, tomorrow. Tell me—"

Rhoswen interrupted, "I will not let that priest talk at me," and slipped away.

Colmcille, leader of the smaller of the two factions of the Irish Christian Church, was pushing his way through the crowd toward the door. Reaching Patrick, he declared, "This should be a Christian wedding."

"Christian weddings are for Christians," replied Patrick. "Besides, pagan weddings are more fun."

"That is all it is to you, isn't it? How much fun you can have?"

"Jesus was always up for a good feast."

"There will be no feast for you in hell," warned Colmcille. "Or for anyone else here."

"I hear that hell features prominently in your sermons of late," said Patrick. "No wonder your congregation is shrinking while mine is growing. You're becoming quite Roman, aren't you?"

"The new Church of Rome will cover the world soon. There's no standing against the true word of God. Look to your own rotting soul, your church is too accommodating— educating women, sanctioning divorce. Your sermons do more harm than good."

"Let's let the Bell decide whose words are true," said Patrick, drawing the Blood Bell from its holster.

"I wasn't going to grace this heathen gathering with my presence anyway," hissed Colmcille as he left.

Patrick noticed that Liam, along with everyone else nearby, was backing away from him. "Don't worry," he said laughingly. "I'm not going to ring it. Let's go find the wine."

· · · · ·

A week later Conor's coat of arms fluttered on a flag above a mounted column of twenty-four Gallowglass. The small force was a gift from King Murchada of Leinster. To this, Murchada added his sealed pledge to support, with his own forces if need be, Conor mac Tadg's right to Dunsany Castle—there was no better way to ensure that the Maolan clan actually turned over the property.

Two wagons of supplies followed, with Tadg's widow driving the first. At the head of the column rode Liam, behind him Aisling and Conor, side by side. Since departing Tara to the cries of a herald, Conor had been wearing the awkwardly furtive smile of a young boy who has been caught eating a stolen pastry, only to learn it was intended for him all along.

The procession had taken the southern road out of Tara. Open fields now lay to both sides. Two curious young shepherds trotted along the side of the road, talking to one of the younger Gallowglass. The road was about to enter Laigen Forest when a Woodwose stepped out.

The air filled with the sharp scrape of swords being drawn from scabbards.

"Hold!" shouted Aisling.

Liam's sword flashed, knocking down an arrow that had already been loosed by one of the Gallowglass.

"Hold!" Aisling repeated.

The Woodwose, an unpainted male wearing a loincloth, carried a severed head. He took several steps forward and tossed the head toward them. It rolled to the forelegs of Aisling's horse and stared up at her with vacant eyes. Aisling recognized the dead face, still contorted, of the Woodwose shaman. She dismounted.

"What are you doing?" objected Conor.

"They seek a new shaman," she answered.

Liam circled his horse back protectively.

Conor studied the Woodwose as Aisling picked up the head and lashed it by its bushy hair to her saddle. He asked, "Why do this? They killed Tadg and almost killed us."

"That's why I need to. They'll follow their shaman to their death without question, so I must become their shaman." Aisling looked up at Conor. "And you must become their lord." She wiped a smear of blackened, sticky blood from her hands. "They'll be a powerful ally for you, to the exclusion of all other nobles. What they lack in organization and weapons they make up for in fearlessness and ferocity."

"She has a point," offered Liam.

Aisling walked toward the Woodwose while Liam watched. Conor pulled his bow from its pouch behind his saddle and fitted an arrow but did not draw. When Aisling stood in front of the Woodwose, he dropped to his knees and bowed his head. A line of Woodwose, men and women, materialized from the trees, moved forward, and dropped to a supplication pose. Then another line, followed by more, until more than two hundred, Aisling estimated, knelt before her.

One hundred forty-six miles north, on the coast of Ireland, large waves crashed through the soaring, arched mouth of Dunkerry Cave, an entrance that rivaled any cathedral's. Its crimson-hued galleries extended far under land, briefly dipping beneath the dark water before emerging to form a vast cavern.

In the cavern, scattered torches did little to push back the darkness. Carvings of the sea-serpent-shaped God Seonaidh glistened faintly on the damp walls. There was just enough light to reveal blood dripping from open wounds on the Fomorian's strong arms and chest, staining his white sable cloak as he sat, for the first time, on the stone throne of the Fomorian high king. At his feet lay the broken body of his predecessor. The new high king reached down, ripped out the single engorged eye of the former ruler, and held it aloft, his own single eye looking out at the four thousand Fomorian warriors kneeling before him.

15

Propped up in bed on a copious pile of purple silk pillows, Queen Anne watched de Vere getting dressed. Opening the chamber door, he glanced back at her. She smiled, a smile he returned, and then he left. Anne looked down at Richard, his head in her lap, eyes closed, and stroked his hair. Richard curled up tighter against her bare body.

"Our pretty king," she cooed. "We hate that Our lovely friend had to run off to a war council meeting. Such a tedious errand."

Richard nuzzled her lap and whispered, "He must prepare for the invasion."

"You and he are spending altogether too much energy on these plans. We are not happy that there is less time for Our games. How hard will it be to defeat the faeries? There cannot be that many of them—We have never even seen one."

Richard opened his eyes. "Our sweet queen, do not be cross. You have not seen a faerie because the Romans drove them out of southern England a millennium ago. However, Longshanks had to fight them in Wales, and he recorded that they were quite fierce. We have been reliably informed that there are a lot of faeries in Ireland, as well as Celts. You would be happy We are making such efforts to protect de Vere's force and make sure he comes back to Us, if you heard what happened during the last attempted invasion. We cannot afford to repeat that disaster."

❧

TWO CENTURIES EARLIER, twenty miles off the Irish coast, gray clouds closed in on the sun, building a midday gloom. A quarter mile ahead of Strongbow's flagship, enchanted waves suddenly sprang up thirty feet and tossed themselves about, forming turbulent fortifications spanning the horizon, blocking the armada's route to Ireland.

"Time to earn your kingdom back," Strongbow said to Diarmait, the exiled king of Leinster.

Diarmait removed his cloak, handed it to Strongbow's marshal, Robert Fitz-Stephen, and strode to the prow. Spreading his arms wide, he began to chant. At first nothing happened, but then a wide channel of calm opened up in the wild sea ahead. Strongbow's armada sailed easily into it.

Pope Adrian IV had issued the Laudabiliter grant authorizing Henry II, the Norman king of England, to invade Ireland. As tempting as the Vatican's offer was, Henry did not act upon it for a decade, not until the apparently blessed event of Diarmait's eviction from Ireland and arrival in Henry's court. By demonstrating a few simple enchantments, Diarmait convinced Henry that he would be able to perform the rite necessary to land an invasion force safely on the Irish shore. So with great confidence, King Henry, having also secured the Vatican's payment for the nine-hundred-sixty-man mercenary army, launched an armada at Ireland under the command of Richard de Clare, second Earl of Pembroke, known as Strongbow. With him went his marshal, Robert Fitz-Stephen, illegitimate son of the constable of Cardigan.

Robert watched as a wave rose up above the port rail only to fall harmlessly away from his ship and, for the first time since hearing of this plan, allowed himself to smile. Clapping Strongbow on the back, he said, "I'm looking forward to plenty of Celtic ale, and I hear their women—" He did not finish.

A loud crash reverberated from off their starboard bow as one of the other ships hit a colossal rock that had not been there a moment earlier. Robert glimpsed two young women astride its peak, their long red hair streaming out behind them in the rising wind. One reached out in the direction from which his ship had come, and her hand made a gesture, leaving a glowing trail in the air. He looked back. A wall of water rushed down the channel behind him and washed over the trailing ships, causing them to flounder, spilling men over the side. The women—Robert saw that they were twins—began to direct a symphony of rising waves and rocks. His flagship tossed and spun. A green-tinged, manlike Fomorian climbed over the rail, seized the sailor at the ship's wheel, and dragged him over the side. Strongbow grabbed the wheel and fought the waves for control.

Robert drew his sword just in time to thrust it into the chest of a Fomorian charging at him. He kicked the dying beast off his blade. The flagship ran up against the side of another ship that was overrun with the creatures, and he heard the screams of its men. Robert severed the head of a Fomorian lunging for Strongbow and yelled, "We have to turn back!"

"Which way is back?" shouted Strongbow.

Both men were knocked to the deck as the ship struck one of the rocks that were now everywhere. With a groan the ship started to list. Strongbow's personal guards gathered around him and were holding their own against the Fomorians. "Get to the longboats!" Robert shouted. They managed to launch two of the boats, carrying Strongbow, Robert, Diarmait, and sixteen other survivors, before the ship sank.

The following dawn Robert squatted in the tree line and looked out across the marshy foreshore toward the water. Waves had driven the wreckage landward, where it clogged Bannow Bay. Throughout the night survivors had crawled out of the bay through the marsh and into the woods, having made it to shore on a collection of planks, longboats, and, remarkably, one almost intact ship. Robert waited another hour, but no one else emerged from the water, so he made his way to back to the clearing where Strongbow and Diarmait had assembled the survivors. In all, about a quarter of the men had made it.

"Any more men?" asked Strongbow.

Robert shook his head and asked Diarmait, "Do you know where we are?"

"I'm sure we're between Wexford and Waterford, Viking ports," replied Diarmait. "There's a dry riverbed just to the west of us that must be the Scar, but it's never run dry before."

"Which port is closer?" asked Strongbow.

"If that's truly the Scar River, then Wexford's less than a day's walk to the northeast."

"So we go to Wexford," said Strongbow, looking up at the clear sky to get a sun bearing. "The Vikings might be persuaded with the promise of enough gold to return us to England. With luck we can slip by the Sidhe and Celts without being noticed."

"There'll be no such luck. They know where we are," said Diarmait. "It was the Morrígna twins that sank the fleet. We won't be able to hide from them."

"We have no choice," said Strongbow. "How are the men set for weapons?"

"They have what they were wearing when we were attacked—a sword or a dagger or both," replied Robert. "We managed to salvage five sets of mail, sixty shields, thirty bows, and maybe six hundred arrows from the surviving ship. But we have no fresh water. Fomorians got to the casks, and they were spoiled."

"Organize the men. We make haste to Wexford. There should be plenty of water on the way."

The company did not find Wexford or water. They walked for ten hours, using the sun for bearing, without seeing a sign of a Celt, a Sidhe, or even a farmhouse. Worst of all were the three wells they found. Sunlight glinted on the water at the bottom—they could smell it, drop a stone and hear it splash—but even with all the rope they could piece together, the bucket always came up dry. At the third well, one man attempted to leap in and had to be pulled back by his friends.

Finally Strongbow called a halt to the slog. They scraped together a meager meal consisting of the last of their salvaged provisions and sucked the moisture out of a few wild turnips and radishes they had found.

A shrill wail penetrated their skulls. Men leaped to their feet, swords in hand, peering around through the gathering gloom.

"What's that?" shouted Strongbow to Diarmait.

"Banshee, messenger of death."

A tall woman appeared, walking among the trees, gray hair floating in the air about her gray cloak over a green dress. She looked at Strongbow with eyes red from weeping. Her mouth opened, became impossibly large, and emitted another wail. Three men rushed at her. They found only mist. The Banshee started up again in another direction.

Surrounded, submerged in wailing, the men tried to cover their ears but found no relief as the cry rose and fell for three hours. Then it stopped. The entire company collapsed, exhausted, in a fitful sleep without even posting a guard.

The sun rose on a fresh crisis. Twenty men were missing. Trails of blood led deep into the trees. A nervous scouting party was sent out and quickly returned to report that the bay where they had washed up the day before was just a hundred yards away. They had been walking in circles.

"Diarmait, this is your homeland. You have to find us water," demanded Strongbow.

"It must be the Sidhe. They're not letting the company leave this wood."

"Then go get water and bring it back."

"I know an enchantment that should enable a few of us to get out," Diarmait said. "No more than five. Me, Robert, and three others. We'll take all the buckets and rope."

The group headed west to connect with the course of the river Scar. When they reached its bank, the riverbed appeared to have been dry for an eon, even though, maddeningly, they could hear water running as if the river flowed just around the next bend.

"Pick a sprig of heather and place it in your hair," ordered Diarmait. "Then remove your boots. We can carry them in one of the buckets."

The men looked uncertainly at one another.

"Do it, if you ever want to leave this wood alive."

Robert found a patch of heather and plucked a sprig. Securing it in his hair, he sat on the dry ground and began to pull off his boots. The other men followed his example. Diarmait drew a six-inch circle in the dirt, had each man gather what moisture he had left in his mouth and spat into it. There was just enough for Diarmait to work a layer of mud, in which he drew a complex symbol. Scooping up the mud, he smeared a small amount on each man's feet, then his own.

"This may get us past the Sidhe and out of this trap," he said without emotion.

"Or get us killed trying," added Robert.

"That's right," said Diarmait. He decided to head north and keep the riverbed close on their left to ensure that they did not again travel in circles. After three hours of walking, never losing sight of the dry riverbed, or escaping the sound of flowing water, they broke free of the trees. Spread out ahead of them were large fields divided by a network of stone walls. A mile or more to the east, away from the river, they could see the top of a round tower that signaled the presence of a monastery. The small group turned toward the tower, sliding along the field walls to stay out of sight.

The medium-size monastery consisted of the tall round tower, a stone sanctuary still under construction, and three thatch-roofed buildings with plaster walls. The largest of these was marked as the old sanctuary by a tall stone Irish Christian cross, a merging of the Roman Christian cross with the Celtic Sun God, some said the Moon Goddess, though it could be both. Perhaps even the cross itself was not from the original Roman Church, as cruciform elements were common in both Celtic and Sidhe ritual practice centuries before Christ was born. The sound of harp music and singing drifted from the old sanctuary. In the courtyard, clearly visible through a wide gap in the unfinished outer defensive wall, was a well.

Crouching behind a hedge, Diarmait whispered, "It's unlikely an enchantment protects their well."

"Let's seize this monastery and shuttle water back to the company," said Robert. "Is the heather still in my hair?"

"That enchantment only hides you from Sidhe and won't work here. Besides, we can't capture this monastery, as Celtic monks are often armed, and we don't know how many there are. We'll just quietly slip in and take what water we can carry."

At that moment a young woman bearing a wooden tub walked out of the smallest building and over to the well. Singing softly along with the drifting music, she unlaced her dress, slipped the top off her shoulders, and rolled it down to her waist. She filled her tub from the shallow well, set it on the stone ring, bent forward, and began washing her long black hair.

Music from the old sanctuary fell away, chanting rose in its place. "We must be quick," whispered Diarmait. "They've started the Sext prayers, and they don't last long. Careful, though, there may be a watch in the tower."

"I'll cover the tower," said Robert, fitting an arrow into his bow. "You three"—he indicated the soldiers carrying two buckets each—"to the well. If it won't let you draw water, make the woman do it. Diarmait, you stay with me, and as soon as we have the water, lead us back to our camp. Go now."

The three men ran to the outer wall, paused, and then looped through the opening, quietly approaching the distracted woman from behind. Before they reached her, a monk leaned out from the tower's highest window, shouting a warning. The woman looked up just as one of the men seized her, pressing his dagger to her throat.

Robert stood and loosed an arrow at the monk. It clattered against the suddenly vacant windowsill. An alarm bell began to clang from the tower. The soldier's grip on the woman slipped on her wet skin as she tried to spin away, but her footing failed in the mud and she fell, sliding her neck along the dagger, severing an artery.

The soldiers stared down at the woman as her life flowed out onto the ground, as did a cluster of monks now congregated outside the doorway of the old sanctuary. One, wearing a blue robe with a cream sash around his neck, stepped forward and pulled an iron bell from a leather pouch on his belt.

Diarmait grabbed Robert and yanked him down behind the hedge. "The Blood Bell," he hissed. "That's Patrick."

Patrick rang the Bell at the soldiers who turned to run, but blood was already flowing from their ears, eyes, and mouths. They fell before they passed the outer wall. Diarmait and Robert fled, crouching low out of sight, back toward the woods.

Diarmait and Robert's return without water and without their men further disheartened the company. They had no food left for a meal that night. In the dawn more men were missing. The only sign of them, other than trails of blood, was Diarmait's head in the wooden tub that had belonged to the young woman whom they had killed the day before, an Irish cross branded into his forehead.

Robert sat, his back against a tree, as the sun rose, vacant eyes staring into the woods, waiting. A battle horn sounded in the distance, then a second, a third. More followed. As the sound built, Strongbow called to him, "Get the men up. The end is here."

Robert slowly rose to his feet. He struck the shoulder of one of his remaining men with the flat of his sword. "Get up, all of you. Do you want to die sitting here or die with a sword in your hand? I don't care how tired and thirsty you are. If you want relief, follow me and you'll soon find relief in heaven." None of the men moved. "Or stay here and find out what the Sidhe will do to you." Men began to stand and gather their meager supplies.

"Leave everything but your weapons," said Strongbow. "You'll have no need for the rest."

They had to walk for only a quarter hour before they entered a meadow. The Celtic force waiting on the far side began to laugh. Many mounted Celts made a show of falling off their horses and rolling around on the ground. Others, on foot, sheathed their swords and lounged on the grass. Some of the female warriors exposed their breasts while calling out to the Normans, asking if they needed milk. On horses in front of the Celtic army sat the same two young women that Robert had glimpsed on the rock before the flagship sank—the newly enthroned Morrígna twins of that time.

"Archers," croaked Strongbow through parched lips.

"All of the bowstrings were cut last night," Robert replied.

"Men, this is the end of your suffering. Gather any strength you have left—we charge to our death." Strongbow tried to put some force behind his voice but failed. Still, the last of his men began to advance at a determined, if slow, pace, though no one would consider it a charge.

"That charge calls for one of our own. Send the dancers!" shouted one of the Morrígna twins. A large group of women detached from the Celts. They were not dressed as warriors. In their hands each held three or four darts that were smaller than spears, more like very long arrows. The women curtsied to the Celtic warriors, who bowed in return and then began to sing. The women spun their skirts and danced toward the Normans. Staying just outside the reach of Norman swords, they danced and spun and hurled their darts.

Normans began to stumble with a dart in their leg or arm or shoulder. Only a few died when a dart caught a throat or a chest—killing someone with a dart opened up the thrower to ridicule back in camp. With his men falling around him and a dart in his own thigh, Strongbow tossed his sword away and went down on one knee.

Eight days later, in a field adjoining the Leinster capital city of Fearna, scores of children sat on the top rails of newly erected pens and watched as the thirteen dozen survivors of Strongbow's invading army were sorted by the skills they plied when they were not fighting: carpenters, blacksmiths, masons, fletchers, and cobblers, though most ended up in the general labor pen. From these pens they were led twenty at a time to the slave market and auctioned off. There was little resistance from the men; they had been relieved to discover that in Ireland most slaves earned their freedom.

Strongbow was penned with Robert and a handful of men who could read and write Latin, along with one musician who demonstrated his skill with a flute. Their sale would be the highlight of the day's festivities, which had a distinctively carnival feel. The auction master had been hoping for a poet, but none stepped forward.

When their time came, the men in Strongbow's group, like the others, were required to remove their clothing before being led into the yard of the slave market. Their hands were bound behind them to a ring in one of the many short posts dotting the auction ground. Interested buyers strolled among them, inspecting the wares, writing their bids in blue paint on a particular slave's chest, crossing out any previous bid.

Aoife was interested. The only daughter of Tigernan Ua Ruairc, the current king of Leinster, she had heard of Strongbow's abnormality. As she walked into the market, she could hear the slave crier: "The Earl of Pembroke! Come see why they call him Strongbow!" A large crowd had gathered to do just that, talking excitedly among themselves. "Buy him for your daughter and your grandsons will be renowned throughout the five kingdoms."

Aoife pushed to the front of the crowd and gave a small gasp.

"Let's see this Strongbow in his full glory," she said to her attendants. "Stroke him."

The two girls moved eagerly forward and, with shouted encouragement of the crowd, began to arouse Strongbow. He raised his head and expressionlessly locked eyes with Aoife. She looked at the long list of bids that already ran down his chest to his abdomen and, turning to the slave master, asked, "How long until bidding on this one closes?"

"If my lady would like to make a fair offer, we'll call the auction complete."

Aoife took the small brush from him, crossed out the last bid, and wrote another, twice as high.

Strongbow's appeal to Aoife extended beyond her bed, for she married him a year later, and a year after that he was elected king of Leinster. When King Henry heard that Strongbow had become a king, he thought he finally had a powerful ally among the Celts. But when his envoy arrived, delivered by the Vikings under a flag of truce, he discovered that Strongbow had become Irish and had no interest in helping the English.

❦

"So that's why Strongbow was his nickname," Anne said with a laugh. She stopped abruptly and frowned. "Are you sure de Vere will be safe?"

"We will make sure of it, my sweet queen, by sending the largest army by far that has ever sailed aginst Ireland, ten times the size of Strongbow's force. All paid for by the pope's Jews."

"But tell Us, Our noble king, does de Vere really have to meet with Jews, and in Our palace? They make Us uncomfortable."

"They bring gold and silver, more than We can trust with anyone but de Vere."

The Jewish financiers were delivering the first installment of funds for the Irish campaign. The Vatican had agreed to send Richard a total of over four hundred thousand pounds, a sum many times more than the Crown's annual peacetime tax revenue. Anne had already ferreted out this information. Resisting pressure from the Exchequer to cut her lavish expenses, which were blamed for the Crown's deficit the previous year, Anne had cornered de Vere a month earlier with pointed questions about the agreement with the Vatican. Looking through the figures during one of their private sessions, she had quickly identified a portion of the budget with the most potential.

"De Vere tells Us that a large amount is being provided for new ships. More than one hundred thousand pounds."

Richard sat up and studied her face. "Does he? Well, We must have a fleet of ships for the invasion. What are you plotting?"

"Our dear king, can you not just press merchant ships into service?"

"Of course. We can do as We like. But, Our clever queen, by building new ships We buy the support of the high guilds, particularly the shipwrights and blacksmiths."

"You are their king. They have no choice but to support you."

"Even a pressed ship has the legal right to a charter fee, and many of them would need expense for refitting."

"We are told that the charter fee is but ten pounds, and how much refitting will really be required for such a short journey?" She slid one of her delicate hands between her legs and began to stroke herself. "We are hoping, Our kind and generous husband, that you will consider transferring forty thousand to Our allowance. It would be but meager compensation for having to suffer through your distraction and de Vere's coming absence."

"No," he said, watching her movements.

She continued to touch herself, looking at him, knowing that his no was a playful no.

He leaned against her body, embraced her. Placing his head against her small, sharp breasts, he said, "We will transfer fifty thousand to your allowance, Our queen."

For the second time that afternoon, Anne brought herself to climax while Richard watched.

The next morning Richard strode into the crowded chamber that had been set up as a war room. De Vere, Mortimer, and the Earl of Nottingham, Richard's appointed war council, were standing at the counting table laughing at some comment when the steward announced Richard's arrival. All in the room hurriedly bowed. With a casual wave of his hand, Richard motioned for them to rise and joined his earls. De Vere would command the invasion with Mortimer as his second, while Nottingham had been appointed marshal and would led the troops in battle.

The chancellor of the Exchequer was laying out small gold and silver bars on one end of the counting table, the bars that de Vere had received from the Vatican's Jews in exchange for an unsigned note from the Crown. Next to them was a stack of wooden bars, blanks, signifying the balance of the funds the Vatican had agreed to provide.

Down the length of the table, squares had been marked off with white paint and labeled by account, including ships, mustering, horses, staples, and supplies. Wages, one of the largest expenses, were divided among knights, archers, infantry, and retainers. At the far end of the table was an unlabeled square, which everyone knew belonged to Richard. The game was simple: the more money that ended up in Richard's square, the more Irish land would be granted to each of the three earls of the war council.

As the chancellor double-checked the stacks of gold, silver, and blanks against his ledger, Richard walked around and stroked the end of the table where his box, waiting for its gold, was marked off. "Chancellor, did you bring your pot of white paint?" Richard asked.

"Yes, Your Royal Majesty, of course."

"Then bring it over here and make another square next to Ours."

The chancellor motioned to one of his assistants, who hurried over with a small paint pot and marked off a new square.

"Not as large as Ours, you fool. All right, now give Us that brush and move out of Our way." Richard scrawled *"50,000"* next to the new square. "Chancellor, this is for Our queen."

"As you direct, Your Royal Majesty."

"Well, go ahead, move counters into it." Richard tossed the brush at the chancellor, who caught it clumsily, white paint splattering onto his sleeve. "And it would be better for you if We did not hear that you are bothering Our queen again about her expenses."

"Of course, Your Royal Majesty. My only concern was for your—"

Richard cut him off with one of his waves and turned away from the counting table to the map table. Fifteen feet long and six feet wide, the tabletop was painted with a map of England and Wales, showing each county and its sheriff. Several scribes hovered nearby with small pieces of parchment on which would be listed directives to the sheriffs or commitments received from them. The parchment notes would then be pinned onto the relevant county.

Nottingham began to speak. "Your Royal Majesty—"

Only to be interrupted by de Vere, who placed a hand on his shoulder and said, "I am sure we will find fifty thousand for the queen."

Richard glanced at de Vere with a smile. "You will find it and more from the ships' allowance. We have decided to press merchant vessels into service."

"What of the shipwright contracts already signed, Your Royal Majesty?" asked Mortimer gently.

"Yes, what of the shipwrights? Tell Us, de Vere, and the promises made to the blacksmiths," Richard replied. Almost half the two-hundred-pound cost of a new sixty-five-ton troopship was for forged-iron clinch nails.

All eyes turned to de Vere. "We will exchange the shipwright contracts for generous licenses for timber from Ireland. Any contracts the shipwrights have already placed with the blacksmiths for nails will be exchanged for arrowhead contracts. We will need—what did you say, Nottingham?—a million and a half arrowheads?"

Nottingham nodded.

De Vere continued, "Also, with contracts for modifications to the merchant ships and orders for new arms, armor, and supplies, the high guilds will be supportive enough of the invasion."

"So We direct," said Richard, and the scribes began scribbling. "Come, Nottingham, show Us how you will prepare."

The men gathered around the map table. "Finding that many suitable ships and making any needed modifications will take some time," said Nottingham.

"You have twenty-four months until the fleet sails, no longer," Richard replied.

Nottingham called his secretary forward and directed while

pointing at the map, "Dispatch surveyors to all ports from Thames to Exeter plus Somerset, Devon, Cornwall, Bristol, and Lancashire. Add the ports in Wales as well. They're to inspect all ships from sixty to one hundred tons and compile a list of those suitable for the transport of troops or horses and any modifications required. A separate list is to be made of ships from forty to sixty tons for the transport of supplies. All reports are to be received by my office within the next three months."

"Good," said Richard, smiling and rubbing his hands together. "This will be a fun game. If Our new Sidhe allies come through, then any old ship can make the short crossing."

"And if these faeries cannot protect our ships, Your Royal Majesty?" asked Nottingham.

"Then no ship, not even those newly built, can survive the crossing, and your son will be most pleased at his early inheritance."

Nottingham laughed, as was required. "On another matter, Your Royal Majesty, may I have your warrant to conscript supplies, men, and horses? An allocation has been drawn up by county, and it just awaits your approval to send word to the sheriffs." Nottingham held out a document, which Richard did not take.

"You can conscript the men and the supplies, but not the horses. We do not want the sheriffs to send us their old, broken-down nags. You will pay one pound apiece for young, fast mounts. And let the sheriffs know that if any but their fastest are sent, they will incur a penalty of Our design."

Richard walked back to the counting table. All squares remained empty except for the queen's, which contained a stack of blanks and two small gold bars from the Jews' initial payment. Richard picked up the gold. "We shall deliver this to Our queen."

The assembly bowed as Richard left. To replace the bars, an officer of the Exchequer set two blanks, each bearing a gold dot, in the queen's square and painted a red stripe on them to signify that payment had been made.

The war council gathered around the counting table and conferred with the Chancellor and his officers. Figures were consulted and discussed. Squares began to be filled.

They knew that transport was not going to be as simple as Richard had said. Tonnage had become the standard measure of shipping, a ton being the capacity to carry eight full wine barrels. While any old ship could indeed act as a troop carrier, it would need to be at least sixty tons to be efficient. The two dozen ships designated for the vanguard would also need bow and stern castles added to protect archers during the landing. However, most of the refurbishment funds would be spent on transports for the seven thousand horses Richard had decided to take.

As strong as they were, horses possessed fragile legs, and any that arrived injured, sick, or even irritable would be useless to the invasion force. Horses were also expensive. While one pound would buy a spry horse for an archer, a knight's warhorse, trained to charge a forest of pikemen and not flee the mayhem of close combat, cost twenty-five pounds or more. For their transport the largest ships were needed, to which would be added sturdy gangways, stalls, and hurdles, as well as dry-storage lockers for fodder. Fortunately, Kellach had assured de Vere that replacement horses could be captured in Ireland; otherwise several times as many would need to be shipped, as horses were killed at a much faster rate than were their riders.

The need to transport thousands of horses came from the battle plan developed by Richard himself. None of the English infantry, and few of its knights, could survive in close combat against the Irish Gallowglass wielding deadly, long-headed axes. Richard reasoned that mounted archers could quickly reposition and flank advancing Gallowglass, so his bold and unprecedented plan called for using mounted archers with longbows for the bulk of the English force. This also helped alleviate Nottingham's expressed concerns about sending infantry against the Sidhe, as he did not know how good Irish faeries were with a sword. On the counting table, the square for archer salaries was filling; these men would not be conscripts.

As for the Irish light cavalry, mounted on fast hobbies, their bows would be outmatched, the English longbow being able to kill men and horses at a much greater distance.

Increasingly, the longbow was becoming the deadliest weapon in modern warfare, and the English were by far the master of the art. Six and a half feet long, the English longbow was carefully cut from the radius of a yew tree, so that the forward face was sapwood and the belly heartwood. This produced a bow so strong that it could not be drawn the usual way, by pulling back the string, without quickly exhausting the archer's right arm. Instead the string was held steady while the archer bent the bow by laying his body weight into it. Using this method, a trained archer could accurately fire up to six arrows a minute over the course of a sustained battle.

Nottingham moved money for sixty-five thousand sheaves of arrows into the square representing the Privy Wardrobe, the office responsible for arms and armor. Each arrow would be made of poplar and tipped with a bodkin head, which was long and narrow with a specially hardened point. Bodkin-tipped arrows fired from an English yew longbow would pierce chain mail at two hundred yards and light plate armor at one hundred.

The most skilled longbowmen came from Cheshire, and Richard kept them as his personal bodyguards—utilizing the fear of quick, inevitable death that a skilled archer struck in his foes. In their green-and-white livery that bore Richard's white-stag badge, his bodyguards did whatever he commanded for one hundred eighty-six pence a month, an amount equal to the income from a small estate. Richard even found them effective in presenting his request to Parliament, as required by the Magna Carta, for new taxes to finance the Irish invasion, the funds coming from the Vatican being a closely held secret. He sent twelve to stand in the Parliament chamber during the vote, longbow in one hand, arrow in the other.

Four Cheshire archers remained in the war room, hovering about the counting table to protect the gold and act as Richard's eyes and ears. Around the table a lively debate was going on about how much money to allocate to salaries. A force of ten thousand men-at-arms would be raised for the invasion, even though the Vatican paid for fifteen thousand. It would consist of sixty-five hundred mounted archers, thirty-one hundred infantry—primarily pikemen—and four hundred knights. Any men not already in the service of the earls or Richard had to be hired or pressed into service, clothed, equipped, and trained. In addition to de Vere—who held the earldom of Oxford—Mortimer—who held the earldom of March as well as being the designated heir—and Nottingham, the earls of Rutland, Huntingdon, and Gloucester had agreed to participate in the invasion. All the fighting men plus squires, stewards, and retainers, along with their horses, arms, and supplies, would need to be mustered, housed, and fed at Milford Haven, the disembarking point for the invasion scheduled for twenty-four months hence.

The decision to invade in late fall and brave the wet, cold Irish weather was also Richard's. He believed that his archers would be at their most effective when the forests and undergrowth were barren. It would also surprise the Irish, since historically armadas sailed in the calm summer months.

In a particularly poetic moment while lounging in bed, Richard mused to de Vere, "I want you to gallop behind a gale of arrows sweeping away the Irish forces and splash through a river of their blood." Anne's slim, pale hands clapped almost soundlessly while de Vere laughed.

16

What peace, so long as the whoredoms of thy mother Jezebel and her witchcrafts are so many?

—2 Kings 9:22, King James Version

And he [Manasseh] caused his children to pass through the fire in the valley of the son of Hinnom: also he observed times, and used enchantments, and used witchcraft, and dealt with a familiar spirit, and with wizards: he wrought much evil in the sight of the Lord, to provoke him to anger.

—2 Chronicles 33:6, King James Version

Paris, France
December 1392

Queen Isabeau of France was dreaming of Ireland before she awoke to flat, silver light streaming into her opulent bedroom. The first full moon following the winter solstice was framed in a floor-to-ceiling window. Tonight she had made sure her husband, King Charles VI—now known more often as "the Mad" rather than his preferred "the Beloved"—was being cared for by her sister-in-law in his slightly less opulent bedroom on the other side of the royal residence, the Hôtel Saint-Pol, in the fourth arrondissement of Paris. While the nominal seat of government and the court of Charles the Mad was at the nearby Palais du Louvre, the true power of the throne lay here, in Isabeau's shadow court, the witch court, known throughout Europe, by those few who knew, as the High Coven, for which she was the Grande Sorcière.

A small clock on the mantel chimed 2:00 A.M., the time for her witches to gather. Before she could join them tonight, she must renew her bond—a bond through blood and time—to the founder of their coven, as she did after each solstice. Though still exhausted from her most recent trip to Norway, she climbed out of her canopy bed and pulled a silk robe over her nightgown. Gliding across her moonlit bedroom, she approached the wall and pressed a piece of molding. With a click a panel swung open.

The Grande Sorcière entered into a perfectly square, windowless room. In the center, on a small gilded table, a single golden candle burned, filling the room with liquid yellow light. The Grande Sorcière knew that as long as she performed the rite, this candle, first lit by her kinswoman Taddea de la Barthe 112 years ago, would not go out and would not burn down. She sat on a plain wooden chair, gazed into the flame, and began the ritual of remembering.

She was rowing a boat up a river of blood under a dark purple sky, where a sun and a moon spun in a tight arc. Along the black sand bank, row upon row of women, thousands of them, each of them on fire, turned their heads to watch her pass.

She tied the boat to a stone wharf and stepped out onto a staircase, which led down farther than she could see.

She walked down the staircase and entered one of the many doors along its edge.

She was in the body of eight-year-old Taddea, standing at a familiar second-story window at the edge of a large square in a town she knew to be Toulouse in 1275.

She could feel the man's rough hand under her chin, squeezing her face, smell the ale and sausage on his breath as he bent down to her. "You must watch," he growled. The Grande Sorcière and her predecessors did not care enough about him to remember the man's name. "See what happens to your kind, what we've done to your mother."

He thought he was forcing her to watch. He was not; she would have watched anyway. "Some, they start off blubbering, some try to be brave, like your mother, but they all end up thrashing in the flames." He laughed as her mother's thin shift burned away.

It was true, the body that had once held her mother, Angéle de la Barthe, was screaming and flailing against its bonds, tied to a stake in the center of the flaming pyre as a large crowd cheered. What was untrue was that a real witch's body writhed in pain at the stake. It flailed in anguish because its spirit had flown, and the body was lost without it. Before the first lick of flame on skin, Taddea had felt her mother's spirit enter her body, her mother's blood surge within her own veins.

The inquisitor, Hugo de Beniols, had convicted her mother of having sexual intercourse with Satan. That was not true. It had been an incubus. As for the charge of kidnapping infants to feed the monstrous spawn of that unholy union, there had been no spawn. Her mother took the incubus purely for her pleasure, and the kidnapped infants were used to create reagents for a variety of enchantments.

"You'll end up on the stake," the man said, his voice softened, "if you don't please your king. You'd be out there burning now if not for his grace." In the square the body blackened, crisped, and finally stopped moving. The crowd, many holding scented linen handkerchiefs over their noses and mouths, drifted off.

"Come along," the man said, moving his grip to her arm and pulling her away from the window toward the door. "As long as your king, Philip the Bold, holds you under his protection, you'll be safe." The Grande Sorcière felt Taddea make the decision that it was not she who would need protection.

The Grande Sorcière withdrew from the candle flame and smiled. She could feel Taddea's blood, renewed, flowing through her own body.

Taddea had been loaded into a carriage, which took her to the court of King Philip III. At first she had performed tricks to amuse the court and, in private, divinations for Philip the Bold. Soon, though, he had become afflicted with debilitating dysentery, and her role evolved. Taddea became his constant caretaker and spokeswoman, bringing other women into the court to help her. Philip was the first of an unbroken chain of nine French kings who suffered mysterious maladies, a chain that continued with the Grande Sorcière's husband. While poison was often whispered about, suspicion never fell on the women of the High Coven.

As the Grande Sorcière stood, a warm, lustful wave washed through her blood. She would summon the king's younger brother, the duc d'Orléans, to her bedchamber later. First she must meet with her witches. Since Taddea had formed the High Coven during her second year at court, it had always been ruled by her direct descendants, three of whom, like the Grande Sorcière, had become queen of France. The Grande Sorcière left the candle chamber and walked out of her bedroom and down the short corridor to her private audience room.

Valentina Visconti, the twenty-six-year-old wife of the king's younger brother, followed her into the room, trailed by Charles the Mad on tiptoes. The Grande Sorcière gave her a questioning look. Valentina shrugged. "I couldn't shoo him away."

"Your Highness." The Grande Sorcière gave an almost imperceptible nod in her husband's direction.

"What? How can you see Us?" Charles cried. "We are made of glass. It must be these clothes, you can see Our clothes." Charles began to pull at his clothing.

"Be careful, Your Highness, you may shatter yourself," said Valentina.

Charles froze.

"Take him over to the corner," said the Grande Sorcière.

"Come, Your Highness, I will help you undress." Valentina carefully led Charles away.

Valentina had come to the Grande Sorcière's attention through the system of lower covens spread throughout Europe. At the age of fourteen, Valentina had poisoned her first son, illegitimate and unbaptized, to harvest his blood and fat to make an ointment that allowed her to travel long distances very quickly without being seen. It was this difficult spell that created the false but growing rumor that witches could fly. At fifteen Valentina was initiated into the High Coven; when Valentina was nineteen, the Grande Sorcière arranged for her to marry the king's brother; and at twenty she was appointed by the Grande Sorcière as the coven's new Keeper of the King.

The other members of the coven rose and bowed to their Grande Sorcière in greeting.

Joanna of Navarre, also twenty-six, had, when she was but seven, sewn her sleeping father, King Charles "the Bad" of Navarre, into his bedsheet, doused it with brandy, and lit it on fire. While her father squirmed, screamed, and burned to death, she collected his flames into blue glass boxes. Death flames were the most powerful reagent that could be extracted from an adult human and were used in spells to make the living do anything commanded, but only for a short time, until the flames consumed their internal organs. They could also be used to make the freshly dead talk.

Béatrix de Montjean, seventeen, nursed her daughter, Catherine. The Grande Sorcière could already sense power emerging in the infant. Béatrix was adept in the preparation of potions and poisons, items always useful at court. She was also the coven's wet nurse. The Grande Sorcière's own infant daughter, Michelle, was sleeping in a crib beside her chair.

From the corner Charles watched Béatrix move her daughter from one breast to the other. "Polish Us," he murmured to Valentina as she carefully removed the last of his undergarments. "We must be perfectly clear."

"As you wish, Your Highness," replied Valentina. "Joanna, please bring an empty vial over."

Matteuccia de Francesco clapped her hands. "Back to your lessons," she ordered the three young girls standing next to her. Matteuccia, a sixteen-year-old former Italian nun, had become known as the Witch of Ripabianca due to her success in necromancy, the art of divining through and animating the dead, even those long passed. She had been brought into the High Coven a year earlier as tutor to the Grande Sorcière's daughters.

The Grande Sorcière sat at a table off to one side of the large room, where Joanna joined her. A young eunuch, illiterate and mute—his tongue had been cut out—served them hot spiced wine while a similarly maimed boy brought a gold platter stacked with small fig pies and balls of puffed dough covered with honey.

"We dreamed of Ireland again," said the Grande Sorcière, selecting a pastry.

"Have you divined meaning in these dreams, Your Highness?" asked Joanna.

"Our spies in England tell Us the Vatican has sponsored a full-scale invasion of Ireland for Richard."

"They could not possibly succeed."

"Probably not. But in war there is always opportunity. We must be vigilant for an opening to extend Our influence into England. Or even, given some weakening in their veil, Ireland itself. That is what the dream is telling Us."

The women paused as a platter of cinnamon-custard tarts was added to the table.

"Our coven in Norway grows powerful within their court," the Grande Sorcière continued. "However, Our trip there showed Us that the Nephilim are almost all gone. The Vatican has done too good a job killing them off. It will not be the rich pickings We had hoped. Ireland would be a true prize. If Richard fails, We must find some other channel into that magical land, while there is still magic there to be taken."

"Just imagine the force of a spell powered by the fat of a pure-blood

Sidhe infant," mused Joanna. "I would keep a clutch of their women just to make them."

"That is but a minor part of what We would gain," said the Grande Sorcière. "You must think in much greater terms. We would force the Sidhe to reveal the secrets of their enchantments and their knowledge of using Ardor. We would become powerful without equal."

It was through patience that the High Coven had been built. Bit by bit, king by king, it gained control of the royal family, then the French Church, then the country, building an unassailable power base for the good of the bloodline. But her patience was being tested. Already she had grown the High Coven more than any since its founder, and she hungered to add subjugation of the Sidhe to her legacy.

Cries of "Yes! Oh, yes, keep polishing," came from Charles, interrupting her thoughts. The Grande Sorcière cast an irritated look at Valentina, who smiled and gave one of her shrugs from the corner. In a few more strokes, Charles ejaculated into her hand, then ran out the door yelling, "We are completely clear! We are clear!" His shouts faded down the hallway. Valentina scraped the royal semen off her hand into a vial and sealed it. While spells calling for the seed of a king tended to be more flash than substance, it was always handy to have an ample supply available. Valentina wiped her hand on her skirt and joined them at the table, helping herself to the pastries.

"Valentina."

"Yes, Your Highness."

"Help Joanna gather more death flames. We may have need of them."

"Certainly." Valentina licked custard off her finger. "It is never hard to find people to burn."

⚬

SHORTLY AFTER SUNRISE, in a forested valley of the Wicklow Mountains in east Ireland, an old Celt trudged up the trail grumbling to himself about Sidhe in general and Sidhe witches in particular. He led a black bull by a rope tied around its neck, the only bull he had left, the other having been taken by wolves the previous winter. Now it was to be killed for nothing more than a single Taghairm divination ritual, which required the practitioner to be wrapped in the hide of a freshly skinned bull. But he would have to be witless to turn down a request from a Sidhe witch, especially one from the Adhene clan, and the farmer did not consider himself witless. *A request my arse,* he thought as he spat on the ground. *It was an order.* Then he looked about to make sure the witch had not seen him being disrespectful. An Adhene witch in her green-and-brown paint could be hard to spot in these woods.

A brown hawk soared along the course of the rain swollen river Dargle as it flowed from the eastern slope of Mount Djouce. With a loud screech, she swooped over the crest of the four-hundred-foot cliff the river tumbled down. She circled once and then flapped her descent toward a clearing along the base of the waterfall. The hawk's talons reached for the ground, touched, leaving Rhoswen walking to absorb the momentum of her hawk form.

Rhoswen searched along the river's edge until she found a slender piece of slate and a granite rock the size of her fist. Using the granite, she chipped the slate and within a few minutes created a sharp, jagged edge.

The old Celt approached, removing his hat. He held the bull's rope in one hand while he worried the hat in his other. Somewhat gruffly he said, "Aren't you required to use a wild bull for Taghairm?"

"Let go of the rope," Rhoswen ordered.

The man immediately obeyed.

"There, now he is wild."

Then Rhoswen addressed the bull. "Your master is unhappy. I must wrap myself in your skin, but that would leave him without your services for his cows. Will you consider just loaning me your skin?"

The bull craned its neck and let out a bellow.

"I hope your master remembers what you have done for him today."

The bull snorted.

"Do not worry, I will shed my own blood so you do not have to." Rhoswen pulled the flint blade across her palm, and a narrow stream of blood splattered on the ground. She smeared her hand across the bull's neck, leaving a red trail, then pressed her palm between its eyes.

She was looking out of the bull's eyes. There was no Sidhe witch standing in the clearing, only an old man with an astonished face. She gazed into the spray from the waterfall, lit with sunlight diffused through thin clouds. White mist filled her vision. She focused on her love for her homeland, and the core of the mist thickened into the shape of Ireland. She asked four questions: When will the English attack? What magical forces aid them? How can the Sidhe stop it? Will Aisling be able to help?

Sections of mist began to solidify and form not one but several shapes. Before they became identifiable, the mist faded from the lower part of her vision as a gust of black wind scattered it from the upper part. Soon only one strand of light was left, squirming like an injured serpent while it illuminated a solitary three-leaf clover, which she, as the bull, ate.

Rhoswen stood again in the clearing, squeezing her fist tight to stop the flow of blood. "The answer to a question I did not ask, few answers to the ones I did," she said to the bull. "I do not know whether to thank you or skin you. Go back to your cows."

The old man walked backward bowing, repeating, "Thank you! Thank you!" He turned and fled, leading his spared animal away.

Rhoswen wondered what she was going to tell her father, King Fearghal. Little had been revealed that would help him prepare the Middle Kingdom. Only that there was more than one threat, that many sources were working to blind foresight of how things would unfold, and that there was no way to predict if the outcome would be good or bad for the Sidhe.

There had been no answers, not even hints, about Aisling, which was not surprising given her transitory state. Aisling's fate was in her own hands—and perhaps the fate of Ireland, at least in the short term.

Rhoswen walked along the river, contemplating the signs. The final vision—the one of her consuming a three-leaf clover illuminated by a strand of light in the form of an injured serpent—appeared to signify that if the Morrígna was ever to fully return, she, Rhoswen, must hold space for the Goddess, but that it would not be an easy task. And there had been no signs to indicate how long this might take—one year, one hundred years, one thousand years—if the Morrígna returned at all.

She had spent her young life, barely two centuries, absorbed in her studies of Sidhe enchantments, and humans were largely a mystery to her. But it did not take divination for her to see that foreign humans would be Ireland's greatest threat over time. If the Morrígna was sending her a message, was truly giving her a mission that might last a millennium, then she needed to learn more about human ways. Maybe it was time, she thought, to take a human mate, or at least one who was half human.

17

The ark was of small compass, but yet even there Ham [Noah's son] preserved his book detailing the arts of magic and idolatry [taught him by Enoch].

—Herbert de Losinga, the first bishop of Norwich (1119)

Before his death, he [Enoch] entrusted it [Book of Raziel] to Shem and Ham, and they in turn to Abraham. From Abraham it descended through Jacob, Levi, Moses, and Joshua to Solomon, who learnt all his wisdom from it, and his skill in the healing art, and also his mastery over the demons.

—Book of Jubilees (circa 100 BCE), Dead Sea Scrolls

Rome, the Papal States
February 1393

Jordan pushed through the tempest. Rain driving horizontally stung his face. Mud sucked at his boots, making each step increasingly difficult, as the ashes of Christians burned on this spot in Nero's Circus attempted to pull him down to join them in the earth of Rome. Lightning lit the world of stark stone temples around him. Darkness returned. Lightning crashed against it; dark pushed back, faster and faster until light and dark existed together, spinning around him. An ancient obelisk of red granite rose behind one of the Christian temples. Lightning snaked from the gilt ball on top and struck his black armor. White fire crawled across its engraved surface, and, to his dismay, his armor began to melt away.

"Are you all right, Marshal Jordan?" asked the legate.

Jordan blinked. He was standing ankle-deep in mud on a clear, windless February morning. Beside him stood the legate, his robes gathered up in both hands, almost to his knees, with a quizzical look on his face.

"I'm fine, just . . . breakfast must have disagreed with my stomach."

The legate gestured toward a shallow ditch on the edge of St. Peter's Square where men and women were squatting to relieve themselves. "If you need to empty your bowels, hurry. The VRS are not men you want to keep waiting."

"No. I'll be all right."

They continued trudging through the mud, weaving between stalls that sold everything from dubious religious artifacts for plague protection to rapidly decaying pig heads for soup. Bordering the square to the west stood St. Peter's Basilica, built over the Tomb of the Apostle by Emperor Constantine in 327 but abandoned while Avignon held the papacy. Clearly in disrepair, its mildew-speckled wooden roof sagged in several places. Since the papacy had been restored to Rome fifteen years earlier, the Vatican had been focused on using its new military force to expand its control in Europe, leaving few funds for restoration. Though Jordan did notice workmen in one corner of the square starting to lay paving stones.

Lurking just to the right of the basilica was a small fortress built two centuries earlier by Pope Innocent III, now the headquarters of the VRS League and residing place of the Ring of Solomon.

Jordan glanced up at the fortress, his destination, and a gale buffeted his soul, lightning flashed in his consciousness, and he understood why Najia had been scared for him, scared of the Ring, scared that he would not leave Innocent's fortress alive. She had spent the night weaving a protective enchantment about him, an intricate spell known as black armor.

⊗

THAT MORNING Jordan had awoken at sunrise in his room at the Palace of the Lateran on Piazza San Giovanni in southeast Rome to find Najia standing at the window, exhausted and angry.

"'In the beginning was the Word, and the Word was with God, and the Word was God,'" Najia recited. "But the Word didn't stay with God, did it? Men took it."

"Is it wise to utter blasphemy here, so close to the VRS League?" Jordan asked, suppressing a yawn as he climbed out of bed. They had sailed from Conwy Castle to Venice, then, after several months awaiting orders, had ridden here, arriving late the previous night.

Najia glared at him, her eyes red and tired from a night of weaving the black-armor spell. "The Church's sorcerers, these exorcists, what power they cannot gather to themselves and control, they seek to destroy." She looked back out the window, across Rome toward the Tiber River and, on the other side, Vatican Hill. "Concealed inside their stone temples, they try to manipulate words of power, words from the original grimoires written by demons and angels. Ever since Archangel Raphael mistakenly persuaded God to reveal these secrets to mortals, mortals who learned them began to think of themselves as Gods. They become corrupted."

"I've read plenty of grimoires, and I've not been corrupted." Jordan unwrapped his new tunic and held it up for inspection.

"You haven't read any grimoires like the ones the VRS possesses. Those books corrupted even Moses and Solomon. No wonder they hid them. But they shouldn't just be hidden, they should be destroyed." Najia held Jordan's face in both hands, stared into his eyes. "Don't let them tempt you with those books. It's important—swear to me you won't read even a page."

"I'm surprised you're more concerned about books than about the Ring of Solomon," said Jordan. He gave her a peck on the lips, then ⁿlled away and put on his boots.

" ᵃ Ring is another too-powerful relic." A shudder visibly passed   'ᵴ body. "Cast by angels, it was never meant to be kept   ⁺ᵴ don't know its subtlety or how to control it. I   said, pointing toward the Vatican. "Like a sandstorm abrading my soul. That's how they use it, as a crude, blunt instrument to repel demons, Nephilim and . . . witches."

"But your enchantment will protect me from the Ring, no?"

"I'm not sure." Najia began to cry, something Jordan had never seen. He gathered her into his arms, held her head to his chest, and stroked her back.

"I'm scared. Aren't you scared? The VRS is growing so powerful," she mumbled, her tears spotting his new tunic.

"What are you scared of?" he whispered.

"I've seen into your soul, seen your connection with Ardor growing. If they see it, if the Ring reveals it to them, they'll kill you. They'll tie you to a stake and burn you."

"They can't hurt me. I'm marshal to the legate." As he said it, Jordan felt his confidence wavering. "I must go. The legate commands it. I'll be fine."

A few more sobs escaped Najia. Jordan led her over to the small table set with breakfast—a round loaf of bread, some slices of prosciutto, and a jug of water. He kissed her forehead and sat her in a chair.

Najia pulled off a piece of bread and chewed on it while sniffling softly. "I don't know which to be more afraid of, the VRS burning you as a sorcerer or you tempted into joining them so you can learn what's in their grimoires."

HAVING NAVIGATED the muddy square in front of St. Peter's, the legate stepped up onto a stone walkway, brushed out his robes, and strode toward Innocent's fortress. Jordan trailed along behind him, teeth clenched. The closer they came to the fortress, the stronger the force of Solomon's Ring became. Jordan's skin crawled and burned as if a plague of fiery insects were swarming across it, eating away at his black-armor enchantment. When his protective spell was gone, he suddenly felt naked and looked down at himself, relieved to find he was still fully clothed in the silk tunic and leather breeches he had set out in that morning. Trotting to catch up to the legate, he noticed his progress was easier, though his nausea was increasing.

Just as Jordan and the legate were admitted through the gate of the fortress, a bald man in his fifties, no more than five foot two inches tall and half that wide, wearing a simple, rough, brown monk's robe, ran up to them. Blotches of darker brown stained the sleeves. Dried blood, Jordan thought.

"Cardinal Orsini," said the legate, giving a bow to the high exorcist.

"Venerable Brother de' Migliorati," responded Orsini, panting a bit, "or should I just call you 'Legate' now? I am so sorry, I seem to be running a bit late. I was having such an interesting conversation with a witch."

"You no longer imprison the witches here?" asked the legate.

"No. No," said Orsini. "There are too many of them these days, and it is much more peaceful and quiet not questioning them here. You know what they say, 'a witch's scream will pierce stone and bone.'"

The legate said, "Allow me to introduce Marshal Jordan d'Anglano."

Jordan bowed. "Cardinal."

Orsini studied Jordan's pallid face. "The steward will show you to my office. Give me a few moments to change, and I will join you." Orsini trundled down a side corridor, adding over his shoulder, "Please have some wine while you wait."

The steward led them across the inner yard, into the central stone building, and up to an opulently furnished meeting chamber on the third floor. He poured them each a goblet of wine, but Jordan declined and surrendered into one of the thick chairs, his stomach churning. He clamped his jaw shut to keep from losing his breakfast and grasped his knees to steady them.

A few minutes later, Orsini rushed in. "My apologies. My apologies again. When I finally get a witch talking, I lose all track of time." He had changed into a black robe with a black cowl hanging down his back, distinctive to exorcists, and a white surplice with a black silk stole. A gold cross and a silver VRS medallion hung from a chain around his neck. Stuck on the crown of his head was the small red cardinal's cap known as a *zucchetto*. He extended his right hand, now adorned with an ecclesiastical ring, which the legate bowed and kissed.

Jordan pushed himself up out of the chair, gingerly bowed, and kissed the ring, wondering how many people had kissed it since the last time it had been cleaned.

"Marshal Jordan," said Orsini, "I have heard so much about you." Orsini smiled, again studying Jordan's face. "You seem to be struggling. I am not surprised."

Orsini led Jordan over to a large painting of an upward-pointing triangle set over a downward-pointing triangle, together forming a six-pointed star. In the center was written the tetragrammaton, the four-letter name of God, יְהֹוָה YHWH. "You are familiar with the Seal of Solomon?"

"Yes, Your Grace."

"Yes. Yes. Of course you are. It is from the Ring of Solomon. It was twenty-two hundred years ago, almost a thousand years before the birth of Our Lord Christ, give or take. Demons and Nephilim were battling King Solomon, preventing him from building the first temple in Jerusalem, until Archangel Michael brought Solomon a ring bearing this seal to protect the construction of the temple. It turned out that the Ring not only provided protection, it also had the power to force demons to follow Solomon's orders, so he disobeyed Michael and kept it after the temple was finished. The Ring is now secured in this very building to protect the Vatican from all kinds of unholy attacks."

Jordan steadied himself with the back of a chair. It felt as if some creature were eating his intestines from the inside. Orsini continued to smile at him.

"Do you know how the Ring came to be here? I daresay there might not be a building standing in the Vatican today without it."

Jordan shook his head.

"Well, Solomon's son, Rehoboam, had seen that the Ring so

corrupted his father that his father even abandoned the One True God, married a Shunammite witch, and began worshipping pagan idols. Upon Solomon's death Rehoboam sealed the Ring in an ivory box and secretly buried it with his father. However, the Ring was unearthed by the Greek sorcerer Toz Graecus, around two hundred years after the birth of Christ. Graecus found that he could not control it, so he decided to bring the Ring to Rome for guidance. But before he got here, a deep scratch he received from a hawthorn tree festered, and he died of a fever in the hut of a farmhand in San Bartolomeo.

"Legate, you know of this farmhand."

The legate looked thoughtful. "Do you mean Fabian?"

"The very same. Farmhand Fabian had the Ring with him when he came to the Vatican to watch the election of a new pope. While he stood in the commoners' gallery with the Ring of Solomon in his pocket, a dove illuminated by golden light—or, as I suspect, by Michael himself—appeared over Fabian's head. The assembly of cardinals was immediately moved by the Holy Spirit—or, as I suspect, the power of the Ring—to proclaim this unknown layman pope. And Solomon's Ring has been in the Vatican ever since. Here it is kept safe."

Orsini regarded the painting. "The Ring is too close to God. Men, even men as holy as King Solomon, cannot wield it without becoming corrupt. The Ring protects the Vatican, but the Vatican and all men must also be protected from it."

"Except for you," hissed Jordan through clenched teeth. "You're holy enough to be immune from such corruption."

"No. No. No." Orsini laughed. "I am not very holy. The Church knows this, which is how it protects itself from me. But unlike Solomon, I know my weaknesses. It is only a group of imperfect but dedicated men, constantly on the watch for our own corruption and watched over by the Church, who are able to utilize knowledge that is so close to God. And there is more here than just Solomon's Ring. But where is my grace? Marshal Jordan, I have let the Ring cause you distress much too long."

Orsini stepped over to a large wax tablet set in a metal frame on a floor stand next to his desk. Picking up an elaborate silver stylus, he inscribed the seal of Solomon in the upper left corner, followed by a string of words in Aramaic.

"Jordan d'Anglano is the name you were given at birth?"

"Yes," whispered Jordan. He collapsed into the chair.

Orsini paused, stylus poised above the wax. "You know, Marshal Jordan, you have an unusually strong natural talent for enchantments. Of course you know that—you have been practicing. And the stronger your talent is, the more Solomon's Ring affects you."

Jordan, bent over in pain, looked up at Orsini.

"All in preparation for the battles ahead, I am sure, to the greater glory of God and all that. In fact, when you finish in Ireland, you must return here and become one of God's holy warriors: an exorcist of the VRS League."

Through a searing cramp, Jordan managed to whisper, "The legate and I already have an agreement for after the war. Besides, I've met some of your holy sorcerers, and I wasn't impressed."

Orsini gave Jordan his biggest smile. "Ah, yes. The two you killed in Oslo when rescuing your giant friend."

"You killed exorcists?" the legate demanded of Jordan.

"Do not concern yourself, Legate," said Orsini. "They were barely novices." To Jordan he said, "You were born with more skill than they would ever learn. It was fortunate you killed them, because that is what brought you to my attention. And as I know you murdered my men, my offer is more than an offer. But we will talk about that when you return."

Orsini finished inscribing Jordan's name in the wax and added one more complex seal. "There, better?"

All at once Jordan's nausea and pain were gone. He eased himself back into a normal sitting position.

"Good," said Orsini. "Now, hand me that fire iron, would you?"

Jordan rose, pulled the iron out of the fire, its large flattened tip glowing orange, and handed it to Orsini.

"I would not want anyone to see what they should not," said Orsini, passing the hot iron just above the wax, causing the writing to flow and disappear.

"Legate," called Orsini cheerfully, "let me refill your goblet while you tell me how the preparations are going for the last great battle with the Nephilim."

Forty-five minutes later, Orsini, the legate, and Jordan were standing in the corridor outside the meeting chamber.

"Thank you for your report, Legate. I am so happy that my plans are working out. Clearly we should proceed with the final phase," said Orsini, handing him a small sealed letter. "Give this authorization to the commissary general, and he will arrange for the transport of the rest of the gold to England." He clapped Jordan on the back. "The True Church is finally going to Ireland, and you will lead us there. But before you take your leave, allow me to show you our small but impressive library."

Orsini and Jordan strode down the corridor in the opposite direction of the legate and soon entered a room where eight guards snapped to attention.

"What have we got here?" asked Orsini, eyeing a basket on the table. "Ah, lunch. Are you hungry, Marshal?" Orsini removed two packets of lamb wrapped in flat bread, then parchment, and tied with string. He handed one to Jordan. "Put this in your pocket for later. The lamb here is so tender it falls off the bone."

Pocketing the other packet, Orsini unlocked a door in the far wall, held it for Jordan to pass through, and locked it behind them. Twenty feet down a curved stone corridor, they came to a second door, solid iron without a handle or an apparent lock.

"The demon Amelouith is bound into this door," said Orsini. "He protects it from anyone who would open it, even me if I gave him the chance."

Jordan took this as a test and began to mutter an enchantment he had used many times before to enter locked rooms.

"Marshal, do not—"

But it was too late. A slender finger of lightning leaped from the door. Jordan cried out and clutched his chest where a hole had been burned through his tunic.

"My, you are having a difficult day. Dealing with demons is not like manipulating inanimate objects. You must be careful; he is not very friendly."

Orsini pulled a small wax tablet and a silver stylus from his pocket. "Do you know how to say the ineffable name of a demon? Of course not. It is, after all, ineffable and cannot be uttered by any human throat. However, it is only by expressing their true names that you gain absolute control over them, control to do things like bind them into a door. Moses taught us that their true names can be expressed with a seal. Here, let me show you."

Orsini inscribed a complex seal in the wax tablet. The door swung open. Inside was a small stone chamber with three walls lined with half-full bookcases and a fireplace set in the fourth, where coals smoldered. In the center sat a table and two chairs.

Entering the chamber, Orsini spread his arms. "'In the beginning was the Word, and the Word was with God, and the Word was God.'"

"So I have been recently reminded," muttered Jordan, recalling his conversation with Najia that morning.

"Every word that God utters contains power unimaginable to men. God's words are gathered in these grimoires," said Orsini, indicating the library shelves. "An angel's true name has power over that angel, even a fallen angel, because God himself named them." Orsini added another seal to his small wax tablet and tossed it onto the coals. An intense blue fire blossomed. "Which is very handy, as demons and angels can do all sorts of things for you if you force them to, like telling me who killed my men in Oslo." Picking up the three books sitting on the table, Orsini tossed them onto the blue flame. Green, red, and gold sparks flew up the chimney.

Jordan watched parchment pages curl, blacken, and begin to disintegrate.

"There are only two original lines of true grimoires on this earth," Orsini continued. "The closer a book is to one of these lines, the more power its words have." He picked up a set of tongs, fished around in the fire, and pulled out one of the books. The cover boards were charred, but the pages were in perfect condition.

"Ah. I thought so," said Orsini. "This is the quickest method I have found to determine the authenticity of a grimoire. Words of true power do not burn." He dropped the book back onto the table, sending a small cloud of ash floating into the air, then opened it and stroked a delicate page. "Such fine work. Virgin vellum made from the amniotic sac of an aborted calf fetus. This one is worth studying.

"Come and sit. Let us have our lunch. Damn, I should have brought some wine."

"Perhaps you could turn some water into wine?" Jordan ventured.

"But we have no water either. Oh, well. As I was saying, there are two original lines of grimoires. The most recent line originated from Solomon himself. Using the Ring, Solomon gained control of thirty-six demons and bound them into bronze vessels. He forced them to reveal their true names, tell him the evil they and their minions were responsible for, and teach him enchantments. All of this knowledge he recorded in his grimoire, called the Testament of Solomon.

"It was Solomon who first used the term 'exorcist,' derived from the Greek *exorkizein,* meaning the ability to command and bind by oath. It is a delightful ability that I will use with my cache of demons to eliminate one final nagging issue before the English sail forth."

"And that would be?" asked Jordan.

"You must leave me my surprises. Be assured it will be quite the unique event, and I am so looking forward to it." Orsini clutched both fists in excitement. "Anyway, it is also from Solomon's grimoire that the Church gets its directive to protect men from such knowledge, for in the end Solomon knew he was becoming corrupt and yet could not stop it. All he could do was write a warning.

"Solomon's son hid the grimoire away with the Ring, and so it passed from Graecus to Pope Fabian and into the protection of the Church. In fact, this book was the genesis of the VRS League. Unfortunately, Graecus made copies of portions of the material, which we are still trying to gather and destroy. Grimoires do seem to multiply like rabbits.

"It is the role of the VRS League, and soon to be your role, Marshal, not only to battle Nephilim—there are merely a few of those battles left to fight—but also to protect men from knowledge that is too powerful for them. As for those already corrupted, we send them on to God's judgment before they can corrupt others."

"The VRS seems to mainly hunt women these days," said Jordan.

"Ah, well. Much progress has been made, but it does seem that women have a strong tendency toward corruption. They are daughters of Eve after all. And you have killed witches."

"Only the one I witnessed with my own eyes practicing dark arts," Jordan snapped back. "She was killing infants."

"I am sure you only did what you had to do, Marshal. Do not worry, we will find some appropriately dark witches for you to fight— perhaps the High Coven."

"What are you going to do about them? Your emissaries in Oslo weren't exactly successful in forcing those two witches to meet with you. They strike me as formidable."

"The Grande Sorcière was too smart to attend a conclave with me. She knew I would have trapped her in Rome. I will think of something else, after I am finished with the Irish Nephilim. We will have to kill off those witches as well, if we are going to subdue the French Church. But let us return to King Solomon. My time is quite limited.

"There is some indication that Solomon may have also read the

Book of Raziel, the other line of true grimoires, the original line, older and more powerful as it is closer to the first words of God. Archangel Raphael, God's general in this war, was frustrated at having to battle both demons and their Nephilim offspring, who were scurrying around everywhere causing mischief. So, six millennia before the birth of Christ, Raphael talked God into allowing him to enlist man's help, at least with battling the Nephilim.

"Raphael gave Enoch a grimoire, written by the Archangel Raziel, describing how to fight the Nephilim. Raziel, as you surely know, was the Archangel Keeper of Secrets. Raziel's grimoire also contained plans for the Ark, which Enoch shared with his grandson Noah so his family could survive the Flood. Raphael said the Flood was coming to wipe out nine of every ten Nephilim. By the way, Enoch is the only man not to be corrupted by such knowledge, and God decided to take him up to heaven before the Flood, without the benefit of death first, to help administer his legions of angels."

"And what of the book that Enoch himself wrote?"

"That is a very important book, almost a grimoire, but Enoch was careful not to record any of Raziel's more powerful enchantments. Fortunately, Noah's sons, Shem and Ham, preserved the Book of Raziel. Ham also wrote a book describing how to work Raziel's enchantments.

"For centuries it was thought that the books of Raziel and Ham were lost in the Great Flood; however, almost three hundred years ago, Herbert de Losinga, the first bishop of Norwich, discovered evidence in the second-century writings of Celsus that the grimoires had been hidden on the Ark and survived."

Jordan leaned across the table. "Can I see these books?"

"We continue to seek them. What we do now know is that Moses studied them while training to be a magus in the house of Pharaoh Chephren, his adopted grandfather. Moses wrote ten books. The first five are included in our Bible, books of history and teaching. In addition to Genesis—which was derived from Jubilees—there was Exodus, Leviticus, Numbers, and Deuteronomy. The next five are grimoires."

Jordan asked, "And the VRS has these books?"

"Yes. The sixth and seventh books contain instruction for the spells Moses used to win the magic contest with the pharaoh's sorcerers and the magic he worked during the subsequent exodus of the Jews. The eighth book explains how to conjure angels and subdue demons using their true ineffable names. The ninth and tenth books, sometimes called the Sword of Moses, contain lists of symbols corresponding to those names."

Orsini shook his head. "But just like Solomon, without the Church to watch over him too much knowledge corrupted Moses. He thought he could prove his power to the Jews by bringing water forth at the rock at Meribah using an enchantment of his own creation, instead of the one dictated by God. So God punished Moses by taking his life within sight of the promised land."

Orsini wiped his hands on his white surplice and stood dismissively, his lamb roll half eaten. "You should keep this in mind, Marshal. No man, no matter how strong a sorcerer he is, can avoid being corrupted by that much knowledge. He needs the True Church to watch over him, to protect him and pull him back from the brink when necessary."

Jordan rose and followed Orsini out.

"When you return from Ireland, you will have access to all these grimoires, within the safety of the bosom of the Church."

"Thank you, Your Holiness," said Jordan. "You are as generous as you are persuasive."

Upon entering the guardroom, they were greeted by a guard holding a rope binding the hands of a young girl, whom Jordan estimated to be around sixteen. Manacles had worn raw and bleeding rings on her ankles, a gag stretched her mouth back, and her red-rimmed eyes were wide with fear.

"What have we here?" asked Orsini.

"The witch Catherine Simon, from Lugano," said the guard. "I thought you might want to see her before I took her to Castel Sant'Angelo."

The girl shook her head violently, tears streaming down her cheeks.

"Such a small, sweet thing," said Orsini. "We will not need much wood to burn you, will we? Tell me, child, have you ever seen a witch die in the flames?"

The girl began screaming, the sound muffled by her gag. The pungent smell of fresh urine filled the air.

"Oh, my dear girl," said Orsini, stroking her cheek. "Perhaps a mistake has been made. Let us have a quick test—almost painless, really. You see, a fully consecrated witch is bound to fornicate only with Satan. If a girl can still give herself voluntarily to lie with a cardinal of the Church, then perhaps she is not too far gone and can still be saved."

Sobbing, the girl collapsed onto her haunches.

"Take her to my personal chamber," said Orsini, handing a small silver soldo coin to the guard as he pulled the girl roughly to her feet. "And have my steward clean her up!" Orsini called as the girl was led away.

Jordan's chest was tight, his hand involuntarily gripping his sword hilt. "Benefits of the position?"

"All for the glory of the Church."

"Has any woman, girl, escaped the fires through this . . . test?"

"Not yet, but you never know, if she is enthusiastic enough. At least until they bring in someone prettier. Now I must attend to my work. You can find your way out, I am sure."

The guards, alerted by Jordan's tense bearing, eyed him suspiciously as he watched Orsini walk away, humming.

Leaving Innocent's fortress, Jordan strode back across St. Peter's Square, pushing his way through the crowded market, his agitation barely contained. *There is nothing I hate more than being forced into impotence,* he thought. He felt he should have done something, anything, to help that girl, but surrounded by guards and exorcists, what was there to do? Breaking free of the stalls at the far end of the square, he felt an itch on the back of his scalp, as if he were being watched. He stopped and turned around. Rising to the left of the basilica was the obelisk. He could feel power radiating from it, the globe perched on its pointed top watching him like a gilded eye. Caligula's obelisk.

Long before a depraved emperor brought the obelisk to Rome, this solid piece of red granite stood in the holy Egyptian city of Heliopolis. It had been quarried on the Nile island of Elephantine while Moses was still deciphering the grimoire of Raziel. Jordan remembered the writings of Herodotus, the first Greek to investigate obelisks in an attempt to unravel their magic.

The Egyptians had embraced the Nephilim as true Gods, which left them with a problem: how to worship Gods who walked the earth but who you did not actually want to show up in your palace or temple. Staring at Caligula's obelisk, Jordan wondered what it was like to be one of the Nephilim in that age of the world, fathered by an angel who had abandoned heaven for earthly pleasures. Loping through the desert at night, what did they see when they gazed up at the stars, how much of the expanded consciousness of their divine fathers did they retain? Could they see past this physical world into other realms? Jordan knew what the Nephilim saw when they looked upon human settlements along the river Nile: they saw food and soft flesh to rape.

Packs of jackal-headed Nephilim, rabid with hunger and lust, drove the Egyptian sorcerers to develop the obelisk. Charged with enchantments and fed with sacrificial blood, it repelled most magical beings. Herodotus had been particularly interested in the metal cap the Egyptian sorcerers placed on the obelisks to magnify their power, a metal called electrum. He never learned the exact formula, jealously guarded as it was, only that it was an alloy of gold, silver, and copper, with some other elements added.

First-century Rome faced a problem similar to ancient Egypt's. Rome's festivals of debauchery and blood sports attracted European Nephilim as unwelcome guests. They moved into the maze of dark alleyways and warrens of sewers and tunnels that underlay the city. From there they crept up to plague slaves and nobles alike. With no other remedy available at that time, the emperors were forced to bear the vast expense of moving fifteen of the most powerful obelisks from Egypt to Rome to protect key areas.

Caligula brought this one to Rome, the centerpiece of the obelisk polygon. Weighing 326 tons, it required the construction of the largest ship the world had ever seen in order to transport it, a ship so big it took three hundred slaves to row. The ship was later filled with rock, scuttled, and used as the foundation for the new harbor at Ostia.

When the obelisk was hauled into Rome, Caligula replaced the electrum cap with a gilded globe filled with blood drained from the corpse of Drusilla, who had been his favorite sister of the three he took as incestuous lovers. Caligula then erected it in the center of his circus, where its power would continue to be fed by sacrificial blood, including—after Nero had renamed the circus to honor himself—that of the apostle Peter, who was crucified upside down at its base. Jordan imagined he could smell the blood still throbbing in the heart of this red stone, though perhaps it was not his imagination.

When the Ring of Solomon was brought to Rome two centuries later, it proved more effective than the obelisks, and now all of them had either fallen or been pulled down, except for this one. Caligula's obelisk had become too powerful for even the Roman Church to abandon. They continued to use it to protect St. Peter's Basilica.

Jordan turned his back on the obelisk and resumed his walk away from the Vatican. The Roman Church was repelling the wrong creatures, he thought. While fallen angels and their Nephilim offspring were kept at bay, human devils were rising up and seizing control. Human devils—the exorcists and their inquisitor offspring—who hungered for power and lusted after women. A lust that had darkened into festivals of torture and death.

Anxious to return to Najia, Jordan quickened his pace.

18

The Isle of Man
June 1394

An Irish Viking longship slipped from the fog that hung like a curtain across the bay's entrance. Fingers of white clung to the ropes and mast as if trying to pull the vessel back, then relented and were reabsorbed into the mist, which was beginning to glow in the morning sun.

Patrick, standing on the prow, glanced over his shoulder, but the longship carrying the Colmcille contingent was still hidden. He nervously fingered the Blood Bell hanging in its holster on his belt. This trip was risky, and Patrick—despite the increasing animosity between the orders—would feel better with the Colmcille force by his side. The Colmcille longship had entered the fog at the same time, but it seemed to be slower to find the bay.

Patrick looked out at Castletown, Isle of Man. Behind him he could hear the Vikings lowering the sail, relying on oars to reach the dock. He thought of his new wife, who had asked to accompany him; she had never left Ireland and was excited by the prospect. He had flatly refused, hardening himself to her rants and tears. There was too much danger. He did not trust the Roman Church.

When an offer to negotiate a truce between the two churches arrived from the legate, his first instinct had been to dismiss it out of hand, but Colmcille had insisted that it was their duty to at least try to avoid a bloody conflict. Patrick requested an update from the Fomorian spies who were keeping an eye on the preparations of the English; the message back had said the armada would not be ready for at least another nine months. Still, he wouldn't have seriously considered the offer had Colmcille not declared that he would meet with the Vatican's representatives—Patrick didn't want to appear cowardly by not offering to go as well. So he had replied to the legate with his terms: the meeting had to take place at a neutral site, the Irish Church's delegation would be armed, and he would bring the Blood Bell. When the Roman Church agreed, Patrick found himself surprised—he had hoped they would refuse.

The Irish Church's contingent consisted of twelve armed monks from each of the two orders, his blue-robed Order of Patrick and the brown-robed Order of Colmcille, along with Colmcille himself.

Disembarking at the Castletown dock, Patrick was met by an old priest standing beside three small donkey carts. Bowing reverently, the priest said, "Welcome, Your Grace. I am the legate's personal secretary, here to provide transport to Rushen Abbey."

Patrick looked back over the bay once again. Colmcille's longship was just emerging from the fog. "Thank you, but we'll wait for our Colmcille brothers."

Pointing at the carts, the secretary said, "The abbey here is quite humble. They barely have enough carts to transport your own brothers. I'll bring them back to pick up the Colmcille brothers just about the time they land."

Patrick relented and climbed onto the front cart. His brothers, each with a short sword strapped over his robes, were barely able to squeeze into the carts for the three-mile ride northeast along a muddy track. Patrick allowed himself a brief smile when he heard small bells jingling on the donkey's harness. They would have been blessed by the abbot to frighten away faeries and were probably completely ineffective, unlike the Blood Bell, which he touched once again to reassure himself that it was still attached to his belt.

Arriving, they were shown into the great hall of the cloister. The dining tables and chairs were pushed back against the eighteen-foot-high stone walls supporting the wooden roof. Small windows set into the tops of the walls cast rays of mild light into the gloom. The monks' footsteps echoed as they walked into the vast, empty space, and Patrick became increasingly uneasy.

The bang of a door slamming closed caused Patrick's monks to spin around. Seven exorcists had entered behind them. Gathering just inside, the exorcists removed their black cowls. The one in front, short, bald, and smiling, spoke first. "You must be Patrick," said Orsini.

"Where's the legate?" Patrick responded, his hand on the Blood Bell.

Orsini spread his arms, palms open. "He will not be joining us, which is unfortunate, as he will be missing quite a spectacle. I am Cardinal Orsini, and I will be directing the . . . events here."

"Are we not talking truce?"

"Regrettably, no."

Patrick pulled the Bell from its holster.

The exorcists flanking Orsini started to chant in Aramaic.

Patrick began ringing the Bell, his arm arching high, low.

Blood ran from the ears, eyes, and mouths of two exorcists, and they collapsed dead onto the stone floor. The others continued to chant.

Orsini beheld his fallen brothers and shook his head. He smiled at Patrick, who was sweating from the effort he was putting into ringing the Blood Bell. "Well, that is a good way to separate the wheat from the chaff," he shouted over the clanging and chanting. "I will have to remember that. I am always looking for better methods to test new exorcists."

Patrick stopped ringing the Bell, seeing that the remaining exorcists were able to protect themselves from it. "It does not matter if you kill me, for my brothers in Ireland will just elect a new Patrick, and the church will carry on as before."

The exorcists ceased their chant. Orsini laughed. "I did not come here to kill you. I could not care less about you. I came for the Bell."

"It will do you no good. Only a Patrick can wield its power," insisted Patrick.

"I simply need for you not to have it. I cannot protect the whole English armada against it. But here, in this confined space, well . . . I believe I have the advantage. Of course, we will kill you, since you are here, just to save time later."

Three of Patrick's monks drew their swords and rushed at the remaining exorcists. One exorcist stepped forward, simultaneously making a complex gesture with his right hand and muttering indistinctly. The monks fell backward, as if they had run into an invisible wall.

"Now, you all just stay there while I invite some . . . well, just watch, you will be astounded," said Orsini.

Two bronze vessels were placed in front of Orsini and their lids removed.

Patrick stretched his neck to look inside. They appeared to be filled with a black liquid.

One of Orsini's men held a wax tablet for him. Orsini removed a stylus from a pocket in his robe and began to inscribe seals. "Just a second," he said, holding up a finger to Patrick. "It has been a while since I have done this, and it is, after all, quite complex." Orsini retrieved a small book from his pocket and leafed through the pages. "Ah, here it is." He resumed inscribing the tablet.

The liquid in the pots erupted into black mist that thickened into creatures standing in the rough proportions of a man. The edges began to firm somewhat, revealing strong legs reminiscent of those of a horse but terminating in large cloven hooves. Muscular arms sported humanlike hands with sharp claws. Small black eyes peered out from intense faces, one like an ape's, the other with the snout of a dog, both filled with long, jagged teeth.

Orsini laughed and clapped his hands. "I love doing this. Meet Furfur, the one with the longer snout, and Nadriel. Both demons of a high order, I assure you."

Patrick stood his ground while the rest of his brothers began to back away, swords in hand.

"They have not been unbound from their vessels for . . . oh, two or three hundred years and must be very hungry." The demons looked around, locking eyes with Orsini. Black saliva dripped from their open jaws, became mist, and merged with their bodies.

Orsini pointed at Patrick, gave him a big smile, and spoke in a language rarely heard since the days of the Tower of Babel.

The demons leaped for Patrick. He recoiled, desperately ringing the Blood Bell. Waves rippled across the demons' skin. They knocked Patrick onto his back and pinned him to the floor, a hoof on each of his wrists, then ripped off his robe as if it were paper. Using their sharp claws in slow, practiced movements, they began to tear off long strips of Patrick's skin, flinging them to the side, to reach the sweeter meat they preferred.

With a look of satisfaction, Orsini watched the demons work. Patrick's screams rose and fell in time with the stripping off of his flesh. Three of Patrick's monks threw themselves against the sealed rear door, two tried to scale the wall toward the windows, and the rest tried to rush past the feeding demons. Each was knocked back into the center of the room by enchantments hurled by the exorcists.

"Bring in the other one, the Colmcille," said Orsini.

Colmcille was pulled into the hall. "Oh, my God! Oh, God. Oh, God, protect me," he kept saying, covering his ears to Patrick's screams and averting his eyes. He dropped to his knees.

Orsini knocked Colmcille's hands away from his ears and, grabbing his head, forced him to face Patrick's agony. "You made this bargain," Orsini hissed. "Now watch its results."

"I never thought you'd do something like this, never thought you'd unleash demons on them."

"I am only doing this for your benefit," said Orsini. "Now you know what will happen if you do not honor your agreement. I have plenty more demons bound up in my storeroom, anxious to get out—and hungry. They like their food fresh and have an instinct for keeping it alive while they feed. Livers, kidneys, and testicles seem to be their favorite bits, though they will eat any organ."

Patrick's screams dissolved into gurgles as the demons reached his lungs. Seeking fresh meat, they straightened up, blood dripping from their faces, looked around, and pounced on a monk trying to scale the wall, dragging him down to the floor. The lump of muscle, tissue, and bone that was Patrick twitched and then was still. Colmcille put his hand over his mouth and swallowed hard. The demons' next meal began to shriek.

Orsini extracted the Blood Bell from the grisly pile and returned to where Colmcille cowered. "Following the invasion you will become bishop of Ireland," said Orsini. He pulled a cloth from his pocket, wiped the muck off the Bell, and held it up to admire the inscribed runes. "In return you will swear allegiance to the Roman Church, and you will surrender all monasteries in Britain and Europe to our bishops. It's that simple. I am sure you will have no trouble. Oh, and make sure you forbid all Irish Christians from fighting the English when they arrive. Now, on your way."

Orsini traced along one of the runes with his finger. "If I can divine which demon is bound into this Bell, I will be able to redirect its power. Oh, well, time enough for that after the invasion."

Colmcille was pulled to his feet by an exorcist. As Colmcille edged toward the door, a young novice monk boldly charged the demon Nadriel, thrusting his sword into the demon's chest. It had no effect. Nadriel knocked the novice to the ground, pulled out the sword, flung it away, then grabbed the novice's left arm just as Furfur grabbed the right. The demons began arguing, in their ancient tongue, about who was going to eat his organs, as he was too small to share.

Colmcille, tears running down his cheeks, croaked, "Are you going to kill them all? Have you no mercy?"

"Not me," said Orsini, keeping his eyes on the carnage. Nadriel had dragged the novice off to a corner, leaving Furfur holding only a torn-off arm, which he angrily threw down, and then began inspecting the remaining monks. "It is you who is killing them. You are the one who came to us looking for control of the Irish Church."

Colmcille took another step toward the door. "And what of the Vikings who brought us here?" he asked. "They may tell the Celts about all this."

"Nothing for you to worry about," replied Orsini. "They have been paid."

◈

ACROSS THE SEA in England, Richard's personal residence, Sheen Manor, sat on the south bank of the river Thames nine miles upstream from the Palace of Westminster. Outside on the riverbank, in the warmth of the early-afternoon sun, children danced in a circle singing:

> *A ring, a ring o' rosy,*
> *A pocket full o' posies,*
> *Ashes, ashes,*
> *We all fall down.*

Inside, Richard, with his fists clenched, stood over Anne's bed, where she lay uncovered from the waist up. Her chamber was filled with smoke emanating from a brazier containing a mixture of powdered amber, balm-mint leaves, camphor, cloves, labdanum, myrrh, rose petals, and storax. Posies of herbs hung from the bed canopy.

As de Vere and Chaucer watched, a physician cut loose the silk scarves that had bound Anne's arms above her head to keep her from rupturing any more of the apple-size, black, bulbous inflammations crowded in her rosy-ringed armpits. More buboes climbed up and blackened the left side of her neck. In the five days since symptoms first appeared, most of these had burst, leaving a spiderweb of red and black under the pale skin of her face. The physician gently placed Anne's hands down by her sides, the ends of her fingers black, the few remaining fingernails curled up. One nail caught on the sheet and fell off. Anne's dead eyes stared blankly at the ceiling.

Tears fell from Richard's eyes. De Vere tried to hold him, but Richard shook off the embrace.

"How can this be?" Richard screamed at the physician. "There has been no plague in London for more than four years. How could you let her die?"

Richard grabbed a dagger from de Vere's belt and awkwardly lunged at the physician, who darted behind a table. "Your Royal Majesty, I assure you—"

Chaucer stepped in front of the physician. "Your Royal Majesty," he said softly, "it must have been a curse that inflicted the plague on Queen Anne."

"Then We shall burn Jews in retribution." Richard threw down the dagger and turned to de Vere. "Burn a thousand Jews. Then round up a thousand more and burn them as well. Have their ashes blessed to keep them from their Jew heaven."

Chaucer held up his hands. "I am sure it was not the Jews this time. It must have been the Sidhe. They are angry at your invasion plans."

Richard swayed on his feet, gave one long scream, and fled the room. De Vere followed.

Richard ran out the front gate, scattering the dancing children. De Vere caught up to him just before he reached the river. Richard collapsed into his arms, and they slid down onto the grass.

"Come with me," de Vere whispered, stroking Richard's hair. "Come with me to Ireland, and together we will kill all the Sidhe."

Richard wiped futilely at his eyes and nodded. "We shall never come here again," he said, looking back at Sheen Manor. "No one shall. Tear it to the ground."

⚘

ON THE COAST of Wales, the high king of the Fomorians, his sable cloak stained with blood and beginning to take on a green mildew tinge, sat on a rock in the garden of Conwy Castle. His two ever-present female attendants squatted at his feet, gnawing on the remains of a stag leg, their English hosts having refused to provide them with a Welsh prisoner to dine on.

"All of the Fomorian clans have pledged their lives to me," he growled. "What do you bring to the fight? War draws near, and I question if it is you who should lead."

Kellach reclined in a low oak bough, gazing west toward the setting sun, toward Ireland.

"Come here," he snapped. Three barefoot Dryads, wearing baggy rough wool tunics over tattered trousers, scurried up and bowed. Peaking at two feet tall, Dryads were the smallest of the Sidhe clans and easily able to hide their slight frames in the bellies of the Irish Viking trade ships still running between Dublin and Welsh ports. Another variety of tree Sidhe, Dryads lived only in oaks and were treated by the Skeaghshee as something between slaves and pets.

"All the Skeaghshee are preparing for my return. My Dryads here tell me that the Grogoch and Wichtlein have pledged to fight for me. Do not worry—my forces will be strong when we arrive," Kellach assured.

"They better be. You promised to keep the Morrígna at bay."

"The Celts continue to put their faith in Aisling, but she is not the Morrígna. Soon you and your people will be able to return to the land that once was yours. That is, the tracts we agreed to."

"I do not trust the English, and I hate the Celts and the Christians," grumbled the Fomorian king, grabbing the meaty leg bone from his attendants and biting off the end.

"Once I return to Ireland and the Celts and the Irish Christians have been killed, the rest of the Sidhe will rise and follow me. We will turn on the English and drive them back out."

"What of Oren, the English's faerie traitor? What if he sniffs out the plan?"

Kellach turned toward the garden doorway to the castle. "What of Oren?" he echoed in a loud voice.

Oren dragged himself out of the doorway and along the grass, propping himself up against a tree. "I vouched for your credibility to the English, though I could tell that you were plotting something. That I have finally betrayed my tormentors brings a lightness to my heart that I have not felt since I was a boy." Oren turned his blind face toward the warmth of the setting sun. "With it has come a renewed hope that if there is an After Lands to journey to, I have earned my place there. There I will be whole again. Once I am rid of this miserable life."

"Happy to assist you," snarled the Fomorian king, rising from his rock.

"Not yet," said Kellach. "Not until the English land their invasion. Oren knows that to betray us is to betray himself and lose this . . . opportunity."

"I still do not trust him." The Fomorian king did not sit back down.

Kellach sent the Dryads to wait on the other side of the wall. "We can succeed only together, so we will bind our agreements, the three of us, by exchanging our true names."

"You are willing to do such a thing?" The Fomorian's growl carried a note of surprise. "In that case so will I, and abide by your leadership in this war—as long as you are winning."

Once they had exchanged true names, each in turn, the Fomorian took his seat again and resumed chewing on the leg bone. Kellach called the Dryads back and instructed them, "Send word to my forces. It is time for them to prepare themselves to fight. They are to gather in Waterford at the beginning of the fourth Roman month hence to secure my arrival."

Each Dryad scurried up a separate tree so thick with rooks that it appeared to have black leaves. Darting from branch to branch, the Dryads whispered to the birds. With a rush of hundreds of wings, the rooks took flight, heading west.

⊲

IN PARIS the witch Joanna held a candelabrum to light her way down a dark corridor of the French royal residence. Her other hand clutched a sheet of folded parchment, its wax seal broken. She entered a large red door without knocking and approached the ornate canopy bed. "Grande Sorcière," she said, shaking the queen's shoulder.

Queen Isabeau awoke with a start. "What? What do you want?" The king's brother stirred next to her. She touched his temple with one finger and hissed a short spell. He stilled.

"The queen of England is dead, Your Highness. The messenger just arrived. It happened eight days ago." Joanna handed her the letter.

"Was it blamed on the plague?" The Grande Sorcière did not bother to read the parchment.

"Richard believes it was a Sidhe curse."

"Even better," said the Grande Sorcière.

"Your Highness already knew?"

"Of course, it was Us. A potion of Our own design. By ensuring that the English queen's throne became vacant, We created the opportunity We were waiting for, and We have such an abundance of daughters."

"But Richard's preference is for men."

"That is fortunate. We do not need to worry about him falling in love with some woman before We can exert Our influence. Love can be such a challenge to overcome."

"Shall I gather your coven?"

"No, not yet. We have plans to make." The Grande Sorcière looked at the man sleeping next to her. "This news excites Us. Leave Us. We desire to wake him up."

19

Aisling awoke to Conor's soft kisses on her forehead. Her eyes flickered open as his lips moved down to her neck. His hand ran over her pregnant belly and, slipping between her legs, stroked her.

"No," she said, rolling over and struggling to sit up. "It was no yesterday, and it's still no today."

"What's wrong?" asked Conor gently.

"I don't know," snapped Aisling, throwing off the covers. "You're welcome to my handmaid if you must quench your desires."

She climbed out of their bed and lumbered over to the fireplace, feeling Conor's eyes follow her. Placing wood on the grate, she spoke a short fire incantation. A single spark fell from the wood and died on the fireplace floor. Aisling gave a deep sigh. "They're sucking all the power from me."

"They?"

"Yes." Aisling turned to face Conor, her eyes suddenly welling with tears. "I'm carrying twin girls. I know I am."

Conor rose, walked over, and embraced her. "That's wonderful."

"Is it? I keep thinking about what happened to me, what happened to Anya!" cried Aisling, relieved to finally unburden herself. "It's making me crazy. I don't want my daughters to go through what I went through. I don't want to lose them to the Sidhe. Or to Tara, where their whole lives will be dictated to them. I have to keep them safe and free somehow."

"Hush," said Conor. "I'll never let anything bad happen to you or our daughters."

"I keep dreading Brigid's knock on our door."

"Don't be silly," said Conor. He kissed Aisling's eyes and stroked her hair. "You know Brigid never knocks."

"You're right about that," said Aisling, wiping a tear from her cheek.

"And why should I knock?" asked Brigid, entering their bedchamber. "Think of all the fun I'd miss."

Aisling took cover behind Conor. "Get out!" she screamed. "Get out of our house! I don't want your news!"

"It's all right, everything will be all right," said Brigid. "I'm not here to tell you your twins are the returned Morrígna. I'm just here to help you deliver. It'll be any day now."

Still hiding behind Conor, Aisling cast a suspicious look at her.

"I keep telling you that the Morrígna can't return to this world as long as you occupy one aspect," said Brigid in a soothing tone.

"What if you're wrong?"

"Have you ever known me to be wrong?" Brigid smiled. "Now, get dressed and let's have breakfast."

Liam stuck his head in the doorway. "Breakfast sounds good. Come on, Brigid."

"What's the latest word on the English?" asked Conor, pulling out a chair for Aisling as they joined Liam and Brigid at the table in the warm kitchen of Dunsany Castle.

"The Fomorians are keeping a sea-level eye on their preparations," replied Brigid. "It looks like they're still planning for an invasion attempt late next spring."

"Makes sense," said Conor. "Who would want to start a war with winter approaching, even if Kellach can get part of their fleet ashore?"

"Can he really do that?" asked Aisling, piling her platter with cold ham, duck breast, bread, honey, and butter.

"He can get them safely through the waves," said Brigid, pouring herself a mug of dark ale. "But I doubt many ships will get past the Fomorians."

"And the Irish Vikings are always itching for an excuse to attack English ships," added Conor. "As for those who make it to shore alive, we'll handle them easily. After the solstice High King Art is planning to—"

"I'm nervous," interrupted Aisling.

"About?" asked Brigid.

"Our strategy, the timing, everything. I can't foresee what will happen, but that may just be my pregnancy getting in the way."

"Between Kellach and the VRS, there's an impenetrable veil covering the English preparations," said Brigid, trying to reassure her. "And there's too much turmoil in the Middle Kingdom. I can't get any help from the Sidhe right now. I'm afraid we have no choice but to rely on spying by the Fomorians."

"I also have a bad feeling," Liam said, putting down his half-drained mug of ale. "Something just seems wrong. Two nights ago I dreamed of clear-cut woods and boiling lakes. So yesterday I convinced one of my Sidhe half brothers to go snooping. There are still a few passages to Wales open in the Middle Kingdom."

"Good thought," said Brigid, carving off another piece of cold ham. Nudging Conor with her elbow, she asked, "How comes your new army, Lord McTadg?"

"He's making some progress in organizing them," replied Aisling.

"The Woodwose may lack discipline, but they excel in enthusiasm. They make great fighters," said Conor. "Though I still haven't heard back from Art on my petition for iron weapons. I think he's nervous about these wild people having sworn allegiance to Aisling and me and not to him. There are over three hundred in the camp now, plus an ever-increasing flock of children."

"Speaking of my Woodwose," Aisling said, leaning in close to Brigid. "How would you like to be treated like a Goddess for the day?"

"I'd like to be treated as a Goddess every day."

"Well, then, eat up and follow me."

· · · · ·

Aisling and Brigid walked west through the gardens behind the castle toward the tree line. It was nine days past the autumn equinox, a brisk October morning. Brigid followed Aisling into the trees, their leaves drifting down to the forest floor, creating a carpet of brown decorated with swaths of gold and red.

Half a mile along the path, just past the staked head of the previous shaman preserved with pine oil, they entered a large clearing, the site of the Woodwose camp. It was rapidly becoming a true village with new, crudely constructed huts. A swarm of boys and girls gathered around them, laughing and practicing their bowing and curtsying, though it was still a bit random as to who did what. Aisling did not bother correcting them today.

When the Woodwose camp had been established, just one day after Aisling and Conor arrived at Dunsany Castle, Aisling had told them that they had new Gods now, ones who did not desire live offerings of their people, a practice that Aisling had been disturbed to find in progress when she entered the camp that day. Instead their new Gods required devotion to her and obedience to her consort to atone for the death of Tadg.

Aisling's appointed attendants, whose fresh white robes contrasted with the animal skins worn by the rest of the tribe, shooed the children away. They escorted Aisling and Brigid a short distance to a second, smaller clearing. On the way Aisling could hear a group of the bolder children sneaking along behind them. As with all things, the Woodwose devoted themselves to Aisling with unbridled fervor, creating this open-air temple for her.

When she and Brigid entered, two men used forked branches to roll large rocks out of a bonfire and into a pool that had been dug at the edge of the clearing, generating loud splashes and brief hisses. Aisling's attendants helped her undress. Using the Woodwose's rough, limited language, Aisling ordered them to attend to Brigid next as she hugged herself to ward off the chill. Another attendant brought over a large pot of honey, clarified to remove the comb, which had been warming at the fire's edge. The attendants giggled as they smeared the warm, sticky honey onto Aisling and Brigid. Infected with their laughter, Brigid and Aisling joined in.

"Gods, this feels good," said Brigid, "but how am I ever going to get my clothes back on?"

"Just wait," said Aisling. "There's more to come."

Brigid leaned over and licked a glaze of honey off Aisling's shoulder, which the attendants found hilarious. "You should teach them to take it off with their tongues."

"After the babies are born," replied Aisling, moving toward the pool. "Follow me." She gently lowered herself into the water, feeling her heavy body become weightless. The hot rocks had barely taken the chill off the pool, but she found that when she rested her feet on their still-warm surface, the heat rose into her body.

The two men who had been attending the fire had become aroused watching the ceremony and took the opportunity to dash over to the attendants, who admonished them to wait. The men threw their animal-skin cloaks and loincloths to the ground and squatted on their haunches, swaying gently. The attendants carefully hung their white gowns on tree limbs and then, with cries of delight, dove onto the expectant men.

Aisling floated beside Brigid, watching the revelry. "Poor Conor," she said. "My babies are sapping all my energy, all my desire. He's had no sex for more than a month."

"I'll bring over one of my novices to keep him contented until the twins are born," said Brigid.

"No. He won't take anyone else. I've tried." Aisling felt around with her toes until she found a warmer rock. "So how long have you known that I'm carrying twin girls?"

"As long as you have, of course."

"And what do you think of me losing my abilities?" asked Aisling. "Is this normal?"

"Normal? No, but I've read of other occurrences," reassured Brigid.

"I can't seem to work even the simplest of enchantments," said Aisling. She rubbed her belly and smiled briefly when she felt a kick. She placed one of Brigid's hands on the spot, but the baby didn't move again.

"I worked so hard to forge a new connection to the Morrígna's power," said Aisling. "Losing it again has been . . . troubling. What do I do if it doesn't come back?"

"Don't worry, your abilities will return, and your girls will become powerful druids. In fact, one may become the next Brigid—hopefully while I'm still young enough to win back Liam." Brigid gave Aisling a sly smile.

"That might not be a good thing."

"Liam and me? Why?"

"No, not that." Aisling hesitated. "I'm not sure I want my girls to be druids. The world's becoming difficult and dangerous for them."

They were interrupted by a group of young naked children sprinting from the woods and diving into the pool.

When Aisling tried to get the children to practice their Gaelic, they ran off. The pool had become too cold and the attendants had once again donned their robes. Aisling and Brigid climbed out of the water and stretched out on the grass in the sun. A warm pot of melted butterfat was brought over, and the attendants oiled their skin.

"Are we coming back tomorrow? I could get used to this," said Brigid, staring up at the sky, where a small flock of rooks circled. As she studied them, her face became concerned. The rooks flew west, then disappeared, apparently dropping into the forest. "We should return to Liam and Conor," she said, gathering her clothes. "Tell your Woodwose to be alert and keep their children close."

Aisling and Brigid walked out of the tree line behind Dunsany

Castle only to see Liam, Conor, and six Gallowglass sprinting toward them.

"Liam's half brother has returned from Wales with word that the English fleet left Milford Haven this morning. We must ride for Waterford," declared Conor as they reached Aisling.

"And the fleet is twice as large as the Fomorians told us," added Liam.

"Which means they must be in league with Kellach," said Brigid.

"I've sent word to Art and the Vikings at Waterford," said Liam. "Can you fight in your condition?" he asked Aisling.

"I can't even get a candle to light," said Aisling. "I will be of no use."

"That's why they're coming now. I should've anticipated this," said Liam.

"How did they find out?" asked Conor.

A dozen rooks passed overhead from the west. One wheeled back and landed on a branch. A drop of blood fell from its beak.

"My Woodwose!" cried Aisling.

Liam and his warriors ran down the path, while Conor and Brigid followed with the slower Aisling. When they caught up, Liam and his men were hacking at branches that had woven themselves into a solid wall around the Woodwose camp. Aisling called the names of her attendants. There was no response.

Liam broke through the barrier, and the group spilled into the hushed clearing, where they found piles of corpses: men, women, and children. Aisling knelt by the small stack of her attendants' bodies.

"Aisling." A voice drifted from across the barrier on the other side of the clearing.

Conor stepped between Aisling and the voice. Two Gallowglass drew their bows.

"Skeaghshee," Liam said to his men. "Save your arrows. They won't make it through the wall."

"Aisling, this is your fault," the voice said. "Had you just let them be, left them scattered in the woods worshipping their old Gods, they would still be alive. You need to learn that you are not strong enough to protect those around you. You failed Anya and Tadg, and now them." Flames erupted from the piles of bodies.

Thrown backward by the force of the combustion, Aisling landed hard. A snap echoed through her bones, and amniotic fluid flowed out onto the ground, followed by a single, powerful contraction. She grimaced. "The babies are coming."

20

Conor clenched his jaw. *What do I want?* he questioned. *Who am I, and what have I become?*

High in the midnight sky, a half-moon cast a slash of silver light down into the forest trail, punctuated with deep black moon shadows. A dark arm swept toward him. He ducked under the branch without slowing his horse—or his thoughts.

Are my daughters born yet? Are they healthy? Questions kept looping through his mind, and his heart ached for Aisling, whom he had left in labor eight hours earlier. He swung his horse around a boulder. There were no calls from rooks in the night. No message from Brigid. For the first time, he really knew what it meant to be an earl: to have an honor price, to owe duty to Ireland, to leave his wife in labor and ride to war. The feeling sat like a stone in his throat.

Moonlight danced upon his chain mail, as shiny as the day it was given to him in Tara. His shimmering form glided above the trail as his black horse merged with the night. A shape materialized ahead, portending something wrong. Conor slowed his horse to a walk as he approached the mass of deep gray in the black moon shadow of a tall rock. Liam's face emerged. He had been scouting ahead. The company of Gallowglass they were leading reined in and paused along the trail behind them.

"What do you sense?" asked Conor.

"To the west of us, a large column of Sidhe are moving south."

"Overland. They must be Skeaghshee."

"Or at least led by the Skeaghshee. Now a group has broken off and turned toward our path."

"How many?"

Liam cast a look back down the line of Gallowglass. "More than we are, but I'd still bet on my men. The problem is that we don't have time to stand and fight. Carlow is less than half an hour ahead. Take the company and ride hard. I'll cover the rear."

Conor urged his horse into a gallop down the narrow path. Black shapes of trees flashed by. Feeling the energy of the forest as he hadn't since becoming lord of Dunsany Castle, he effortlessly maneuvered his horse over fallen trees and dodged boulders; the Gallowglass directly behind him copied his every move, and so it went down the line. A flash of green light overtook him, but he did not turn to look.

Breaking from the forest outside Carlow, Conor could see that the village was alive with torches, while a few faerie lights flowed down from the Sidhe rath, an earthen fort crowning a hill to the east. Conor wheeled his horse to face the path they had exited, and the rest of the company took up positions beside him.

Liam did not ride out. Several of the Gallowglass looked from the trail's mouth to Conor and then back, their horses snorting restlessly. Conor's chest tightened. *All I want is to be with Aisling*, he thought, *out of that castle and back in the woods, fighting threats one on one.* Face the enemy, kill the enemy, then face the next.

I knew this day would come, he thought, glancing at Liam's men. *I thought I was ready, but I was ready to lead my Woodwose, not a company of Gallowglass who've had more training than I'll ever have. What'll they think of me as a leader? Curse the Gods, Liam, don't leave me here alone.*

Conor walked his horse out in front of the company, toward the trail mouth, and drew his sword. *For Aisling and for my daughters*, he thought, *if I am going to leave them to fight, then by the Goddess Morrígna I am going to fight hard and lead the best I can.*

Liam rode out of the trail, his horse in a limping trot, an arrow protruding from its rump. Wiping the blood from his sword, he sheathed it and said, "As soon as they discovered they could not catch our company, they turned back toward the main column. I tried to take one alive, but he fought to the death."

Concern for Aisling surged in Conor's mind. "Do you think they could attack Dunsany?"

"Don't worry, that column is heading to Waterford," Liam said. "If Skeaghshee do show up at our home, Brigid and the men we left behind can hold the castle against any threat, at least long enough for us to return."

Conor sheathed his sword and turned toward the village. Carlow Castle guarded the end of a long stone bridge spanning, by way of a small island, the river Barrow, Ireland's second-largest river. Having left their men at the edge of the village with instructions to find a replacement horse, Liam and Conor wove their way through crowded groups of mustering Sidhe, Celts, and Gallowglass; female warriors made up one-quarter of the humans, one-half of the Sidhe. At any other time in her life, Aisling would be here, Conor thought.

Outside the castle they intercepted King Murchada of Leinster, his long hair swinging as he strode forward, leading them into the great hall, where High King Art and King Turlough of Meath were bent over a map.

"Where's Aisling?" Art demanded of Liam.

Conor answered, "In labor."

"Probably one of the reasons they're coming now," said Liam. "Brigid is with her."

"How could we be so unprepared?" said Art, shaking his head. "Do you think the Fomorian high king is part of their betrayal, that all the Fomorians are joining the English?"

"We're about to find out," Liam answered.

Turlough spoke up. "Are you sure they're headed to Waterford?"

"Yes, my half brother confirmed it himself. He was able to interrogate one of their captains, captain of one of the five hundred ships in the armada."

"That many," Murchada said. "I had not heard. How many men are they bringing?"

"Based on the size of the armada, around ten thousand," said Liam.

"Unbelievable!" Art exclaimed. "Not in my wildest estimation would I have thought Richard would muster so large a force." The tense looks exchanged throughout the assembly indicated it was a shock to all.

"Thankfully, we caught a break," continued Art. "King Myndill is already in Waterford, where his son Geir is hosting a feast to celebrate his election as the Viking marshal. Myndill has all twenty-five longboats with him. That plus the twenty-two that Geir has can defend the harbor. In a fight, one longboat is worth at least ten cogs."

"Not necessarily," said Liam. He opened his mouth as if to go on, then shut it, deferring to Conor.

"Liam is right," said Conor, stepping forward, his anxiety in his position fading. "This has been too well orchestrated. If the Viking king is in Waterford, then the English planned for him to be there when they land."

"You don't know that," replied Art.

"Otherwise why would they be sailing to Waterford? It is the last harbor they would attack. For five hundred years, the Vikings have fortified it as their sanctuary. Now it's by far the most secure port in Ireland."

Conor placed a finger on the map at Waterford. "Here the bay is pinched into a narrows by two low hills at the mouth of the river Suir, and only one ship can enter at a time." He traced his finger along the line of the river. "Past the hills the river swells again here, where a small fleet of defensive ships can wait and pick off invaders easily. Ten Viking ships could hold that narrows from the inside, fewer with archers on the hills spanning it. Even if invading ships make it past the narrows, they'd have to launch tenders to tow them around this sharp turn before getting to the port fortifications, all the while under attack."

"The shore is gentle. They could land and assault the city from the south," said Art, indicating coastline on the map.

"You've never been to Waterford, have you?"

"No reason to."

"To the south is all bog. As I said, it's the easiest port in all of Ireland to defend. The only reason the English would sail there is that they are sure of taking it and then that they will be able to defend Waterford against us."

"Are you saying the Vikings have betrayed us as well?"

"I don't know, but clearly the English have made arrangements to take Waterford."

Art nodded in agreement.

"That can't be right. King Myndill would never side with the Christians. He would die first!" exclaimed Turlough.

"But what about Geir?" asked Liam. "He did let Colmcille build a monastery in Waterford, the first in any Viking city."

"Where are Colmcille and Patrick?" interrupted Murchada. "Patrick should be here with the Bell."

"Colmcille has decided this is not the Christians' fight, and he sent word that Patrick has not yet returned from Rome," replied Art.

"Patrick is dead," came a voice from behind them, "and the Blood Bell is captured."

Fearghal had entered the room with several of his Sidhe captains, his right arm bandaged at the wrist where his hand used to be.

"My friend," said Art. "An assassination attempt?"

"They did not try to kill me. It is better for the Skeaghshee if I am less than whole and no longer fit to be high king, to stir discord when there is no time for a new election."

"Does the Sidhe army still follow you?"

Holding up his empty wrist, Fearghal said, "This is the latest, but the least, of the Skeaghshee treachery. They have been fomenting rebellion for over a year, though most Sidhe do not want to fight on either side, not without the Morrígna to bind them to their oaths.

Many decided that it is time to explore paths through the Middle Kingdom to other worlds, time to abandon this world that is being consumed by Christianity."

"Are you saying the Sidhe will not fight with us?" asked Art.

Fearghal sighed. "Those who have passion enough left to fight mainly want to win Ireland back for the Sidhe only. Few are willing to fight to maintain things as they are."

"How many?" asked Art.

"I have pledges from only two thousand and but one thousand with me tonight."

The group stood in stunned silence.

"Tell me you at least have Fire Sprites," said Liam.

Fearghal shook his head. "I have not seen a Fire Sprite in the Middle Kingdom in two months. The Sidhe setting out on paths to new worlds enlisted them, the Skeaghshee made sure of that. Those with me are mainly Devas and Adhene—it is hard to abandon a kingdom you rule. We will see if they still know how to fight. And a few Brownies."

"A thousand Sidhe," repeated Conor. "There were almost that many in just the one column of renegades from the north that we detected. How many Celt and Gallowglass warriors have we mustered?"

"My company plus the forces that have arrived with Turlough and Murchada total around twenty-five hundred," replied Art. "Forces from Connacht and Ulster will not arrive for two days. Last time I received word, Queen Gormflaith is leading a force from Munster of around one thousand that should make it to Waterford before sunrise, though there have been no messages for many hours."

"Few messages will get through tonight, not this close to Waterford, not with the Skeaghshee stopping them," said Fearghal.

"So in total we have thirty-five hundred mustered here, plus Gormflaith's thousand or so coming from the west," said Conor, "facing some unknown thousands of Sidhe, probably a Fomorian force, perhaps all of them, and the English."

"And we don't yet know what to expect from the Vikings," added Liam.

"What do you advise?" the high king asked Liam.

"Our advantage is that the English will be most vulnerable when they try to land," said Liam. "Our disadvantage is that they seem to have allies both in the sea and on shore. But we don't know their plan, and even if it's a good one, something could go wrong. I say we ride as fast as possible to Waterford and try to beat the opposing Sidhe forces there. Then, if the Vikings are preparing to hold the port against the armada, we join them, and if we're very lucky, we take the high ground above the narrows. Then we can hold Waterford until the rest of the Irish forces can be mustered."

"That's a lot of luck to count on."

"What other option is there? If Waterford is captured, the English will have their toehold in Ireland, and we'll be forced to withdraw and regroup."

Art stood looking at the map, anger filling his face. "We can't wait any longer, then. Rally all that are here and ride for Waterford," he commanded. "Fearghal, how will your Sidhe travel? You could be in Waterford before any of us."

"Unfortunately, it is best for us to move overland with you. If we try to traverse the Middle Kingdom tonight, much will happen to delay us."

Conor became aware of a presence. Glancing to his left, he was surprised to see Rhoswen standing close to him.

"Thirty minutes ago Aisling gave birth to twin girls," she announced.

"Are you sure?" demanded Conor, his heart pounding.

"I have just come from her side. Brigid asked me to tell you all are healthy and safe. She said it would help you to know."

"It does." Conor let out a long sigh. He felt light and strong again. "Thank you for bringing word."

The group gathered around Conor, congratulating him.

"Enough!" announced Art. "There's no time for celebration. We must make haste to Waterford."

Fearghal asked Rhoswen, "Daughter, you made fast time. Did you travel through the Middle Kingdom? What is happening there?"

Rhoswen shook her head. "I took a witch path."

The sunrise was blotted out by an overcast sky as a Viking longship rowed through the river Suir narrows toward Waterford Bay. Flat and gray, the sea ahead would have been indistinguishable from the clouds if not for the mass of English cogs creating a dark artificial horizon, their sails billowing.

The Viking king Myndill glanced up at the empty hills spanning the narrows. *Damn the Celts,* he thought, *where are they? Damn Kellach, who stilled the sea and slacked the tide that should have been running out, should have been giving speed to my ships and taking it from the English.* "Odin, damn the Fomorians to Hel's realm," he cursed aloud as his brother joined him on the bow, "for letting the English through."

Myndill's longship entered the bay and glided to a stop followed by five others, three of which were commanded by his son Geir, the new marshal of Waterford. Shouts, too distant to decipher, drifted across the water from the English armada and Myndill knew they were alarms, warning of the dragon ships. He smiled. His dragon figurehead was fitted to the prow, signaling to all that his ship came for battle, not trade.

Ninety-eight feet long and twelve feet wide, Myndill's longship, a *skei* design built two years earlier in Dublin, held eighty warriors. Sixty of the warriors sat poised with their oars raised, each oar a custom length to match its position on the ship. The mast and the square sail were unneeded and left on shore. A colorful line of round shields, painted with the red, yellow, and black family emblems of the rowers, ran down slots in the gunwale rail. Graceful, elegant, highly maneuverable, and very fast, his ship was deadly, at least when not faced with five hundred lumbering English cogs. *Even the fiercest dragon can be crushed by a stampede of cows*, Myndill thought.

"Best to meet them one at a time back on the other side of the narrows," his brother said. His brother's long mail shirt, falling almost to his knees, and iron helmet were a contrast to Myndill's lack of armor. Myndill believed that the Gods would decide when he was to die.

Myndill studied the English armada. Ten ships had sailed out ahead of the fleet and were gaining speed toward the Vikings, the lead ship of the vanguard flying Richard's standard. "No," Myndill growled. "We'll sink that arrogant king's flagship and block the approach to the narrows." He called out his order: "Fire arrows!"

A dozen bows were pulled from a sea chest and passed out. Irish Vikings' poor bowmanship was the source of many Celtic jokes, such as, "You are more likely to be hit by lightning than by a Viking arrow." To kill a man face-to-face with a sword or an ax brought honor and the favor of the Viking Gods, to kill a man from a distance with a bow did not. Consequently, the Irish Vikings rarely practiced. However, it did not take much skill to hit a target as large as a ship at short range. Fire arrows were unwrapped from thick oilskin coverings. Each iron arrowhead bulged out at the base, forming a basket of metal fingers. Into this basket was stuffed wool soaked with a mixture of pitch, sulfur, and lime, so that the flame would not be extinguished by water.

"Full stroke!" Myndill cried out. Sixty oars moved as one, and the longship sprang forward, followed by Myndill's two other ships.

"You son doesn't follow," his brother said.

"That boy wants to die in front of his hearth," Myndill grumbled. "Halt!" he ordered his rowers, and he turned to see Geir's three ships just floating, their limp oars resting in the water.

A large Fomorian scaled the bow of his son's ship and stood beside him, a dilapidated sable cloak hanging off the creature's shoulders, patches of white fur showing through the caked mildew. Geir pulled on a chain around his neck, and a large crucifix emerged from under his tunic, which he let fall to sway in front of his chest.

"Traitor!" Myndill roared at his son. "You'll never join me in Valhalla."

"I'll look down from heaven and see you burning in hell!" Geir retorted.

Fomorians surfaced and seized the oars of Myndill's longships. Others scaled the sides and swarmed inside. Myndill swung his ax, killing a charging Fomorian. A Viking drew his bow only to be knocked down, the fire arrow striking the stern of the longship, setting it ablaze.

Myndill cut off the head of another Fomorian. Pulling a spear from its place of honor in a holder attached to the rail, its oak shaft inlaid with woven gold-and-silver cord, he looked out across his ship. His men were cutting down the Fomorians, but not as fast as they were leaping over the gunwale. He cried out, "Odin, are you watching? I dedicate my last battle to you!" and threw the spear over the embattled deck.

Drawing a short sword with his left hand, his right holding the ax, he began slaughtering the green creatures climbing onto the prow. One managed to duck under the ax, swinging his clawed hand. Myndill's belly erupted in fire. He stabbed the Fomorian, dropped his sword and pushed the loop of intestine back into the wound, held it there and hacked at more advancing creatures with his ax. Three of them jumped him from the left, knocking him to the deck. Pain swept a fog across his vision as his gut split further open. He felt the deck sliding beneath him.

"Odin," he whispered, "I'm the last of the Viking kings to come to you." He felt himself falling, the frigid water of the bay engulfing him, then the pain fading.

Conor, Liam, and a Brownie watched from up in a willow tree on the bay shore. Richard's flagship glided by Myndill's now-empty ships and dropped its sail. A rope was thrown to one of Geir's ships, which took it in tow toward the narrows and the port beyond. Conor and his companions scrambled down from the tree.

"Return to High King Art," Liam directed the Brownie. "Tell him Waterford is lost. We'll wait for Rhoswen and join them soon." The Brownie slipped off.

All the previous night, the Skeaghshee forces had harried the Irish column with hit-and-run tactics. Casualties had been light, but progress toward Waterford had been slowed. When it became apparent that the army was not going to reach Waterford before sunrise, Conor and Liam led a scouting party ahead. The Irish forces would proceed to Slievecoiltia Hill, just north of Waterford, and wait for word.

Conor and Liam crept along the shoreline, surveying the arriving English ships. Grogoch and Wichtlein climbed out of the bog across the bay and mounted the hill west of the narrows. Skeaghshee broke from their hiding places in the woods to the east of the narrows, rushing up the other hill, calling out welcomes to their king, Kellach, who stood in victory on the prow of Richard's ship. Richard, de Vere, and Mortimer could be seen in the aftcastle.

Rhoswen emerged from the shadows beside Liam, a sheen of red blood covering the green and brown body paint on her left arm.

Liam saw that Rhoswen had already plugged the wound with clay, and he asked, "Did you locate Queen Gormflaith?"

"She lies dead in Rathgormuck Forest, along with half her force. The rest have retreated to Tipperary."

"A great loss," said Liam, looking back out over the bay. The longship of Geir, now the Viking king, turned to follow Richard's flagship.

Conor took the bow from his back, drew an arrow from its quiver, and held it out to Rhoswen. "For Kellach," he said.

"It will never be allowed to reach Kellach," she said. Taking the arrow, she dragged its shaft across her neck, leaving a trail of pale skin showing through her body paint, then held it close to her ear. "It desires to find the Viking who betrayed its land." Handing it back to Conor, its iron tip glowing faintly, she added, "The traitor Geir will have no Sidhe protection."

Conor drew his bow and, aiming high, released the arrow. It seemed as if it were going to rise forever until, suddenly turning, it plummeted at unnatural speed, piercing Geir's neck. He fell in a spray of blood to the laughter of the Fomorian high king still standing beside him.

"That may slow them down," said Conor as he sprinted through the woods toward where they'd left their horses.

"At least he'll carry the stigma of having the shortest reign in Viking history," added Liam, running beside him.

21

Outside Waterford, Ireland
The Next Morning

Alone, Jordan rode his horse through the forest north of Waterford as the rising sun promised a clear, crisp day for killing. All the drudgery and anticipation of preparation, followed by the tedious journey to Ireland with the English, had finally given way to the first morning of war.

Times of feasting and fucking have never brought such fierce ecstasy as days of carnage, Jordan thought. The feel of bloodlust rising hot with the cry of battle horns. The ring of sharpened iron against iron as each man desperately seeks to be the first to find that weak spot in the other's defense. The cries of "Help me!" from nobleman and peasant alike as they attempt to drag themselves from the field without their severed limbs. The quick prayer snatched from the slit throat of the pious. The thunder of riderless horses, crazed from their wounds. The distinctively sweet smell of blood mixed with sweat on the victors, the stench of guts spilling from the losers as the cry of havoc goes up. *This is what I have craved.*

Facing another man, knowing that only one of us will survive the next few heartbeats, feeling his life flee as I push my blade into his body—that's when I've felt most alive. Like an opium addict constantly drawn back to the poppy, he had been drawn to killing.

Until today. Until I arrived here.

A gust of wind sent yellow leaves cascading down about him. Jordan dropped the reins and held out his hands, each leaf tingling as it brushed across his skin. He closed his eyes, spurred his horse into a trot, then a canter, then a gallop. He did not retake the reins. The feeling had started with his first step from the ship and had built ever since. The energy at the heart of the world—Ardor—flowed through this land as he had never felt before, eclipsing even the rush of a life ended at his hand. It was as if he'd been searching for this feeling each time he'd killed. Now he swam in Ardor.

He kept his eyes closed and arms extended as trees and boulders flashed by. He knew where they were without having to see them. His horse followed instructions without his giving them.

Jordan finally, truly understood why the Roman Church had tried to keep people out of Ireland, why they were determined to destroy its Ardor now. How could they be the exclusive voice with and for God when God was so clearly everywhere here? How could kings claim divine selection when so much divinity was in everyone and everything?

Jordan halted his horse, opened his eyes, and gathered up the loose, swaying reins. He found himself sitting just inside a large clearing, facing a ring of standing stones around a low mound with a stone-rimmed opening. He sensed rather than saw hostile intent. He pulled on the reins, causing his horse to back into the tree line. Turning, he urged his horse into a respectful trot toward Waterford again. He felt nothing follow.

When he left Waterford that morning, the day after the English landed, most of the ships had been unloaded. By this time Jordan was sure that a second flotilla would be hovering off the bay, waiting for its opportunity to dock. These smaller vessels, chartered by merchants, blacksmiths, and tailors, would have products and services to sell, at a premium price, to the English soldiers and, if they slipped in and out quietly enough, to the Irish. The merchants' empty ships would be refilled with plunder purchased from those same soldiers for meager sums.

Today the decks of these trade ships would also be packed with paying passengers eager to rush ashore, an assortment of wives, lovers, and, primarily, whores. There was much profit to be made from war. Jordan suspected—hoped even, he admitted to himself—that

Najia would be among the passengers, though he had ordered her to wait in Milford Haven.

The English camp was rapidly sprawling outside the walls of Waterford as Jordan rode up. Local cattle had been commandeered and butchered, chunks of the meat boiling in bags made of their own hide, hung over campfires on tripods of freshly cut poles. The smell reminded Jordan that he had not yet had breakfast. Outside the city gates, Nottingham was conferring with Kellach and a group of young knights, second sons of English high nobles, first sons of low nobles, all seeking the king's favor and perhaps estates of their own in the soon-to-be-conquered country. Meanwhile their fathers rested inside the city walls, the earls of Rutland, Huntingdon, and Gloucester; the knights Despenser, Percy, Scrope, and Beaumont.

"There you are, Marshal," called Nottingham. "Come join us."

Jordan dismounted, handed his reins to a squire, and joined the group.

"King Kellach's allies say the Irish high king, along with the Morrígna's consort, has withdrawn to muster their army. The king of Leinster remains behind with a small army of Celts and some number of Sidhe, apparently in an attempt to hold us here as long as possible. He's moving his forces to the north."

"And not far to the north," said Jordan.

"You have been scouting as well," said Kellach. "That is brave, or perhaps foolhardy. Until all of the Sidhe have been brought under my control, perhaps you should leave that to my followers."

"I prefer to see for myself," Jordan snapped back.

"Do we know where the Sidhe high king is?" asked Nottingham.

All eyes looked at Kellach. He hesitated and then said, "My allies are not certain, but he does not seem to have withdrawn."

"Well, we had better go stir them up before they've a chance to establish defensive positions," Nottingham said. "The pikemen will remain behind to fortify and protect the camp. We'll take six companies of mounted archers. Rutland and Huntingdon, you each take a company shallow east and deep east for a quarter of a mile, then loop north. Gloucester and Scrope, the same move to the west. I'll take two companies of Cheshire archers straight north. When you hear my horn, converge on the sound. Soon we'll find out how well Richard's strategy works in battle.

"Kellach, your . . . what do I call them, your men?" asked Nottingham.

"I will deploy my followers. Do not concern yourself with them. They will be where they need to be."

"Well, yes, I'll leave that to you, then. We move out in half an hour."

"I'll ride with you," said Jordan to Nottingham.

"Most welcome," he replied. "Though I wish you had brought some of the VRS League with you."

"Our agreement with Kellach forbids it."

"Still," whispered Nottingham. He looked around, but Kellach had already disappeared. "He makes me nervous."

Cries flowed around the camp as men were organized. Archers led horses from the holding pens into their section of camp. The horses pranced, hopped, and pawed the ground nervously, as if testing its soundness after the unpredictable decks of the ships. Jordan watched as an archer sought to calm the horse he had selected, stroking its face and whispering in its ear. The horse's wide eyes began to soften, its hooves steady. The man strapped on the saddle. His wool tunic, green on the right side and white on the left, distinguished his status as a Cheshire archer. As with all the army, on his left chest was sewn the badge of King Richard II, featuring a white stag reclining on grass. This archer's badge was fringed with blue, indicating his rank as captain. The tunic hung almost to his knees over his brown hose and leather boots. A simple wool cap, fastened under his chin, kept his hair bound and his ears warm.

He wore no armor, only a linen gambeson, a jacket densely padded with cotton and wool weft, under his tunic. On his hip hung a buckler, a round shield merely eight inches across, and a short eighteen-inch sword. His entire livery, as with all the mounted archers, had been set in close consultation with Richard himself to facilitate rapid mounting and dismounting, a key element in Richard's strategy.

Dressed lightly, Richard's longbowmen relied on mobility for their defense. They could slip off their horses, fire several times with great accuracy at an enemy over two hundred yards away, remount, and be on the move before the Irish bows came within range. At least that is how it worked in their drills. For enemies at a shorter range, or to volley into a group, they could fire from a stationary horse, or even while galloping if required.

Finished securing his saddle, the archer strapped a bracer onto his left forearm to protect it from the snap of the bowstring and to keep his sleeve from interfering with the arrow. He secured a quiver of twenty-four arrows behind his saddle. Another quiver was attached to his back with a double cross-wrapped leather belt about his upper waist. The quiver was a band of sheepskin, wool nap facing in, covering a third of the shaft between point and feather. In battle he would grasp the point and pull the arrow down and out, let it slip through his hand to the feathers, then notch it to the bowstring and fire. After half the arrows were gone, he would tighten the leather belt to keep the quiver secure.

Expecting the Irish to be close at hand, he took the precaution of unwrapping the covering of his bow and handing the linen to his squire. Placing one end against the inside of his foot, he leaned on the other end, grasped the loop on the hemp string that hung about the bow's midsection, and slid it up to the horn notch. Holding the ready bow in his left hand, he mounted his horse, took the reins in his right hand, and swung around to muster his men.

Jordan mounted his horse. Knights began to ride out with companies of archers followed by squires. Jordan could tell the financial standing of each knight by the amount of newly developed plate armor he wore. Nottingham rode up covered head to toe in plate, his visor up.

His large warhorse was itself draped in mail. Noticing Jordan in his simple mail vest, he said, "Is that all you're going to wear?"

Jordan thought about the set of new plates waiting in his tent. "I believe it will be most important to remain nimble today," he replied. In this land he did not want to cover himself with metal and would have discarded even the mail, but he could not afford to be thought completely mad. He directed his horse into a walk north.

"Your choice, of course, Marshal," said Nottingham, riding beside him as two companies of archers fell in behind.

Nottingham urged his horse into a trot, and Jordan followed suit as they headed deep into the woods he had explored earlier that morning. This time the beat of all those English hooves seemed to be trampling down the Ardor.

Out of the corner of his eye, Jordan caught a glimpse of giant birds to his right; however, when he turned to look, it was Kellach and his new Skeaghshee entourage flitting from tree to tree. On the ground beneath them, lumbering Grogoch gave Jordan a strong impression of boulders rolling along. They carried large hammers, and Dryads rode on the backs of several. He was surprised they could keep up. He spotted a group of Wichtlein loping along like small trolls but with long, skinny legs, their weapon of choice appearing to be the javelin.

He was checking to see if other Sidhe were joining the procession when a vibration swept through the air. Leaves were torn off the trees and flew sideways into Jordan's face. Grogoch sat heavily on the ground while the Dryads scurried down to squat behind them, jabbering to one another in nervous, crackling voices. Wichtlein formed into a knot, javelins pointing forward.

The forest in front of them seemed to compress and flatten as if it had become a painting with no perspective. For a moment Jordan thought he saw an edge begin to curl and believed he could see bright light begin to slip around; he held his breath as his pulse quickened. The flat world was rent down the center, trees thrust to each side.

Kellach screamed as if it were his own skin tearing. Regaining his composure, he whispered an enchantment into his hand, then hurled it into the widening gap.

The tearing sound stilled. The trees no longer moved, having stacked themselves around a large grassy meadow, about three hundred yards square, the land rising gently to the back in full perspective. In the center waited the Irish.

About a thousand mounted Celts, Jordan estimated, brandishing their swords, bows, and spears. Standing in front of them were half as many Gallowglass in a two-deep line, their long-handled axes relaxed on shoulders, large oval shields not yet formed into a wall, their horses gathered behind the Irish forces. There were also Sidhe moving about, maybe two hundred or more. It was hard to tell with them.

Nottingham began shouting orders. One company of archers dismounted and hurried into a line three deep; the other company remained mounted and split to each side of the line. The clatter of arrows being pulled from quivers and fitted to bows was overwhelmed by Nottingham's lieutenant sounding a horn, calling for reinforcements.

Murchada, king of Leinster, and Fearghal, Sidhe high king, strode forward through the Gallowglass line. Murchada stopped while Fearghal continued toward the English.

"Kill him," Nottingham ordered the captain of the dismounted company of archers. The captain leaned into his longbow, swept it up, took careful aim, and let the arrow loose. All eyes watched as its shallow arc turned down toward the walking Fearghal. The arrow continued down, getting smaller with the distance, long after, Jordan realized, it should have struck Fearghal, or at least the ground. Soon it was lost to sight.

Nottingham wheeled his horse to directly address the line of archers. Pointing at Fearghal, he shouted, "Kill him!" A volley of arrows, too thick to count, sailed forth and met the same fate.

Stopping fifty yards from the English line, Fearghal spoke, and his voice sounded as if he were standing next to them. "Welcome home,

Kellach, though you seem to have forgotten that you were banished from the mainland, forgotten that the Adhene rule the Middle Kingdom and that I am their high king."

"You are no high king," spat back Kellach. "Not anymore."

Fearghal held up his stump of a wrist. "Yes, there may now have to be a new election. However, the Middle Kingdom clans have gifted me with the opportunity to first take a replacement hand. From you."

Kellach walked a few steps in front of the English line, made a point of looking over the Irish and Sidhe forces, and laughed. "I have many times your number. I will take your other hand, then your life, and then all Sidhe will follow me. The Skeaghshee will rule the Middle Kingdom, and I will be their high king."

The trees that encompassed the meadow leaned in, appearing to Jordan to be about to rush into the center, then leaned back, swayed, and stilled in a swarm of falling leaves.

Kellach reached toward the ground. A thick tree root wriggled up to the surface. He pulled it free, deftly molded it into a javelin as if he were working with clay, and hurled it at Fearghal. Just before reaching its mark, the javelin flashed into a cloud of ash that drifted to the ground around Fearghal.

From his belt Fearghal pulled a small ax that grew into a battle-ax as he raised it above his head and threw it at Kellach. Kellach spoke the name of the ax, "Dilgendfir," reached toward it, and drew a symbol in the air, his fingers leaving a short trail of green light. The ax flew straight at Kellach, rotating head over tail, once, twice, then seemed to rotate into itself and vanish.

An unnatural stillness settled on the meadow. Fearghal and Kellach stared at each other. Horses got nervous legs. Men pulled on their collars, suddenly warm as the air between the two Sidhe radiated heat. Fearghal strained under some unseen load. Sweat dripped off Kellach's face. Jordan closed his eyes, and a vision sprang into his consciousness of two beings spitting lightning at each other, the space between them full of thunder, flash, and smoke, but without effect.

Nottingham leaned forward in his saddle and asked Jordan, "What's going on?"

Jordan pulled his gaze back into the physical world. "It's a faerie standoff," he replied as he swung out of his saddle to the ground. He walked toward Kellach.

Nottingham, weighed down by his armor, eased from his horse with help from his squire and hurried to catch up.

Kellach broke first and turned to face them. Jordan saw Fearghal stumble out in the meadow, then catch himself.

"What now?" Nottingham asked.

"I haven't eaten today, so I propose lunch," offered Jordan.

"Now you and your men go kill the Celts," Kellach snarled. "I cannot do all the work for you."

"If our arrows will not reach them, what hope have we?" Nottingham asked, reassessing their adversary. "We may overpower this lot, but what do we do when they assemble their main army? If you cannot help us, as you said you could, you'll not get your throne."

Kellach glared at him. "Fearghal may still have enough power to protect himself, but he cannot protect all those Celts, I guarantee that. My followers and I will neutralize whatever enchantments his lackeys throw up." Pointing at Nottingham, he added, "Then I will see if the English are as good as they think they are at killing Celts face-to-face."

"Hmmm. Are you sure your Skeaghshee can handle their enchantments?" Nottingham asked. "It didn't look like it."

A cry rose from the Irish forces, followed by the clatter of Gallowglass shields forming into a wall. Jordan glimpsed English moving in the trees to the right of the meadow. Two hundred Celtic cavalry broke from their formation and charged at the new arrivals. Fearghal and Murchada rushed back toward the Irish lines.

"It's time to find out," said Nottingham. He lumbered back to his horse, shouting orders to his captains. Archers snapped to the ready position, while squires scurried to stand behind their lines, arms full of quivers.

"The rest of the Irish cavalry will soon break for the woods," called Kellach, "where they will try to flank your men and force them into close combat with the Gallowglass."

"That's not going to work," said Jordan, mostly to himself. Standing his ground in front of the lines of English archers, he felt more than saw Kellach's Sidhe followers fanning out into the trees.

The initial Celtic charge had almost made it to the right tree line when the first volley of English arrows streaked from the shadows, felling a quarter of the horses and tumbling their riders to the earth. Jordan was surprised by how quickly the next volley followed, striking before the fallen riders could pick themselves up or even raise their shields to protect themselves. A third volley felled more men and horses, who were trying to maneuver around those already flailing on the ground. In the span of thirty seconds, more than half the Irish charge was down when the rest reached the trees.

Bellowing out clan war cries, the main Irish formation thinned as lines of Celtic cavalry, this time joined by Sidhe cavalry, streamed toward the left and right tree lines. The Gallowglass shield wall began to slowly advance down the center.

Companies of English archers, called by Nottingham's horn, established formations along the meadow edges. Volleys of arrows leaped from their lines. Second volleys took flight before the first volley arced down toward the charging Irish. Only this time the Irish Sidhe were prepared, and large groups of arrows stopped short and tumbled out of the sky as if they had struck something immovable in the air. Other arrows flamed into ashes; some sprouted wings and soared off harmlessly. Less than a third of the first and second volleys completed their flight. Shouts from the charging Irish rose to a roar, voices that began to be cut off as half of the third volley reached its mark. Jordan could sense the Skeaghshee counter-enchantments growing.

Arrows sailed over Jordan's head and crashed like iron rain against the Gallowglass shield wall. Holes appeared in the barricade as arrows found small gaps and Gallowglass fell, only to quickly close as the wounded were dragged to the back and replaced. The Gallowglass halted their slow advance and tightened their shield wall.

Jordan knew that when the Archangel Azâzêl came to earth, he had taught men to work iron into weapons, thereby imbuing a desire for violence into the metal itself. With enchantments flying in both directions—to both destroy and protect the English arrows—the iron arrowheads exerted their innate will and tipped the scales in favor of bloodshed. It would take enchantments more powerful than anyone here could wield to overcome the will of so much iron, to stop this many arrows, Jordan thought.

Almost all the English arrows were now penetrating what was left of the Irish Sidhe enchantments, turning back the cavalry charges. Struggling to deal with the dead and dying underhoof, the remaining cavalry were pressed into clusters on the left and right by the constant volleys. But with the English now in range of the Irish bows, the Irish cavalry began to let fly deadly volleys of their own. The Irish formed teams of three, an archer and two shield holders.

Nottingham ordered his longbowmen to turn from the Gallowglass line and direct their fire at the Irish archers' horses. The Irish could not protect themselves and their horses at the same time. Injured horsed panicked, slamming into one another and breaking the Irish formations. Horses and their riders fell onto those already down who were trying to draw their bows or retrieve their shields.

Behind Jordan the triple line of English longbowmen were steady in their work and eerily quiet except for the count of the captain pacing his men at four arrows per minute. Frequently the cry of "Quiver!" would send a squire weaving through the lines to deliver more arrows. They were careful not to interfere with any bowman's shot, as that would result in having an ear sliced off as punishment.

Soon the quantity of dead warriors on the ground, flailing horses, and blood-generated mud made any Irish offensive formation impossible. A horn sounded from the left, then the right, two short notes followed by a long one, and those still able to ride or run broke for the Gallowglass line. The retreat left a trail of dead and injured as arrows continued to find flesh. The Gallowglass shield wall curved back around the few cavalry that reached them, and the combined force began to withdraw.

"Horse archers forward!" ordered Nottingham. The mounted archers charged into the meadow. Other commanders followed Nottingham's lead. Circling the Irish formation, just out of effective range of the Irish bows, the English were able to stop the retreat and rain down more deadly volleys. Horses were brought up for the lines of standing archers behind Jordan. They mounted and galloped past him to join the attack.

Celts and Sidhe abandoned their remaining horses, driving them away with slaps to their rumps, and then joined the Gallowglass in reinforcing the shield wall, now forced into a complete circle. A Celtic horn sounded three melancholy notes, repeated. The four Irish standards that still flew were lowered through the shields and held out parallel to the ground.

"They've lowered their standards," said the captain to Nottingham.

Jordan's feeling of relief disappeared when Nottingham replied, "Have the men press on, Captain."

The captain shouted, "Press on!" to his signalman, who gave two short horn blasts, which were quickly repeated around the meadow, eliminating any doubt that might have been in the minds of the English and Irish alike.

Jordan did not want to watch the futile stand of the Irish, but he was unable to make himself look away. Occasionally an arrow would disintegrate into ash, but not enough to make any difference. The Irish formation collapsed in on itself, men—and women, he now saw—staggering backward up the growing pile of their fallen comrades, holding aloft their shields against the deadly rain. Seeing that hope was lost, two dozen mounted one last charge but did not get ten yards.

"Shall I give the order havoc?" asked the captain, inquiring if it was time to release the men from military control, allowing them to plunder from the fallen and take hostages of the living.

Nottingham surveyed the battlefield. A small group still huddled behind shields, most of them probably wounded. Other wounded crawled along the field or held up their hands in submission. Some called for mercy. Some called to their God or Goddess of choice—Lugh, Dagda, or Danu—to bear them to Tír na nÓg, the After Lands of eternal youth. Most just stared at the English, stoic, resigned.

The captain waited patiently, knowing that to cry havoc before the order was given by the highest commander in the field was punishable by a slow death.

"Yes, havoc," said Nottingham. "But no hostages, not this early in the campaign, except for the kings. Bring me the kings, if they still live."

The captain, disappointment on his face, asked, "What of the women? There are women in their forces. Can we take them as hostages?"

Nottingham stood in his stirrups to have a clearer view of the blood-soaked meadow. "The men may do with them what they will, but only out there. Do not bring them into camp. Do not leave them alive. There should be plenty of whores in camp by now."

"Havoc!" cried the captain, a cry that was picked up and carried with fervor by the victorious soldiers. "No quarter!" added the captain, signaling they could not take hostages for the customary ransom of one-quarter of the captive's pay, a cry carried across the field with much less enthusiasm.

Nottingham added, "Captain, when all the Irish are dead, have our arrows retrieved and cleaned. I'll authorize payment of one penny for each two dozen that are still in good condition."

"Yes, my lord," replied the captain. "The men will be grateful."

"Kellach," Nottingham called, "have your men—or should I say forces—finish off the opposing Sidhe. They may still be a danger to my men."

Kellach, already fading into the forest, did not answer.

Nottingham turned his horse south and rode back toward Waterford at a trot, his squire and bodyguards following.

Jordan listened to the calls for mercy, the offers of gold, cut short. The battlefield had become a killing field. He had seen mass slaughter before, been part of it, but here it was different. Here the land itself was dying with each fresh flow of blood, the pale red of Sidhe, dark red of Celt and Gallowglass. Ardor was rotting away, and he had made it happen.

Flocks of ravens swooped in, seeking tender morsels to feed on, bits of hacked-off flesh, open chest cavities, eyes—black scavengers who flapped about, calling their irritation as English soldiers claimed corpses for their own. The dead were stripped of torcs, armbands, weapons, armor, boots, and other items of value, items the English would trade among themselves or sell for pennies to the merchants waiting back at camp.

Finally Jordan turned from the carnage, mounted his horse, and nudged it into a slow walk toward Waterford. Everything he had obtained this morning while riding alone—that connection to a potent source of Ardor, feelings of being energized and empowered—had bled away.

22

Returning to the outskirts of Waterford past nightfall, Jordan observed that the English encampment had swelled further, lit up with cooking fires, torches, and moonlight. He rode between the tents, clustered by lordly allegiance around banners bearing coats of arms, and past a drinking canopy set up by some enterprising merchant, its crude tables and benches already packed with noisy victory celebrations. Jordan reached his small circle of tents that bore no insignia, as if they belonged to an unbounded tradesman, and gave his horse to a squire. Squatting close to the fire, he tried to expel the chill that had taken hold of his bones.

"Congratulations," said his cook, handing Jordan a tankard of dark ale and a steaming plate of boiled beef topped with a hunk of rough bread.

Jordan did not even acknowledge him as he took the food. Chewing a piece of beef, he noticed that his page and the page he had left with Najia in the armada's Milford Haven embarking port were sitting to the side of Jordan's tent playing chess, an increasingly popular adaptation of the Persian game *shatranj*. Najia's fingers eased open the tent flap a few inches. Jordan could just discern her eyes shining in the glow from the fire, and his heart lightened. He placed his plate on the ground, drained his ale, and stepped toward the tent.

"Marshal d'Anglano," called a young page running toward him.

"What?" Jordan snapped.

"Lord Nottingham commands that you come immediately."

"Commands?" scoffed Jordan. "I'm the high representative of the

Vatican. I don't take commands from any other authority." He continued toward Najia and his tent.

"My deepest apologies, Marshal," said the page, bowing. "It was my mistake. Lord Nottingham told me to ask you to join him. Please don't tell him I said it was a command."

Jordan looked at the frightened boy, not more than twelve years old, and gave him a soft kick in the ass. "There, you've been punished. No more will be said. Now, go away. I'll see Nottingham tomorrow."

"Excuse me, Marshal, but it's about a king. We have captured one of their kings," the page said, shifting from one foot to the other.

"Which one?"

"I'm sorry, I don't know, Marshal."

Jordan glanced at his tent—the flap was closed, and there was no sign of Najia. He gave a sigh of resignation and motioned the page to lead on.

Nottingham's ring of red-and-white-striped tents was awash in torchlight. The page led Jordan across the central area to a medium-size tent next to Nottingham's large personal one. Upon entering, Jordan felt his hope to meet the Sidhe high king vanish when he saw a Celt, who would be King Murchada of Leinster, slumped in a chair.

Murchada's tunic was ripped open and gathered at his waist, his long black hair matted with blood and mud. A nasty gash in his right shoulder oozed past the rag he pressed against it. He must have torn out an arrow in the heat of battle, thought Jordan. Murchada's right arm hung at an unnatural angle, indicating that it was fractured in more than one place. The stubs of two broken arrow shafts protruded from his left leg.

"Keep him alive, for a while." Nottingham gave the order to a man whose green-quartered cap and leather apron identified him as a barber-surgeon.

"I just need to stop the bleeding," replied the barber, drawing a short iron from a brazier, its tip glowing hot.

"As king, I merit a quick death," said Murchada with pain, but no fear, in his voice.

There was a commotion outside. Richard strode in, followed by de Vere and Mortimer; the rest of his large retinue gathered about the entrance. "Your Royal Majesty" rolled around the tent as all bowed, except Murchada.

"Really, Nottingham, a barber-surgeon? You must upgrade your servants. Bring in Our surgeon," ordered Richard.

A man emerged from the crowd at the entrance, his long orange garde-corps distinguishing him as a master from the great medical school of Salerno.

"I want no mercy from you," spat Murchada.

"And you will receive none," Richard replied as he stood over Murchada. Richard pulled Murchada's hand away and studied his wounded shoulder closely. "There will be plenty of time to kill you later, in one fashion or another."

Murchada gritted his teeth in pain, glaring at Richard.

"But this war will be over soon, and then We will need kings to run this land for Us. Perhaps when you see the outcome, see your fellow kings pledge their allegiance to Us, you will decide the best course of action is to pledge as well. You never know. We will see. Then you will want the use of this arm and that leg."

Richard turned away and led Nottingham aside. "Describe the battle to Us."

The surgeon examined Murchada's wounds and instructed one of his apprentices to boil a pot of elder oil and the other to bring pliers, silk, and a needle. As they left to do his bidding, he called out, "And a vial of opiate."

Jordan was sure Murchada looked relieved.

A fresh hubbub arose outside, and Jordan followed Richard and Nottingham out. Two horses were being led into the torchlit ring of Nottingham's tents, the first with the body of a knight draped over it and the second with the bodies of two archers. Two men followed on foot, their hands bound to a rope trailing from the second horse.

Nottingham approached the dead knight, whose simple armor spoke of his status, and raised his head. Jordan recognized the face as belonging to the young man he had fought alongside in last week's tavern brawl back at Milford Haven. He was nineteen-year-old John of Exeter, the bastard son of John Holland, Duke of Exeter, and Isabel, wife of the Duke of York.

"Well, York has his revenge," said Nottingham. "Boil the flesh off and ship his bones back to Exeter for a Christian burial. Add the other two to the pit." Turning to the captain leading the horses, he asked, "What happened?"

"My lord, a company of Celts surprised us in the east wood. The young lord charged them bravely. Too bravely. He was ahead of the protection of my men and didn't survive the first exchange. My men were able to kill ten of them and capture these two. Do you wish to question them?"

"There's no need," replied Nottingham, drawing his sword and approaching the captives.

"Stay your hand a moment," ordered Richard. "We are in a new land. There may be new interesting ways for Us to discover." Turning to his retinue, he called, "Lord Alrik!"

Jordan did not recognize the Viking who stepped forward. Perhaps he was to be yet another replacement Viking king.

"Yes, Your Royal Majesty," said Alrik with a bow.

"How do your people kill someone when they want to set an example? Something slow, extraordinary, and . . . playful."

"We would use the rite of the blood eagle, Your Royal Majesty."

Richard walked up the captive, who was wearing seven colors. "What is your name?"

Straightening up, the captive replied, "I am Lord Reily of Kilkenny, and you must be King Richard."

"You will refer to Us as Your Royal Majesty King Richard." There was a moment of strained silence. "Well, never mind that now. Why did you attack your king's forces and kill the Bastard Exeter?"

"You are not my king. That knight was an invader, and he presented himself for the killing."

"We became your king the moment We set foot on this island." He turned to Alrik and said, "Proceed with your blood-eagle rite. We expect to be entertained."

"Bring me a hammer, chisel, and bowl of salt," Alrik called. "Strip off their tunics and stake them to the ground facedown."

The English soldiers, joking and laughing in anticipation of a good show, followed Alrik's instructions.

Early the next morning, Jordan emerged from sleep knowing that it was not yet dawn even before he opened his eyes, knowing that Najia was no longer pressed warmly against his skin in their small cot. His body was still exhausted, heavy. The screams of the prisoners from the night before had returned in his nightmares, along with the disembodied laugh of Richard. Jordan, when he was a condottiere, had always killed quickly, turning down any job that required a slow death for the victim, as torment reminded him too vividly of his plague-riddled childhood.

Opening his eyes revealed Najia, fully clothed, standing in the light of one lamp she must have lit. Something was wrong. Jordan eased himself into a sitting position.

"Are you ready for the English to win this war? For Irish Ardor to be snuffed out? Is that not why you're here?" demanded Najia.

"No. I don't know," mumbled Jordan. "I'm starting to think I never should have come here. I need more time to figure out how I feel, to decide what to do."

"You're about to run out of time. Unless you intervene, the English may end this war this morning when they capture the Celtic high king."

Jordan swung his legs over to sit on the edge of the cot and tried to rub the sleep off his face with both hands. He noticed there were twigs in Najia's hair and dirt on her shoes. "Tell me what's going on. Where have you been?"

"I've been exploring the Sidhe witch paths, and I've learned that the Celtic high king—"

"Art MacMurrough," interrupted Jordan, yawning.

Najia continued, "—has stopped at his lover's cottage, hidden with enchantments in the great wood of Leverough, but Kellach has revealed its location to Nottingham. He rides there now with a company of his men."

Jordan rose, walked over to the small table, and studied the precious map of Ireland, provided yesterday by their new Viking allies. "How long ago did he leave?"

"Two hours."

"And you're just telling me now? I'll never catch up with him."

"I can show you a faster way to Art's cottage. There are many paths for someone like you to travel in Ireland."

Jordan pulled on leather trousers. "You could've stayed away. You didn't have to come back here. I'm sure the Celts would have welcomed someone with your talents."

Najia stroked Jordan's face, interrupting his buckling on of a sword belt. "Our fates are locked together. It would be foolish of me to anger God by leaving you."

Najia led him a short way out of the English encampment and into the woods. They came to a fat old oak tree on the top of a small mossy mound with a wave of roots exposed down one side. She indicated an opening between two particularly thick roots.

"That hole isn't much larger than my head. I can't fit through there," said Jordan. "What is it, a tunnel?"

"Just go," said Najia.

Jordan got down on his hands and knees. He reached into the hole and felt around. It seemed to be larger on the inside, as he could feel nothing past the throat. He pushed in his head, one shoulder, then the other, and slid his body in. It was not nearly as tight as he had expected. Suddenly he realized that he was not climbing into a hole, he was climbing out of one, on the side of a mound with an oak tree perched on top. A hint of deep blue in the sky spoke of the sunrise to come while the moon made for the treetops, shining in the smoke rolling from the chimney of a small stone-and-thatched-roof cottage.

Jordan stood, brushed himself off, walked up to the door, and mumbled a brief incantation, which caused it to swing open silently. He stepped inside, where coals glowed in the fireplace and smoky tallow candles cast a yellow light throughout the room. A female Sidhe, still dressed in the mud- and bloodstained clothes she must have fought in the day before, lay curled up asleep on top of a pile of covers on the small bed. Art, bent over a bowl of stew, sat next to a human woman at a table in the center of the room. A large dog lying in front of the fire looked over to Jordan and let out a deep growl.

Art grabbed his sword off the table and charged Jordan in a move so quick that he had no time to draw his own sword. *I'm about to die*, Jordan thought as Art's blade swept down toward his neck. The sword's momentum, coupled with the unexpected lack of resistance, carried its arc all the way to the floor, where it sparked on the stone.

Art looked at his sword in surprise—he could not have missed. He then stared at Jordan as if he expected Jordan's head to topple from his shoulders. Jordan, also shocked, felt his neck, and then, leaving his own sword sheathed, he opened his hands, palms toward Art. The Sidhe woman leaped from the bed and gathered up a dense golden ball of light that hissed and sparked in her right hand, preparing to hurl it at Jordan.

"Hold!" cried Art, still staring at Jordan. "Who are you? What are you?"

"I need time to figure that out," said Jordan. "I need it not to end like this."

Art stepped back. "End like what?" Behind him the human woman was brandishing a knife.

A horse whinnied outside. There were the faint clinks of riders in mail and plate approaching. Jordan spun around and shut the door. "Nottingham's here. Is there a back door or a window?"

"After a fashion," said Art. The Sidhe made her threatening orb disappear and walked to the center of the room. Reaching down with her delicate arms, she inserted slender fingers into a seam and tilted up a four-foot-square flooring stone that must have weighed twice as much as she did. The human woman jumped into the hole that the stone had been covering. Art motioned to the Sidhe to enter next.

She shook her head and said, "I want to kill some English first."

Art nodded and said to Jordan, "If I can get all the Sidhe to think like that, we'll butcher the invaders." Then he jumped into the hole.

Jordan followed him, expecting to be instantly jumping out of a hole somewhere, but instead he found himself standing in an ordinary dirt hollow with a tunnel leading off. Total darkness engulfed him as the stone was pivoted closed. He felt his way forward, trailing the sounds of the other two.

Nottingham burst through the door of the cottage, followed by three mail-clad men.

"Welcome to Ireland!" shouted the Sidhe as she hurled a sparking ball of light at him. Nottingham ducked, and it struck the man behind him, who fell to the ground screaming, snakes of golden light eating away his flesh. There was a flash, and a second man fell. Nottingham dived back outside. Another flash and more screams followed.

The Sidhe woman risked a glance around the doorframe. Nottingham shouted to a pair of Grogoch that were just trundling up, "Seal her in there! She must not escape!" A faint song began to rise from deep in the throats of the Grogoch. The door slammed shut. The Sidhe heard Nottingham shout again: "Burn it down!"

She bent down and heaved on the stone covering the tunnel. It did not move. Through the window she could see fire arrows flying toward the thatched roof. She closed her eyes and held her hands out over the stone. Strands of light dripped from her fingers and crawled along the edges of the stone. She tried to lift it again but failed. She screeched in frustration as flame started to lick down through the thatch above her.

Sunrise was streaming through the trees when Jordan climbed out from the tunnel. Art was standing next to a horse. A quarter mile off to the right, the cottage was engulfed in flames.

"What's your name?" asked Art, his hand ready on the hilt of his sword.

"Jordan d'Anglano, marshal of the Vatican."

"Does this mean the Vatican wants to join our side?"

"No. This means that I'm not yet ready to see you captured or killed."

"Why?"

"This land isn't as I expected. There's much I'm struggling to understand, and I need more time. Now you had better go. We'll meet again, then we'll either fight, or . . . well . . . only time will reveal what is to come."

"Until then," said Art, untying his horse from a tree. "But don't expect any leniency if we cross swords." He swung up, followed by his lover, and rode quietly off.

Jordan turned and looked at the burning cottage in the distance, hoping the Sidhe had made it out. Then he crept around to the tree on the mound and climbed into and out of the witch path to where Najia was waiting.

The sun had risen high in the sky when a small Irish company including Conor, Liam, and Rhoswen rode over the crest of Linsigh Hill, ten miles south of Tara, and down its gentle slope, where they found Fearghal squatting at a spring beside the road. He had stripped to the waist to wash, the icy water leaving his pale skin pink, his new wounds bright red, though none appeared deep. The stump of his right wrist had already sealed over with fresh skin.

"Where is the high king?" asked Fearghal.

"Art will meet us at Tara," replied Liam.

"Tell him that King Murchada is captured and his entire force slaughtered."

"Even the Gallowglass?"

"The English sent death on black winds of iron. Kellach was too strong, his followers too fanatical, for loyal Sidhe to stop them. Many of my Sidhe fought to the death alongside the Celts. In the end no quarter was given."

Fearghal addressed Conor. "I would be dead myself if I did not need to deliver this message. Our only hope is the Morrígna. Has Aisling reconnected with enough of the Goddess's power?"

"Aisling will be enough," said Conor. "She defeated the demon Semjâzâ. She can handle Kellach."

"When her powers return, now that the twins are born," added Liam.

"Let us hope her powers return before Richard reaches Tara," said Fearghal. "Let us hope the new twins do not keep the powers for themselves. I will return to the Middle Kingdom and gather what forces are still loyal to Ireland, still true to their vows. We will join you at Tara when it is time."

Rhoswen dismounted and handed the reins of her horse to Liam. "I will see you again on the battlefield." She held his gaze for a long moment.

"Count on it," said Liam. In her eyes he saw a look that reminded him of the one his Sidhe mother gave his father. Under different circumstances he would be drawn to Rhoswen, he thought, as he watched her and Fearghal disappear into a nearby Sidhe mound.

Turning to Conor, Liam said, "You might as well split off here to Dunsany. Tell Aisling that I need you back as soon as possible."

. . . . .

Richard had established his quarters in Reginald's Tower, named after the Viking who had founded the fortified port of Waterford in 914. In the great hall, Oren sat propped up at the end of the lunch table. A purple robe draped over his shoulders fell all the way to the floor, a fool's hat cockeyed on his head, as Richard had taken to dressing up the Tylwyth Teg for meals.

Richard abruptly stood, causing his chair to tumble behind him, and shouted at Nottingham, "Art was not there? How could he not be there?"

De Vere put down his wine goblet.

Nottingham shifted uncomfortably in his armor. "The only occupant of the cottage was a female Sidhe, whom we burned."

"We do not give a damn about burning another faerie." Richard leaned forward with his fists on the table, glowering at Kellach, who sat without plate or goblet in front of him. "You said the high king would be there."

"He was there. He must have slipped out when Nottingham arrived," said Kellach.

Nottingham stiffened. "We had the cottage surrounded. And you assured me all the passages in the area to the Middle Kingdom were sealed."

"They were sealed," said Kellach. "However, if he was escorted, he might have used a witch path."

"Witch path! Witch path!" shouted Richard, now pacing around the table. "There are witches as well as faeries in this country?"

"Among the Sidhe, powers vary," said Kellach. "Sidhe who dedicate themselves to the study of the old ways can become very powerful witches, able to travel between worlds and within worlds in ways others cannot."

"Well, it does not matter, a minor irritation," said Richard, his pace increasing, with arms swinging and hands clenching, releasing. He looked toward Oren. "Do We still need that faerie?" he asked to no one in particular. Striding over to Oren, he asked, "Do We still need you?"

Oren turned his blind face up toward Richard, causing the fool's hat to slide off. "No," he replied. "You no longer need me."

"Good," replied Richard. He pulled Nottingham's sword from its scabbard and took a wild swing at Oren, catching him in the shoulder. Oren gave no cry, a look of peace on his face. Richard changed to a two-handed grip on the hilt. With three more swings, Richard had Oren's head off.

"There, let no one say We do not keep Our promises. Now, put it on a spike somewhere."

23

Next to a giant bonfire on the bank of the river Boyne outside Trim Castle stood Turlough, king of Meath. It was the eve of Samhain festival, marking the beginning of winter, halfway between the autumn equinox and the winter solstice. Tonight the veil between this world and the After Lands would thin, and feasts and sacrifices would need to be dedicated to ancestors to avoid suffering a visit from their annoyed ghosts.

Turlough remembered the Samhain eves of his youth, when he would throw the bones of livestock, slaughtered to fill the winter larder, into their bonfire as an offering. The bonfire beside him required no more bones: the pyre was stacked with burning Fomorian bodies, more than a hundred.

Turlough ordered his captain of the guard to line the bridge with torches and secure it with fifty warriors each night. "It must be kept open, Captain," said Turlough. "Let the creatures have the ford after dark. We can take it back with ease each morning if we have to."

"Yes, sire," replied the captain, immediately making his way toward the new stone bridge, finished less than a year earlier just upriver of the ford. A steady stream of refugees flowed north across it. After the English invasion, Turlough had suspended the toll of one-half a silver penny.

Liam and Conor rode around the corner of the castle, following the outer edge of the moat, leading a company of frayed and tired Gallowglass. On seeing Turlough and the pile of burning bodies, they reined in their horses.

"King Turlough," Liam said. "Looks like you had a difficult fight."

"Indeed," confirmed Turlough. "The Fomorians overran the ford and the bridge. We counterattacked. It was a long and bloody night. When the sun rose, my archers on the castle walls were able to drive them off with impunity. Now that we know, they'll not catch us by surprise again. We'll keep the bridge open."

"Were many of your people killed?" asked Liam, his brow furrowed.

"Twenty-three warriors died fighting. Most of the wounded will be ready to fight again soon," said Turlough. "What word of the English?"

Advancing north from Waterford, Richard was copying the slash-and-burn policy of *chevauchée* that his father, the Black Prince, had employed so successfully in France. Turlough last heard that Richard had skirted the Wicklow Mountains, leaving them to his Sidhe collaborators, and that he had captured and fortified Jerpoint and Kilkenny while burning all other villages to the ground along the way.

"We just withdrew from Leighlin," said Liam. "It's Richard's now."

Turlough nodded, watching the refugees plod across the bridge.

Art was not making a stand in the south. Instead he was harrying the English in an attempt to slow the enemy's advance while the Irish armies mustered at Tara and to give Aisling time to recover her powers. Art maintained that Aisling was their only hope to defeat Kellach and the English. Meanwhile Irish casualties were mounting, mostly the result of the English longbow's lethal reach.

"The land will be thick with ghosts tonight," said Turlough, inclining his head toward the line of refugees. "Few have time for a feast or even offerings."

"Too many new ghosts," said Liam.

"Do you know how long it will be until I have to move my forces to Tara?" asked Turlough.

"The English will need to take the bridge at Carlow next. We can slow them down there for a while. And Art won't attack before Richard moves north of Dublin, so as not to become trapped between him and his Viking allies. You still have a few weeks to finish preparations."

"We'll be ready," said Turlough. "Will Aisling be ready?" he asked Conor.

"Yes."

"Tell her . . ." Turlough paused. "Tell her how much we're counting on her."

"She knows," replied Conor as he spurred his horse and splashed across the ford, followed by Liam and the Gallowglass.

A wagon lightly loaded with supplies lumbered toward the castle gate. *Tonight's feast will be meager,* Turlough thought. Still, a king owes hospitality to his subjects, and the gate would be open to all who wished to attend. A shallow smile crept onto Turlough's face as he thought of his required, ritual intercourse with the symbolic Earth Mother—a welcome distraction, particularly with the beautiful priestess who had agreed to conduct the ceremony. His smile vanished as Mamos walked through the smoke toward him.

As a young boy, Turlough had been afraid of the gruff druid of Trim, old and weathered even then. Time had not improved Mamos's disposition, and Turlough hoped Mamos would not insist on being one of the witnesses at the Earth Mother ceremony. That would take all the fun from it and even risk its success.

Without greeting, Mamos declared, "Aisling no longer brings enough of the Morrígna into this world to save Ireland from Kellach or the English."

Turlough clenched his fist, dried Fomorian blood flaking off his glove, and wished he could hit Mamos for the insult to Aisling. But it was unwise for anyone, even a regional king, to strike a druid as powerful as Mamos, second only to Brigid. Instead he said, "Aisling is all we have."

"We have her new twins. They've drawn the power from Aisling, and it's said they're slow to return it. What if these twins are the next incarnation of the Morrígna arriving, as it's called for, in our greatest time of need? Perhaps Aisling is the only thing stopping the twins from bringing the Morrígna back fully into this world."

"Brigid has said that the Morrígna can't return as long as Aisling is alive. It's unknown if the Morrígna can ever return after what happened to Anya," Turlough said.

"The Morrígna can do anything the Morrígna wishes. Remember when the Goddess first appeared to us, in that time of dire need. She manifested into human form from nothing but her own desire. Are we in less need now?"

Turlough stared into Mamos's eyes. "What are you suggesting?" Turlough thought he knew. The faction calling for Aisling to retire to the Otherworld—so there could be at least a chance that the Morrígna would return to this world—was rapidly growing and had become more vocal. As one of the most respected monarchs, he had been approached several times already to see if he would join their ranks. He hoped he did not have to.

"There are Sidhe other than the Devas and Adhene that don't wish to see Kellach rise to power, some even within the ranks that Kellach considers allies." Mamos lowered his voice. "I've received word that they wish for a meeting. What I'm suggesting is that you come with me, and we shall learn what they propose."

Ignoring the chill of the first winter night, Aisling walked barefoot in her thin night shift along the tree line behind Dunsany Castle. She watched ghosts drift between the trees, so many seeming lost. Thinking of her sister, Anya, awoke that familiar pain in Aisling's heart, as if the arrow had never been pulled out. A tear slid down her cheek, cooling as it went. She thought of how, when Anya and she were young, they would sneak out in the dark of Samhain and chase the ghosts. She remembered how she had learned an enchantment to reveal their features and how Anya could make them talk, always tales of loss, regret, and loneliness. Tales that the girls, in their innocence, so confident that such misfortune would never happen to them, would giggle at as the ghosts drifted off.

Now she ached to talk to Anya's ghost, but all her attempts had failed. Anya should have returned to the Morrígna in the Otherworld, to wait for her there. But could she, with her heart destroyed? Was Anya just gone, never to return to the Morrígna, or pass to the After Lands, or even to haunt this world? Just gone?

Aisling stopped at the trailhead that had once led to her Woodwose camp. The Woodwose believed that after death they would be reborn as animals, echoing how they had lived—wolves, bears, or foxes, they hoped. Aisling saw nothing down the dark path. When she died, where would she go? she wondered. Would she, too, just be gone? Turned to nothing, without Anya's heart to call her home to the Morrígna? The pain in her chest doubled, causing her to catch her breath. She did not want to hear any stories from the dead tonight—or any night. She circled back toward the castle and increased her pace, trying to keep her fears at bay.

Since the English landed, thoughts of Anya's loss had been returning too often, bringing with them the old dark visions and making it impossible to ignore the emptiness inside herself. The invasion was a bitter reminder of what she was meant to be and what had been taken from her. With all of Ireland counting on her, the ground under her feet felt less solid. Her sleep was plagued by nightmares of Conor being killed in battle, of herself falling back into her internal blackness. She fell and fell, and in the dream she could not tell if it was a nightmare or if she was trapped once again in that hellish place. She would awake screaming and flailing for something to grasp on to. When Conor was home and she felt the nightmare waiting at the edge of her exhaustion, she would force herself to stay awake all night to keep it at bay. She did not want him distracted by her fears while he was fighting the English.

As Aisling approached her home, the rear door swung open and cast a warm light out toward her. Conor, still grubby from the ride back and cradling a daughter in each arm, smiled warmly at her. Her pain eased as she ran to him. His absences were particularly hard, given that she could not work enchantments to watch over him. Reaching the stairs, she longed to ask him to stay with her, to not return to the war, but she knew she could not. She was born to her duty to Ireland, but she had thrust position and duty upon him. It would be too much of a betrayal to ask him to abandon those responsibilities now.

☙

IT TOOK FIVE WEEKS before Turlough was ready to accept the dissident Sidhe's invitation to meet. He had urged Art to storm Dublin and take it from the Vikings before Richard reached it, but Art continued to wait for Aisling. Now Richard had arrived at Dublin and had added Carlow, Castledermot, and Connell to his chain of fortified villages, linking it to Waterford, burning the twenty-three villages in between that he did not consider strategic enough to hold. If something was not done to stop Richard soon, he would roll over Tara and be at the gates of Trim Castle in a month. Not even Trim could stand long against an army as large as his.

Tonight the road northeast was a ribbon of black rain wandering through a darker black forest. Turlough had been following the hint of gray that was Mamos's horse, which had now stopped. Turlough dismounted, tied his horse to a tree next to Mamos's, and pulled a torch from behind his saddle. He struck a flint a few times, but the sparks were doused instantly in the rain. Mamos spoke a few words, and his own torch flared up. Abandoning his efforts with the flint, Turlough lit his torch from Mamos's, then followed the old druid down a narrow path into the thick forest. He could hear Mamos muttering an enchantment of concealment, keeping other druids and Sidhe witches from sensing their location or intent.

The path opened into a large field, where a few cows along the edge huddled together against the cold, wet night. In the center an

earthen ring rose waist high. Large retaining stones set lengthwise
in the earth were carved with star trails, the eighteen-year-long
cycle of the moon around the earth and, some said, maps through
the Middle Kingdom to new worlds known only to the Sidhe. The
ring glowed, as if lit by moonlight, though the moon was well hidden behind thick clouds. It looked empty.

Taking over the lead from Mamos, Turlough sloshed across the
field and around the ring to the gap in the far side. He drew his sword,
stuck it into the soft ground, and then jammed the base of his torch
into the earthen ring above a retaining stone. Once through the gap,
he found that it was not raining inside and saw, as he knew he would,
that the faerie-lit ring was full of Sidhe.

Eight squat Grogoch and three diminutive Dryads awaited his
arrival. One Grogoch stepped forward. Turlough had the impression
that he was older than the rest, though, truthfully, it was hard to tell;
perhaps it was just that he was a bit wider than the others. He was
called Eldan. Turlough recognized him from negotiations about the
construction of the new stone bridge at Trim.

"King Turlough, thank you for agreeing to see us," rumbled
Eldan with a bow.

"Eldan," replied Turlough with a nod of his head. "It doesn't surprise me that you're not aligned with Kellach, though I'm surprised
you're still here."

Eldan rolled out a deep sigh. "I thought to leave, as so many have,
but who knows if a new world will have stone as loving as in this
world? Or harsher masters? Ireland is my home. Best to protect this
land from Kellach, for the tree does not respect the stone; rather it
seeks to break it, turn it to earth, and consume it."

"How do you propose to stop Kellach?" asked Mamos, in a tone
belying the fact that he already knew the answer.

"The Morrígna must return fully."

"The Morrígna must return," echoed the gravelly voices of the
other Grogoch and the squeaky voices of the Dryad.

"Aisling still lives. And even if she didn't, Anya's heart was destroyed," Turlough said, repeating the old familiar argument.

Eldan trundled over to one of the inner retaining stones and sang to it. Reaching his stubby fingers into the stone as if it had softened to clay, he tugged open a chamber, then stepped back.

Mamos pulled a candle from his pocket, lit it with whispered words, and held it up to the opening. Turlough bent to look inside and gave an involuntary intake of breath at what had been concealed: a shriveled thing, brown like a piece of dried meat, no more than a small bite. Turlough had been at the Ceremony of Hearts when Aisling and Anya were but seven and knew that this must be the missing piece of the Morrígna heart, the piece entrusted to the Skeaghshee—thought to be from the previous Anya incarnation.

Turlough straightened up quickly, instinctively surveying his surroundings, straining to see into the dark beyond the ring. He reached for his sword, but his hand found only the scabbard.

"Do not worry," said Eldan. "Kellach cannot afford to draw attention to this place by having it watched. He killed the Grogoch who created this chamber for him. Her name was Raisie, and I was the one who taught her our songs when she was young. . . ." Eldan's voice trailed off.

"She told you of this?" asked Turlough.

"She became concerned about betraying the Morrígna and planned to tell Aisling. She was a solid girl," replied Eldan. "Kellach thinks he owns us. We are one with the stone, and you do not own stone, you do not own something that outlives you, you just get to use it for a while. It is time for Kellach's life to end, for the allegiance of the Grogoch and the Dryads to return to the Morrígna."

Turlough reached toward the chamber's opening, but Mamos grabbed his wrist. "No. It's protected." It was then that Turlough noticed the faint blue sheen across the mouth of the enclosure.

"I can break the enchantment," said Mamos, "but doing so will alert Kellach. We must wait until we're ready to act."

"Ready? Ready for what?" asked Turlough, hoping he was not about to hear what he suspected was coming.

"Ready to perform the Ceremony of Hearts with the new twins," replied Mamos gravely.

"For which we will also need Aisling's heart," added Eldan.

"In her death," said Mamos, "Aisling will perform her greatest service to the Celts and the Sidhe. Her spirit will join with the Morrígna only to immediately return in the twins. It will be more of a birth than a death for her."

"What if you're wrong?" argued Turlough. "Then we lose all hope for the Morrígna's help in defeating the English."

"The Morrígna will provide an irrefutable sign."

"And how will this sign come to you? In a dream? Or are you going to meditate by a waterfall?" Skepticism rose in Turlough's voice.

"The sign will come to you, not me," said Mamos, "when we submit Aisling's twins to the Test."

"And will you bond the Test with your life?"

"In this war what matters the life of one old man or one infant?"

"Yes, they are but infants, too young for the prescribed Ceremony of Hearts. That is, if they survive the Test. Even if they bring the Morrígna fully back into this world, what good can infants do us now?"

"Knowledge of the Morrígna's return, even in infant form, will call the Sidhe away from Kellach and bind them to their old oaths. It will draw many back from their new worlds, binding them to this world again. The Morrígna will empower the Celts and the Sidhe to keep fighting the English until the twins are old enough to drive them out completely."

"Mamos speaks with truth," said Eldan, smoothing closed the stone chamber, leaving no trace of its existence.

Aisling awoke shivering. She slipped from under the covers of their bed and stood in the darkness. She concentrated. A glow rose in the hearth, surrounding the stacked wood. She concentrated harder. There was a spark, a sudden whoosh of air, and the wood burst into flame, bringing a smile to her face.

"Your power is returning," mumbled Conor from the bed.

"That's not all that's returning." A candle on the bedside table sputtered, then lit. Aisling pulled her night shift off over her head and crawled back into their bed.

Two hours later she untangled herself from Conor and padded across their bedchamber to the crib.

"Ah, the joys of making up for lost time," said Conor, propping himself up. Aisling picked up one of her daughters, Deirdre, whom she had heard moving, but not crying. Both Deirdre and her sister, Uaine, rarely cried, which worried Aisling. Climbing back into bed, she held the hungry infant to her breast.

Conor rubbed her shoulders as the baby suckled. "The whole country has been waiting for you."

"I'm not sure I am ready to fight yet."

"The English will soon sweep through and destroy our tiny castle," said Conor softly. "There's little time left. I will be by your side to protect you, and I will make sure Liam and Art provide a large guard."

"I'm not afraid of dying. It was not long ago that I yearned for it," Aisling reminded him, inhaling the sweet fragrance of her daughter's head. "I'm afraid of losing you. The Skeaghshee were right—when I fight, people around me die. People I love."

Conor stroked Deirdre's dash of red hair until the baby unlatched from her mother, having fallen into a deep sleep. "We will just have to protect each other." Conor took Deirdre from Aisling and replaced her with Uaine, whose arms were outstretched.

"This land brought me only misery," said Aisling, directing a nipple into Uaine's eager mouth. "Until I found you. You mustn't die, for our girls' sake as much as for mine. If you leave me for the After Lands, I'll plummet back into my dark half. I know I will. I can feel its edge even now, and then what kind of life will our daughters have? Better I die than you."

"We can't hide from Richard in any castle, and we can't hide from Kellach in any forest. They're coming for you, and they will have to go through me." Conor knelt in front of Aisling and kissed her palm. Taking the candle, he gently blew against the flame, which streamed over and swirled into a small ball in her hand. Conor stopped blowing, yet the yellow sphere of flame continued to grow. "We have to fight them. Defeat them. You and I together."

Aisling closed her hand, and the flame disappeared. "I know." She sighed. She stroked Conor's cheek, her hand still warm. "I go to battle to protect you. I'll not let you leave me, and I'll not let our daughters lose their father." She kept her voice steady with deliberate effort.

When Uaine was finished, Conor returned her to the crib, gently placing her alongside her sister, where their tiny chests rose and fell in unison. Aisling stood to follow but was overcome with the sudden vision of a fate worse than losing Conor—losing her daughters. She grasped the bedpost and took several deep breaths, but she quickly realized that the vision did not have the feeling of true foresight, and she dismissed it as the normal anxiety of a new mother.

24

Tara, Ireland
December 26, 1394

Liam walked down the Hill of Tara in the frosty morning and into the Gallowglass encampment. All of the warrior schools had brought their students with at least five years of training to join the established Gallowglass companies—although one look at the faces gathered around the campfires told Liam that more than a few younger than thirteen years old had slipped in as well. *They will not be students after tomorrow,* he thought.

Reaching the center of the camp, he strode into the giant common tent searching for his niece, Treasa, to whom he had given his Sgathaich Scoil warrior school. Liam found her with Earnan and a scrivener, signing a one-year-and-a-day marriage-contract renewal.

"Another year? I thought the previous one was the last for sure," declared Liam.

Earnan pulled open his tunic, revealing a fresh wound among the scars. "We fought for it, and she won again." Leaning into Liam, he whispered, "It's how I keep her renewing."

Treasa glanced up from the document. "No use signing a longer contract, as you're probably going to get yourself killed in this war."

"I left all my property to Liam. I don't want you motivated to let me get killed."

"You don't have anything I want."

"We'll have to feast to your happiness later," Liam interjected. "All Irish forces are moving south to Ratoath village today. The English have finished their God's-birth celebration and are advancing up Slige Cualann." Slige Cualaan was the kings road south, from Tara past Dublin.

"What kind of people worship a God that has only been born once?" asked Treasa.

"Have your students ready to leave in an hour," said Liam. "Your school will ride with my companies."

Treasa gave Earnan a long, hard kiss. "About time we got the chance to kill English." She bounded out of the tent with Earnan following. Cries could be heard rising through the camp as similar orders were received.

At the Meath embassy in the Tara royal enclosure, Art stood beside the druid Mamos and looked down at Turlough, whose bedcovers were soaked in sweat. Turlough mumbled incoherently as Mamos placed a wet rag on his feverish forehead.

"He may not survive the day, even with my treatment," said Mamos.

Art frowned. "Do what you can, but meet us at Ratoath by dawn tomorrow. We will need you. More is at stake than one life, even a king's life."

"Trust me, that's something I understand," replied Mamos.

Aisling, dressed in riding attire and a warm cloak, stood holding both Deirdre and Uaine in her Dunsany Castle bedchamber. She gently rocked them while softly singing an Irish lullaby. Brigid, wearing her white robes, walked in followed by a wet nurse. Through the window the afternoon light darkened as sleet began to fall, carried on the east wind.

"We need to go," said Brigid, putting her arm around Aisling's shoulders. "Richard has started up the kings road and will be here in two days, at Tara in three, if we don't stop him."

Aisling hugged her daughters tighter. "I keep having this feeling that it's wrong to leave them, that I should be doing something different to protect them."

Brigid rested a hand on each tiny head and closed her eyes. "I have no foresight of any danger to them. They'll be safe here."

Reassured by Brigid's words, Aisling felt her anxiety ebb. She kissed each of her daughters and handed them to the wet nurse just as Conor entered carrying her sword. "The horses are ready."

"Remember, no unnecessary risks," Aisling commanded her husband. "We both must survive this." She accepted her sword and cast a final longing look back at her twins.

Night had fallen when Turlough forced down the foul-smelling drink that Mamos held to his lips. Half an hour later, he was standing, shaky but able to dress. "Did you have to make my illness that bad?" he said, more an accusation than a question.

"It had to be convincing to Art and any druids he brought," replied Mamos.

"He did not bring any druids."

Mamos shrugged.

"Get me some ale and bread." Turlough's order was stern enough that Mamos bowed and hurriedly left for the kitchen.

By four in the morning, Turlough and Mamos were once again slogging toward the earthen ring, this time in sleet rather than rain. A glow rose from within it, illuminating the ice forming on the trees surrounding the field. Hesitating at the entrance and eyeing the small group of Grogoch and Dryads waiting inside, Turlough asked Mamos, "Are you sure this is the only way? You are staking our lives on it."

"We are staking more than our lives on it," replied the old druid. "The time is upon us. We must act."

"What do you think Kellach will do when he feels you break his enchantment protecting the heart segment?"

Dawn was more a rumor than true light when Jordan pushed open his tent flap and stepped out. The wind had died, and sleet had given way to heavy snow. His squire was working to get a fire going. His small camp was set off by itself north of Clonee, a village on the kings road that had been so overwhelmed by the English encampment that it was no longer possible to tell village from camp. Citing the role of the Vatican as an observer, Jordan had taken to keeping his distance from the English army. Najia emerged from his tent and bent to help with the fire. Miraculously, it roared to life. The real reason Jordan kept his camp well away from the others: there was growing talk among the English that Najia was a witch.

Feeling restless, Jordan pulled his cloak tighter and headed north. His boots crunched upon the frosted grass. The fate of Ireland was about to be decided, and, to his surprise, he was no longer conflicted. It was not just his distaste for Orsini's blackmail, trying to force him to join the VRS League when he returned to Europe, nullifying the legate's promise of land and title. No, it was Ireland itself. Every day he sensed Ardor evaporating, like a river in a drought, but there was still more here than anywhere else. It made Ireland feel like home. And there was Najia to consider. Europe was becoming an increasingly dangerous place for women like her. He was not sure she could ever return safely. The light in the eastern sky grew, along with his certainty: he wanted the Irish to win. Now, what to do about it?

He passed through a gate in a low, gray stone wall and started across a large field with a hawthorn tree in the center. Spying a figure standing under the barren tree, he diverted toward it. Kellach, staring uneasily to the northwest, did not acknowledge Jordan's approach. It was the first time Jordan had seen him concerned.

"Worried about the battle today?" asked Jordan.

"Which side are you hoping will win, in truth?" asked Kellach.

The man and the Sidhe stood under the tree in silence as snow fell down around them. Jordan slowly edged his hand toward his dagger. Out of the corner of his eye, he saw Kellach's hand move to rest on the hilt of his sword. That was unfortunate. Jordan wished he had thought to bring his sword on his morning walk. He considered making a move anyway, but knew it would be foolhardy, he had seen how deadly a fighter Kellach was. Jordan, then Kellach, allowed their hands to drift back down to their sides.

Kellach broke the silence. "The Celts have found the hidden heart segment and will try to recall the Morrígna." He turned toward Jordan and smiled. "There was a time when that might have helped them, but it is too late. The seeds of my victory are sown, even if the Morrígna returns." Kellach walked back toward the English camp.

"Seeds may sprout, but they can still be torn from the earth," Jordan called after him. Kellach did not respond.

When Jordan returned to his camp, he found Najia packing their horses for travel, not battle. His squire, cook, and two pages were standing off to the side, watching. *Trust Najia to take decisive action,* he thought.

Najia kissed him and said, "No matter who wins today, the English will no longer tolerate a reputed witch in their presence. I've learned that a trial is being planned, and you know what the verdict will be. It's time for me to go." She placed her hand on his chest. "Besides, neither you nor I belong with the English anymore. Come with me. Somewhere in this land there's a place for us."

Jordan covered her hand with his. "I was thinking the same," he said. He stepped away from her, opened his horse's saddlebag, and retrieved a leather pouch, one of the few things he was carrying with a Vatican seal on it. From inside he selected six gold nobles and two dozen silver pennies, which he dropped back into the saddlebag. He handed his squire the pouch, still round and heavy with coins. "Divide the rest among the four of you as promised," he said. "My gratitude for your loyalty—and your discretion."

"Thank you, my lord. Good luck to you." There were handshakes all around, though none of them offered to join him.

Later that morning the snow had slacked to drifting flakes. South of Ratoath Village, Conor, Aisling, and Brigid rode up the low, broad hill, passing a group of Sidhe Devas carrying down the bodies of fallen comrades. At the summit was a small Sidhe rath with half its earthen walls destroyed and a pile of bodies—the Wichtlein who had tried to defend it. On the other side of the rath, Liam, Fearghal, and Rhoswen sat on their horses studying the landscape below. Swirls within swirls of blue paint engulfed half of Liam's face, flowed down his neck, and disappeared under his cloak. Aisling recognized the motif; it belonged to his Sidhe mother's clan.

To the south, Aisling could not see the kings road, only—at the very edge of sight—a line of movement: the English army. To the right was a dense wood; to the left a wandering bog; down the middle, all the way to the English, stretched wide fields crisscrossed with low stone walls.

"Perfect," said Conor. "Richard's dream battlefield. Open ground for his archers, trees for his Skeaghshee."

"Which is drawing him north off the road," replied Liam. "Aisling and our druids benefit from the open as well, and we have the high ground."

"Kellach will have told Richard that," said Conor.

"Perhaps," said Fearghal. "But Kellach does not care how many English die as long they defeat us. Richard believes momentum is on his side, and he's overconfident that he will win this war. Besides, they both know, as we all do, that this battle is inevitable."

"So we fight today," acknowledged Aisling. "Now that I can see the terrain, show me where our forces will be deployed."

"You, Brigid, and the rest of the druids will work from here," replied Liam. "Conor, your Gallowglass and two companies of Celts will protect this hill while Aisling holds the enchantment. Art will lead the main force of Celts down the left center, and I'll lead the Gallowglass down the right center, straight at the English front line." Liam swept his arm along the line of fields. "We'll break the English formations and destroy the bulk of their forces."

"You're going to have to work fast. I don't know how long I can hold an enchantment of this power," said Aisling.

"We mount one massive charge. There'll be no standing formations," said Liam.

"My Sidhe forces are already concealed in the bog," added Fearghal. "When the English pass that old Christian church"—he pointed to an abandoned stone building three-quarters of a mile south—"half of my Sidhe will sweep behind the English to the trees, engaging the Skeaghshee and whatever other Sidhe are hiding there while blocking any English retreat. The other half will attack the main body of the English from the left."

Aisling's eyes turned to Liam, who for her entire life had been by her side. "Just come back alive."

"Just keep those arrows off me," replied Liam.

"May the Morrígna protect us all," said Fearghal solemnly. With a nod to his comrades, he urged his horse into a trot and started down the hill, with Rhoswen following.

Brigid slid her horse alongside Liam's and leaned into him. "I've decided that after this is over I'll pass on the mantle of Brigid to one of my priestesses. I've accepted the position of druid of Connacht, which doesn't require celibacy."

Liam kissed her forehead, eased away from her, and galloped after Fearghal.

From the foot of the hill came the sounds of the Celtic forces moving into position under the command of Art. To one side the Gallowglass companies, distinctive from the cloaked Celts, were not outfitted in their normal heavy mail and iron helmets. Today was not a day to stand and fight; today was a day to charge and win—or die. All of the Gallowglass, men and women, had stripped to their waists, with their torsos, arms, and faces painted in the complex blue patterns of their own clans and Gods. Steam rose from the mass of bodies. One hand held their shield and their horse's reins, most choosing to fill their other with a sparth, a six-foot-long battle-ax with a foot-wide blade. Aisling watched as Liam galloped to the front and threw his cloak to the frozen ground, revealing the rest of his blue motif. Treasa and Earnan moved in behind him.

Conor took Aisling's hand. "We're both going home when this is over, home in a land that's safe for our daughters. I'll not let any harm come to you."

Aisling nodded, desperately wanting to believe him. Her brow furrowed, she stared out across the coming battlefield, pristine white in snow.

Turlough rode toward Dunsany Castle. Mamos, riding beside him, was mumbling words to further strengthen the enchantment that had been hiding their intent from the foresight of others, particularly Brigid and Rhoswen. Turlough rode in silence, sure that neither would be casting her inner sight in this direction today. And if the Test of the twins was successful, no enchantment could block the sudden knowledge among all Sidhe and druids that the Morrígna was returning.

As they approached, the gate opened and Dunsany's steward walked out to greet them. "King Turlough," the steward said with a bow. "I am sorry, but Aisling and Lord Conor left to join High King Art yesterday."

"We're aware of that," replied Mamos. "Art sent us to ensure the safety of the twins."

The steward looked from one to the other. "Of course," he replied, and motioned them inside.

A procession of two packhorses loaded with wood and nine white-robed druids reached the top of the hill. There should have been ten.

"Where's Mamos?" Brigid called out.

"He hasn't arrived yet," replied a young druid from Meath.

"No great loss," whispered Brigid as she and Aisling dismounted. "The old relic's powers are fading anyway." They joined the others in the construction of a large bonfire. Once it was ablaze, Brigid called everyone into a circle and began a chant.

A series of loud rumbles drew Aisling's attention back toward the English, where Grogoch lumbered along in front of advancing lines of horse archers and a scattering of armored knights. Each swing of a Grogoch hammer demolished fifty feet of wall, sending stones flying.

Suddenly Fearghal's forces—Devas, Adhenes, Brownies, and a few Leprechauns—rose from the bog and streamed on foot behind the English. Before they could reach the tree line, Skeaghshee and Wichtlein charged out, crashing into them. The day's first ring of blade on blade rose up to Aisling, and fear caught in her throat, fear for those she loved around her, fear for her daughters, fear she would fail them all.

As the last wall fell, English archers reined in their horses and let fly a volley of arrows. Aisling gasped in surprise that the arrows were able to reach all the way to the Irish lines. Even though the Irish threw up their shields into a wall, men and horses fell.

"Aisling!" shouted Brigid.

"Yes, I know," Aisling snapped back. "You suppress any Skeaghshee enchantments, I'll take care of the arrows." Aisling scooped up a handful of firelight and held it out toward the battlefield. She began reciting an enchantment in the original language of angels while slowly closing her fingers around the ball of light. It infused her hand.

"Azâzêl," Aisling called out, "master of iron, patron of the Celts before your corruption, I know your true name." Aisling spoke a sound like metal cleaving bone. She felt the most delicate of touches from Anann in the Otherworld, and a fringe of green circled her gray irises. Around the top of the hill, the gently falling snow began to seethe. With her glowing hand, Aisling traced a complex symbol in light that continued to hang steady in the turbulent air. "Azâzêl, I bind you to this place and time, to preventing any iron from flying." A disturbance radiated through the snowfall, out from the hill and across the fields.

Below, companies of English archers drew arrows in their longbows and released. The arrows dropped to the ground at their horses' feet. They quickly tried again, with the same result. No iron flew.

From the Irish, horns sounded only to be immediately drowned out by the roar of warriors as they charged forward, smashing into the English lines. Fearghal led the rest of his Sidhe forces out of the bog and into the English's right flank. Skeaghshee enchantments soared from the trees toward the hill, only to be repelled by Brigid and her druids.

Jordan and Najia galloped around the north end of the bog and reined their horses into a skidding stop on the frozen ground. Spread out to the south, the battle had become a melee. Waves of enchantments rolled through the snowy air, dashing into one another in sudden, fierce swirls, each canceling out the other. Gallowglass and Celt were cutting through the English archers, overpowering their light swords and small shields. Fifty English knights, with armor and broadswords, bravely mounted a charge to protect their men.

It was the light—a warm glow radiating from a low hill not far away—that alerted Jordan to what was suppressing all flying iron, arrows or javelins. *It must be Aisling,* he thought, astonished by the strength of the enchantment she was maintaining. His heart pounded against his ribs, hope surging through him for the first time since landing in Ireland.

Movement in the trees at the base of the hill caught his eye. Kellach came into view. Jordan could not hear what Kellach was calling, but a company of Skeaghshee broke from the forest and rushed the hill on foot. Conor led a mounted charge of Celts down to intercept them.

Aisling, her face illuminated by the glow of Azâzêl's symbol floating before her, saw Conor lead the charge down hill. She began an enchantment of protection for him, and as she did so, the luminosity of Azâzêl's symbol dimmed.

"Aisling!" Brigid called out to her in alarm. "Maintain your connection to Azâzêl! Don't let him become unbound!"

"I have to protect Conor," Aisling called back, not taking her eyes off her husband.

"You are protecting Conor from the English archers—that's critical."

Aisling abandoned the new enchantment. She refocused, reached out, and retraced Azâzêl's symbol. It returned to full brightness, but it took everything she had to maintain it, and her face dampened with cold sweat. She thought she heard an infant start to cry and glanced around for the source of the sound. She realized it was in her mind; it was one of her daughters. The cry abruptly stopped, and a searing pain struck her heart. She screamed and fell to her knees, clutching her chest. She tried to see Conor through the fog of pain, tried to call out to him, but her throat would no longer respond.

Conor turned toward the scream that had pierced the cacophony of battle and saw Aisling rise unsteadily. She stumbled back toward her horse, out of sight over the crest of the hill. Brigid called for her to return. He felt the whisper of a sword through air and brought his shield up to take the blow. His horse plunged to the ground as its legs were cut down by an ax. He rolled free and came up, thrusting his sword under a Skeaghshee's shield into his groin. Another lunged at Conor, who parried, cut across the Skeaghshee's sword arm, then slashed his throat. Conor risked a look back up, but Aisling was gone and light was dripping off Azâzêl's symbol. Brigid was struggling in vain to renew the enchantment as it melted away.

Conor could hear Kellach close at hand calling for archers. One arrow flew, then another. "Brigid!" Conor shouted. "Get her back!" He turned and struck down another Skeaghshee to reveal Kellach advancing toward him across the red snow, a sword in each hand.

Liam was killing his way into the English lines. Progressing steadily, he used his half-Sidhe ability to anticipate the moves of each successive foe and had established a rhythm of delivering the lethal strike on the third blow alternating with the second. He felt a compulsion to look back toward the hill. There was no sign of Aisling, only Brigid bursting into her swan form, her robes collapsing onto the ground.

Worried, he heard the English commanders shout new orders. Over the battlefield he spied a small volley of arrows taking flight.

"Dismount, shields up!" he shouted. The Gallowglass around him jumped from their horses and pulled them into a tight formation, slamming their shields into a wall. The *whack, whack* of iron arrowheads striking wood washed across them, intermingled with curses as arrows found gaps and struck flesh. Several wounded horses reared, jerking their reins free, and fled.

"Something's happened to Aisling," Liam said to Treasa, who had crowded in beside him. "If the archers start up in force, we're going to be in a very dangerous position."

"Let's charge farther into the English," she said. "They'll not rain arrows onto us if we're centered in their men." A second, much larger volley of arrows fell on the front lines, striking Irish and English alike.

"That's not going to work," said Earnan from the other side of Treasa, adjusting his shield to catch an arrow.

There was still no sign of Aisling or Brigid on the hill, but Liam spotted Conor facing off against Kellach. Conor made a move. Kellach parried and circled away, as if waiting for something. Two short notes sounded from an Irish horn, followed by a long note, the signal to withdraw. The Gallowglass started to back up while trying to protect themselves and their horses from the now-steady rain of arrows.

"Follow me and keep those arrows off my back." Liam set off at a run toward Conor. Treasa and Earnan followed close, swinging their shields to block arrows. Together they wove through retreating Celts, knocking down or cutting through any English who tried to obstruct their path.

On the hilltop an arrow struck down one druid, then another, and the rest ran for cover on the far side of the crest. Liam realized that no more counter-enchantments would be coming from them. He had to make it to Conor in time, fight through the chaos that stood in his way. He wanted to shout at Conor to retreat, but he knew it would be futile over the din of the battlefield.

A smile crawled up Kellach's face, and his lips moved, and the wood of Conor's shield rotted away to dust. Conor threw down the limp bindings and raised his sword in a high guard. Kellach lunged toward him. There was blade against blade, back and forth for a frenzied minute. The sword in Kellach's right hand parried a thrust from Conor, engaging him just long enough for Kellach's other sword to slip inside Conor's guard and plunge up under his mail vest. Kellach yanked out his blade and pushed Conor to the ground, where he lay gasping, blood bubbling from his mouth. All Liam could do was continue to fight his way forward. Kellach looked over at Liam, then led his Skeaghshee up the hill.

Upon reaching Conor, Liam went down on one knee. Conor grasped Liam's arm, tried to speak but only coughed up more blood. Treasa and Earnan hunched over them, shielded them from arrows. A wolf howled in the distance. Liam did not turn to look, holding his friend and keeping his gaze locked with Conor's as life faded from his eyes.

From the northern edge of the bog, Jordan and Najia saw Aisling gallop away and, a minute later, Brigid burst into her swan form, robes collapsing onto the ground, to fly after her. A group of Skeaghshee arrows sailed toward Brigid. Both Jordan and Najia raised their hands and flung enchantments, knocking down all the arrows except one, which struck the swan in the side. The swan tried to keep aloft but began to flutter toward earth.

"Come on!" shouted Jordan, spurring his horse into a gallop.

They found Brigid, back in her human form, crawling in the snow. Jordan dismounted, covered her with his cloak, and said, "Be still, we're here to help you."

"No," gasped Brigid, "I must catch Aisling."

"Not until we get this arrow out of you."

Jordan and Najia eased Brigid down flat on her stomach. Najia gently probed around the arrow shaft with two fingers.

"Well?" asked Jordan.

"Shhh," hissed Najia. Shutting her eyes, she held her hand next to the wound, then bent down and placed her ear against Brigid's back. She sat up and stroked Brigid's cheek.

Brigid asked, "How bad?"

"The arrowhead is lodged in a major vessel. You're bleeding inside."

Jordan reached to pull out the arrow, but Najia grabbed his hand. "That will make the bleeding worse, and she'll be dead in minutes."

"What then?"

"I'm going to try to bind the vessel to the arrowhead. It won't save her, but it'll slow down her departure."

"Please," said Brigid. "Do what you can. Then take me to Dunsany Castle. You must hurry."

Jordan retrieved a clipper from his saddlebag and cut off the arrow shaft at the skin. Najia held her hand over the wound and mumbled an enchantment. There was a whiff of burning flesh as the gash closed, and Brigid grimaced in pain, then lay quiet. Helping her stand, Jordan tightened his cloak around her. Brigid staggered and leaned against him. When she was ready, with much help, she mounted Jordan's horse, and he swung up behind her.

"Slow and smooth," said Najia. "That's her only chance to get there alive."

At the sound of a howl, Jordan turned toward its source. A giant red she-wolf now stood at the north edge of the bog where he and Najia had first spied the battle.

In the center of the melee, Fearghal was swinging his long, slender blade in graceful, deadly arcs that severed English arms and legs. Without a second hand to hold a shield, he was forced to knock down an arrow with his sword, then sidestep another before he could duck behind the shield wall that three companies of dismounted Celts had formed around their high king. "The day is lost," he said to Art.

"No, we cannot retreat now. We're too close to victory."

"Aisling is gone. There will be no victory today. Save as many of your warriors as you can."

Art peered between the shields. The air was thickening black with arrows. "Sound withdraw!" he shouted to his horn bearer. The call of two short notes followed by one long one was taken up by other Irish horns. "Have your Sidhe fall back to Tara," Art said to Fearghal.

Fearghal shook his head. "My time in this world has come to an end, as has the time of all loyal Sidhe. I have passed the word, all who now wish to seek a new world, withdraw to the Middle Kingdom. Those ready to travel to the After Lands, stand with me and fight to the death."

"My king," said Rhoswen, who had just slid behind the shield wall to join them, "I will not abandon this land. I believe the Morrígna will return, and I know there are others who believe the same."

"My daughter, I do not see that, but my sight has grown dim. Choose that path if you wish, but do not die on this field today."

"We may all have no choice but to die here," said Art, surveying the English movements. Their captains had restored order among the mounted archers, and a troop was already moving around to cut off the Irish vanguard's retreat.

A howl pierced his thoughts. He spotted the giant red she-wolf as it raised its head and let out a louder howl, compelling English and Irish alike to take heed. A vast pack of gray and black wolves took up the cry, carrying it forward as they swarmed past the red wolf toward the battle. Horses reared in blind terror as the pack closed in. Others spun as their riders tried to regain control. Men fell to the ground. Just before reaching the first of the English, the wolves rose up and finished the charge on their back legs, with human faces howling.

"Wolfcoats! Berserkers!" shouted Art.

"The last of the Woodwose," said Rhoswen. "I sense their lust for revenge."

The Woodwose, dressed in wolfskins with razor-sharp claws strapped to their hands, bounded into the English, tearing the bellies out of horses, the throats out of men. A desperate sword stroke cut the skin-draped arm off a lead Woodwose. The crazed look in his eyes intensified as he raked the face of his attacker, blinding him before lunging for another.

"This is your chance," said Fearghal. "Be quick and get your warriors out. It will not be long before the English regroup."

Art clasped Fearghal on the shoulder. "Kill all you can."

"Go. When it is your time, I will meet you in the After Lands, and we will feast as if we had won the day."

∝

AISLING STUMBLED up the stairs of Dunsany Castle and flung open the door of her bedchamber. She stepped inside and paused, trembling. King Turlough rose from the chair where he awaited her. His bloodstained sword fell from his hand and clattered on the stone floor next to the decapitated body of Mamos. Mamos's head sat on a table in the center of the room.

One daughter was wailing from her crib. Only one. It took Aisling a moment to force her eyes to focus on the other one, Uaine, lying dead on the table next to Mamos's head. A dagger was beside the infant—a few drops of blood had fallen from the blade onto the wood. Aisling gasped for air. "Why?" was all she could get out.

Turlough handed her the dried-up piece of heart. "I am sorry. We thought . . . I thought . . . It was the Test. To save Ireland. My life is yours to . . ."

Aisling screamed at him, bending over with the effort. Turlough's skin turned the black of absence, his chest caved in, his shoulders folded together, his body crumbled and disintegrated into a patch of dark mist, which was sucked into the fireplace and up the flue. Silence fell. Deirdre had stilled. Aisling gripped the piece of heart in her hand, rough and leathered with age. Tears flowed down her cheeks. "Never again," she whispered, flinging it into the fire, which erupted in blue flame and then went out.

Dark had settled in when a procession of riders led by Art approached Dunsany Castle by torchlight. Treasa rode with one hand on Conor's back, his body draped in front of her over her horse, Earnan riding beside her. Liam was cradling Brigid tight against him, breathing warm air into the cloak wrapped around her. Even with all his efforts, he had felt her body cooling as they traveled. When Liam had overtaken Jordan and Najia, he'd been prepared to kill them both until Art vouched for Jordan, convincing him to spare their lives. "Now we're even," Art told Jordan.

When they reached the castle, the steward and the servants, who had been squatting by a fire outside, rose.

"We're here," Liam whispered to Brigid, who opened her eyes but said nothing.

Earnan dismounted and tried the door. It was bolted. He pounded on it. Aisling appeared at an upper window, her gray eyes ringed with red, lips tight. She clutched Deirdre against herself with both hands.

"Aisling," called up Liam. "We bear Conor's body to you."

"You think I didn't feel his passing? I'll have no more death, no more pain in my home. Take it away."

The steward approached Art's horse and silently handed a cloth-wrapped bundle up to him. Art, the day's events hanging on his face, took the parcel, the size of a loaf of bread, and began to unwrap it. The others watched in silence. Art froze when a dead Uaine was exposed. "The Morrígna has abandoned us," he said softly, rewrapping the bundle.

"Aisling," called Liam. "Let me help you, let us in."

Aisling stared down, silent.

"At least help Brigid, I beg you. She's badly wounded."

"I can do nothing more," said Aisling, withdrawing from the window.

"We have failed." Brigid's words slipped out on a wisp of breath. "Aisling is lost to this land." She turned her eyes to Liam. "I'm sorry, I tried to help her."

He hushed her. "You did all anyone could do. Save your strength."

"I wish I could stay. How I long to be with you." Brigid closed her eyes, and Liam felt the last of her life drain away.

. . . . .

On the order of Art, the steward retrieved axes from an outbuilding, and trees were cut and a simple pyre built. Moonlight glowed faintly through the overcast as Earnan placed Conor's body on top. Treasa climbed up and carefully positioned his daughter in his arms. She paused there for a moment, then climbed down and took Earnan's hand. Liam laid Brigid's body next to Conor, kissed her on the lips, and said, "Until I join you." The wood was green and damp, but with an enchantment from Najia flame roared to life, lighting up the front of the castle. They all watched it for a while; dense smoke billowed up in the firelight, disappearing into the night sky.

"What are you going to do now?" Art asked Jordan.

"I've come to believe there's a place for me somewhere in this land."

"You'd be welcome to join me in Tara. I could use your knowledge of the English."

"I've had enough of kings for a while," Jordan responded without malice. Then he and Najia mounted their horses. "Which way?" he asked her.

"The Sidhe believe that magic comes from the west," she replied, and they rode out of the firelight.

A horse was brought from the stable for the steward, and a team was hitched to a wagon for the servants. Art led the ensemble north toward Tara—all except Liam, who insisted on standing a solitary vigil for the dead.

Sun broke through the clouds as noon approached. Wisps of smoke still drifted from the smoldering ash of the pyre when Aisling came out the door wearing her finest gown. She was carrying Deirdre and a large leather satchel.

Liam emerged from behind the stable. "Where are you going?"

"I'm going where I need to go to protect Deirdre, to the English camp. She's all that's left in my life now."

"You think it'll be better there, that she'll be safe with them?"

"Safer there than with the Celts or the Sidhe. They murdered my daughter and took everything from me—my husband, my sister, my friends, my followers, my very purpose. Everything I ever valued! The English know nothing of the Morrígna. They won't sacrifice an infant in a futile attempt to bring a Goddess forth for their own greedy desires. They have no need for Goddesses. They have no enchantments to hide their evil intentions. I can handle their dull mortal senses."

"You can't abandon your people," said Liam. "We're still at war. You're still very much needed."

"The war's over." Aisling ran into the stable.

When she rode out, Liam blocked the horse's path. "Many said that you should have been killed years ago and returned to the Morrígna with your sister, to let the Goddess reincarnate fully. I chose to stand by you instead. I believed in you."

"You made a mistake," Aisling replied, swinging her horse past him.

From within the trees, Kellach watched Aisling ride away. Moving from tree to tree, he followed her for a while. He could sense that the heart segment that had once been in his keeping was destroyed. She had done to herself what he had failed to do, for when he stretched out his consciousness, she no longer glowed as a beacon to the Sidhe; she felt cold and dead. Kellach quickened his pace and moved ahead, making sure the English sentries did not stop her along the way. By the time Aisling reached the edge of the English encampment, Kellach was waiting for her with Nottingham and a company of guards.

"What do you want?" demanded Nottingham.

"Nothing," said Aisling. "Nothing but safety for my daughter." She surveyed the men in front of her. "Who will take us in? My daughter seldom cries." She unwrapped her cloak. "I'm twenty-one and well experienced in pleasing a man. Doesn't one of you want to marry me?"

"Quiet!" barked Nottingham to his men, who had begun talking among themselves. "Stand to order."

"She poses no more threat to us," Kellach said. "Particularly if she comes into the bosom of your king. Better a living symbol of defeat than a dead martyr."

Nottingham turned to the captain of the guard. "What's your name?"

"Captain John Cooper, my lord."

"Are you married, Captain Cooper?"

"No, my lord."

"You are now. Take her back to Dublin and make sure she does not cause any trouble."

John did not look displeased. "Perhaps there should be an adjustment in my pay for such a duty?"

"Yes, yes, an extra sixty-two pence per month, and tell the chamberlain I said to conscript a house for you to keep her in. Now, you and your men escort her to Dublin. Today, Captain Cooper."

Kellach could not help but laugh quietly as Aisling was led away. He walked back into the woods, his mind already deliberating on how to defeat his next enemy, a much weaker adversary—the English. He was so absorbed in his thoughts that he failed to notice the spread wings soaring high above.

Rhoswen, in her hawk form, watched Aisling ride off with a group of English soldiers. When Kellach disappeared into the trees, she swooped down upon the riders with a shrill screech. Several of the English ducked as she let one talon brush across Aisling's hair. Aisling did not flinch. Rhoswen banked and flew up, then turned west. The contact had brought a clear vision: Aisling might want her involvement with the Irish struggle to be over, but it was not.

25

Tara, Ireland
January 1395

For two weeks envoys had journeyed back and forth between Tara and Dublin. The English army had halted its advance and established an encampment at Kilmessan, just three miles south of Tara. Richard had been clear that this truce would be canceled if talks broke down. In a field outside Tara, a dozen large tents had been erected, crowned with Richard's banners, a white stag on green and blue. Across the field, a hundred yards away, their backs to the Irish capital city, stood three smaller tents bearing the banners of its high king, five ravens soaring over a crescent moon on a green background.

From the center Irish tent, Art looked out toward Richard's camp, watching the snow fall. It had been an unusually harsh winter, blown in on the east wind, just like the English. He longed for spring, for this all to be over. Turning to the table, he picked up the negotiated *comairce* agreement and skimmed the pledge of fealty once again. A group of English and Irish scriveners waited, along with his youngest brother, the twelve-year-old Dermod. *Gods,* Art thought, *Richard loves his flowery language.* At any other occasion, uttering these words would make him the laughingstock of Tara, but he would say them now. With Aisling gone there was no standing against the English archers, and so the only alternative to surrender was death, his and his remaining fighters'—a noble death but a useless one, he reasoned. He read further down the document to confirm the compensation he would receive for being Richard's lapdog: eighty pounds of silver per year and forty-three thousand acres south of Kildare, comprising the newly delineated barony of Norragh; his request for an earldom had been soundly rejected.

Grabbing the offered goose-pinion pen, dunking it in ink, and leaving a trail of black drops from the well, Art scrawled his name on the parchment and threw the pen on the ground. His personal scrivener applied the Irish royal wax seal. The Irish captain of the guard stepped outside the tent and sounded his horn. Art stared down at the agreement he had signed, then turned and strode out across the fresh snow. His brother trailed a few feet behind, creating a second set of tracks. An English scrivener gathered up the document and trotted after them.

As they approached, Richard emerged from the most elaborately decorated tent, followed by his retinue. Art stopped in front of a green-and-white-striped canopy, just large enough to cover the small table and the large chair under it. Richard paused, looking annoyed, as one of his pages rushed forward and brushed a trace of stray snow from the chair, then sat down. Behind him stood de Vere, as well as the now-ex-kings Murchada of Leinster and Niall of Ulster, who had already finalized their *comairce* agreements. Queen Gormflaith of Munster was dead, as was, it was presumed, King Turlough of Meath, though no body had been found. Only the young Queen Mael of Connacht still held out, her forces continuing to fight the Fomorians, who were striking inland from the west coast. In some ways Art envied Mael, who was still in the fight; in other ways he did not. The Fomorians were not known to accept surrender.

Nottingham took the agreement from the scrivener, checked the signature, then held it toward Art. "Kneel and read the pledge."

Art batted it away. "As if I'll ever forget what I must swear to today." Art dropped to his knees in the snow, grateful that at least it was not red, bowed his head, and spoke in a loud, clear voice. "I, Art MacMurrough, pledge my fealty to my most excellent lord, His Royal Majesty Richard the Second, true divine king of all England, Wales, and Ireland, to his successors, and to whomever they are pleased to appoint as their Crown representatives in Ireland. I am filled with joy to drink at the fountainhead of royal justice. I pledge obedience to Crown laws, compliance with Crown decrees, and I pledge to come when summoned, all this without complaint, and bind all my issue as well as all men who are subject to my will to do the same. I will collect the Crown's taxes and submit them without offset. As my king's faithful liegeman, I will aid him in all fights against his worldly enemies, and I do bind my liegemen to do the same, even to death. I seal this pledge with my property, my lands, my life, and the life of my brother Dermod, whom I love dearly and give as hostage."

Nottingham cried out, "Let it be so transcribed on the memoranda roll of the Exchequer!"

Contrary to the instructions he had received, Art raised his head and watched as Richard leisurely signed the document and the chamberlain applied the privy seal.

"Thanks to the Lord for such pleasant news," said Richard. "Baron Art MacMurrough, We welcome you into Our Royal protection, the glow of Our mercy. As Our vassal—oh, Nottingham, add 'vassal' to that pledge when it is recorded—as Our vassal, We are sure your only desire now is to obediently watch over Our interests."

Richard walked around to Art, extended a hand, and pulled Art to his feet. "Rise. Come join Us in a feast in your honor." Richard made a sweeping gesture toward the long tent to his right.

Three hours later Richard sat in the middle of his English lords on a raised dais watching the surviving ex-kings of Ireland grow increasingly drunk and loud, none more so than Art. The Irish high lords' dais sat perpendicular to Richard's, at half the height. Tables were set on the ground around it for guild heads and minor lords, now even more minor than they were before.

I hold the Irish queens above the kings, Richard thought, picking at the roast beef in front of him. Neither had surrendered. One queen died in battle, the other, if not dead already, would be soon. He leaned over to de Vere. "It would have been so much more fun to have executed the kings. We loved that blood-eagle thing."

"Let's do that, then. Shall I call the guards?"

"No, unfortunately, We do not have enough loyal English lords willing to stay in Ireland, so We need these Irish chieftains to help keep Our peace. The secret will be for you to find ways to encourage them to hold one another in check so none becomes too strong again."

"Me? Am I not coming home with you?"

Richard gripped de Vere's knee under the table. "My sweet man, We could never let anything bad happen to you, yet your enemies in court have rallied during Our absence. There is even a rumor being spread that you died of some foul disease already. We are told that a plot is in the making to have you assassinated on the journey home. You must stay here with members of Our most trusted Cheshire guard."

De Vere turned away from Richard, drained his goblet, and refilled it. When he turned back to Richard, his eyes had grown moist. "What shall I do here without you?"

"You must help young Mortimer. While We are appointing him as lord lieutenant for Ireland, he is in truth too inexperienced. You must advise him, teach him how to handle such as these." Richard inclined his head toward the Irish lords, who had broken into some kind of song.

"If I must stay here, why are you not making me lord lieutenant?" De Vere drained another goblet.

Richard slid his hand along de Vere's thigh. "Because We will be bringing you back to Us soon, as soon as We have ferreted out and dealt with those that would do you harm."

"As Your Royal Majesty commands." De Vere drummed his fingers on the table. "What of the Sidhe? They expect you to turn over Ireland to them. Kellach is already furious with you for not killing Art and the others. Yesterday he took his Sidhe followers and disappeared. God only knows what he is up to."

"So We were informed. It will not matter. The legate has sent word that the Vatican is providing a replacement for their wayward marshal, someone of higher rank. The Sidhe are the Vatican's responsibility now, not Ours."

"Well and good, but he'd better arrive soon to protect Your Royal Person, and mine, from the sorcery of these creatures."

A platter stacked with roast pigeons crashed from the hands of a page, sparking a fight with the drunken squire who had tripped him. Several Celts, whose station did not merit a seat on the dais, threw food in appreciation of the brawl.

"How long do we need to stay?" asked de Vere.

"Until We see which of the Irish chiefs passes out first. Make a wager with Us."

Twilight was settling over Dublin quay. A dozen Viking guards huddled around a glowing brazier at one end, anxiously talking among themselves while watching the Fomorians at the other end tear apart the body of a Celtic prisoner, the nightly offering. Their snarling came to a sudden stop. Still and quiet, the Fomorians looked toward the sea. One barked a command. Although unintelligible to the Vikings, it carried a clear tone of fear, and the creatures slipped into the water, leaving much of their victim behind. A ship's bell sounded.

The Vikings took up their shields and spread out along the quay, though not too close to the bloody pile of flesh and bone. A war galley emerged from the gloom, its rowers straining in their stations. The Vatican flag flew from the ship's mast, its linen sail furled and its prow dominated by the figurehead of an angel holding a flaming sword. Bolted to each side of the bow was a large medallion on which the initials VRS glowed with an unnatural light. In the forecastle stood black-robed and -hooded figures. The Viking closest to the entrance of the quay shouted, "Treat them as royalty if you wish to keep your newly won soul!" Then he sprinted toward Dublin Castle.

∝

IN THE FOREST west of Dublin, a towering oak spread its bare winter branches above all others of its kind. Its name was Gormghiolla, "the Gray Servant," though the memory of how it became so designated was long lost to the Skeaghshee.

Kellach woke with a jolt shooting through his body as if he were falling. The oak remained in its deep winter sleep, safely cradling him in an upper bough. Kellach felt exhausted and angry: he had fallen asleep angry, and his troubled dreams had not helped, dreams of shadowy creatures pursing him, creatures with axes for arms.

Resting one hand on the trunk, Kellach pushed himself up to face the sunrise breaking through the last trace of the snow clouds that had finally exhausted themselves. The life-giving light on his skin chased away the lingering dreams. In the trees around him, he could see his Skeaghshee warriors awakening and knew they would be doing so throughout the forest, raising their arms and giving thanks to the sun and the earth for, first, the trees and, second, for him, their liberator, their king. As the drone of their ritual chant reached him, he could feel their gratitude, their loyalty. It gave him strength.

Wichtlein, difficult Sidhe to lead but savage fighters when it suited them, dotted the ground, still asleep. They were creatures of the night when left to their own devices. Kellach called down to their general, or at least the one he had appointed as their general, and saw him stir toward wakefulness. Savage fighters yes, but vehement fleers as well. It seemed they had only those two modes, Kellach thought. *I just need to keep working them up into a blood frenzy. Today I will gather them all together and inform them that the English who were their allies are now their enemies.*

The Christian English are impotent, Kellach thought, laughing to himself. *They have no true power.* He had already sent his Grogoch and Dryads into the Middle Kingdom to call the other clans back from their travels. It was time for Ireland to once again be exclusively the domain of the Sidhe. Now that the Celts were defeated and the Morrígna vanquished, it would be easy to drive out the deceitful English. *I could do it with the warriors I have,* Kellach thought, *though it would be best to lead an army composed of all the Sidhe clans, as it will solidify my position as their new high king.*

Kellach jumped down to a lower branch, only to find he was still standing on the same one. He smiled at his misstep, leaped again. He did not leave the original branch. Stretching his leg out, he felt resistance. He tried simply stepping off into the air but immediately slid back onto his branch.

"My king!" shouted a neighboring Skeaghshee. "I cannot leave this tree!"

"Nor can I!" shouted another. Commotion spread throughout the forest.

Kellach closed his eyes, blocked out the noise, and began a counter-enchantment.

Six hours later, sweating and drained from the effort, he was still unable to negate whatever force was holding him in the tree. The surrounding Skeaghshee watched him, waiting. A new commotion rose from the east, heading his way. Several Wichtlein rushed into view, darted past, and kept going. The Wichtlein around his tree held out their javelins and raised their small shields. The pounding of hoofbeats approached. Arrows flew. Wichtlein began to fall. His general glanced up at Kellach and then ordered his remaining forces to retreat, which they did with enthusiasm. English mounted archers galloped by in pursuit. Half a dozen members of the VRS League rode up in their black-cowled robes and stopped. Behind them rode more peasants than he could count from his perch. Not peasants, realized Kellach. Worse. They were woodsmen, glinting axes strapped to their horses. Empty wagons rolled up.

Orsini dismounted beneath the giant oak and gazed up at him. "You must be Kellach, king of the Skeaghshee and, so I hear, new high king of all Sidhe, though I am not sure they all know that."

"What have you done?" hissed Kellach.

"Impressive work, is it not?" Orsini glanced around at the trees full of Skeaghshee. "You will discover that you and I did this together."

"You cannot keep me here. No human can maintain an enchantment of this magnitude for long. Then I will kill you."

"I simply— Well, it was not that simple, but I did bind you into that tree. Now that it is done, you will stay bound unless I undo it. Do not worry yourself. It requires no further effort from me."

"I do not believe you. You would have had to know my true name to have such power over me."

One of Orsini's brothers handed him a small ivory box. He opened it, revealing a single, grossly enlarged eye. "Your friend the Fomorian high king made the mistake of believing me when I told him I had the power to put it back in his head if he would only reveal your true name."

Fear struck Kellach's heart and exploded into terror. "I am a much more powerful ally," he pleaded. "I will give you the Fomorian's true name."

"His true name is of no use to me now, or to him." Orsini dumped the eye onto the ground, flicked it away with his foot.

Kellach tried to hurl an enchantment at Orsini, but it faded away in the branches.

"It would not be much use to bind a Sidhe, just like binding a demon if they could still spit out enchantments. Nothing of yours can leave this tree that you love," said Orsini, stroking Gormghiolla's grand trunk. "The real joy of this exorcism, the part that I was not sure would work, was binding your compatriots. But it did work. That is where you were of such help." Orsini spread his arms wide, spun around. "You bound them to you with their oaths to you. As long as you are bound into your tree, and as long as you are alive, they, too, are bound into theirs. They will die with their trees."

Orsini's spin caused the robe to ride up his arms, revealing small dark stains under his skin. Orsini quickly pulled down his sleeves.

"My followers will rescue me!" Kellach's voice rose to a scream. "You cannot cut down all the trees!"

"Ah, but you will learn that we can. You are going to feel each one,

I am afraid. The forests of Ireland have been sold to the shipwrights and coopers of England." He patted the giant tree. "Yes, when your time to die comes, this will make many fine barrels." Orsini turned to his brothers and said, "Have a stockade built around this tree and make sure it is not cut down until all the other Skeaghshee are dead. Use the trees around here. It is a good place to start."

Orders were shouted. The woodsmen dismounted and began to unstrap their axes.

26

Then certain of the vagabond Jews, exorcists, took upon them to call over them which had evil spirits the name of the Lord Jesus, saying, We adjure you by Jesus whom Paul preacheth. And there were seven sons of one Sceva, a Jew, and chief of the priests, which did so. And the evil spirit answered and said, Jesus I know, and Paul I know; but who are ye? And the man in whom the evil spirit was leaped on them, and overcame them, and prevailed against them, so that they fled out of that house naked and wounded.

—Acts 19:13–16, King James Version

Be sober, be vigilant; because your adversary the devil, as a roaring lion, walketh about, seeking whom he may devour.

—1 Peter 5:8, King James Version

Galway, Ireland
Two Months Later

On the west coast of Ireland, the kingdom of Connacht crawls from the Atlantic Ocean with craggy bays giving way to thousands of dark lakes, called loughs by the Celts, woven together with rocky streams, punctuated with bogs and low, gray, stony mountains. The soggy westerly half of this kingdom is divided from the rest by a chain of giant loughs that snake from its capital, Galway, to the northern sea: Lough Corrib, Mask, Curra, Cullen, and Conn. It was this rough west land that Kellach had promised the Fomorians, and while the other four kingdoms were busy fighting Richard, they took it. Now, with the Fomorian high king dead, they fractured into tribalism, with petty chiefs fighting each other over every lough and bog, pausing only to pursue their greatest love, killing Celts.

Queen Mael had quickly grown to look older than her years. She returned to Galway every day with blood on her sword and fewer warriors than she had when she left. One morning she rode out at the head of a relief column for the besieged Renvyle Castle, which her only son was trying to hold against the Fomorians, and she did not return. No one returned. The people of Galway retreated behind their city walls and waited for whatever end their Gods decreed. And so when Nottingham's army rode up in a March sleet storm, the surviving townspeople did not know whether they were opening their gate to their salvation or their final doom. When a long line of wagons followed the soldiers inside, each driven by a black-cowled exorcist, they suspected the latter.

Orsini climbed down from the lead wagon, snatched a rag from his pocket, and coughed, staining the cloth with flecks of black. He tucked it away. "Take me to the queen's chambers. I shall rest there," he ordered the town's bailiff, who was kneeling in the mud before him. That evening orders were issued to the townspeople to strip the great hall of all furniture and build a dividing wall in the middle by morning. There were plenty of newly empty houses to tear down for construction materials, and the wall was completed on time.

At noon the next day, the sleet had given way to rain, and Orsini and Nottingham entered the great hall, now split in two, and wiped the mud from their boots. Several hundred barrels stood end up on the flagstone floor, their lids removed. Behind them the makeshift wall rose to the timber roof. In front of the barrels waited the members of the VRS League. One brought forward a large Bible and held it for Orsini. The rest dropped to their knees.

Orsini opened the Bible to where it was marked with a red ribbon at the book of Ephesians, spread his hands shoulder-high, and read in Latin, "'Put on the whole armor of God, that you may be able to stand against the schemes of the devil. For we do not wrestle against flesh and blood, but against the rulers, against the authorities, against the cosmic powers over this present darkness, against the spiritual forces of evil in the heavenly places. . . . '" Orsini rushed through the familiar text, his mind elsewhere. "'. . . take up the shield of faith, with which you can extinguish all the flaming darts of the evil one.'"

Calls of "Amen" echoed off the walls as the exorcists rose to their work, half going into the newly created room beyond the wall, closing the door behind them. The rest went from barrel to barrel, making the sign of the cross while mumbling in Latin:

> *"We invoke upon this oil the name of him who suffered, who was crucified, who arose from the dead, and who sits at the right of the uncreated. . . ."*

"What are they doing?" asked Nottingham, following Orsini around the room, inspecting the barrels.

"These contain olive oil from my own orchard. My brothers are infusing a blessing," replied Orsini.

> *". . . may every evil spirit be put to flight. . . ."*

Carrying an iron pot, one brother carefully ladled a small amount of different, amber-colored oil into each barrel, releasing a sweet, musky odor.

"Smells good," said Nottingham, peering into the pot.

"Spikenard oil. It was what Lazarus's sister anointed Jesus's feet with after Jesus raised Lazarus from the dead. I hope it will provide some extra punch to the olive oil."

"And this concoction will drive off the Fomorians?"

"It would, but that is not our aim, is it? We are here to kill them. Come into the next room." Orsini opened the door. "Be quick. I would not want any of the blessings to slip in."

The second room was also full of barrels with their tops removed.

"Remember that Fomorians are Elioud, only one bloodline removed from the fallen angels that sired them," continued Orsini. "They are still bound by the ancient laws."

In this room the exorcists were not mumbling but rather shouting their Latin:

". . . I exorcise thee, unclean spirit, whoever thou art among issue of the original serpent, his apostate angels, and his diabolical legions. . . ."

White gleamed from inside the barrels.

". . . Make way thou wicked creature, make way thou profligate monster for Christ's true love of man. I restrain the force of the adversary's dominion and break his deceitful snares. . . ."

"You're exorcising salt?" asked Nottingham, shouting to be heard.

"Not precisely," replied Orsini. "I am having an exorcism infused into salt. Salt is wonderful that way, a true boon from God."

". . . The descent of the Holy Ghost grants me power to tread upon serpents and dragons and upon all powers of the infernal adversary. . . ."

"And what are you going to do with all this?" asked Nottingham.

"Between the blessing in the oil and the exorcism in the salt, the Fomorians will literally be torn apart. We need only to wait for a clear day," said Orsini.

". . . Hence, pay heed and tremble, pestilential creature, as I castrate your strength and bind you to this salt even as it dissolves. I strip you of your might and lay waste thy Kingdom. In the name of Jesus the Christ, let all enemies of the one true God be shattered. . . ."

Two days later the clouds finally gave way to blue sky. Orsini knelt in sunlight streaming through the window of the ex-queen's receiving chamber and prayed: prayed that God would allow him to finish what he started, prayed for strength to get through the next ten minutes. Pulling his robe over his head and placing it to the side, he heard a gasp and made a mental note to chastise the brother who had made it. Under Orsini's skin, scattered across his body, were black blotches the size of pennies, except for one on his lower back, which was as big as a hand with black tendrils stretching out like a hundred legs.

Behind Orsini, in addition to the soon-to-be-repentant brother, there were two other exorcists and the legate, who had arrived in Galway the previous day. The legate bent and spoke softly into Orsini's ear. "Are you sure this has to be done here, now? Let me take you back to Rome. Your brothers can finish with the Fomorians."

"No. Do not tempt me." Orsini's voice trembled, a tremor that seemed to run from his throat down through his body. He regained control with effort. "Just think of it, Legate, the last major race of Nephilim are within our grasp. The great test given by God to Enoch shall be completed. We will have proved to God that we are his one True Church. All other churches will fall before us and become no more than dust. I must remain here, must make sure my process works. It is the culmination of my life's purpose."

"As you command, Your Eminence." The legate straightened up and stepped back.

Orsini prostrated himself on the floor. "Just drive enough of the corruption from me to allow me to finish."

The legate picked up the sword from the table, unsheathed it, and directed the point toward the exorcists, who joined their hands to form a ring around it. They began an enchantment in Aramaic.

"Legate, these are my three most accomplished students," said Orsini. "If I should . . . if I should lose control of my holy self, make sure they are allowed to finish my work. Saving me is of little concern." Orsini began reciting the Lord's Prayer.

The sword tip had brightened to an orange glow. The legate pressed the tip against the large blotch on Orsini's back. A thin stream of black smoke rose. Orsini prayed louder. The blotch wriggled, crawled under his skin up his back to his shoulder.

"Good," sighed the legate. "It is clearly smaller."

"Again," ordered Orsini.

After the fourth application, the black blotch had been reduced to half its original size and was no longer animated. "Enough!" cried Orsini, struggling to a sitting position. "Enough. Thank you, my brothers, and you, Legate. I shall be able to serve a bit longer now, I should think."

While Orsini was preparing himself, all the residents of Galway were at Mass. They had been ordered to attend under penalty of death. The small Christian chapel overflowed into the square, where the bulk of the populace, hearing little and understanding none of the Latin service, fretted. Looking up, the prayers they did make were not offered to the Christian God but rather to their own Gods, beseeching them to keep the sky clear, for the people had come to know that Fomorians avoided direct sunlight whenever possible and, on this bright day, would be slumbering in the depths of their loughs. When the Mass was finally over, the city gates were opened, and the people cautiously ventured forth in large groups to harvest peat for their hearths and fish the shallows for their tables.

As the sun approached its zenith, Orsini left the city by wagon with his companions and a small contingent of guards. *I did not realize that there were this many Celts left alive in Galway,* the legate thought, looking at the work parties. *That is good. After they see Orsini defeat the Fomorians, they will not have to be ordered to Mass, and they can carry the good word through the rest of this pagan country.*

They took the north road along the bank of the river Corrib, veering off just before it reached Lough Corrib. Within an hour they arrived at the smallish Lough Aceelagh.

"This is our test lough," said Orsini, climbing down from the wagon. "Bring one barrel of oil and one of salt."

"How many Fomorians are in here?" asked the legate.

"Reports say twenty to thirty," replied Orsini.

Guards dragged the barrels to the shore. "Oil first," commanded Orsini. A guard used his dagger to pry off the lid. As the oil was poured into the lough, a sheen spread, rainbowed in the sunlight.

"Now the salt."

For a moment the water was still. Then a short wave rose and rolled across the lough, leaving eddies and whirlpools in its wake. The turbulence grew. A Fomorian crawled up the far shore and ran off. Others followed along the shoreline, four or five, the legate estimated. Another emerged halfway out, only to collapse on the bank and let loose a deep-throated scream. Using his arms, he dragged himself up a little farther, revealing that he no longer had a lower body, and died. No others emerged.

The legate watched the churning water with fascination. Within fifteen minutes it calmed once again. "What are those?" he asked, pointing to white specks floating to the surface.

Orsini ordered one of the guards to collect some. When the guard hesitated, Orsini gave him a shove. "You will not be hurt, unless you disobey me." The guard cautiously dipped his foot into the water. When nothing happened, he waded out and collected a handful. They were teeth.

Orsini slapped the legate's shoulder. "It worked. We will exorcise all the loughs."

"Some did escape," said the legate.

"But a few, but a few. I will just have to provide more incentive for them to stay in their lough, by the promise of a worse death." Orsini called, "Bring me some vessels."

Wooden crates were pried open in the wagon. "How many does Your Eminence want?" asked one of his brothers.

"Twelve is always a good number." Twelve bronze vessels were placed in a line on the ground in front of Orsini. He read the name engraved on the first, then drew his journal out of a pocket and consulted it. "Glasya-Labolas, he is a perfect one for this. How exciting."

Taking the wax tablet handed to him, Orsini pulled a silver stylus from his pocket and inscribed a symbol representing the demon's true name while chanting in Aramaic. Black mist streamed from the vessel and formed into the shape of a large dog with the wings of a griffin.

"Go," ordered Orsini, in a language too old to have a name. "Keep the Fomorians in their loughs. Skin and consume any that escape." With a snarl the demon took off in the direction of the escaped Fomorians.

Orsini moved down the line, releasing the demons one at a time, giving them their orders, each time his voice weakening a shade, until he reached the twelfth. He slowly stood up from reading the name. He did not have to consult his journal.

"Vepar. I should have checked them all. I should have handled him first." With his dagger he cut a vellum page from his journal and handed it to his exorcist brothers. "This is Vepar's page, in case you need it. Have your tablet and stylus ready."

"Are you all right?" asked the legate. "Perhaps this one should be left in his pot."

Orsini shook his head. "There was a time I could handle demons of his rank like kittens. I can deal with him still." He began the ritual. Vepar formed, a giant worm with the head and shoulders of a man. Orsini issued his orders. Vepar began to slither off, then reversed himself. Orsini repeated his orders. Vepar smiled, baring his fangs. Orsini quickly began to redraw Vepar's symbol. "I bind you back—" But before he finished, Vepar reared up and struck, becoming mist once again and flowing into Orsini's mouth. Orsini collapsed.

No one moved.

Orsini sprang up and ran.

"Stop him!" cried the legate. A guard swiped his sword at Orsini, catching his ankle, severing the Achilles tendon. Orsini fell to the ground again. A black hump rose from his back, bursting through his robe. The guards dropped to their knees and started praying fervently for their own salvation. The exorcists completed Vepar's symbol and began to recite the words on the page. Black and gray mist swirled around Orsini's flesh, obscuring it. The chant of the exorcists rose in volume. Mist streamed from Orsini's robe into Vepar's vessel. As the robe collapsed, the mist dragged a small, flickering ball of light into the pot. Then the robe was empty of Vepar and Orsini, the vessel still.

The legate and the exorcists panted as their terror subsided. The guards' frantic prayers filled the air. "Silence!" shouted the legate. Addressing the exorcists, he said, "Have the rest of the barrels brought out and start working through the loughs. I'll take Orsini back home to Rome. There the Mother Church may be able to restore him." The legate gingerly picked up the vessel and peered inside. There was black moving within black and a hint of a flickering light a great distance away.

IN ROME THAT MAY, the legate and four exorcists were ushered into the office of Pope Boniface IX. The exorcists carried a glass case etched with runes, which contained a bronze vessel. The procession stopped and waited for their presence to be acknowledged. The pope, flanked by two secretaries, sat listening to a commissary read out the terms for the sale of an indulgence. Pope Boniface himself was illiterate, the legate recalled.

"That is good. That is good," said the pope. "Make sure you get all the gold before you turn over the document."

One secretary signed the pope's name to the parchment, and the other applied the seal of the Apostolic See. Upon the commissary's departure, the pope waved the legate forward. "Tell Us, Legate, is the Irish Church now Ours?"

The legate advanced and kissed the pope's Ring of the Fisherman. "There is no longer an Irish Church, Your Holiness. All of the monasteries in Ireland, as well as those in Britain and Europe that were once theirs, are now in the possession of your bishops."

"And the Sidhe, they are all dead?"

"Like rats you can never kill every last one. However, the few remaining cower in their holes and hold no sway in Ireland. They will not trouble Your Holiness further."

"Well done, Legate. So many new monasteries to fatten Our purse. And what is this? Have you brought Us a present from Ireland?"

"This is the vessel containing the demon Vepar, Your Holiness."

The pope shrank back in his chair. "Why would you bring it before Us?"

"Regrettably, Your Holiness, Cardinal Orsini was captured by Vepar and now also resides in this vessel."

"Really?" The pope rose and cautiously approached the glass case. He leaned down and examined the bronze vessel it held. "Orsini is in there? How interesting."

"Your Holiness, I request permission to have the VRS League try to get him out."

"We must not risk freeing the demon. Leave him in there until We appoint a new high exorcist. He will be able to free him."

"Yes, Your Holiness. Please do not wait long. It is impossible to imagine the anguish Orsini's soul must be undergoing, being bound with Vepar."

The pope watched the legate and the exorcists carry the case out. "We are famished. Have Our lunch brought in," said the pope to one secretary. To the other he whispered loudly, "Frankly, Orsini always made Us feel . . . uneasy. With the Sidhe defeated, We do not think We need a high exorcist for now. Strike this meeting from the record."

27

Joanna's sitting room was larger than those of the other witches of the High Coven who resided in the Paris royal residence, as befitted her new station as Second Sorcière. A eunuch threw open the door, and Queen Isabeau, the Grande Sorcière, swept in. Joanna, dressed in a night shift, rose from her chair by the fireplace.

"It is done," announced the Grande Sorcière. "We have finalized terms with Richard." She took the seat Joanna had vacated as the eunuch gathered clothing from an armoire.

"Then we will have Ireland as well?" asked Joanna. She pulled off her shift. Thin trails of smooth pink scars snaked up her right arm, across her shoulder, and wove around half her torso; they spoke of the high cost of learning flame enchantments, paid early in her training.

"We must be clever and patient," replied the Grande Sorcière, and she sipped from Joanna's half-drained wine goblet. She had always found Joanna's scar work eerily beautiful, like an elaborate tattoo. "It was a miracle that Richard prevailed in Ireland, but he has become unloved by many of his lords at home. Not only will we have to control him, we must gain control of the English royal court, and then Ireland will be open to Us."

The eunuch helped Joanna into a floor-length yellow chemise—silver thread woven into its lace collar and sleeves long enough to cover her scars—then belted on a purple velvet robe. The High Coven's witches forwent the restrictive fashions of the day for their private nighttime gatherings. "How many Sidhe do you believe are left there?" Joanna asked.

"Enough for Our purposes, not enough to resist Us. We could not have hoped for better. We will enslave them, break them, and take their magic. Then We will not have to hide Our coven behind these pathetic kings. No one will be able to stand against Us, not even the Vatican."

"The VRS will be a fight." Having checked herself in the mirror, Joanna followed her queen out.

The Grande Sorcière waved her hand dismissively as she glided along. "Orsini has disappeared. They can do nothing to stop us."

The eunuch, carrying a candelabrum, illuminated their path down a long hallway. He pushed open the door to the private audience room and bowed deeply as they entered.

The Grande Sorcière's three oldest daughters and their tutor, the Witch of Ripabianca, sat around a chalk circle drawn on the floor-boards in the center of the room. The tutor was showing Joan how to prepare a viscous, dark potion in a bowl made of ash wood. Five years old, Joan was promised for a summer wedding to John "the Wise" of Brittany. Marie, four years old, squirmed restlessly, unable to follow the complex procedure, unlike the oldest daughter, Isabella, six. In the center of the circle lay a lamb, its throat slit open, its blood drained, and its skin flayed. The tutor handed the bowl to Isabella, who slurped in a mouthful of the thick, green liquid. The child closed her eyes, and the Grande Sorcière knew she would be visualizing what she wanted from the lamb. Isabella snapped open her eyes, pursed her lips, and sprayed the lamb corpse with the now-red liquid.

"*Réveillez!*" she commanded.

The wide, lidless eye swiveled, then settled on Isabella.

"*Soulevez!*" she said, straightening her own spine and lifting her palms.

The lamb struggled onto its legs like a newborn, stood shakily, and gave a wag of its skinned tail.

"*Marchez!*"

With dainty clicks of cloven hoofs upon the wooden floor, the lamb almost made it around the circle before it tripped and crumpled to the floor in front of the Grande Sorcière.

Marie and Joan clapped their hands enthusiastically. "Very good, Our little dove. You're getting much better," said the Grande Sorcière. "Now, gather around, We have great news about England."

Isabella spoke up, her voice hoarse from the effort of her incantation. "Does this mean that negotiations are complete, Mother?"

"Yes, Our little dove. We have bribed Richard to take you as his new queen." The witches erupted in laughter, which the Grande Sorcière could not help but join. "For one hundred thousand francs per year," she managed to get out, "and a promise of peace." The laughter intensified. Isabella jumped up and hugged her mother.

In November, upon receipt of payment, Richard married Isabella, making her queen of England, Wales, and Ireland, and the youngest queen in the history of the realm. It was five days before her seventh birthday.

On the morning of Isabella's departure from France, the Grande Sorcière had summoned her daughter to issue final instructions to her. Leading her into the secret chamber where Taddea's candle burned, the Grande Sorcière began, "Always remember that the blood of Our coven's founder, Taddea, runs in your veins, a coven that has been unassailable for over a hundred and twenty years." From her pocket she removed a small red glass box that she had enchanted earlier. She carefully lifted the lid a fraction and flame streamed inside the box from Taddea's candle threatening to douse it, but the lid clicked shut first.

A glow flickered faintly through the opaque glass as she handed the box to Isabella. "You are to build your coven within the English court the same way Taddea did here. However, their royal bloodline is more fractured than the French was. Many families harbor claims to the throne. You must be thorough in establishing a foundation of control and power. When you have done that, make a candle from human tallow and light it with this flame. We will know and will send more of Our witches to join you at the English court. Then We will move on to Ireland."

"Yes, Mother," replied Isabella, fidgeting with excitement.

☙

THE FOLLOWING YEAR on the outskirts of Dublin, a woman wearing a floppy bonnet and a frock and holding a basket of turnips watched a plain post-and-wattle house from the shadows across the dirt road. A three-year-old girl with wild red hair played in the October mud of the unkempt yard. Beyond her a woman's muffled voice could be heard yelling inside. When the door opened, the yelling spilled out in full volume, and Captain John Cooper beat a hasty exit. "Make sure you spread my sheltering water or you'll be sorry!" shouted Aisling behind him, her voice rising to a screech. "And when you get back—" John slammed the door closed without saying a word, causing Aisling's voice to become indistinct again. Dutifully, he carried an earthenware jug and splashed its bright yellow contents around the yard. The woman in the floppy bonnet knew it was a potion consisting of Aisling's urine, steeped with crushed hawthorn leaves for seven days, then infused with a curse—an old method used to prevent Sidhe from stealing human children.

John shook out the last of the liquid and the used leaves, then quietly set the jug beside the door. He walked over to Deirdre and took an apple out of his pocket, cut it, and placed half into the girl's outstretched hand, smiling at her. She beamed, and he ruffled her hair, then strode briskly toward Dublin Castle, eating the other half.

The woman, her face hidden beneath the ample bonnet, retreated in the opposite direction. Two miles down the road, she veered toward a farm. Rounding the stable, she found Liam and Earnan sitting on a log, talking to the farmer and his wife, awaiting her. Treasa removed the borrowed bonnet and handed it to the farmer.

"She's getting worse," said Treasa, pulling the baggy frock over her head and revealing her own mail vest. "We should just kill her. I know her husband would be grateful."

Liam handed Treasa her sword. "That decision was made long ago, right or wrong."

"Wrong, I think," said Earnan, giving Treasa a quick kiss.

Treasa grabbed Earnan's collar and drew him in for a long kiss. "If you go crazy on me, I'll not hesitate to slit your offending throat."

"And Deirdre?" asked Liam.

"Seems happy enough. John clearly dotes on her."

"Good." Liam sighed.

Having made his periodic check on his former charge, a lingering duty Liam could not bring himself to abandon, the three mounted their horses and rode west toward home, careful to stay off the road and avoid English patrols.

Treasa had left Aisling's house before seeing Deirdre wander over to a scrubby bush where John had splashed some of the sheltering water. Curious, the child reached toward the plant, still wet with urine. A small spark leaped out and bit her index finger. She snatched her hand back and, angry that the bush had done such a thing, frowned at it. Threads of fire blossomed, dancing among its leaves. The bush crackled, crinkled, and died before her eyes. With a satisfied smile, Deirdre returned to her mud pies, not understanding what she had just done.

Half a day's ride through the stubbled remains of clear-cut forests brought Liam, Treasa, and Earnan within sight of Kellach's solitary, giant oak, Gormghiolla, silhouetted on the horizon by the sunset, the stockade ringing its base. Leaves had never returned to its branches.

"There's a Skeaghshee who deserves to die," said Earnan.

"The VRS continues to toy with him," said Liam, turning from the sight. "I'm sure he wishes for death by now." They directed their horses north to look for a place to camp for the night.

The next day they skirted Tara, which had been abandoned on Richard's orders. All governing functions had been moved to Dublin, while the guild headquarters were relocated to Galway. Most of Tara's buildings were already in ruins, the English having pulled them down and hauled off the stones to build their own castles and manor houses. The only activity on the hill was the construction of a new Christian monastery, adjoining what was once Tara's main gate, to house the VRS League.

Three more days brought them to the Derryveagh Mountains north of Donegal, the sparse and rugged northwest corner of Ireland, where the English rarely ventured. They rode along the shore of Lough Dunlewey, located at the foot of the glittering quartzite peak of Mount Errigal, then followed the river Owenabhainn upstream into Nimhe Glen, where Liam had built a one-room stone-and-thatch cottage. Liam drew his dagger, stuck its point into his thumb, and gave it a quarter twist to ensure a good flow of blood drops onto the ground as he approached his home, an offering to the earth spirits he had asked to conceal its existence. Treasa and Earnan did the same.

The next morning Liam, lying on a pallet stuffed with wool set on the floor and covered with his cloak, awoke to rustling sounds coming from the bed, which he had given to Treasa and Earnan. Deciding to allow them some privacy, Liam donned his cloak and braced himself for the cold. Outside, a tinge of blue in the eastern sky hinted at the coming sunrise. He walked down to the riverbank and sat on a boulder, waiting. The sun eventually cleared the valley wall, and he turned his face to it, feeling the warmth.

When sunlight had crawled down to the river, Liam removed his clothes, carefully folding and stacking them on the boulder, and waded out into the waist-deep center. He eased himself down until the water was up to his neck. He felt the heat of his body fight the frigid water, watched the sunlight fill the valley, and wondered what was left for him in this life.

The English lords, never happy with the size of their new Irish lands, were contracting with Gallowglass companies, but as a cross-breed he was less than welcome. He would not have worked for them anyway. Their petty fights seemed pointless.

Perhaps Fearghal had been correct. Perhaps it was time to move on from this life to the After Lands, or Tír na nÓg, or whatever truly came next. For that he would need an epic battle, one worth dying in. During practice fights it had become clear that his original half-Sidhe ability to anticipate the moves of a challenger had become unreliable, like the Ardor of Ireland, leaving him vulnerable. He laughed to himself. Hopes and dreams still lingered in this defeated land, but they had decayed into such thin desires. It's possible, he thought, that even today news of such a battle might be coming, brought to him by those he sensed moving up his valley. There were two of them, he determined as he focused on their energies, one a Sidhe. He had not encountered a Sidhe for almost a year. Deciding to wait in the river for his visitors, he rose enough to let the sun warm his chest and arms again, the water that dripped down his body shimmering in the light.

Liam was pleased to see that it was Rhoswen who rode up the riverbank. She led a second horse on which slumped an exorcist, his complexion ashen, mouth gagged, and wrists bound. All ten of his fingers had been hacked off, the stumps black and red and swollen, crudely cauterized. Her Adhene witch's body paint was not as crisp as when Liam had last seen her, as if it had not been refreshed recently. Rhoswen slid off her horse and waded into the river a few feet from Liam. She scooped up a handful of coarse river sand and began to scrub off her paint, revealing fair skin.

"I was beginning to think the last of the Sidhe had finally departed," Liam said, breaking their silence.

"Some remain," Rhoswen replied. "Those few of us still loyal to our vows, those who still believe the Morrígna will return fully. We hold the vigil."

"Not much of a vigil as long as Aisling's alive."

"She will not be forever."

"I'm surprised that the Sidhe allowed her to live this long."

"If we were to take her life, I fear the Morrígna would never return to us. We must wait for the Morrígna to take Aisling herself. In the eternity of the Goddess's eyes, one life is but a blink."

"Until then you hunt exorcists to pass the time," said Liam, wading toward the hapless man.

"He crossed my path."

"Your path to talk with me?"

"Yes."

"Great Mother Danu!" Liam exclaimed upon reaching the horses. "He stinks."

"He fouled his robes when I removed his fingers. I could not have him tracing symbols at me."

"I'd better give him a bath, then." Liam pulled the exorcist off his horse and dragged him into the river. "If the Morrígna returns, will she deliver Ireland back to the Sidhe?" he asked, thrusting the exorcist up and down in the water as if he were a piece of laundry.

"Was Ireland ever truly ours?" replied Rhoswen. She was scrubbing her head, revealing that a stubble of hair was beginning to grow. "The Sidhe took it from the Fomorians. The Celts seized parts of it from the Sidhe. And now the English have conquered most of it. Whatever the Morrígna's purpose is when she returns, the remaining Sidhe will be here to serve her."

Liam considered her words but was distracted by the sight of her freshly scoured body—naked, pale, and pink. Rhoswen returned to her horse, where she untied a large cloth bag and pulled out buckskin boots, a simple black wool tunic, heavy green leggings, and a brown cloak, clothing of three colors that would mark her as someone of indistinct middle status. As she dressed, Liam felt desire rising hot through his body for the first time since Brigid's death. He was grateful for the cold water and the exorcist in his hands, or he might have had to hide an erection.

"Have you come to ask me to join the vigil?" he asked. "I was hoping you brought news that a battle was brewing and a Sidhe army gathering." He dragged the gasping exorcist up onto the bank.

Rhoswen fastened the cloak about her shoulders with a plain

iron brooch. Holding out her arms and pretending to be human, she asked, playfully, "What do you think?"

Liam, in the process of donning his own clothing, replied, "It suits you."

"We Sidhe need to learn how to blend in with humans if we are going to survive." She moved closer to Liam. "There's no battle coming. What's coming is much more dangerous. Even in the faded light of the remaining Ardor, the threat radiates in my visions. I've confirmed it with information from a faerie witch I trust in Normandy."

"So what is it?"

"Dark, malevolent creatures. A coven of human witches from France, large and well organized. They've ferreted out bits of the ancient knowledge and corrupted what power it has brought them. Now they're in the process of seizing control of the English throne—one has become the new queen. But their ultimate plan is to take Ireland. They lust after it, after Sidhe knowledge, the enchantments they would force us to reveal. They believe they will be able to tap into Ardor here. And into the energy residing in Sidhe bodies. They will kill us to harvest it."

The exorcist finally stopped gasping through his gag and propped himself into a sitting position. Rhoswen observed him for a moment. "With Orsini gone, and no new high exorcist here, we Sidhe can hide from the likes of him. But the High Coven will bring an English army to hunt us down and enslave those of us who do not flee this world. They'll use their coarse magic to rip whatever power they can from us. Then there'll be no Sidhe holding vigil for the Morrígna. Ardor here will truly and finally die. Ireland will become just a lump of rock in the sea."

Liam's heart sank. "This isn't my type of fight. I'm not sure how to help you."

"The Morrígna herself, while I was performing Taghairm, charged me and my descendants with preparing for her return, no matter what we have to risk to do it and however many years or centuries it takes. Your mother was a Sidhe. Will you not be true to the Morrígna now?"

Liam rubbed his face in contemplation. "There's a couple I can introduce you to who know much more about these sorts of things than I."

Rhoswen nodded, then placed her hand on his chest. "I felt your body warm as you watched me in the river." She leaned in and kissed him. "I also want you to show me how to be more like a human woman."

28

Leaving Treasa and Earnan at the cottage, Liam, Rhoswen, and the exorcist rode out of Nimhe Glen toward the Rock. As they traveled through central Ireland, the harsh, staccato sounds of wood-cutters plying their trade became common background. Skeaghshee screams, though, were absent. The trees they had been bound into, and died with, had long since been harvested. When Liam passed a group of woodcutters returning to their camp, axes resting on tired shoulders, he was surprised to hear them speaking in French. Richard's new relatives were already exerting their rights.

After several long days of riding, the trio saw the Rock emerge on the horizon. The size of a hill, it had been torn from a mountain twenty miles away and hurled here during a fierce battle between the original Patrick and an Archdemon, reputed to be Samael. A druid had tricked Patrick—who had newly founded his Irish Christian Church—into the fight, yet Patrick had prevailed and gained his first royal patron, the king of Munster. The king christened it the Rock of Cashel and built his principal castle on top, along with a monastery for Patrick—but everyone simply called it the Rock. *A monument to what has been lost,* thought Liam. A sorcerer could no longer tap into enough Ardor to defeat a demon, and there was not enough Ardor to draw demons to live here. A tragedy on both fronts, his heart told him. The days of epic magical battles were gone. Unless Rhoswen's belief that the Morrígna would return was borne out—an event that she, with her long life span, might experience, but he doubted he would.

His thoughts turned inevitably to Aisling, the last to defeat a demon. How much of Ireland's downfall could be laid at his door for allowing her to live and not rejoin the Morrígna when Anya did? A lot, he conceded. Each decision seemed honorable at the time, but looking back he could see that he had been trapped by his oaths to protect her. Those were the thoughts that haunted his worst nights.

Both the Rock's castle and its monastery had been abandoned after the English invasion. As Liam rode closer, it became evident that the buildings were in ruins. "Stone scavengers?" he asked Rhoswen.

"No. There's more at work here. An enchantment of some kind."

As their horses walked up the steep path to the gate, Liam saw she was correct. It appeared that the structures had been in ruins for hundreds of years, not three, the edges of broken stones softened by weather and covered with moss. Liam asked the exorcist, "Is this the work of your kind?"

Still gagged, the exorcist could only shake his head.

They rode slowly between the rubble, looking for signs of occupation. Alerted by a grating sound, Liam looked up to see a stone wobble on top of a wall that must once have been part of the keep. It fell, striking the exorcist on the shoulder and knocking him off his horse. The exorcist struggled to his feet, his dislocated shoulder hanging low, and began to run. As he passed a standing corner of the monastery, another stone tumbled. This one split his head open.

Liam dismounted and nudged a boulder with his foot. "Was that really necessary?"

The boulder uncurled into the Grogoch Eldan, who replied, "Orders of the Lord of the Rock. No English, and particularly no exorcists."

"The Lord of the Rock?" said Rhoswen.

"Is that what Jordan's calling himself?" said Liam. "You had better take us to him. And we were saving that exorcist to ransom back to the Church."

"They may pay for him still," replied Eldan, his gravelly voice flat. He led them through the empty doorway of the ruined keep. "Best not to call Jordan 'Lord of the Rock' to his face. He hates that nickname."

"Are you responsible for all this?" asked Rhoswen, indicating their decayed surroundings.

"Keeps the English and the Christians from trying to use it." Eldan more mumbled than sang a brief enchantment, and two large floor stones slid back, revealing a stairway. Warm light glowed from below.

"How did you come to serve Jordan?" asked Liam, following Eldan down the stairs.

"It is my penance, serving a human, and one that is not even a Celt."

"Penance for what?"

Eldan glanced back over his shoulder. "I will keep that to myself and thereby keep my head."

The procession reached the bottom of the stairs, which led directly into a well-appointed chamber carved out of the solid rock. Liam recognized the tapestries, carpets, and furniture as having once graced the castle above. Faerie lights hovered near the ceiling, illuminating several passages leading farther into the rock. Eldan guided them to the right, past a chamber still being molded from the rock by two singing Grogoch, and into a room whose walls were lined with shelves. Crates of books and scrolls and piles of vellum manuscripts occupied the middle of the floor. Dryads scurried about, sorting the documents and carrying them up onto the shelves. Through a far door was the final chamber, also lined with shelves, these already filled. At a table in the center, Jordan and Najia were hunched over a papyrus scroll.

"Liam, it's so good to see you again," Najia said, rising and extending her hands. "Last time was such a . . . a tragedy."

A vision of Brigid's body being consumed by flames evoked a familiar ache in his chest, but it also reminded him of all that Najia had done for her at the end. "Greetings, Najia," he replied, taking her hands. "I would like you to meet Rhoswen. You've much in common."

Najia bowed. "I could never hope to have much in common with the skill of an Adhene, much less an Adhene witch."

"Thank you. I've heard of the respect you show the Ardor of my homeland," said Rhoswen, returning the bow. "It's those human witches that seek to control Ardor and corrupt it for their own ends that we've come to ask for your help with."

Liam placed his hand on the small of Rhoswen's back. "If you're going to pass as human, you'll have to learn the art of social conversation before asking favors."

"Rhoswen and I have too much to discuss to worry about such conventions," Najia said.

Jordan hurriedly finished transcribing a line and finally looked up, greeting Liam with a nod. "Please excuse me. It's imperative that I finish this section," he said, his index finger still marking his spot on the text. "If you'll stay for lunch, I'll join you shortly."

Najia led them back to the great chamber, where two Dryads stacked the lunch table with Sicilian wine, fresh roast pork, fine white bread, honey, and sweet salted butter. Two hours slipped by, the conversation flowing with the wine, mostly talk of the ills that had befallen Ireland, before Jordan joined them, the scroll rolled up in his hand, as if he could not bear to part with it. He kissed Najia on the cheek. "I'm sorry for being late. Became absorbed in translating."

"I take it that means you received my message about Brigid's library at Druim Criaidh?" asked Liam.

Jordan dropped into a chair and poured himself a goblet of wine. "Yes. With the help of our Grogoch friends, Najia and I were able to rescue all the grimoires before the VRS League found the place. We also liberated Patrick's library at Armagh. You should have seen the exorcist's face when he opened the chamber door to find that Patrick's complete library had disappeared in the night." Jordan pulled off the end of a bread loaf and smeared it with butter. "There's much research to be done if we're to find a way to preserve the remains of Ardor. I could spend a lifetime down there and not get through it all."

"I'm not going to spend a lifetime in this hole," said Najia.

"Of course, my love. I'm sure we'll be able to find a safe place aboveground, eventually. Liam, you should see these diagrams." Jordan partially unrolled the scroll on the table. "I believe this document is originally from the Library of Alexandria. It must have been taken, perhaps stolen, before that great library's destruction a millennium ago. Najia and I are still working to decipher the accompanying text, but it appears that the Egyptians were also concerned about the loss of Ardor when the Romans wiped out their Nephilim."

"Anything we can use there?" said Liam, catching Jordan's enthusiasm.

"They had some theories that may help," replied Jordan. "I'll try to find records of the actions they took and what, if any, success they had. It'll take a lot more study. Let me read this bit to you—"

Najia placed her hand over the papyrus. "Rhoswen and Liam have come with a more immediate problem. They're asking for our help against a group of French witches who're planning to attack the Sidhe."

"That must be the High Coven," said Jordan, rolling the scroll back up.

"Are you still corresponding with your contacts in Europe?" asked Liam.

"Of course," replied Jordan, starting in on the roast pork.

"Then you know the High Coven has infiltrated the English court already."

"That's what I hear. Isabella is the new child queen. It's causing quite a stir. But remember, as formidable as the High Coven is, they're still just human witches. Witches don't concern me," said Jordan between chews. "Except, of course, you," he hastily added to Najia. And then, under Rhoswen's glare, he added, "And certainly you, but you're not human."

"The High Coven has become more powerful than you realize," said Rhoswen. "Once they control England, they'll bring the English army and capture the remaining Sidhe. There aren't enough of us left to fight them, not with Richard's archers at their side. Those they don't enslave or kill will finally leave this world. Then no free Sidhe will remain in Ireland, and what do you think will happen to the Ardor you hope to preserve?"

Jordan took a long drink of wine.

Liam asked, "Could we get to Richard and assassinate him?"

"Probably," replied Jordan. "But Richard has recently designated a new successor, who's already been enraptured by Isabella. As this successor is but five years old, Richard's death would only serve to strengthen the High Coven's grip on the throne. Killing Richard may even be part of the High Coven's plan."

Najia stroked the back of Jordan's neck and leaned closer. "If you did decide to help stop these witches, what would your plan look like?"

"Well, any strategy would be risky, but it would have to involve getting the English nobility to do what they do best: fight among themselves and change the line of royal succession. The throne would have to be taken from Richard's line, controlled as it is by the High Coven, and given to a family not under their control. Perhaps to a family that doesn't even support the occupation of Ireland." Jordan leaned back in his chair. "There're those within the English nobility who believe their military resources would be better served subduing Scotland." He stared up at the rock ceiling, lost in thought.

The others watched Jordan think in silence for a few moments, and then Najia and Rhoswen drifted back into conversation. Liam became occupied with thoughts of his own, not thoughts of protecting Ireland from the High Coven but thoughts of revenge. Revenge for Brigid. Revenge for Aisling. Revenge for all that had been taken from his land. A renewed feeling of purpose swelled in his chest.

Late that night Jordan walked through the cold and darkened ruins atop the Rock. Sitting on a fallen stone, he pulled off his boots and placed his bare feet on the ground, curling his toes into the thin layer of dirt. He felt thin tendrils of Ardor course up through his body. The moon was not yet out. The countryside spread out below him was a sea of black under a dome of bright stars, connecting in a ragged horizon. He felt the earth of his new homeland and watched the sky. A radiance of deepest purple emerged in the east, a hint of color distinguishable only in contrast to the black around it. The purple brightened to a deep blue. Eventually a trace of silver emerged and grew to reveal a waxing moon rising. Najia, wrapped in a heavy cloak, approached silently and sat beside him. The moon cleared the horizon, sweeping away stars before it.

"I once lived to join fights like the one Liam has proposed," said Jordan. "To sail off to another land to subvert, manipulate, and kill. Now I just want to stay here, immersed in what's left of the Ardor of Ireland." Najia took his hand. Jordan asked, "How dangerous do you think the High Coven has really become?"

"It sounds as if their magic is crude and often poorly controlled, but strong in a brute-force kind of way," said Najia. "They wield it without mercy, seeking only to expand their power. I believe it'll be very hard on the Sidhe, and on us, if they move on Ireland."

"Are there any enchantments we can work from here to stop them?" asked Jordan, looking up at the moon.

"I doubt it," said Najia. "The Ardor has faded too much, and the High Coven is too strong. They'll deflect any spell that comes straight at them. Any attempt would also alert them that we're trying to thwart their plans, and they'll become more vigilant."

"That's how it seems to me as well," said Jordan. He pushed dirt around with his toes. "Then I have no choice. If there's any chance I can stop the High Coven from destroying what I love most about this land, I must go and try."

"It's dangerous for you in England and Europe. The Vatican will pay handsomely for your capture, then they'll burn you as a traitor and a sorcerer."

"That's why you must remain here."

"Do you remember when you ordered me to remain in Wales?

You seemed happy when I didn't follow your instructions. Am I still your slave, or did you truly free me?"

"You know you're free."

"Then I'm coming with you."

Jordan looked into Najia's eyes, barely visible in the moonlight, and knew it was useless to argue. "You do have certain unique powers that could prove useful." He put his arm around her and kissed her neck. "Tell me the truth—did you cast a spell on me that day you were loaded onto my ship?"

"Perhaps I've a spell on you still," said Najia, and she returned his kiss. "No. I sensed immediately that you'd be able to tell if I attempted any enchantment, and I didn't want to provoke Ty to crush me into jam. I came to you as myself. Everything between us is true." She pulled back from him a few inches. "Unless you cast some sort of spell on me."

Before he could reply, Liam and Rhoswen emerged from the darkness and joined them. "Any ideas?" asked Liam. "Or do I just round up warriors and attack whatever witches the High Coven sends?"

"That won't work," replied Jordan. "If we wait for them to arrive, it'll be too late. Do you think you two could cause so much trouble that Richard himself will be forced to return with an army?"

Liam looked at Rhoswen, who nodded. "It'll certainly be fun to try," he said. "What then?"

"The Lancasters have been sniffing around the throne for two generations. Lately their patriarch, Henry of Bolingbroke, has been stirring up discontent, asserting that Richard has grossly mismanaged the realm. If you can draw Richard out of England, I may be able to convince Henry that the king's absence is an opportunity to seize the Crown."

"Surely it'll be difficult to get to him, with both the Vatican and the English after your head?"

"There's one Lancaster who owes me a favor," said Jordan. "Thomas of Arundel. He was archbishop of Canterbury until being exiled to Florence and is no ally of Richard or the pope."

"A friend you can trust with your life?" asked Rhoswen.

"I trust his fear. I caught him practicing witchcraft, and he knows I can prove it. I have kept his secret, preferring to have him in my debt than watch him burn. You see, Thomas had a habit of falling in love—that's how he put it—with newly married women who came to him for confession. But the poor man was and remains strikingly unattractive—repulsive, really. He learned two spells: one to make him irresistible and the other, for afterward, to make the women forget their transgressions. He'll get me a meeting with Henry."

"So we thwart the High Coven's plans by igniting a rebellion in England? Long odds at best," said Liam. "But even if it's successful, won't the new king turn his greedy eyes back on Ireland?"

"It'll at least buy us some more time," replied Jordan.

"And perhaps we can help some of the Lancasters' enemies while we're at it, and distract the new king further," added Najia.

"All right," said Liam. "I'll do my part. It's certainly a noble enough cause to die for."

Rhoswen placed her hand on Liam's cheek. "A noble enough cause to live for."

"Yes. To live for if we're successful. Or to die for if we're not."

Three days later, through a rainy dawn, four riders left the Rock. Jordan and Najia rode southeast toward the small harbor village of Ardmore to secure passage to Europe.

Liam and Rhoswen rode northeast to the barony of Norragh. When they approached the former high king's manor house south of Kildare, Liam said, "Last time I saw Art, he was in no state to help anyone. This may be a waste of time."

"If we raise an army to fight the English," said Rhoswen, "we'll just be bandits and criminals. If the high king does it, we'll be rebels and patriots."

"Art is a baron, no longer a high king."

"If he were still king, we would not need to be rebels."

Liam smiled at Rhoswen. "You are learning human ways."

Rhoswen urged her horse into a gallop toward the manor house. They found their own way into the great hall without fanfare. There were few servants about, and those ignored them. The hall was filthy. Cheap tallow candles smoked in their holders, adding to the reek of spoiled food and urine, some of it from the dogs that chewed bones under the table and some of it, Liam suspected, from Art himself.

Art, even fatter than the last time Liam had seen him, was fumbling about on the table, apparently scrounging to find something still edible among the scraps. When he noticed them, he seemed to shrink into his chair. "Liam, what are you doing here?"

"We come with a proposal, if the spirit of a king still lives in you. Though that appears unlikely."

Art slapped his hands on the table and tried to rise but fell back into his chair. He grabbed a pitcher of wine and, forgoing any of the dirty goblets scattered around, gulped down some while spilling most. Fortified, he tried again and this time successfully got to his feet and walked unsteadily around the table to greet them.

"You are welcome, but I don't need your insults." Art looked about as if registering the state of his hall for the first time. "My apologies for the mess. I had to let most of the servants go."

"What of all the English money?" asked Liam.

"Damn English. Taxes and administration fees, they say. Money for protection. Little ends up in my purse." Art wobbled a bit. "Doesn't matter, as long as I've enough left for wine, cheap wine." Art gagged, retched, then fell to his hands and knees as the contents of his ample stomach spewed onto the stone floor, a foul-smelling lake.

Stepping into the vomit, Rhoswen placed her hand on the nape of Art's neck. His retching became more violent, his spine arching from the effort. A thin stream of clear liquid, smelling of alcohol, flowed from his mouth, making a pool within the pool on the floor. When no more could come out, Art crawled backward away from the mess and sat on the floor panting with exhaustion. "What was that you did to me?" he gasped.

"Granted you a moment of clarity," Rhoswen said, retreating as well. "Don't worry, you can undo it and drown yourself in wine again."

"This is no way to live," said Liam.

Art wiped his mouth with the back of his hand. "You're right about that," his voice stronger, his eyes clear, "but there's little to live for."

Rhoswen retrieved a dirty goblet from the table, cleaned it with the hem of her tunic, and filled it with wine. Looping back, staying to dry stones, she held it out to him.

"Do you want to die in here?" asked Liam. "Or out there, fighting for your country? If protection money is to be paid, it needs to be paid to you."

Art did not reach for the goblet. "You know, they said my little brother died of dysentery on the journey back to London. Liars. Richard probably buggered him to death. Do you have a plan?"

Liam could hear the desire in his voice. "Much of Richard's army returned to England with him and his lords. Let's strike where the remaining English forces are thinnest, then disappear before they can send reinforcements. We'll wear them down. You will reassert your right as high king."

"And what's to stop Richard from returning with his army and killing us all?" Art rose to his feet, almost steady this time.

"That's our goal: Richard's return," said Liam. "It's essential to our plans."

Art gazed at the squalor around him. "Just promise me there will be no surrender this time. We fight to the end."

"You have my word."

29

Kellistown, Ireland
July 1398

Dressed in his finest armor, helmet hanging in his hand, de Vere looked out the second-story window and across the scattered houses of Kellistown. All the houses were new, as was this one, the house of a wealthy English wool merchant and the only two-story structure in town. Kellistown, halfway between Waterford and Dublin, had been razed during the invasion and was being rebuilt by the freshly appointed baron of Forth—a land grant to a minor English lord's son. The new timber-and-plaster buildings showed what English rule could bring to this backward country, de Vere thought, if only Richard would send reinforcements. Mortimer and he had been making the same fruitless demands for the last seven months: for Richard to send more fighting men or money to hire mercenaries. In his last letter, de Vere had pleaded with Richard to return himself with an army.

Art's annoying hit-and-run raids had grown into a full-blown rebellion. De Vere pressed his lips together and shook his head. Art, who should have drunk himself to death by now, was forcing English-occupied towns and villages to pay black rent, protection money to guarantee against attack.

Well, I prohibited young Baron Forth from paying Kellistown's black rent, de Vere thought, *and today Art will be in for a fatal surprise when he arrives to forcibly collect it.* De Vere made a mental inventory of the pikemen on the floor below, the longbowmen hiding in two adjacent houses, and Mortimer waiting with a company of mounted archers in the stables and wool sheds. He felt confident of victory.

There was movement in the distance. Yes, it was Art, and a surprisingly small group of rebels. De Vere's pulse quickened. *Once Art is dead and the rebellion broken,* he thought, *I'll return to London. I don't care if Richard has not sent for me. He is enthralled with that little eight-year-old bitch of a queen. She probably still looks like a boy. Poor, dear Richard, so susceptible to anyone who charms him. I'll return and win back his heart. That little girl can't know how to please him the way I do.*

De Vere watched Art cautiously approach the outskirts of town. Shouting came from the floor below. He flashed to anger; he had not given the command to attack.

De Vere turned from the window and froze. Liam was behind him. The helmet slipped from de Vere's hand. He did not hear it land on the floor. The room had become suddenly silent and bright, every detail in sharp focus: the texture of plaster walls, the grain of wood beams, the sharply angled features of the Sidhe woman near the far wall. Why was Liam standing so close, as if he were going to lean in for a kiss? De Vere felt a compulsion to look down. He saw with surprise that Liam's sword was thrust up under his breastplate. The thought that it must be in his belly wandered through his mind. Fascinated, de Vere watched as Liam withdrew the sword, blood streaming down the groove in the center of the blade. Then pain, as viscous as syrup, flooded up from his gut through his chest, arms, neck, face, head. The stench of his own bowels filled his nostrils. De Vere tried to scream, thought he should be screaming, but he had breath enough only to release a weak groan. He pushed both hands under his breastplate against the wound and took a step past Liam toward the door. His legs failed, and he fell to his knees. He felt Liam grab his hair and pull his head back. De Vere looked into Liam's eyes and saw no mercy. Terror multiplied the pain. With a surge of desperate strength, he gasped, "Please, no." Liam's sword flashed down toward his neck. His pain vanished with the light.

In London, Richard skipped into his private meeting chamber holding the hand of his newly designated heir, six-year-old Edmund, son of Roger Mortimer. Shortly after marrying Isabella, Richard had changed his will, replacing Roger with Edmund as the next king. Rumor was that when Richard died, Edmund would inherit more than just the throne, that he would also inherit Isabella as his wife and queen.

Queen Isabella, now eight, sat on a miniature replica of the throne, dressed in her royal robe and holding a small scepter, waiting for them. "What are you wearing?" she demanded of Richard.

"Our royal robes, Our sweet queen," Richard replied, stopping mid-skip.

"You call those royal?" Isabella sneered. "They are not fit for Our husband or the heir. Take them off. All of them."

Obediently, Richard and Edmund stripped, tossing their clothing into a corner.

"Parchment and paint," ordered Isabella.

The naked king and boy complied and fetched a stack of parchment and a box containing paint and brushes from a cabinet. She pointed to the floor. "We will describe how a king should dress." Richard and Edmund plopped down on their stomachs and unpacked the supplies. As Isabella described fanciful robes, they began to paint crude representations of them.

Chaucer threw open the door and rushed in, then halted, embarrassed by what was before him. It was not the first time. "Your Majesties." Chaucer bowed to Richard, then Isabella. "I bring grave news."

"Get out," said Richard. "We are busy."

"My most sincere apologies, Your Royal Majesty. I must report that Roger Mortimer has been murdered in Ireland," said Chaucer. "A foul death, little Lord Edmund, to befall such as your beloved father."

Edmund continued with his painting, the news of his father's death having no apparent effect. Richard glanced up. "Have de Vere take over as Our lord lieutenant of Ireland."

"No," said Isabella firmly to her husband. "We do not—you do not—love de Vere anymore. Send someone else."

Chaucer inched toward Richard. "Your Royal Majesty, there is more I must report."

"We are becoming tired," said Isabella, with a dismissive flick of her tiny hand. "No more news today."

"De Vere was also killed," Chaucer blurted out, "by a band of rebels led by Art MacMurrough. He is calling himself high king again."

Richard ceased painting, a visible tremor running through his body.

"My sweet king, de Vere does not matter to Us," Isabella said.

Richard crumpled up his parchment, smearing wet paint on his hands, and threw it at Chaucer. He scattered the rest of the parchment pages while letting out a scream. Leaping up, he shouted, "We will kill Art Ourselves! Muster Our armies! Assemble Our ships!" Richard pulled on his clothes.

That night Isabella wrote a letter to her mother. The Grande Sorcière's reply instructed Isabella to do everything in her powers to delay Richard until she could gain control over more of the English court.

Isabella persuaded Richard to hold extended auditions for minstrels, ostensibly to accompany him back to Ireland. There was also a nationwide competition for a new royal embroiderer, followed by work on a portable diptych depicting the Virgin Mary, a Mary bearing a striking resemblance to Isabella. The need to raise taxes to fund a new army postponed Richard's departure as well; the Vatican, having already taken firm control of all the monasteries that once belonged to the Irish Church, felt no compulsion to finance another war.

During these months, as Richard's mind slipped further from his grasp, it also slipped from Isabella's. So she switched to potions, but they seemed to have no effect. It was as if all her efforts were being countered by some force, some witch or sorcerer whom she could not identify. The other lords and ladies of the Court whom she tried to influence were also strangely resistant to her enchantments. She resorted to gold, and bribed a guard to steal an infant from an orphanage so she could render the child into tallow for a coven candle, which remained unlit.

Finally, desperately needing help and not being able to fulfill the requirements for lighting her candle, Isabella sent an urgent plea for help to her mother. The High Coven dispatched Joanna, the Second Sorcière, to London with her magic flames. But in a sudden rush, in early June 1399, Richard loaded his most loyal lords and knights, led once again by Nottingham—plus his new embroiderer and minstrels—onto a small fleet and sailed for Ireland before the witch could arrive.

⚭

ART AND LIAM had established their base of operations on a crannog—a man-made island fort—in a marsh outside Kildare. In the small, crowded hall, Rhoswen handed Liam a note from Najia in London: "*Richard is on his way without Isabella. Jordan will soon sail for England from the coast of Normandy with Thomas of Arundel and Henry of Bolingbroke. They are joined by a group of disgruntled earls and barons. Their army is small, but Jordan believes it to be sufficient. Stay safe—Richard will have his men hunt for you.*"

"This fight is about to become a lot more dangerous," said Liam, folding the note into a small square and tucking it into his pocket.

"I think it's time," said Rhoswen.

"I still disagree."

"We need Aisling on our side," she pressed.

"You haven't seen what she's become," Liam said. "She has nothing left to offer us."

"On the day Aisling rode into the English camp, I foresaw that she still had a role to play," Rhoswen said. "Trust me in this. There is something she has to do—I don't know what—for you to succeed with the rebellion."

"Us, you mean."

"It related to you."

"That's it, no other details?"

"No."

"And no premonitions since?"

"No," Rhoswen admitted. "But that one was very strong. It still feels true."

"All right," Liam said. "I should at least warn her Richard's returning, for Deirdre's sake."

"Do you want me to come with you?"

Liam shook his head.

Twilight settled on the trail through one of the last remaining woods in an area still firmly controlled by the English, northwest of Dublin. A pair of grouse broke from an elderberry bush with a flurry of wings. Aisling climbed out of a witch path, brushed the dirt and twigs from her black wool dress, and sauntered down the trail. She came to a cleared area, a stone-walled field where a dozen dairy cows grazed, their udders full in anticipation of the evening milking.

Aisling reached an open hand toward the herd, called out, "*Siccata peri*," and half closed her hand while twisting it. A cow let out a woeful *maaawwwuer* as its udder shriveled. It collapsed, convulsed, and then stilled, its eyes open and its thick tongue lolling out onto the grass.

Aisling laughed. She became aware of a presence and added, "Not like fighting demons, though."

"No," said Liam, approaching from behind her.

"No, but it has its charms. You see, the lord next door covets this farmer's land. With the loss of his cows, he will be forced to sell cheap."

"Why do you bother with this?"

"For silver, of course." She pulled out a handful of coins. "Or maybe just because I can. I'm not really sure." She let the coins slide through her fingers onto the ground.

"Richard's coming back," Liam said softly. "I thought you should know. There'll be more fighting. If he decides that you're a risk—if he even thinks you might become one—he'll have you imprisoned or killed. Even Deirdre is in danger."

Aisling twisted her hand, and a cow lowed in pain and died. "Are you having fun with your little rebellion?"

"Aisling, come away from the English." He touched her shoulder, but she twitched off his hand. "You don't have to be the Morrígna or even a priestess. Just come be with your kinsmen."

"I don't have kinsmen!" Aisling shrieked. "I am not a Celt, or Sidhe, or even human. I was a Goddess." She spun to face Liam. "I was a Goddess until you failed me and left me as this half-dead thing. You let Anya die, but then you didn't let me die." She turned back to the field. Another cow collapsed.

"I tried to live up to my vows, tried to protect you."

"Stop watching me. Go fail someone else."

Liam turned away from her and left.

As soon as he was gone, Aisling thought of all she wished she had said. *Kinsmen? How dare he suggest I return with him?* Two cows crumpled. She vibrated with frustration. How dare he make any demands of her? *No. No*, she thought. *He cannot leave yet. He must repent for all he did to me.* Enraged, she spun and ran down the path, changed her mind and cut through the trees. A vision rose unbidden, of her and Conor gliding through the woods together hunting a stag. She forced it back down.

Approaching the edge of the woods, she spied two Cheshire archers just inside the tree line. In the open beyond, Liam swung up on his horse. She eased behind the men.

"Recognize him?" whispered the first archer.

"Never seen him, and he is not wearing the badge of any lord," replied the second. "Must be Irish."

"You know what that means?"

"Target practice."

"A flagon of ale says mine strikes closest to his heart."

"Let's make it two."

They plucked arrows from their quivers.

Not like this, Aisling thought. *Liam can't die like this.*

The archers drew their longbows and aimed for Liam's back.

Aisling, acting on instinct, thrust out her hands, and the bow-strings disintegrated, the bows snapped forward with a loud *thwack*, and the men stumbled with the sudden release. Aisling leaped forward and broke the neck of one with a touch, the back of the other. A feeling of exhilaration rushed in along with another memory, a memory of her and Conor fighting Woodwose. As the surviving archer struggled on the ground, Liam disappeared over a hill, unaware that Aisling had saved his life.

"I like killing men more than cows," she said to the archer who was trying to drag himself away. "Makes me feel a bit more vital. Or was it saving that miscreant's life? Better check. How did I kill that one Woodwose?" She brushed her hand across the archer's back, and his heart jerked to a stop. Aisling tried to suppress her laugh, yet a snicker forced its way out.

"Sorry," she said to the dead man, "but that felt . . . right. I was trained to be a warrior, you know, born to it. Better than selling spells. People are always wanting one to bring a disfiguring goiter to a rival. What use is that? Doesn't make me feel like this."

She paused. *What am I saying?* she thought, and she leaned against a tree, sighing heavily. *What did I just do? My darkness is leaching away the last of my will. Too often I don't recognize my actions as my own anymore.* To her surprise she found herself contemplating joining the rebellion. Might it give her a purpose that she could hold on to while she still had some access to her old self remaining? Killing brought its own power—the corpses at her feet reminded her of that. Could she use it to channel her darkness into a different outcome? At the thought of rejoining the Celts, fear rose in her throat, tasting of bile. *No, I cannot do that, not reconcile with them, not yet,* she thought. She had to protect Deirdre above all else.

She looked at the dead archers and made a decision. She would work from within and attack the English when their backs were turned, as with these two, or in the night. First she would have to hide Deirdre somewhere away from the English and the Celts. Liam would help with that. Even if they were not reconciled, he was that type of man. She hurried toward the witch path, anxious to make a start before she changed her mind.

She was about to climb in when her dress snagged on a low tree branch. She tugged at it. Another branch coiled around her arm. She tried to pull free. A tangle of branches and twigs wrapped around her and pulled her against a fragmented trunk, each branch a composite of bits of wood, the whole thing resembling a haphazard puzzle. She cast a spell, shattering a number of limbs. They quickly reassembled and reconnected with the tree, drawing her in tighter.

"You will not escape," said a Skeaghshee appearing from behind the tree.

"What do you want?" Aisling demanded.

"To fulfill my king's last wish. I constructed this tree from broken pieces of those felled by the English. I animated it by releasing the latent hate each shard bore from the Skeaghshee who died with it. Then I bribed that farmer to hire you, so you would come through this path."

"Order this tree to release me or I'll burn you where you stand. You don't have the power to bind my enchantments."

"None can stop what has started. This tree wants nothing more, and nothing less, than your death. And it will have it. I am the last of my clan. This was my last task. I go now to the After Lands." The Skeaghshee pulled a dagger and slit his own throat.

Aisling cast enchantment after enchantment. Branches broke and reformed, flashed to ash and regenerated, each time tightening their grip upon her. She abandoned that tactic. "Please," she pleaded with the tree, her breath labored. "Please. I have decided to fight the English, those that hurt you. Give me one more chance to help your land. Help our land. Please."

The tree was pitiless. It closed its branches around her, crushing her. She attempted to send out a call through the Ardor, but the tree was drawing all in the area into itself. The limbs squeezed, and she felt a rib crack. She tried to cry for help, but it came out as a gasp: "Liam . . ."

⚛

UPON ARRIVING at Dublin Castle, Richard immediately ordered de Vere's body brought to his bedchamber. Members of the VRS League carried the coffin up from the cellar and placed it on two trestles in the center of the room.

"Remove the lid," Richard ordered. "Now get out. Get out! Get out!" The exorcists retreated from Richard's flailing arms and out the door. He stooped over the coffin and stared at his old lover. How could he have forgotten this man? How could he have left him here?

One of de Vere's cheeks was mostly gone, revealing emaciated muscles and black teeth. Despite the cold of the cellar and the best efforts of the VRS League, without Orsini's knowledge of the Egyptian method to preserve the dead, de Vere's body had begun to rot. Richard pulled off his gold ring and placed it on de Vere's finger, carefully positioning the withered hand so the ring would not slide off. Then he kissed what was left of de Vere's lips.

Richard's troops received no orders from their king and so were content to limit their patrols to the lowlands around Dublin in an attempt to avoid skirmishes with the rebels. Emboldened by Richard's unexpected lack of offense, Liam and Art soon harried the English even there.

It had been three weeks since Richard reached Dublin, but he had not left his bedchamber when Nottingham brought unwelcome news. Richard was lying on the floor next to the coffin. The diptych depicting Isabella as the Virgin Mary sprawled broken in the corner. "Why do you disturb Us?" Richard mumbled. He pushed himself up, stood in his disheveled robes, and gazed down upon de Vere's decaying face.

Without formality Nottingham said, "A messenger just arrived with news that Henry of Bolingbroke has landed in Yorkshire and marched unopposed to London. He is accompanied by Thomas of Arundel."

Richard looked up, confused. "Henry? Landed?"

"Yes. Of the Lancasters. Remember, you exiled him and Thomas?"

"Unopposed?" Richard's stance straightened.

"All those lords still loyal to you accompanied you here," said Nottingham. "Henry's allies are burning out the last of your vassals in Cheshire. Henry has already petitioned Parliament to name him king. He has imprisoned your heir and the queen."

"No. No. No. This cannot be happening." Richard pounded both fists on the edge of the coffin until it tipped off the trestles, spilling de Vere's body across the floor, causing one if its arms to break off.

An eerie calm settled over Richard. He walked around the broken body to within inches of Nottingham's face. "Ready Our ships," he ordered.

"Your Royal Majesty," said Nottingham, reverting to a formal tone and taking a step back, "we cannot sail against London. Where will we go?"

"Do We still control Wales?" asked Richard.

"Wales? I have no word of fighting in Wales."

"Well, go find out," Richard commanded.

Less than two months after he had left in a fury for Ireland, Richard returned to Britain, landing in Wales on July 24. He climbed the sea stairs and walked across the garden and into the back gate of Conwy Castle. His ship was anchored in the estuary. No other ships accompanied it. Previously, upon hearing that Parliament was likely to side with Henry's claim to the throne, all the loyal lords and knights who had sailed with Richard to Ireland abandoned him and pledged their fealty to Henry in an attempt to keep their stations and their heads. Many had taken ships and slipped off in the night. Nottingham and a few others who still valued their honor had told Richard to his face that they were disavowing him. He had accepted their betrayal with uncharacteristic grace. Now, holed up in Conwy Castle with only two companies of his Cheshire archers, he would await the coming siege. He did not have to wait long.

Five days later sixteen ships arrived flying Henry's banner. The estuary was blockaded while companies of fighting men disembarked and took the walled port town without resistance. A siege line was set outside the castle's main gate. Thomas of Arundel's ship arrived the next morning. After meeting with his captains at the inn that had been conscripted for his headquarters, Thomas retired upstairs to his private chambers.

Jordan and Najia rose in greeting when Thomas entered, slamming the door behind him. "I should have known—no, you should have foreseen that Richard would hole up in Conwy," fumed Thomas. "We don't have time for a siege! Every day that Parliament does not finalize Henry's right to the throne increases the chance that the earls opposing Henry will mount a counteroffensive. They may even try to rescue Richard to use as a puppet. Richard needs to abdicate or be killed—quickly."

Thomas sank into a chair at the table and poured himself a goblet of wine. "Just before I left London, Henry summoned me. He expressed . . ."—Thomas searched for the right word—"a distaste for further use of your magic. He also told me that the Vatican had offered to recognize him as the true king if he turned you over."

"Henry was happy enough with our magic while we suppressed the spells and potions of Isabella, but now he plans to betray us?" said Jordan, stiffening. "If we burn, you burn."

"It's not yet time to worry. I convinced Henry that you and your woman remain more useful than the Vatican in his quest to be king." Thomas drained the last of his wine. "Now prove me right."

Najia leaned over and whispered in Jordan's ear. They conferred for a moment.

"Thomas, does Richard still trust your word?" Jordan asked.

"Richard knows I'm true to my bond."

"Then swear to him that no man will harm him if he comes out for a conclave."

Thomas fetched a sheet of parchment, a quill, and ink from the sideboard and scratched out a letter. "If this works, you'll both need to return to Ireland as soon as possible, for your own safety as well as mine. Now tell me what we do if Richard comes out for this conclave."

30

London, England
February 1400

"Have you come to be my valentyne?" asked Richard, breaking into manic laughter as Najia entered his dark, windowless cell in the undercroft of Pontefract Castle, Yorkshire, carrying a torch and a small wooden box. His laughter stumbled to a halt as Najia closed the door and set the torch into a wall bracket.

At the same time, in the grand hall of the Palace of Westminster, London, Chaucer was standing at the podium reading his seven-hundred-line poem: "'Ye knowe wel how, seynt Valentynes day . . .'" It was one of Chaucer's favorite days of the year, as it was for much of the English court: February 14. Years earlier he had persuaded the now-usurped Richard to allow him to designate a date to celebrate courtly love. His new king, King Henry IV, was a strong proponent of the emerging English language, going so far as to give his coronation address in English instead of French, the first king to do this in over three centuries, so he had retained Chaucer's services as Poet to the King, and the holiday had survived.

Chaucer spied yet another couple slipping through a side door of the hall as he continued reading: "'Ye come for to chese—and flee your way—your makes, as I prik yow with plesaunce . . .'"

"Plesaunce" was one of the hundreds of words he had proudly added to the new English, this one meaning to give pleasure to the senses but without sustenance. Indeed, this was the day when all were liberated from their vows of marriage or betrothal and permitted to seek physical diversion with whomever they chose. For his festival of debauchery, Chaucer had selected the ancient feast day of St. Valentyne—who, in the third century, had given parchment hearts to Christians about to be sent to their death in the arena. Chaucer was looking forward to finishing his reading so he could join the men and women of the court, each with red hearts stashed about their persons. A heart, when offered and accepted, secured a few minutes of passion in one of the many nooks and crannies of the palace.

Richard's cell stank of rotting straw, the waste bucket in the corner, and Richard's unwashed body. His robes were mildewed and shabby, and a long chain led from one bloody ankle to a bracket in the wall against which he sat.

As he watched Najia, his thoughts turned to the last time he had seen her, seven months earlier, when Thomas of Arundel had mis-led him. "Tricky Thomas," he quipped to himself, and his laughter sputtered out again. He had known he would be able to defend Conwy Castle for months, even with his small force of archers, but Thomas had sent a letter: "*I only wish to negotiate your abdica-tion,*" Thomas had written. "*You know I hold no love for you, but you also know of my unwavering love of Christ, and I swear on the True Cross that no man shall harm you or lay hands on you if you come out for a conclave.*"

So he had gone out, dressed in his most regal robes, and this woman—his valentyne—had approached him. He was enraptured by her deep eyes and gorgeous swarthy body, a feeling he was not accus-tomed to with women. She reached out and stroked his neck, sending tingles of excitement down his spine, unexpected and delicious. The tingles grew almost to the point of pain. He had wondered what was happening, until he fell to the ground, conscious but immobile. This woman then bound him and dragged him into an open wagon.

Richard's laughter turned to sobs. Tears carved tracks down his grimy cheeks.

. . . . .

Najia watched Richard cry. She did not hate him. He was a king and did what kings do—invade and destroy. But he had not invaded Damascus or enslaved her; others had done that. He just needed to disappear in order to protect her new adopted land, the land that had freed her and freed her lover from a slavery he had not even known he was bound by.

Najia squatted down, opened the box, and removed the seven candles it contained, standing them on the stone floor in front of Richard. They were not quite clear, just so pale that the torchlight glowed through them. Richard stopped crying and watched her.

"You were once brilliant and brave," said Najia. "You once inspired loyalty in many of your lords and fear in the rest. I cannot free your body, but I can free your spirit to fight once more."

"I will not fight for Henry," Richard croaked.

"Good. I offer you the chance to fight against the usurper. But you must want that with all your heart. You must be willing to leave your body behind. I cannot work this enchantment without your desire for it."

Richard regarded her, considering her proposition. "There is nothing I desire more than revenge against Henry, even if I have to get it as a ghost."

Feeling the truth of his wish, Najia touched her left index finger to the wick of the first candle and said, "Battle." A stream of light flowed from Richard's chest into the candle, filling it with red. He looked down at the light and smiled. She touched the second candle and said, "Cunning." Light streamed from one of his eyes, filling the candle with black. Najia touched each candle down the line in turn. Light flowed from Richard's other eye, his mouth, stomach, genitals, and finally, his forehead. He did not struggle; he just withered.

Najia placed the candles carefully back in the box. Three were deep red, three were the dusty black of shadows, and one was solid white. She removed the torch from the wall bracket and paused, looking down into Richard's eyes, which stared back with the peace of indifference, dead eyes in an emaciated corpse.

Jordan was waiting for Najia outside with their horses, still weary from his long, secret journey from Scotland. Najia pressed the box into his hands and leaned in for a kiss, relieved that they had made it this far and that, finally, the end was in sight. They rode back north toward the home of Robert Stewart, illegitimate brother of Robert II, king of Scots. Stewart was known to experiment with enchantments in his duties as Protector of the Kingdom.

After a withered, unidentifiable corpse was discovered in Richard's cell, speculation became rumor, and soon a story circulated that Richard was alive and well and allied with Scotland. Newly crowned King Henry was determined to subdue Scotland before diverting resources to put down Art's Irish rebellion, a strategy developed by his trusted adviser Thomas of Arundel—who had quietly received it from Jordan back when they were plotting to usurp Richard's throne. However, each time Henry's army seemed about to defeat the Scots, a young knight would ride forth and turn the tide, a knight who seemed to glow with an inner fire, a knight whose fighting skills and innovative battle tactics were reminiscent of a young Richard, when he was whole in body and mind. The knight would not stay long—only so long as a candle might burn—but faith in him kept the Scottish forces energized. The myth that Richard lived would plague Henry throughout his reign, and he would never lead an army back to Ireland.

TWO MONTHS AFTER Najia and Jordan transported candles possessed by the spirit of Richard to Scotland, they departed the port of Stranraer in a chartered boat for the short crossing to the north of Ireland. It was a bright April afternoon; Najia put her arms around Jordan's waist and kissed his neck, which was salty and wet with spray. Just ahead lay the Irish fishing village of Larne and, beyond that, home.

"Was this our last war, do you think?" she asked. "I've missed Ireland, though not our underground cave. It's time for us to find a true home."

"So long as it can hold all my books. Do you think my library missed me?"

A brown hawk circled the mast, calling down to them, and then flew toward shore.

Reaching the wharf, they disembarked to find Liam and Rhoswen waiting. Jordan was surprised to find Rhoswen holding an infant. "Yours?" he asked Liam, as Rhoswen let Najia hold the baby.

"Ours," replied Liam, smiling at Rhoswen.

"He's beautiful," said Najia, looking tenderly at the baby now cradled in her arms. "More Sidhe than human, I think."

"A splash of human blood will surely help him in this increasingly Christian world," said Rhoswen.

"His name is Lasair. We named him after Brigid; her birth name was Lisir," added Liam. But the women were not listening. They had wandered off the wharf, cooing and playing with the baby. Jordan stared after Najia, enchanted by the sight of her with a child.

"You don't have to say it," said Jordan.

"It's time you had one of your own." Liam said it anyway.

"You're right," said Jordan. "I'm just waiting on Najia to agree. Perhaps she will now that we don't need to hide belowground."

They followed Rhoswen and Najia, Jordan savoring wisps of Irish Ardor. Liam, understanding, walked silently beside him.

"What news of Aisling?" Jordan finally asked. "Are you still checking on her?"

"She hasn't been seen since Richard's aborted return."

In the light of the next full moon, John Cooper was awakened by a pounding on his door. On his doorstep was a dark-skinned woman, who said her name was Najia, claiming to have news of his missing wife. She urged him to grab his ax and follow. Deep in a wood, they joined a Gallowglass and a Sicilian who were already hacking at the tough, dense knot of branches on a strange, dead tree. There was another woman helping who he suspected was a Sidhe. After an hour of intense effort, they were able to pull Aisling's mangled body out. John gave them the privacy they requested to say their pagan rites over her, but then they avoided his questions, leaving him to bear his wife home alone. Her body was so broken that he did not notice the fresh cut where her heart had been removed.

The priest prohibited John from burying Aisling in consecrated ground before he could even ask, but John knew she would not have found rest there anyway, and he found a beautiful meadow for her grave. He did not delude himself, thinking he had loved her, but he wished her peace in her afterlife, a peace he had never known her to have in this life. It was Deirdre he loved, deliberately forgetting she was not his own daughter.

When his company had been dissolved, the men ordered back to England, he had planned to take her with him. At that time Aisling had long since disappeared, and he thought her dead. However, when the time came to go, he could not bear the thought of parting Deirdre from her homeland, so he had stayed and bought an inn.

Now John stood in the meadow watching a plain coffin being lowered into a hole, while five-year-old Deirdre clutched his pant leg from behind. The gravediggers began shoveling dirt onto Aisling's coffin, and the mourners—all hired, as Aisling had no friends—tapped a cask and filled their cups. As the ritual toasts to commemorate the dead commenced, a brown hawk landed in the grass behind the group. It stood watching Deirdre until she turned, meeting its eyes. Unnoticed by John, she let go and took a few cautious steps toward the bird. It hopped away. She took quicker steps. It stayed out of reach. Soon they were in the trees.

Deirdre watched as the hawk stretched into a woman. Rhoswen picked up her cloak, which she had left folded on the ground with her other clothes, and wrapped it around herself.

"Were you a real bird?" exclaimed Deirdre.

"Don't be scared. I am an old acquaintance of your mother."

"I'm not scared. I know you won't hurt me."

"And how do you know that?"

Deirdre drew her shoulders up in an exaggerated shrug. "How'd you become a bird?"

"Did it look like fun?"

Deirdre nodded vigorously. "Show me how to do it."

"Well, that's my special skill. It may not be yours," replied Rhoswen. "Didn't your mother teach you about such things?"

Deirdre shook her head.

"Would you like to learn what your special skill is?"

"Oh, yes, please. Does everyone have a special skill?"

"No, but you're not like most girls."

John's concerned voice came, calling for Deirdre.

"Whenever a hawk swoops down and brushes against your hair like this . . . follow it. It will be me, and I will teach you. Now, go back to your father."

Deirdre hesitated.

"Go on."

Deirdre bounded through the trees toward the funeral and was quickly out of sight.

"Was that really wise?" asked Liam, emerging from the shadows to join Rhoswen as she dressed. "I thought we were meeting here only to pay our respects."

"Deirdre is carrying great power and has no one to teach her. She'll need to learn to control it, or it may become a problem for her. Most of Ireland is safe enough again for a witch. Besides, I am sure the Morrígna wants me to watch over her. She conveys the bloodline of the Goddess into the future."

They waited in the trees until the mourners dispersed, followed by John and Deirdre. Then Rhoswen and Liam approached Aisling's grave, marked with a stone, not a cross.

"I'm glad we sought her body out," said Rhoswen. "Not just to retrieve the heart but for her husband and Deirdre. They deserved the chance to say good-bye."

Liam sighed. "In truth, I don't know what to say or what to feel."

"When we found her body, I sensed that her part in our rebellion had been fulfilled. Aisling must have done something for us that we will never know about," said Rhoswen. "Whatever it was, I am grateful to her."

"Then I will try to be grateful as well," said Liam. "I should have brought an offering, to leave in the grave."

Rhoswen took his hand. "I have a better idea. Help me protect her daughter."

On Samhain, the last day of autumn of the following year, Eldan trundled into a half-built library and handed Rhoswen a stone box. She slid the lid open and placed Aisling's dried heart inside.

"You are supposed to divide that between fourteen custodians," rumbled the Grogoch.

"And which fourteen would you pick?" said Rhoswen. "That's too risky."

"Shall I sing to seal the box closed?"

Rhoswen shot him a look out the corner of her eye.

"How long until I have your trust?" protested Eldan.

"A millennium, maybe." Rhoswen sealed the box with an enchantment of her own. "Is the slab ready?"

"Of course, but you should have let me make it bigger and mold a design in it."

Rhoswen ignored his grumbling and headed out into the twilight. She and Liam had decided to make their new warrior school much smaller than his previous one, so they could focus on raising a large family. They needed to build the school away from Dublin, where petty lords continued to fight over the small area controlled by the English, and away from the loughs of Galway, where the occasional pack of Fomorians still caused trouble. This island, Innisfallen in giant Lough Leane, southwest Ireland, fit their needs perfectly. As it did for Jordan and Najia, who were constructing the library. They intended to continue studying and experimenting, seeking ways to preserve the Ardor of Ireland and encouraging the last of the Sidhe to remain.

Eldan lumbered after Rhoswen. "Have you heard the latest Aisling myth?"

"I want to hear," said Najia, joining them on a path toward the center of the island.

"It maintains that her ghost still travels Ireland. Appearing solid, it seduces a new man every night, only to kill him in the morning. Christian wives in Dublin are telling it to their husbands to stop them from bedding Irish girls," rumbled Eldan.

Najia laughed. "How do you hear these stories?"

"From the stones of their inns. Some still talk to me," replied Eldan.

"Any ghosts about for Samhain?" asked Najia.

"Only one," replied Rhoswen.

The last of the sunlight had disappeared when they arrived at an opening in the trees, too small to be called a clearing, where Liam and Jordan awaited them with lit torches. On the ground was a small, rough stone slab with a square hole. Rhoswen knelt down, slid the box she'd been carrying into the slab, and bound it there by tracing a symbol on the stone. The slab then appeared solid.

"The heart will be safe here until it is needed," she avowed to her friends, to herself, and to the Morrígna.

An apparition in the shape of a swan circled overhead, shining in the torchlight.

Epilogue

And I, the Sage, declare the grandeur of his radiance in order to frighten and terrify all the spirits of the ravaging angels and the bastard spirits [Nephilim], demons, Lilith, owls and jackals, and those who strike unexpectedly to lead astray the spirit of knowledge.

—Dead Sea Scroll 4Q510–511, Fragment 1 (circa 300 BCE)

A Ferry on the Irish Sea
2016, The Night Before Sara Hill's Body Was Found

Exhausted from the prior sleepless night hunched over her grandmother's secret cache of photographs and translations of the Qumran Scrolls, Sara Hill had splurged and taken a single cabin on the ferry to Ireland. But it was no use; she was too anxious to sleep. Worries for her grandmother's safety, coupled with images of Nephilim, swirled through her restless mind. Still fully dressed, she rose from the bunk. Through her porthole she saw that the lights of Liverpool had receded, and now only the yellow lights of the ferry danced upon the dark waves. The ship began to roll as a wind blew in. Sara decided to go topside for some fresh air.

She pulled on her coat and tucked her leather satchel, laden with her grandmother's illicit materials, under her arm and left the cabin. A short distance down the passageway, she climbed up the steep, narrow stairs to the enclosed main deck. Here travelers without cabins had staked out territory, their sleeping bags rolled out on benches or clustered on the floor. Those still awake, mostly young, played cards or read. Sara wove through the crowd and pushed open the heavy bulkhead door to the outside walkway. The cold, salt wind mussed her hair and cut through her wool coat, but it felt good all the same. It cleared her mind. Alone on the walkway, she leaned against the rail and looked out into the dark.

She had thought she was alone. Sara felt someone passing by brush against her shoulder and take a spot at the rail beside her. Sara glanced over. A woman turned and smiled at her. Grandmother? No, it was someone who looked like old photographs of her grandmother.

"Hello, my dear," the woman said, as if they knew each other.

Sara took a step back. "What do you want?"

"You're walking into a trap, my dear. A group of Sidhe are lying in wait for you in Belfast. They're after what you're carrying. And they won't be pleased to find you've read through it."

"Sidhe?" gasped Sara, clutching her satchel against her chest.

"A small gang of militants who will do anything to keep their secrets—Brownies and Leprechauns, mostly. Violent and unpleasant as they are, it's understandable considering all they've been through. My sister never should have brought you into this."

Sara took another step back. "Your sister?"

Something over Sara's shoulder caught the woman's attention, and Sara spun around. Behind her stood the most beautiful man Sara had ever seen. Terror commingled with instant physical attraction and rendered her breathless. He was a Sidhe; she did not know how she knew, but she knew. "What are you going to do to me?" she managed to whisper.

"We're not going to hurt you, my dear," came the woman's reassuring voice from behind her. "Don't be scared. I'm your grandmother's twin, Claire. I know I look strange to your eyes, too young, but aging progresses a little differently where I have been."

"What happened to you? Does Grandmother even know you're alive?"

"My sister might have been close to Dr. Allegro, but I was one of the students actually working on his scroll team. I learned much more about the Nephilim than she ever did. When a Sidhe approached me—her name was Rhoswen—I went willingly. But I couldn't tell my sister. She'd given up on Allegro and fallen madly in love with your grandfather. She had dreams of starting a family once she graduated. If I'd shared too much, she, too, would've had to leave all that behind."

"But what about now?" interrupted Sara. "Is she safe?"

"She is, don't fret. I collected her myself this morning," said Claire. "There is much more to talk about, but we must hurry and decide what to do about your situation."

The Sidhe spoke with a voice rich and full. "We've come to offer you another way out."

"This is Lasair," explained Claire. "Rhoswen's son, a bit human and you won't believe how old. Together they lead an alliance of Sidhe and crossbreeds unrelated to the militant group who plan to do you harm—those others will stop at nothing to conceal all knowledge of your photographs. Rhoswen's faction takes a more peaceful approach. They continue to hold vigil for the Morrígna's return. I've been living with them."

Sara struggled to take all this in. One thing she did grasp was that she had been right—this gorgeous man was a Sidhe. How old could he be? As her fear receded, her attraction grew. She wondered if he was casting some sort of Sidhe spell on her, then decided she didn't care. She forced her attention back on Claire, who was still talking.

"It's up to you what happens next, my dear. You can take your chances with the militant Sidhe, which won't end well. Or you can come with us. We'll bring you to a place where we can protect you."

Lasair gave her a sideways smile. "I'd like to show you my home." He extended his hand.

Sara took it without thinking. "I'll come with you, then."

"Wonderful," said Claire. "Now, we must be quick. The militants may well send a Fomorian or two to intercept the ship." She glanced nervously over the side, then walked off.

Lasair led her back to her cabin. She did not ask him how he knew the way or how he opened the door she knew she had locked. "What did you bring?" he asked.

"Just that," she said, pointing to her small, battered suitcase in the corner.

"Good. You'll have to leave it. Now I need your clothes."

"They're all still packed in there," she replied hesitantly.

Lasair smiled at her again, a smile that made her wonder when she would get a chance to seduce him, or the other way around. She found out, in part.

"No. I need the clothes you're wearing," he said. "It's important."

"All right." She removed her coat, sat on the bunk and kicked off her shoes and socks, stood, wriggled out of her jeans, pulled her sweater over her head, unbuttoned her blouse, slid it off, and dropped it on the pile.

He looked at her. She met his gaze. "All of them," he said.

Sara cocked her head at him. She went up on her tiptoes and kissed his lips. He returned the kiss, which to her felt like kissing chocolate, chocolate that melted into her. "There, now I've a reason to undress," she said, adding her bra and panties to the pile, and then she looked up into his eyes, hoping for another kiss.

Instead Lasair sorted through the pile of clothes and began reassembling them, laying them out on the bunk. He placed panties into jeans, bra into blouse into sweater into coat, until he had everything arranged perfectly, including her shoes. He bent and breathed into the sleeve. To Sara's amazement her clothing inflated like a balloon and then not a balloon—it became her, or rather a specter of her, lying there on the bunk.

The door opened, and Claire squeezed into the cabin. "My, you've grown into a beautiful woman," she said, handing Sara a stack of folded clothes with shoes on top.

The thing on the bed that looked like Sara rose. In the confined space, it bumped against them as it wobbled toward the open door, then walked haltingly down the passageway toward the stairs. Claire closed the door behind it.

"Where's it going?" Sara asked.

"It's going to fall overboard, my dear. Now, put on those clothes. We won't be able to slip you out unnoticed like that."

Suddenly remembering that she was still naked, Sara hurriedly dressed. "How did the militants find out about Grandmother and me?"

"There was a renovation at the Shrine of the Book, and someone discovered a children's book of faerie tales among Allegro's old papers. He must have overlooked it, or died before he could stash it. The shrine is always under surveillance by the militant Sidhe. They became suspicious as to why he would have such a thing. They found its hidden photos and traced the connection."

"I can't believe all this is happening," said Sara as she laced up her replacement shoes.

"Your bloodline, our bloodline, has always been drawn into events involving the Nephilim, even when unconscious of the connection. It's more than fate," said Claire.

"My bloodline?"

"That's why Rhoswen's group has been watching over you. They're the ones who made sure your grandmother escaped. But you must move now. We'll talk of all this when we arrive, my dear."

Sara followed Claire and Lasair out of the cabin, her satchel tucked firmly under her arm. "Where are we going after you sneak me off the ship?"

"To the Middle Kingdom, of course."

Geoffrey Chaucer died eight months after Richard II, leaving his magnum opus, *The Canterbury Tales,* unfinished. Cries of murder were largely ignored. Chaucer was the first writer interred in the area of Westminster Abbey known as Poets' Corner.

The legate, Cosimo de' Migliorati, was elected pope on October 17, 1404, his reward for bringing the Irish Church into the Holy See. He took the name Pope Innocent VII, but his turbulent reign was cut short when he was found dead just two years later.

Cardinal Orsini, previously high exorcist of the VRS League, remains in the cellar of Innocent's fortress on Vatican Hill, bound into the bronze vessel with the demon Vepar. When the legate became pope, he had intended to have the VRS League try to extricate Orsini, but he died before he got around to it. The Orsini family faded from prominence, losing much of their land and power, due to a curious inability to produce male heirs.

Isabella, no longer the English queen, was released from prison to return to France once the new king, Henry IV, was in firm control of the throne. Little is known of what happened to her there, except that the VRS League had possession of her body upon her death at the age of nineteen. They bound it with linen straps coated with silver, an ancient technique to prevent witches from returning from the afterlife, then interred it in the abbey of St. Laumer in Blois. In 1624, responding to reports of Isabella's reappearance, the Vatican opened the tomb and found that her body was perfectly preserved, as if she were sleeping. For security, the body was moved to the Church of the Celestines in Paris, where the bodies of many women of the High Coven were interred and guarded. Though, for some, just their entrails were secured there. At the time the VRS League believed that it was impossible for a necromancer to resurrect a witch who did not possess her entrails, and the guts took up so much less room than a whole body.

Queen Isabeau of France, the Grande Sorcière, made two more attempts to gain permanent control of the English throne. **Joanna of Navarre,** the Second Sorcière, murdered her husband so she could marry Richard's successor, Henry IV, in 1403. Shortly there-after Henry IV developed a disfiguring skin disease and began having seizures, often leaving his new queen to speak for him. After Henry's death Joanna was tried and convicted of witchcraft. She was imprisoned in Pevensey Castle, Sussex, England. Then Catherine of Valois, another daughter of Queen Isabeau, was sent to seduce and marry Henry IV's successor, Henry V. Henry V died of an overdose of one of Catherine's potions in 1422, two years after their marriage. Catherine was killed by Owen Tudor when he discovered her practicing witchcraft.

Valentina Visconti, the High Coven's "Keeper of the King," was accused of using a tarot deck and witchcraft by the Duke of Bur-gundy, who was plotting to usurp the High Coven's power over the French throne. Valentina was exiled and died of unknown causes.

The Vatican attempted to crush the power of witches in Europe by orchestrating a series of extensive witch-hunts, culminating in the Valais witch trials of 1428. Hundreds of witches and sorcerers were burned to death. Thousands more were imprisoned, fre-quently dying there, often under torture. The trials were run by Cardinal Gabriele Condulmer, legate to Pope Martin V. Legate Condulmer was later elected pope himself, Pope Eugene IV, by promising all the other cardinals that half the revenues of the Church would be distributed to them.

Matteuccia de Francesco, the Witch of Ripabianca, tutor to the children of the High Coven, was captured and burned alive the first year of the Valais witch trials.

Catherine de Thouars, who was nursing at the breast of **Béatrix de Montjean** when Isabella was still studying in the High Coven, escaped the witch trials by marrying Gilles de Rais, marshal of France. He had been declared a hero of the Hundred Years' War for fighting alongside Joan of Arc. Catherine taught Gilles the dark witchcraft practices. He was later hanged for the sadistic murders of over eighty children, whose body parts were used in the rites of witchcraft and the raising of demons. Once again Catherine escaped trial.

Joan of Arc was rumored to be the illegitimate daughter of Queen Isabeau of France, the Grande Sorcière; however, there is no record of Joan's ever attending the High Coven.

Catherine Simon, the young girl who Cardinal Orsini accused of being a witch but promised to save from the fire as long as she was his sex slave, might not have been a real witch when she was taken to the Vatican. However, during her two years in Orsini's chambers she learned enough enchantments to escape while he traveled to Ireland. She practiced her new craft in Andermatt and Wallenboden and taught it to her daughter, until they were both captured and burned at the Valais witch trials.

Brigid, Patrick, and Colmcille (later Anglicized to "Columba") were canonized as saints by the Vatican in an attempt to pacify the Irish population and to reshape history into myth.

Colmcille returned to Ireland from the Isle of Man and established the Monastery of the Holy Trinity in Dublin. Tortured by nightmares, he lived in constant fear of demons and never again left the city walls. Eventually he confined himself to the monastery and then, for the last five years of his life, to his chamber. For centuries after his death, many a monk claimed to hear his pleas for forgiveness echoing down the stone passageways.

Patrick's Blood Bell (also called Bell of the Blood, or Clogh-na-fullah) disappeared for over four hundred years until it resurfaced in 1841—sealed in a jeweled reliquary made of iron, silver, and gold and protected by enchantments—in the possession of Reverend Marcus Beresford, who rapidly rose in prominence to become archbishop of Armagh and Primate of All Ireland. Today the Blood Bell can be seen in the library of Armagh, Northern Ireland.

Fomorians are still occasionally sighted in the loughs of Galway. There were too many bodies of water for the exorcists to find and kill them all.

Johannes Gutenberg, in 1448, invented a system involving movable metal type and a new design of printing press that together could mass-produce inexpensive books. A single press using this system could print thirty-six hundred pages per workday on cheap paper (rather than expensive vellum). The resulting flood of books and pamphlets broke down the Vatican's control over literacy, and with it their ability to reshape history as they wished also faded, though they continued attempting to do so for centuries.

ACKNOWLEDGMENTS

MAGIC IS REAL! There is no other explanation for how I ended up with the talented and passionate team who brought this book to completion and to market.

Long before *The Last Days of Magic* was a novel, when it was still just an idea and a few rudimentary chapters, Adrienne Brodeur believed in what it could be. Over the years her guidance, editorial acumen, and friendship kept me writing. This book would not be in your hands without her support. I am indebted to Tim Ryan and the rest of her family for their willingness to sacrifice time with her as she worked on this project.

What inspired Carole DeSanti, vice president and executive editor at Viking Penguin, to chase down and capture the original manuscript is hard to fathom. I am fortunate to have her as an editor and grateful for all the times she locked me in various (admittedly nice) rooms, refusing to let me compromise on any chapter, paragraph, or word. My thanks go as well to Christopher Russell for his timely input and all the heavy lifting required to get this book out into the world. For their hard work and enthusiasm, my gratitude goes out to the rest of the Viking Penguin team including: Brian Tart, Andrea Schulz, Kate Stark, Carolyn Coleburn, Lydia Hirt, Lindsay Prevette, Allison Carney, Angie Messina, Tory Klose, Maureen Sugden, Francesca Belanger, and their colleagues in publicity, marketing, sales, and production.

Stephanie Cabot is a literary agent extraordinaire whose insights were as invaluable in polishing the manuscript as they were about the marketplace. My thanks go to the entire Gernert Company team, including Ellen Goodson, Anna Worrall, Rebecca Gardner, Seth Fishman, and Flora Hackett, who have facilitated everything from social media to marketing to foreign rights.

The programs and staff of Aspen Words, the literary arm of the Aspen Institute, served as midwives to this novel. Special thanks to Maurice LaMee, Jamie Kravitz, Caroline Tory, and Renee Prince.

My deep appreciation goes to those uniquely generous people who took the time to read and comment on a manuscript that I thought was finished but they knew was not: Lisa Kessler and Jenna Johnson. For their bravery, my thanks to even earlier readers: Tom and Bridget Tomlinson, Kathy Naumann, Barbara Bends, Jonathan Young, Mary and Larry Tompkins (my loving parents), and Cherie Tucker.

In Ireland, Deirdre Wadding shared a treasure trove of information on Irish faeries and magic. Dr. Andy Halpin, with the National Museum of Ireland, was quick to turn around valuable answers to my befuddled questions.

Victoria Haveman and John Beatty let me encamp in the corner of their inspirational café, Victoria's Espresso, in Aspen, Colorado, where most of this book was written. Without their caffeine and pastries, the Gods only know if I would have ever actually finished. I also have a special fondness for Café Du Marché on Rue Cler, in Paris, where for a week I sat and scratched out the original outline.

For his wonderful personal support, both while I was writing and long before, I will always be grateful to my dear friend Rick McCord.

This novel is dedicated to my wife, Dr. Serena Koenig; she knows why.